Massacre

AN EDWARD HUNTER SPY ADVENTURE

Massacre

AN EDWARD HUNTER SPY ADVENTURE

DOUG ADCOCK

Massacre: An Edward Hunter Spy Adventure
Copyright ©2018 by Douglas Adcock

DougAdcockAuthor.com

ISBN-13: 978-0-9976867-1-5

Published by CreateSpace

Cover jacket design and map by Cathy Helms www.avalongraphics.org
Interior Design: Tamara Cribley www.TheDeliberatePage.com

To

Jonah Henry Payne

I wish you had stayed to read this and hundreds of other books, so we could have talked about them. I wish I could have shared Paris with you.

-Grandad

Dramatis Personae

Historical characters are in **bold**. Dates included where known.

Edward Hunter—protagonist. Born 1550 to Henry Hunter and Agnes Gifford Hunter.

IN ENGLAND

George Babcock—uncle to Edward Hunter. Member of Mercer's Guild and Merchant Adventurers Company

Katherine Gifford Babcock—aunt to Edward Hunter

William Cecil, Lord Burghley (1520-1598)—Queen Elizabeth's most trusted counselor, Lord High Treasurer

Captain Bartholomew Tide—captain of the barque *Constance*

Timothy Gain—Tide's first mate

IN PARIS

GENERAL

Don Diego de Zuñiga (1525-1577)—Spanish ambassador

Jacques Crespin—guide and informer

Justin Lepage—lawyer and notary who arranges practical matters for the English Embassy

Antoine Izard—a militia captain and drawer of gold thread

François Martin—militia ensign

Captain Girard—militia leader on the Left Bank

Nicolas Colin—printer at the Cardinal's Hat

Father Antoine—priest of Saint-Gervais

Pierre Merlet—Huguenot merchant

Georges Landon—mason, stonecarver

Gilbert Vasse—leather worker

Robert—leader of a street gang

Armond—treasurer of the gang

AT L'ÉCHIQUIER

Marguerite Moreau—innkeeper of *L'Échiquier*

Laurent & Martin—servants at the inn

Auguste—the inn's cook

Pierre—his son

Bernard—ostler

Bertha—ostler's wife

Marie and Jeanne—chambermaids

Bernard Coran—guest from Gascony, accompanied Henri of Navarre to Paris

Guillaume Poudampa—guest from Gascony, accompanied Henri of Navarre to Paris

Vincent de Galion—guest from Gascony, accompanied Henri of Navarre to Paris

Guy Mongaston—guest from Gascony, accompanied Henri of Navarre to Paris

Georges Grattard—merchant from Bordeaux

AT THE ENGLISH EMBASSY

Francis Walsingham (1532-1590)—English ambassador to France from January 1571 to April 1573.

Robert Beale (1541-1601)—his secretary

Ursula Walsingham (?-1602)—wife to Francis

Anne—her maidservant

Frances Walsingham (1569-1603)—daughter of Francis and Ursula Walsingham

Barbara—her nurse

Henry Roberts—clerk

John de Russe (Jack)—valet of Walsingham

Thomas Howell—Beale's servant

Ned—his son, assists in the kitchen.

Gilbert Morin—embassy cook

Pierre—porter

Jean—usher

André—butler

Jonas—servant

Étienne—kitchen lad

Philip—stableman

Jacob—coachman

Alain Brune—porter, replaces Pierre

Christophe—porter at courtyard gate

ENGLISH CATHOLIC EXPATRIATES

Roger Barnes—befriends Hunter

Sir Gregory Wilkes—leader of expatriates, sends Catholic literature to England

Sir James Kempson

Simon Lodge

Barnaby Timmons—student

Timothy Heath—student

Thomas Fisher

George Pickering

AT THE FRENCH COURT

Charles IX (1550-1574)—King of France (1560-1574), House of Valois, second son of Catherine de Medici and Henri II

Catherine de Medici (1519-1589)—Queen Mother to Charles IX, wife of Henri II (1519-1559)

Henri, Duke of Anjou (1551-1589)—brother of Charles IX, third son of Catherine de Medici and Henri II

Francis, Duke of Alençon (1555-1584)—brother of Charles IX, fourth son of Catherine de Medici and Henri II

Margaret of Valois (1553-1615)—Princess of France, second daughter of Catherine de Medici and Henri II, also called Margot, married to Henri of Navarre 18 August 1572

Henri of Lorraine, 3rd Duke of Guise (1550-88)—prominent member of ultra-Catholic noble family

Anne d'Este, Duchesse of Nemours (1531-1607)—mother of Henri de Guise

Louis de Gonzaga, Duke of Nevers (1539-1595)—a member of the King's Council

Gaspard II de Châtillon, Lord of Coligny, Admiral of France (1519-1572)—Huguenot leader

Henri Bourbon, King of Navarre (1553-1610)—Huguenot, king of a small kingdom in the south of France

Jeanne d'Albret, Queen of Navarre (1528-1572)—Huguenot leader, mother of Henri Bourbon

Gabriel, Count of Montgomery (1530-74)—Captain of Scots Guards who injured King Henri II of France in a joust, member of the Huguenot party

Charles de Téligny (1535-1572)—son-in-law of Coligny

François de Beauvais, Lord of Briquemault (1502-1572)—noble of the Huguenot party

Charlotte de Sauve, Viscountess de Tours (1551-1617)—lady-in-waiting to Catherine de Medici

Madame Marie Challon—lady-in-waiting to Catherine de Medici

Viscount Harduin—financial advisor to King Charles IX

Viscount of Beaulieu—a *maître des requètes*

Estienne Thibaudoux, Sieur de Prideaux—secretary to a *maître des requètes*

Louis Moutonnet—accountant to the Duke of Nevers

Juliette Moutonnet—his wife

Pierre Delorme—Gentleman of the Chamber and former diplomat

SIDNEY'S PARTY

Philip Sidney (1554-1586)—son of Sir Henry Sidney and Lady Mary Dudley, heir to Robert Dudley, Earl of Leicester, on an educational tour of continental Europe

Lodowick Bryskett (1547-1612)—his traveling companion

Griffin Madox—Welsh, his secretary

Harry White—valet

John Fisher—servant

EARL OF LINCOLN'S PARTY

Edward Fiennes de Clinton, Earl of Lincoln (1512-1585)—Lord High Admiral of England

Gregory Fiennes, Lord Dacre (1539-94)

Francis Talbot (c. 1550-82) Lord Talbot, son of George Talbot, 6th Earl of Shrewsbury

William Sandys, 3rd Lord Sandys of the Vine (1545-1623)

Sir Arthur Champernowne (1524-1578)—Vice-Admiral of the Devon Coasts

Sir Henry Borough

Sir Jerome Bowes (?-1616)

Henry Middelmore

REFUGEES SHELTERING IN THE ENGLISH EMBASSY

Leonard Halston—survivor of the Battle of Saint-Ghislain

Philip Wharton, 3rd Baron Wharton (1555-1625)—son of a Catholic privy councilor, studying at Jesuit College in Paris

Timothy Bright (1550-1615)—student from Trinity College, Cambridge, studying medicine in Paris

Edward Cope (1555-1620)—son of Lady Lane (Mary Heneage) by her first marriage

John Watson, Dean of Winchester (1520-84)

Nicolas Faunt (?-1608)—student temporarily in Paris

Pietro Bizari (1530-1586)—historian, poet, intelligencer from 1570

Walter Williams—one of Walsingham's agents

Jacomo Manucci—another of Walsingham's operatives

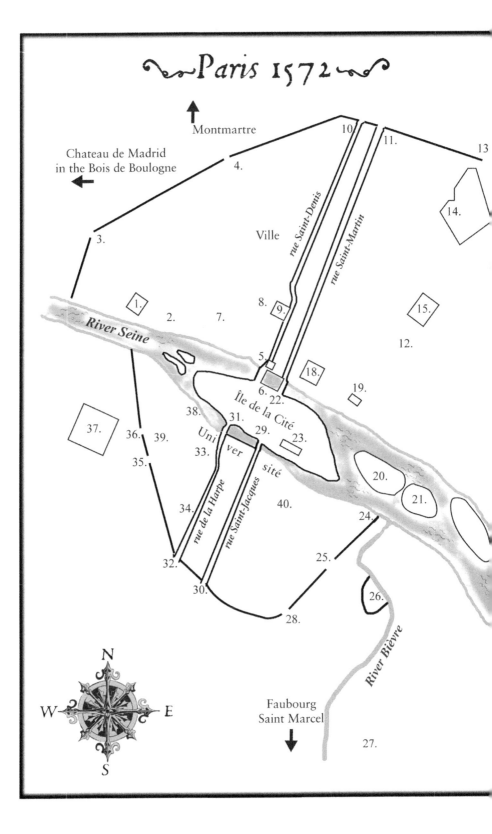

Paris 1572

Montmartre

Chateau de Madrid
in the Bois de Boulogne

4.

Ville

rue Saint-Denis

rue Saint-Martin

10

11.

13

14.

3.

1.

2.

7.

8.

9.

15.

River Seine

5.

18.

12.

6. 22.

19.

Île de la Cité

38.

31.

29.

23.

20.

37.

36.

39.

Uni ver sité

33.

35.

34.

rue de la Harpe

rue Saint-Jacques

40.

21.

24.

32.

25.

30.

26.

28.

River Bièvre

N

W   E

S

Faubourg
Saint Marcel

27.

Key

1. Louvre Palace
2. Saint-Germain l'Auxerrois
3. Porte Saint-Honoré
4. Porte Montmartre
5. Châtelet
6. Pont au Change
7. Rue de Béthizy
8. Les Halles
9. Cemetery of the Innocents
10. Porte Saint-Denis
11. Porte Saint-Martin
12. L'Échiquier
13. Porte du Temple
14. The Temple
15. Hôtel de Guise
16. Bastille
17. Porte Bastille
18. Place de Grève
19. Saint-Gervais
20. Île Notre-Dame
21. Île aux Vaches
22. Pont Notre Dame
23. Cathedral of Notre Dame
24. Tournelle
25. Porte Saint-Victor
26. Saint-Victor Abbey
27. English Embassy
28. Porte Bordelle
29. Petit Pont
30. Porte Saint-Jacques
31. Pont Saint-Michel
32. Porte Saint-Michel
33. The Antelope
34. Church of Saint-Cosme-et-Damien
35. Porte Saint-Germain
36. Porte de Buci
37. Saint-Germain-des-Prés Abbey
38. Quai des Grands-Augustins
39. Residence of Sir Gregory Wilkes
40. Place Maubert

17.

 16.

Prologue

Sunday, 24 August 1572, Saint Bartholomew's Day

HUNTER LIFTED HIS FOOT. THE MUD STUCK TO HIS SOLE. THE PARIS STREETS were no longer running with blood, at least not the rue Vieille du Temple. Here the blood had congealed. To his left another pile of naked male and female bodies lay twisted together in macabre embraces. The face of the young woman nearest him had been beautiful. Now her vacant eyes gazed up at the window from which she had been hurled. Sensing movement beyond the bodies, his head jerked back to street level. Figures in the distance slipped furtively away. A scream echoed from farther north, beyond the Hôtel de Guise. So the killing continued.

The city had become a slaughterhouse full of Protestant carcasses. If he encountered a neighbor who recognized him as the Englishman lodging at the Chessboard Inn, he would become another corpse, killed to advance that neighbor's reputation for religious zeal. Even if he did not meet anyone who recognized him, he doubted he could he reach the Seine without confronting someone who would demand to see what the two bundles he carried contained—one of bloodstained clothes and the other the head of the first man he had killed.

CHAPTER 1

A Mission

Wednesday, 27 February 1572

A THIN-FACED USHER WEARING THE QUEEN'S LIVERY OPENED A DOOR. Hunter's heart drummed a rhythm of fear and excitement. He had waited over a year for the opportunity to serve Queen Elizabeth and prove himself worthy of Mary.

Behind the desk sat a middle-aged man dressed in black. A fur-lined gown, a high-ruffed collar, and an old-fashioned coif afforded him protection from the damp of the Palace. His full moustaches obscured his upper lip and flowed into a graying beard brushed into two points, the swallow-tail style. He scanned a paper on his desk with weary eyes, as though he had been reading late into the night for many nights.

He looked up. Sharp eyes gleamed beneath bold eyebrows, revealing an intelligence that had allowed him to endure in high office through the court intrigues of three sovereigns and the tempests of religious change. Here sat the most powerful man in England, William Cecil, Lord Burghley.

At a nod from Burghley, the usher and the clerk left the room. His eyes fixed on Hunter, weighed him up, and appeared to reach a decision. "Master Edward Hunter."

"Your Lordship."

"Pray be seated." Burghley rested his elbows on the desk and joined his hands in a pointed arch. "Master Hunter, are you prepared to serve your queen loyally with all your ability?"

Hunter swallowed. "Yes, my lord."

A slight smile crossed Burghley's face. "You are here as the result of chance. I received letters from Ambassador Walsingham and the Earl of Rutland on the same day. Walsingham needs a trustworthy Englishman fluent in French to look into some matters in Paris. Lord Rutland met you in Yorkshire. He believes you have a talent for spiery. Of course, Rutland is young and easily impressed."

Hunter flushed. Rutland was only a year older than he was.

"Lord Sussex also spoke well of your efforts during the Northern Rebellion." Burghley unclasped his hands and glanced at a letter "'Able to sustain an assumed character. Posed as a servant and a rebel. Quick-thinking. Physical endurance.'"

"A few days later, I met your uncle and another of the Merchant Adventurers who wish to take advantage of the treaty we are negotiating with France. Their syndicate proposes establishing a staple in Rouen. He said he had convinced you to work in Paris as an agent."

Uncle George had certainly tried to. He nodded.

"All this is good, yet I am not convinced you are the ideal man for this assignment."

Hunter's heart sank. What could he say to convince Burghley? "I would be honored to serve Her Majesty. If I have shortcomings, I will endeavor to mend them."

"You were in Yorkshire, I understand, because of close ties with Richard Spranklin, the son of Sir Lawrence Spranklin."

"Yes."

"Sir Lawrence has served Her Majesty as a justice of the peace, but he is generally acknowledged to be a church papist." He paused a moment. "During the insurrection in the North, one of his sons rode with the rebels, and is now reported to be in Flanders."

"Yes, my lord. That was Walter. His other son, Richard, who is my friend, held a commission from Lord Sussex and led a company against the rebels." Hunter's mouth was dry.

"Having two sons of a family fight on two sides is a frequent theme in our history. It makes for good politics, but does not reveal a man's conscience." Another pause. "Since the Bishop of Rome issued his bull claiming to excommunicate Her Majesty the Queen and ordering good Catholics to renounce her authority, have you heard either father or son make a statement that would indicate what their conduct would be, should a foreign army arrive in England to enforce that bull?"

"I have not seen Sir Lawrence Spranklin since I left Yorkshire two years ago, my lord. But Richard has said that both his father and he regret the actions of the Pope"—Burghley raised one eyebrow—"or rather the Bishop of Rome. He said the bull was foolish, and harmed Catholics in England by asking them to betray their sovereign." Why had he said, "pope?"

"That does not precisely answer my question."

Despite the coolness of the room, Hunter's armpits grew damp. "At the time of the Northern Rebellion, when we thought the Duke of Alva might aid the rebels by landing an army, Richard was ready to fight any such invasion."

"Yes, but that was before the *Regnans in Excelsis* bull."

How ironic, if his friendship with Richard jeopardized his chance to serve Her Majesty and prove himself worthy of Richard's sister. "I cannot imagine the loyalty of either Richard or his father was changed by that."

Burghley stroked his beard. "But they did recognize that the bull presumes that one cannot be both a loyal subject of a lawful queen and a faithful Catholic."

Beads of sweat gathered on his upper lip. "From their words and actions, I believe both feel they can in conscience be loyal subjects and be true to their own faith."

Burghley nodded. "You know from your time in the North that half Her Majesty's subjects cling to the Old Religion. Ridolfi's plot shows that many conspire to murder Her Majesty. We are only a few drops of poison or a pistol shot away from chaos. If such a calamity were to happen, which I pray to God it never shall, how many who believe they are loyal subjects and true Catholics would reconcile both roles in the person of Mary, Queen of Scots?"

Hunter could not answer Burghley's question. No man could.

Burghley perused the papers again. "You have been at Gray's Inn. Through your grandfather and uncle, you have connections with the Mercers' Company and the Merchant Adventurers. Your father and brother are gentlemen in Hertfordshire. Childhood on the Continent, mostly Geneva." Burghley looked up and stared hard at Hunter for a moment, then his face relaxed. "Well, I must tell you of your mission."

Hunter exhaled. He had been holding his breath without realizing it. "Thank you, Your Lordship." He would have a chance to prove himself.

"For the next month, you will disappear and assume another identity. Let us call him Master Adams, an agent of the syndicate promoting the

5

establishment of a staple in Rouen. He will carry letters from the syndicate to officials in Paris. He will meet with officials and merchants, explaining how beneficial trade with England will be. He will have a chest of quality English cloth to impress them."

This was the role Uncle George had been pressing on him.

"Adams is also a secret Catholic," Burghley continued. "He will contact English Catholics living in Paris for advice on printing a seditious tract and shipping it to England. Our hope is that Master Adams can uncover not only the source of the seditious pamphlets that have surfaced in London, but also who transports, receives, and distributes them. Of course, if the expatriate Catholics discover he is a spy, it may cost him his life."

Cost him his life? That was the threat he had lived with in Yorkshire. But there he had only acted a servant. He had relied on an experienced spy to guide him. Alone, and in a foreign country, could he act the convincing Catholic? One slip would betray him. But Burghley was speaking again.

"Your background is both a benefit and a disadvantage. In Geneva you learned French, but Geneva also filled you with John Calvin's theology. That may be useful for speaking to Huguenot merchants, but you will need to master the vocabulary and attitudes of a zealous Catholic to carry off Master Adams. Do you have a preference for a Christian name?"

The façade of St. Paul's Cathedral swam into Hunter's head. "Paul."

"Good. Your transformation from Edward Hunter to Paul Adams will take place in Kent, at Glasswell Manor, during the next month. You will be instructed in Catholic doctrine, in the politics of the French Court, in the Catholics of London we suspect are distributing tracts, and in the qualities of the cloth you will be promoting."

Hunter sighed inwardly. The work he faced dismayed him as much as the danger. The door latch behind him clicked. The thin-faced usher glided in.

"I am pressed with other matters just now," Burghley said. "Your mission may take you to France for six months to a year. The syndicate will support you during that time. Are you ready and willing to undertake this?"

Hunter stood. However difficult this mission, he would succeed—he hoped. "I am honored by your trust in me, my lord. I hope I will prove worthy of it. I am willing to do my best."

"That is all any of us can do, Master Hunter. Derrick, introduce him to Master Coughlin."

"Yes, sir." Derrick stepped towards the door.

Hunter bowed. "Thank you again, Your Lordship."

In his chamber, Derrick wrote on a small square of paper and folded it into quarters. At the meeting tonight outside the Three Tuns Tavern, he would slip it to the clerk of a Spanish merchant, in exchange for a gold angel. As he was better paid by King Philip than by Burghley, so it was only fair to keep Ambassador de Spes informed of any new intelligencers going abroad. Of course, the Ambassador was now in Brussels, dismissed for his part in the Ridolfi plot, but he had left a network in place in London. Although Derrick could not report what Edward Hunter would call him- self in France, he could describe Hunter. Those who paid him well could keep watch for Hunter.

CHAPTER 2

A Sea Crossing

Thursday, 3 April 1572

THE ISLE OF WIGHT SLIPPED BY WITHOUT HUNTER ACTUALLY SEEING IT. The mission he was commencing would change everything. When he returned, perhaps Lord Burghley himself would tell Mary's father of the trust he had placed in him, and how well he had done. How could Sir Lawrence then refuse to accept him as her suitor?

The barque *Constance* cleared the lee of the Isle of Wight, and heeled to larboard. The crew scrambled to adjust the sails. Captain Tide barked orders to his men, then caught Hunter's eye, crossed to him, and asked, "What do you think of her?"

"She seems to respond quickly, and your crew works her well."

"They do. I'm proud of her. She'll do ten knots on a reach. My brother and I, sailing with my father, took her as a prize from the papists in sixty-two, when the Queen sent soldiers to Newhaven and licensed us to take French ships. Not ships from La Rochelle, of course, but those sailing under the orders of the Duke of Guise."

"Then this ship was built in France?"

"That she was. She looks like a French barque, until you get close enough to see St. George's cross there."

Hunter looked up at a weather-beaten pennant. A ship would have to come very close to make out the faded red cross. "Does that cause problems?"

"Not for us," Tide said with a smile. "Did you find room for your gear below?"

"I did," Hunter said. "Though the smell was infernal." The cargo of sheep hides the captain had been waiting for had become soaked during the rainy days before their sailing.

Tide laughed. "You get used to the pelts. Relax, Adams. A passenger should take his leisure during such a smooth passage as we have today. April in the Narrow Seas is usually much rougher." Tide walked aft.

Hunter strolled to the starboard side to watch the wake spreading behind them. Gulls followed, hoping to spot some morsels thrown overboard. A pinnace from the Isle of Wight raced towards their stern. Someone was standing in its bow, holding...a piece of glass? a mirror? Light flashed—three times. The first mate, Gain, standing at the stern, waved back. The pinnace tacked east into the wind and headed away from them. A signal had been passed, but to what effect?

A cry from the main top startled him. The man aloft pointed off the starboard bow. Captain Tide shouted orders, and crewmen rushed to trim the sails. In the haze on the starboard horizon, Hunter strained to make out a white speck. As minutes passed, the speck resolved itself into triangular sails. A murmur of excitement rippled through the crew. He stopped a passing sailor. "What is that ship yonder?"

"That's the Spanish caravel," he answered, then scurried to descend into the hold. He had said *the* Spanish caravel, as though it was expected. The reality of his situation struck him as a cold shower of rain. Captain Tide did not buy his fancy doublets by carrying passengers, or even smuggling hides. He was sailing with a pirate, who was about to plunder a Spanish vessel. And this was the man Lord Burghley had chosen to convey him to France.

The seaman who had identified the Spanish caravel emerged, carrying two arquebuses, and placed them on a rack near the foremast. Men lifted canvas covers from the falconets, lugged them to the bulwarks, and mounted them on swivels. Others carried kegs of gunpowder, swords, helmets, and breastplates. They did not hurry; it would be some time before the *Constance* intercepted the caravel.

The caravel altered her course from northwest to southwest, towards the French coast now visible on the horizon. At Tide's order, crewmen climbed the shrouds and unfurled the topsail. Every minute that the operation took, the caravel slipped further away. If Tide intended to intercept her, why had he delayed adding sail? It was clear the *Constance* would miss her to windward.

When they had closed to within a quarter mile, Hunter made out Spanish arquebusiers. Tide's gaze seemed focused on a point of land beyond the caravel. If she rounded that point, might she find safety? Were they near a harbor? On the point, a flash of light, then another. A moment later, four flashes. Tide, smiling, bellowed another order. Sailors adjusted the sails, and the *Constance* slowed. What was going on? If Tide was a pirate, he seemed to be a poor one.

The crew erupted in a cheer. Hunter followed their gaze. A ship slid out beyond the point of land where the caravel was heading. Was this friend or foe?

"Dutch," said a seaman beside him.

Spying the Dutch vessel in his path, the caravel's captain tried desperately to veer off to the north, but the confused crew mangled the job. Yards jerked into contradictory angles. Sails flapped. The caravel was trapped between the *Constance* and the Dutch ship. Someone on the caravel's deck fired a shot.

"Get below, Adams," Tide ordered. "Now!"

Hunter regretted missing the action, but could not argue. In the dark hold, he stood tense on the ladder with his head near the hatch, listening so hard he hardly noticed the stink of the sheep pelts.

A distant cannon boomed. Had the Dutchman fired on the caravel?

"Wait!" from Captain Tide.

Popping sounds in the distance. Sailors' feet thudded overhead in response to indistinct orders. Metal crashed on the deck as the crew abandoned their weapons to grasp lines and maneuver the ship. Then rattling and thumping as they collected their weapons anew.

More gunfire, closer now. Shouted orders, clomping of feet, and clattering of arms, repeated several times.

Behind these irregular sounds, the steady creaking rhythm of the ship's timbers continued, its tempo slowing as the *Constance* approached the caravel. A cheer erupted. Had the caravel surrendered?

Tide ordered, "Ready grappling hooks." The *Constance* lurched sideways, then, with a bump and a groan, her starboard flank slid alongside the caravel. Cries and curses poured from the crew. They slipped over the side and dropped onto the caravel's deck. Cries of "*Abajo!*" as the Englishmen ordered the Spaniards below decks.

With a crash, the *Constance* leapt backwards. Hunter lost his grip and fell off the ladder onto a bale of sheepskins. What had happened? A stink from the crushed pelts rose around him. The Dutch ship must have struck the caravel from the other side. A hawser ran out through the cat-hole as the *Constance* dropped anchor.

The hatch opened. First mate Gain grinned down at him. "Cap'n said to let you up. The papist pigs are all locked below, so you'll come to no harm."

Hunter climbed out and crossed to the railing overlooking the caravel. On its deck, Tide faced an elegantly dressed Spaniard with a haughty expression. Three crewmen of the *Constance* surrounded him, swords drawn. Two more English sailors emerged from the hatch of the caravel, one pulling and the other pushing a short Spaniard carrying a leather box. On the far side of the caravel, Dutch sailors leapt onto her deck. Two attached a ladder for their portly captain to descend, while others swarmed below.

"Van Tassel," Tide shouted to the Dutch captain.

"Captain Tide," van Tassel replied. "Great news. La Marck has captured Brill."

Hunter knew this name. William de la Marck was the most famous of the Dutch Sea Beggars, who had fled the Duke of Alva five or six years ago, and found refuge in Dover and the Cinque Ports. Although the Sea Beggars held letters of marque from the Prince of Orange that authorized them to attack Spanish ships, they had become increasingly indiscriminate in their choice of victims and the Queen had ordered their expulsion from England at the beginning of March.

"When?" Tide asked.

"Two days ago. Alva's soldiers had left the town."

Tide roared, "Gain!"

Gain scuttled past Hunter. "Here, Captain!" He swung over the side, a black leather case around his neck. His long, thin frame clambering down resembled an ape at Bartholomew's Fair.

"Master Adams," Tide shouted. "Do not stand gawking. Come here to see that this will all be done lawfully."

Hunter arrived as Gain handed Tide a folded sheet. With a flourish, Tide thrust it in the face of the Spanish captain. "Señor Martinez, my license from the Prince of Orange to seize vessels of his enemies. Here is his hand and seal."

Captain Martinez glanced disdainfully at the letter of marque. At this moment, van Tassel reached the group and presented his letter.

"Captain van Tassel, this is Paul Adams, a passenger and a near lawyer. He can swear our dealings are correct, if need be."

"Your servant," Van Tassel said. He spoke in Spanish to Martinez, who turned to the short man with the leather box. He opened it and handed the captain several sheets of paper.

"Their manifest," Tide explained. He and van Tassel put their heads together, reading down the list of cargo and turning pages.

Hunter strained to remember what he knew of maritime law. He had not attended Admiralty Court, but he knew actions backed by letters of marque were questionable.

Angry cries erupted from the caravel's hatch. Three Dutch sailors sprang out, spun around, and leaned back into the hold. They yanked a Dominican monk out with such force he appeared to fly from the hatch, his black and white habit exploding around him. The mariners on deck surrounded the monk, brandishing knives and swords, shouting, knocking him down, and kicking him. A sailor emerged from below holding a rosary and shouted to van Tassel in Dutch.

"They found the monk hiding below," he explained in English. "Another damned Dominican swelling the Inquisition." He listened to a question from the sailor and shouted back, "*Ja!*"

The seamen pulled the monk to his feet and prodded him towards the bow. Two held his arms while the others hacked at his black cloak with knives and ripped it from him. The monk's face was a study in fear.

The Spanish captain directed a torrent of words at van Tassel. The Dutch captain slowly drew his sword and placed the tip under the Spaniard's chin. Hunter's stomach clenched.

The sailors manhandled the monk towards the bow. One flung the rosary into the sea, amid cheers. His mate yanked off the monk's cincture and threw it overboard. Two held the monk fast, while a third poised a knife above his head.

His cry of "*Jesu! Maria!*" soared above the shouts of his tormenters.

The knife descended.

Hunter gasped.

The blade sliced through his white garments rather than his flesh. The English sailors crowed in delight.

The Dutch sailors tore off his slit habit and then his tunic and undergarments. He stood before them, naked and shivering. They mocked him and spat on him.

Such hatred. Surely they meant to kill him.

Two men lifted him onto the larboard bulwark and gripped him tightly on either side. He began a *pater noster*, but the flat of a sword smashed into his mouth and struck him silent. Blood ran from his lips.

Four sailors now stood behind him in a line and drew back their swords. One nodded. They stabbed forward. The swords sliced through the monk's body and jutted from his chest and stomach. He screamed. So did the secretary standing next to Martinez.

Hunter shuddered.

Blood streamed down the monk's body. The sailors withdrew their blades. The two holding the monk tossed him away from the ship.

He seemed to drop slowly. The splash as he entered the water sounded unexpectedly loud.

Brother Robert, the confessor to Mary and her family, had laid healing hands upon Hunter. He had vowed he would die for his beliefs, but would not kill for them. If he had fallen into these sailors' hands, he would surely have died for his religion. The rebellion in the Low Countries, the strife in France—how could his love for Mary withstand the flood of hatred between Protestant and Catholic that flowed over Europe?

Captain Martinez, van Tassel's blade still under his chin, slowly spat out icy words. Van Tassel touched the blade to his chin, but said, "No, *señor.*" He turned to Tide and Hunter. "He asks for a duel with me. I will not give him such satisfaction." He looked at Hunter. "You are troubled by that monk?"

"Yes," Hunter replied.

"Those two brothers, the ones wiping blood off their swords, are from Valenciennes. Their parents were executed four years ago for heresy. They avenge themselves on any priest they find." He turned to Tide, still holding the caravel's manifest. "No gold or silver?"

"Not listed."

"My men can ask each Spaniard until one tells us. They can be very persuasive."

Tide turned to Hunter, apparently unshaken by the murder of the monk. "Spices, iron, wine, some silk...and no doubt Captain van Tassel and his men can convince someone to reveal where some gold escudos have been hidden. That was worth a day's delay, was it not?"

Now Hunter understood. The stinking pelts had been intentionally held outside Portsmouth, so Tide could delay his departure and capture this caravel. Word of her arrival had been passed up the coast via fast boats and mirror signals.

Tide continued. "Occasionally foreign ship owners raise complaints in Admiralty Court. You can attest this is no piracy. I acted under the prince's letter of marque. We did not fire a shot."

In Brussels, former Spanish Ambassador Guerau de Spes studied the square note. Burghley was sending out another intelligence agent. Damn him for his spies! It was hard to know whom to trust—Mather, Hawkyns, even Ridolfi himself might have been acting for Burghley when they outlined their plans to him.

But this Hunter was headed to France. He considered sending a copy of the note directly to Don Diego de Zuñiga, the new Spanish Ambassador in Paris, but hesitated. He did not know Don Diego's alliances at Court. Was he closer to the Prince of Eboli or the Duke of Alva? He could not afford to make enemies of either of them. He could simply tell Alva himself, but Alva had opposed every action he had urged upon the King while he was ambassador to England. Although Alva provided him food and lodging here in Brussels, he made it clear that he considered de Spes a fool. No, better to include this information in the letter he would send directly to Madrid, addressed to the King. He would recount to His Majesty the abominable treatment the English had shown him and protest their imprisonment of his servant Borghese. Although he knew he had always acted in the best interests of King Philip, there were those at Court who might criticize him and present his dismissal from England as a failure.

No. It was better not to write Zuñiga directly. Let His Majesty share this information of a new spy with whomever in Madrid or Brussels he saw fit, then send it to Paris.

CHAPTER 3

Arrival in Paris

Tuesday, 8 April 1572

THE AFTERNOON WAS WARM. RELAXED, HUNTER SWAYED IN RHYTHM WITH his horse. Thomas and Pierre, servants the Rouen merchant Boutilier had sent to see him safe to Paris, rode silently ahead and behind. Hunter's thoughts drifted again to Mary. Where would they live after they wed, he wondered? Yorkshire held no attraction for him except Mary Spranklin, while she longed to see London. Surely when he had earned the confidence of those at Court, as he was likely to do on this assignment, and gained her father's consent to his suit, she would be happy to live in London with him. Perhaps, when his brother Henry inherited their father's estate, Hunter could purchase his house in Hertfordshire...but a needle of doubt pricked his daydream. What right had he to assume his performance on this assignment would please anyone?

Hunter's downward spiral of self-doubt halted when the servant in front of him reined in. Beyond him, a small man with a scraggly beard slouched on a sway-backed roan. Addressing him in French, Thomas said, "Stand aside."

The man fixed his eyes on Hunter. "I am looking for Master Paul Adams, an Englishman. I am to guide him to Paris."

Hunter surveyed the man cautiously. He had not expected anyone to meet him outside Paris.

"He has two of us to see him safe to Paris. He has no need of you," Thomas said.

The man fished a letter from his doublet and held it out. "*S'il vous plait.*"

Thomas studied it with knitted brows and slowly moved his lips. "*Eh, pour vous, monsieur.*" He handed the letter to Hunter.

Hunter broke the seal of the English Embassy, and read:

To Master Paul Adams,

The bearer of this letter, Jacques Crespin, is well known to us, and has instructions to direct you forthwith to lodgings at the Chessboard Inn, in the rue Saint Croix de la Bretonniere.

Neither Ambassador Walsingham nor myself is able to wait upon you today. Pray excuse the brevity of this message. I hope to meet with you soon to discuss the Rouen Syndicate's goals.

Paris, 6 April 1572

Your servant,
Robert Beale, Secretary to the Ambassador

The seal and message appeared genuine. "This man bears a letter from the embassy. He is to guide me to my lodgings."

"By your leave, Master Adams, we were directed to take you safely to Paris," Pierre said.

"So you will, Pierre. I will not deprive you of a night in Paris. But instead of proceeding to the embassy, we will follow"—Hunter glanced at the letter—"Master Crespin to my lodgings."

Jacques Crespin walked his horse forward. "I am at your service, Master Adams," he said in English. "Do not be surprised. I was raised in Calais, of an English father and a French mother. The embassy pays me to meet Englishmen who arrive—Scots and Irish, too. I offer to show them Paris and interpret for them if they speak little French. So I get remuneration from them as well as a reward from the embassy for information about them."

"And will you be informing them about me as well?" Hunter asked.

"I will tell you more of my duties soon," he said.

Hunter and Crespin rode ahead, with Boutilier's servants following.

"Just ahead you can see the basilica of Saint-Denis," Crespin began. "We can stop to view the tombs of the kings of France and admire the style of architecture Abbot Suger introduced here four hundred years. Of course, it is out of fashion now that the Italian style has become..."

"Master Crespin," Hunter interrupted, "I would rather press on just now than take in the sights."

"As you wish," Crespin shrugged. "You must excuse me. I have my little speeches for all the places that visitors want to see, and I have been told I love the sound of my own voice."

"I am disappointed that I cannot speak with Ambassador Walsingham today," Hunter said.

"The ambassador and secretary are meeting now with Sir Thomas Smith, busy with the final stages of negotiating a treaty. But we can send a message as soon as we arrive, requesting a meeting tomorrow."

"Then I will hope for tomorrow."

"I assure you that St. Denis is very interesting." Crespin glanced expectantly, then added, "But perhaps we can ride out later. I understand you may be with us for some time."

How much did Crespin know about his mission?

As they rode, Crespin asked about Hunter's journey from Rouen, his Channel crossing, and when and how his possessions were coming to Paris. Interspersed with his questions was a constant refrain. "You should gain your first view of Paris from Montmartre...All visitors are impressed with the panorama of Paris from the abbey on Montmartre...You will never forget the sight of Paris from Montmartre." Then, to the guards, "Have you seen Paris from the top of Montmartre? Yes, it does involve a ride up the mountain, but I know a shop that serves excellent wine, and I will buy you drinks to compensate for your climb, although the view will be compensation enough. You will all thank me when you behold Paris from the mountain."

Crespin's repeated offers of alcoholic refreshment won the servants to his side. On top of Montmartre, they stood near the walls of the abbey and looked out. "Here we are, Master Adams. Paris lies before you."

Hunter had to admit that the view was impressive. The faubourgs pressed against the walls of Paris. Within the walls, the roofs of the city reminded him of mosaic tiles depicting the waves on a lake. Above the geometric waves rose the steeples of churches, the turrets of grand houses, the towers of palaces and monasteries. He wished he could describe it to Mary, but she thought he was going to Emden.

"Look," Pierre said. "There at the center is the Cathedral of Our Lady."

"And the Châtelet and the Palace." Thomas joined him in pointing.

"See, sir." Pierre said. "You don't need this Jacques as a guide. Me and Thomas can show you all the monuments of Paris."

"Those towers there are the Louvre," Thomas said.

"And there's the gallows on Montfaucon." Pierre pointed east. "See, we are showing you for free. Crespin there will expect you to give him a sol for every word, I reckon."

"Shut up!" Thomas turned on him. "Where's your manners? Don't insult a man who's going to buy us drinks."

Pierre's satisfied smile turned sheepish. "Sorry."

"I take no offense," Crespin said. "And I will keep my bargain. Step this way and you can see a windmill beyond the abbey walls. See the stall just next to it?"

"Yes, Master Crespin," Thomas took a deferential step forward.

"This should buy you several cups of wine." He handed Thomas a coin. "Relax and enjoy yourselves. It will take me some time to point out the antiquities and singularities to Master Adams."

As the servants walked away, Crespin said in English, "Let me show you Paris in an orderly fashion. It has three parts, the island in the Seine, where Paris began, is *la Cité*; north of the river on the right bank, *le ville*; to the south on the left bank, *l'université*. Below you, the road we will follow to the Porte du Montmartre. To the east is the Porte Saint-Denis then Porte Saint-Martin." Here he glanced at the retreating backs of the servants, and abruptly his manner changed.

"Master Adams, I have been at some trouble to draw you away from those two servants since we met at Saint-Denis. But no matter. If you nod occasionally as I talk, and I point, it will convince Pierre and Thomas, and anyone else watching, that I am identifying the landmarks of the city to you."

Surprised at his serious tone, Hunter nodded.

"I should first clarify our relationship. Ambassador Walsingham has entrusted me not merely to guide you, but to assist you. I know that Paul Adams is an assumed name..."

Hunter was on his guard again.

"...but I do not know your true name, nor should I. As a guide, I will orient you to the city of Paris. As an assistant, I can direct you to the haunts of expatriate Englishmen, acquaint you with various printers, and even cart about the chest of cloth samples you have brought to show to merchants. I may even be able to advise you on Catholic forms of worship."

So Crespin knew he was posing as a secret Catholic. There was obviously more to this man than Hunter had realized.

As two brothers in Benedictine habits emerged from the abbey's gate, Crespin pointed east again. "There you see the towers of the Temple. Since the suppression of the Knights Templar by King Philip, the Knights of Malta have occupied the Templars' buildings. I will show you where Philip the Fair burned Jacques DeMolay when we tour the city."

With a nod of greeting, the monks descended the slope. The Benedictine stripped of his habit and stabbed on the deck of the Spanish caravel flashed in Hunter's mind.

"What is the matter?" Crespin asked.

"Nothing. Pray continue."

"You are wise to keep your counsel with someone you have just met," Crespin said, "but you may ask the Ambassador if I have served him well when you see him."

"Your offer predicts his answer."

Crespin smiled and bowed slightly. "I am to tell you of the mood of the city as well as its topography."

"And what is its mood?"

"The people of Paris are angry," Crespin responded. "Angry at the high price of wood and bread. Angry that the king demands a tax, which he styles a 'free gift.' They burn above all with hatred of the Huguenots. They believe everything that is wrong is connected with those damned Protestants."

"Even the price of bread?"

"Everything. You see, the very existence of these heretics endangers the immortal soul of each Parisian. Their preachers tell them each week that the Huguenots are cancerous limbs, which must be cut off so the body of Paris may survive. During the last war, when these heretics dared raise their arms against His Most Christian Majesty, they were driven out of Paris. And did not God show his approval of this act by granting the royal armies victories at Jarnac and Montcontour?"

"I suppose you could say He did."

"Now, as it was clear that God was against the Huguenots, ordaining their defeat in battle, you would expect them to be punished by any treaty ending the fighting. But, no! The Peace of Saint-Germain gave them cities to fortify and said that those Huguenots who had been driven from Paris had a right to return to their homes and shops, and even to regain the offices they had held. You can imagine the anger of those good Catholics who had moved into their houses and purchased their offices."

"I can."

"Parisians are not only angry at the Huguenots, but also at the king, who agreed to such a treaty. It must be, they say, the influence of the Queen Mother and her Italian favorites. They were already hated for grasping high offices and receiving titles over good, honest Frenchmen."

"Does it not matter that the Italians are good Catholics?"

"Not much. The morals of the Borgia and Medici popes are well known. But let me return to the Protestants. After this hated peace treaty was proclaimed, the people of Paris saw the Catholic paragons, the Duke of Guise and the Cardinal of Lorraine, leave the King's Court. In their place, the Protestant Admiral Coligny came to advise. And they heard rumors of a wedding between the Duke of Anjou, the king's brother, and Elizabeth of England, another heretic."

"But that has come to naught."

"You and I know that, but do the vegetable sellers of Paris? And there is the rumor that Princess Margot will marry Henri of Navarre!"

"But the price of bread?"

"I'm coming to that. So the House of Valois appears to turn its back on the Holy Catholic Church and to tolerate, or perhaps even promote, heresy. And the 'free gift' the king demands is used for these ends. People say, 'We paid to fight the war against the Huguenots, and now we must pay for the privileges the peace gives them.' It is clear to Parisians that all these acts cannot please God, so He is punishing this disobedient kingdom by sending bad harvests, floods, and severe winters."

Hunter nodded. "And the price of bread rises. As a Catholic, Paul Adams can only applaud such logic."

"But as an Englishman, Adams is suspect. The Parisians are ready to hate Englishmen as much as Italians. If the treaty with England is signed, it will be seen as another example of tolerating Protestants."

"Does the French Crown not have a treaty with the Turk?"

"Yes, to frustrate the Habsburgs. But Parisians reckon the treaty with Constantinople as another blot on the House of Valois." He glanced up at the returning servants. "But here are our friends, and I have not named half the monuments." He raised his voice. "There is the abbey of Sainte-Geneviève on the hill on the Left Bank…"

"*Voila, L'Échiquier.*" Crespin pointed at the sign of the chessboard hanging before the four-story timber-framed inn. In its doorway, a sandy-haired boy jumped to his feet and shouted. Two other urchins materialized to hold the reins of their horses, and another ran out of the inn to greet them.

Hunter dismounted, aware that a silence had overcome the men. He followed their gaze to the doorway of the inn. There stood a woman, wearing a black gown with a white ruff at her throat. A black French hood with a white coif beneath sat high on her jet-black hair. The black and white of her attire framed an oval face with full lips, a thin nose, and green eyes that did not glance down demurely, but looked out at the men before her with—what? Was it merely confidence, or was there an air of defiance? Crespin had said she was a widow, and managed the inn alone after her husband's death.

"Madame Marguerite Moreau," Crespin said, "this is Master Paul Adams. Master Adams, this is your hostess, Madame Moreau."

Her mouth curved into a slight smile. "*Enchanté,*" she said, bowing. "I have been expecting you."

Hunter bowed in return. "I am pleased to be in Paris with you." He was drawn again to those green eyes with long lashes staring directly back at him. Madame Moreau could not be judged as beautiful as Mary. Her skin was too dark, almost olive in comparison with her white ruff. Her lips were too large. What a contrast. Mary was fair, blonde, and young compared to Madame Moreau's dark maturity. Not that she was old—perhaps thirty.

"I have a chamber ready for you. It is not large, but there should be enough space for…" She looked beyond him. "I was told you would be staying some time and would have much luggage."

"It is coming by barge in a few days."

"Of course," she smiled. "And I understand you brought no servants?"

"I will be looking after Master Adams in Paris," Crespin interjected.

"Ah, Jacques Crespin, guide extraordinaire and master of two tongues," she said in English.

"*Et vous aussi?*" Hunter asked.

"No, no," she said, lapsing back into French. "I speak only a few words of many languages. I can say, 'Pay your bill now,' in many tongues."

They laughed. Her green eyes could be playful as well as challenging.

Pierre cleared his throat. "We will ride on to our lodgings on the Left Bank."

Hunter understood. He reached into his purse and handed each servant a silver teston. That should buy each of them several bottles of wine or a cheap whore. Both bowed their thanks and mounted. One of the boys, having marked Hunter down as generous, fought for the reins of his horse and handed them to Pierre. He and his friends looked up expectantly.

"Avarice is a sin, boys," Crespin said. "And you've done but little."

Their faces fell.

"May it please you, Master Crespin," the sandy-haired servant from the inn said. "They are my friends, and we have an agreement."

"Master Adams is no party to your agreement, Laurent," Crespin said.

Hunter stepped close to him. "They have earned a small vail, but I have only a demi-teston."

"That is too much." Crespin reached in his own purse and extracted a coin. "Here is a dixaine to split among you. Armond, you will be fair." He handed the shortest street urchin the coin. "Now, Laurent, you and Martin pick up those saddle bags and earn your own vails."

Marguerite Moreau's gown swayed agreeably as she led them up two flights of stairs and opened a door. Hunter entered his chamber, and the boys and Crespin followed with his baggage. To his left, a window opened onto the street. Opposite the door, a paneled wall stretched from the fireplace to a single bed with a canopy. A brass candlestick stood on a small table beside the bed; a stool and desk occupied the wall near the door. The furnishings were simple, but the carving on the fireplace and the paneling gave some touches of elegance. There would be space for his chests. "I thank you. This should do well."

Marguerite Moreau's smile said she knew his room was exactly what he needed. "You may wish to change now. Martin, fetch Monsieur Adams some water and a cloth."

Crespin said, "If you can spare Laurent, Madame Moreau, I am sure he might reach the embassy with a message more quickly on foot than I might on horseback at this hour."

"If you are willing to take his place moving a barrel of wine from the cellar, he can deliver a message."

"Agreed," Crespin said.

"Laurent, fetch Master Adams pen and ink," she said. "After you have penned your note and refreshed yourself, if it please you to come down, I will introduce you to my chef Auguste."

Half an hour later, having changed into his light blue doublet and venetians, Hunter descended. Madame Moreau looked him up and down, and smiled. "How pleasant to have a guest who dresses so well."

"This is the fashion my London tailor favors," Hunter said. "I do not know if it will impress anyone in Paris."

"It did last season," Madame Moreau said. "But come." She led him down the corridor to the kitchen. The aroma of a beef stew, heavy with onions, filled the air. A heavy man with salt-and-pepper hair and a moustache, but no beard, turned around. Beside him, a boy of about fifteen did the same.

"Master Adams, this is Auguste and his son Pierre. Auguste is the reason our dining room is full each midday and evening, even when the inn is not."

"You are too kind, madame." Auguste's brown eyes sparkled at the compliment. Pierre's smiling face was a copy of his father's.

"I look forward to sampling your fare," Hunter said. "It smells delicious."

"Thank you. I hope it will not disappoint."

"The dining room is this way." Madame Moreau led him back down the corridor. "Laurent and Martin, whom you have already met, sleep there." She pointed to a door next to her office. "Auguste and Pierre live nearby. I will introduce you to Bernard, the ostler, and his wife Bertha later. They lodge in the courtyard."

They passed her office, turned right at the inn's entrance, and entered a large dining area, well lighted by windows that opened onto the street on one side and onto the courtyard on the other.

Madame Moreau spoke quietly to him. "Ambassador Walsingham requested you have a room to yourself. Likewise, that you take your meals in your room for a few days until you are settled. Though you might gather information from travelers, gleaning information from guests is what he trusts me to do." Their eyes met. She smiled with self-satisfaction.

So, Walsingham was unsure of him.

Behind a bar at the near end of the room, Martin topped up Crespin's cup. "Excellent wine," Crespin said. "Well worth the sweat needed to haul it up."

"You may consider that one cup payment for your effort," Madame Moreau said. "The second cup you must pay for."

A flurry of giggling behind them caused Madame Moreau to twirl around.

"Girls, some decorum before our guest! Master Adams, these are the chambermaids, Marie and Jeanne."

Marie, a slight girl of perhaps seventeen, dropped a curtsy. Her large blue eyes looked up at Hunter from a thin face, and she smiled awkwardly. "Good day, Master Adams," she said. Her thin nose looked as though someone had pinched its bridge. Her curly blonde hair escaped on all sides of the simple linen coif she wore.

Beside her, Jeanne, shorter, with dark, straight hair, a fuller body, and an attractive face, also dropped a curtsy. Her brown eyes glanced at Hunter with interest before she looked down. "Sir," she said.

"If anything is amiss in your chamber, let me know," Madame Moreau said. "Girls, it is time to prepare bowls and plates for the evening meal, and several of Auguste's pots and pans will need washing."

Marie's smile turned to a frown. Jeanne kept her gaze on the floor, but her shoulders slumped. "Yes, mistress."

As the girls passed him, Crespin drained his cup of burgundy and addressed Madame Moreau. "When Laurent returns, pray send him to tell me what is happening. Master Adams, I shall call upon you at eight in the morning. If you have an appointment at the embassy, that should allow us time to reach it. If you do not, we can begin your introduction to Paris."

Wednesday, 9 April 1572

Hunter, wearing his black fustian suit and carrying letters from England in his satchel, left the Chessboard Inn far in advance of his ten o'clock appointment at the embassy. Crespin insisted he needed time to point out landmarks on the way.

"What is that smell?" Hunter asked, as they stepped into the street.

"Smell?" Crespin looked puzzled.

"Yes. Like a rather ripe privy."

"Oh, that," Crespin said. "It's the famous *boue de Paris.*"

"Paris mud?"

"It's mostly shit in reality—horse shit, donkey shit, dog shit, and, of course, human shit. Add in a little dust and some crumbs, mix with dew, blood from the butchers, and urine from everywhere, and *voilà—boue de Paris.* Hercules, who founded the city, would find it harder to clean Paris than the Augean Stables."

"What a gift you have for describing your city's virtues," Hunter said. "But I did not notice it yesterday."

"It rained a little last night. That makes it worse. But you'll get used to it."

They cut through the market in the Old Cemetery of Saint-Jean, "The gathering place for this quarter of Paris when Protestant troops under Coligny besieged the city."

"Was that when he was condemned?"

"No, two years later. Of course, now he is at the king's right hand."

"I fear it will take me a long time to understand French politics."

"I don't think anyone does," Crespin said. He led Hunter past the Saint-Gervais Church and through an archway into a large square.

"Here we are at the Place de Grève. There is the Hôtel de Ville. We will walk downwind of the gibbet, by your leave, or the smell will be much worse than 'Paris mud.' We can stand by the cross."

They mounted a few steps at the base of a tall cross, and Hunter regarded the hollow-eyed corpse twisting in the breeze.

"Only an apothecary who poisoned his wife," Crespin said, "but there have been important executions here. Louis of Luxembourg had his head chopped off for plotting against Louis XI. Anne de Bourg was hanged and burned here for telling Henri II he should not persecute Protestants. And Admiral Coligny was hanged in effigy three years ago."

Hunter grunted. "A gruesome place. Is violence a theme of your tours?"

"Most clients find it intriguing," Crespin said. "Don't you?"

"Less and less."

They crossed the pont Notre-Dame to the Île de la Cité. The uniform façades of the shops were a contrast to the jumble of London Bridge.

Crespin insisted they pause before the façade of Notre-Dame, and he began to describe the carvings on the portals, but Hunter was eager to reach the embassy.

They crossed the Petit-Pont to the Left Bank. Crespin could not resist a few gory stories as they passed the empty gibbet in the Place Maubert, then he rattled off the names of each college they passed as they climbed toward the Abbey of Sainte-Geneviève. His stories of the times she had answered prayers and protected Paris lasted until they reached the English Embassy.

"Good day, Pierre." Crespin greeted the embassy's doorman. "This is Master Paul Adams. He is expected."

Pierre was the sort of formidable presence you would want guarding your door, but the eyes in his round face did not quite focus on Hunter's as he touched his hat. He directed them to a seat and climbed the impressive staircase leading to the first floor, where a gallery circled the large entrance hall.

"The ambassador, his secretary, and their clerk have their offices up there," Crespin said. "Their private apartments are on the top floor."

Pierre returned with a shorter man, dressed in a plain brown tight-sleeved doublet with a small ruff and matching hose. "I am Thomas Howell, Secretary Beale's servant. If you follow me, he will see you soon, Master Adams. He asks only a few moments to peruse any correspondence you have brought from England." It was clear from his manner that Crespin was to wait.

"Certainly," Hunter drew the letters from his satchel, handed them to Howell, and followed him upstairs and down a corridor to a bench beside Beale's office.

After some moments, Howell returned. "Secretary Beale will see you now."

Beale was a stout, solidly built man with a short beard, dressed in a black doublet with silver thread embroidered around the cuffs and collar. "Welcome to Paris, Master Adams. Pray be seated. I trust you found your accommodations suitable."

"I did."

"We debated whether to lodge you on the right or left bank. The left bank would put you nearer the embassy, the printers, and English expatriates. But as your alleged purpose is to convince merchants and officials to favor the Rouen Syndicate's staple, we decided that the right bank was more appropriate."

"Although I scarcely know Paris, the distances do not seem too great," Hunter said.

Beale leaned forward on his elbows. "Let me explain our situation. I must apologize for the ambassador, but he is even now at Blois with Sir Thomas Smith, meeting with members of the King's Council. We are having some difficulty in the treaty regarding Scotland. As you can imagine, we are unwilling to have Mary mentioned as the rightful queen, but the French will not recognize her son James and his regent. But I am sure we will find a way.

"The conclusion of the treaty will be the beginning of the trade negotiations. A clause calls for the establishment of a staple for English goods in France, but it is vague. The location is not named and of course none of the details. But you should know there are some in the City of London and at Court that oppose this staple, and they have allies in the French Court as well."

Hunter nodded. His uncle had spoken of the resistance of some Merchant Adventurers.

"You must wait a few days, until this treaty is agreed and signed, before approaching anyone. Some merchants with close connections to Rouen already know of the proposals, but there has been little reaction among the bourgeoisie of Paris. We want to keep it that way until the treaty is agreed."

"In the meantime, I might occupy myself with contacting some of the English Catholics and Parisian printers," Hunter suggested.

"You might. But I advise you to move slowly there, as well." Beale pulled a thin packet of papers from the left side of his desk. "In January, one George Pickering, whose family holds land in Herefordshire, came to see me. He claimed to be a student at the Collège Mignon, in desperate need of funds. It appears that his family, although they are Catholic, did not approve of his leaving England, and they cut him off. He claimed he was a member of a group of English Catholics here in Paris and was willing to give us information regarding them, their conversation, and any plans they might have that were a danger to Her Majesty."

Hunter had a sinking feeling. Beale was about to tell him he was superfluous. He must pack his bags and leave. He would be unable to prove himself worthy of Mary. Perhaps, so that his trip would not be a total loss, he would surrender himself to Crespin for a few days and listen to descriptions of every building and violent encounter in Paris.

"I asked Master Crespin to enquire as to the truth of Pickering's story. So far as he could tell, Pickering was telling the truth. We agreed to help him financially, and he provided us with this information." Beale presented a folder of papers.

Hunter ran his eye over a list of names with annotations next to each. "Am I to gain the acquaintance of these men?"

"Perhaps, but you need to know more. Over a fortnight ago, we asked Pickering to enquire of these 'friends' of his about the printing of pamphlets or broadsides destined for England. He agreed to do so. Two days ago, he was to report what he had found out. But at the appointed time, he did not appear. Crespin went to his lodgings, asked his landlady, and enquired at his favorite tavern, but no one had seen him. It seems Master Pickering has disappeared."

CHAPTER 4

Explorations

HUNTER TOOK A MOMENT TO ABSORB THE NEWS. PERHAPS HE WOULD HAVE more to do than he expected.

"You see why I advise you to move slowly when asking about printers," Beale said. "Such questions may be dangerous, at least among self-exiled English Catholics."

"Crespin did not tell me about Pickering," Hunter said.

"I asked him not to mention it," Beale said.

Hunter leafed through the reports.

"Those are copies for you, Master Adams," Beale said. "Be sure to keep them hidden. After you have read them, you should have a better idea of how to present yourself to these English exiles as a sympathizer. But have patience and proceed with caution."

"So, I am to delay speaking to merchants and officials concerning the Rouen staple and to move slowly among the English Catholics." Disappointment colored his words.

"This may go against your nature, but relax and play the curious traveler for a fortnight," Beale said. "By that time the ambassador will have returned."

If he said he must bide his time for two weeks, he was sure Crespin would fill it all.

After they left the embassy, Crespin said, "I assume Master Beale told you of an English gentleman who has recently gone missing."

"Yes, Pickering. I would be glad to learn more of him," Hunter said.

"No need to mention the gentleman's name," Crespin said. "At least not on crowded streets. I can tell you more at your lodgings. Always assume we are being observed. By sunset today, the Queen Mother will know who has visited the English Embassy. So will the Duke of Guise and the Spanish ambassador."

"So our visit will bring attention to us?"

"Not particularly. It is natural a recently arrived agent for a merchant group would visit the embassy. And I am there all the time, eager to milk English visitors for as much money as I can."

Hunter raised his eyebrows.

"Do not worry. My services to you are being covered by the embassy. Let us return to the Île de la Cité, the oldest part of Paris.

"Lead on, then."

Lead on he did, through the narrow streets and alleys of the Île de la Cité, naming each of its close-packed parishes. Hunter mentally replaced the small steepled drawings of churches he had studied on the map at Glasswell Manor with images of solid stone and mortar. They marveled at Notre-Dame's stained glass windows. After a midday bowl of pottage, Crespin led them to the Grand Hall of the Palais de Justice, where he reeled off a history of France, pointing to the statues of kings atop columns, from the Merovingians through the Carolingians and Capetians to the House of Valois.

"Stop!" Hunter threw up his hands.

"You wish to remain ignorant of French history?"

"Can you just give me the high points?"

Crespin gave him a disappointed frown. "All right, but it gets complex now. With Philip of Valois our troubles with the English began."

"I thought you were half English."

"I am, but my French half is talking now. Philip of Valois was a nephew of Philip the Fair, but Edward III of England was a grandson."

"Ah, ha! A more direct line."

"No. Edward's claim was through his mother, and the French Crown cannot pass through the female line. I am sure you know of the ensuing wars. The English defeated the French at Crécy, at Poitiers, and finally, at Agincourt, Henry V of England defeated Charles VI—that one there." Crespin pointed at the statue. "When Charles went mad, a civil war started between the Armagnacs and the Burgundians. Paris took one side then the other. I will show you some of the slaughter sites."

Hunter sighed. "You can draw me a diagram over a cup of wine at L'Échiquier."

Both were on their third cup of wine when Madame Moreau and Laurent carried in trays with their supper. As she left, Hunter's eyes followed her. Crespin said, "Many regular visitors to Paris stay at L'Échiquier just so they can watch Madame Moreau walk through the dining room."

"She moves very gracefully." Hunter flushed. He should be thinking of Mary.

Crespin laughed. "So we would all agree. Some women are a pleasure to look at."

"I am surprised she has remained a widow. Has she had offers?"

"Several. A beautiful woman and a thriving inn are two prizes in one. But she enjoys her independence more than she desires a husband."

Hunter regarded Crespin's diagram, covered with names and arrows. "Well, you have talked me through your mad king, Charles VI, and the slaughters of Armagnac and Burgundy. Let us abandon history for a moment so that you can tell me about George Pickering."

"Master Pickering, so far as I could discover, has been in Paris about two years. The youngest son of a Catholic family in Herefordshire. He saw coming here as a courageous act, proving he was a more devout Catholic than his older brothers and his parents. From what he said, they conformed by attending services at their parish church, but had a priest say Mass at their house."

Hunter nodded. Like the Spranklins.

"He was a student at Collège Mignon for a while. He never had the wealth or family status to impress the English Catholics here, but he tried. He wore the latest fashion and tried to contrive introductions to French aristocrats, but when his family cut off his money, he drifted to the margins. When he came to the embassy, I think he just wanted to go home."

"Did you know him?"

"Only in the last few months. We would arrange meetings and he would pass sealed letters to deliver to the embassy. The English exiles here do not need my services, so I have no reason to associate with them."

"So you could not question them after he disappeared."

"No. I presented myself to his landlady as a creditor trying to find him. I was not the only one looking for him. And he owed her two months' rent as well. She had not seen him since Easter. He may have simply left town to abandon his debts. His landlady said his clothing and some papers were still in his chamber. She threatened to sell them and rent the room to someone else if he did not return and pay her soon."

"Secretary Beale seemed to think that he may have been in danger because of some enquiries he was making," Hunter said.

"Although I do not mingle with the expatriates at the Antelope, a server there trades information for silver. He understands little English, but he can recognize an argument in any language. He had not witnessed any conflict involving Pickering."

"Perhaps you are right," Hunter mused. "Debt may have led him into more trouble than spying. I'll read his reports, then approach my countrymen at the Antelope."

Thursday, 10 April 1572

Crespin guided Hunter to the Grand Châtelet ("A court, a prison, and a morgue, all in one") then strolled leisurely towards the Louvre. There, he expounded on the Italian style of Lescot's new wing and disparaged the turrets of the old palace. They bought pies from a stall in Les Halles. Hunter examined the cloth in the drapers' stalls, comparing it with the English textiles he had brought.

Crespin led him to the Cemetery of the Holy Innocents. "The earth came from the Holy Land. It is so good at eating away flesh, that after a week here, only the bones will be left."

"You return to your usual jollity," Hunter said.

Crespin remonstrated. "Can you expect me to avoid the subject of death at a graveyard?"

"Why should you start now?"

Crespin disregarded his jibe. "At the far corner is the church of the Holy Innocents and before it is the Cross of the Gastines."

"The cross of the Gastines?" Hunter said.

"They did not tell you in England? A family arrested for holding a Protestant service in their house. There was a riot and people were killed. Afraid of the mob, the Parlement ordered the Gastines executed, their house torn down, and that huge stone pyramid erected on the site."

"But it is here in the cemetery."

"Because, after the Peace of Saint-Germain, the king orders all monuments to the destruction of Huguenots are to come down. But the city magistrates make excuses a full year, fearing the mob. Admiral Coligny presses the king. Finally, they say they will move the cross to the Cemetery of the Innocents. The priests howl. The mob howls. So they move the cross in the dead of night last December. Next morning the mob attacks houses of Huguenots. Montmorency had to bring in the troops to restore order."

"But the cross was only moved."

"The story tells you about Parisians. Any concession to the Protestants is seen as a defeat."

Crespin assumed his official-guide-speaking-from-rote manner. "One of Paris's most famous sights, the *Danse Macabre*, is in the *Charnier des Lingières*." He led Hunter to the right.

They passed two boys throwing an oddly shaped ball back and forth, to keep it from a third. As it tumbled through the air, Hunter realized it was a ball joint, broken off the top of a thighbone. Beyond, piles of skulls were packed above the arches and beneath the eaves of the charnel houses, as far as the eye could see in either direction, staring out hollow-eyed. Something grasped Hunter's right arm. He jumped back with a cry.

Crespin laughed. "You must watch where you are going, Paul. You almost stumbled into that hawthorn."

Hunter blurted a nervous laugh. "I was distracted by all the skulls."

"The unconsecrated ground where they bury the unclaimed dead from the Châtelet is over there," Crespin gestured. "And here is the *Danse Macabre*."

They walked slowly along the mural. Others brushed past, looking at the paintings, reading the verses, and laughing nervously. Skeletons led a pope and an emperor in their dance, then a cardinal and a king, and so on down the social hierarchy, each one mocking the vanity of the living. "You will want to note the lawyer in the next arcade," Crespin teased.

"He is paired with a musician." The exchange between Death and the lawyer was full of legal terms. The lawyer feared divine justice, without a defense or chance of appeal.

"Take a memory with you," came a voice near at hand. Hunter turned to see one of the dancing skeletons come to life. The old man's deep-set eyes, sunken cheeks, and pallid face made it easy to imagine the skull beneath his shrunken skin. "Buy a picture to take home." The gaunt figure gestured to prints of the *Danse Macabre* hanging on a line beneath the arch.

"No, thank you." Hunter backed away from the print seller. "Let us go see Goujon's nymphs on the fountain. You said they are better than his sculpture at the Louvre."

"I said more beautiful and graceful, not better."

"Beauty will be a great improvement."

Madame Moreau herself served Hunter a chicken stew, and said in a teasing tone, "You look tired. I had heard that Englishmen have great stamina."

"Who told you that?" he asked.

"An Englishman."

They both laughed. "Paris is a large city," he said.

"Ah, bigger than London, I hear. Which part did you see today?"

"The Louvre, some hôtels of your nobility, Les Halles, the Cemetery of the Holy Innocents, several churches, the monastery of Saint Martin..."

"Does your queen have a palace in London as grand as the Louvre?"

"She has no palace in London, but many nearby—Whitehall, St. James, Greenwich, Richmond, Hampton Court. They are all quite grand, but none is as modern as the new Louvre."

"Our king has many châteaux along the Loire. They are some days' journey from Paris, and they are of surpassing beauty. Are those of your queen beautiful?"

"I think grand is a better adjective than beautiful. I have heard different opinions."

Laurent appeared at the door. "Pardon me, Madame, but Auguste has asked for you in the kitchen."

A look of annoyance crossed her face. "Excuse me. Enjoy your meal, Monsieur Adams. You must tell me more of your impressions tomorrow."

Friday, 11 April 1572

After recounting in detail the arrest and torture of Grand Master Jacques DeMolay at the Temple, Crespin led Hunter to the Hôtel de Guise and explained the complex coat of arms over the portal. "The family has so many claims to territory and titles—Lorraine, Aragon, Naples, Hungary, even Jerusalem—they needed to squeeze them all in." He turned. "Across the street, at the Chapel de Braque, Jehan le Retif preached reform. Of course, Guises would say he preached vile heresy."

"What would you say?"

"I am a good Catholic, but as a guide to English Protestants, I must keep an open mind."

"You are a chameleon," Hunter said.

"Like the English who lived through the reigns of King Henry, King Edward, Queen Mary, and Queen Elizabeth," he said. "Flexibility of belief can be a useful trait."

"A cynical, churlish chameleon."

"Around the corner stood the Hôtel Barbette, where Queen Isabelle of Bavaria lived. She took many lovers. One, Louis of Orléans, was attacked by the henchmen of the John the Fearless. First they chopped his arms with axes, so he couldn't fight back, then they stove in his head. That was the start of the war between the Armagnacs and the Burgundians."

"I remember that story from the other night."

"I am glad a few facts stuck."

"There were too many names and alliances and treacheries and glasses of wine that night."

They arrived at an area where new hôtels were rising in the Italian style. "Here stood the Palais des Tournelles, where Henri II was mortally wounded in a tournament. The lance of Count Montgomery shattered, and the splinters ripped through the king's eye. He lingered nine days in extreme pain."

"Yet another jolly tale to cheer up visitors."

Crespin shrugged. "Most of them like gory details, and I can add omens and prophecies of Nostradamus for those who like the occult."

"I am sure you can."

"At any rate, here we are on the rue Saint-Antoine. To your left, the Bastille, built two hundred years ago."

"Must we walk around it? My feet are sore."

Crespin shook his head in disapproval. "Very well. We will head back. Over there is the Hôtel de Birague, where the Keeper of the Seals lives. He said the last war would be settled not by soldiers, but by cooks."

"You speak in riddles, or Monsieur de Birague does."

"Poison," Crespin explained.

As they walked west and the rue Saint-Antoine narrowed, they heard a commotion. At the corner, they were almost bowled over by a man is a black doublet, pursued by a crowd of jeering boys crying "Heretic! Blasphemer! Dog!" and pelting him with stones.

"What is that?" Hunter asked.

"They are baiting a Huguenot. Down that street is a shrine to the Virgin," Crespin explained. "The local boys amuse themselves by inviting any passerby they believe is a Protestant to kneel and pray to Our Lady and, of course, to donate an offering. When he refuses, they set upon him."

That evening, Hunter felt disappointed when Laurent, serving him carp with a sauce of onions and herbs, said that Madame Moreau was otherwise engaged. But, as he was finishing, she knocked on his door and entered.

"I hope you had a good day."

"A fine day, and less tiring than yesterday."

"Perhaps you were fortified with the excellent food of L'Échiquier."

"I am sure that made all the difference. Tell Auguste the fish was excellent." He lifted the last bite to his mouth.

"And what did you see today?"

He told her a brief version of his peregrinations with Crespin.

"Do the nobles of England have such fine hôtels in London?" she asked.

"Few of the hôtels of our nobility—we just call them houses—are in the City of London. Most are to the west, along the Strand."

She wrinkled her brow.

"The great houses—Leicester House, Arundel House, Somerset House, the Savoy, Durham House, York House—are along the Thames," he explained.

Her puzzled expression held.

"Here, I will show you." He grasped a chunk of bread and drew a rough map in the sauce. "This is the Thames, our river. London lies to the north of it, as *le ville de Paris* lies north of the Seine." He drew a semi-circle above the line of the river.

She pulled up a stool and sat beside him.

"In the east, where you have the Bastille, we also have a fortress, the Tower of London." He pinched off a crumb and placed it appropriately on his sauce map. "Now in the west of Paris is your royal palace, the Louvre. Our royal palaces, Whitehall and St. James, are not inside London's walls. They are out here, down the river at Westminster." He tore off two more pieces of bread and placed them on the plate.

Marguerite Moreau giggled. "Not very impressive palaces."

"Well, as I said yesterday, we English have not learned to build in the Italian style yet."

"And these hôtels...or 'houses' you mentioned?"

"Here, along the river between the City and Westminster." He placed several pieces of bread in a line.

"Is this an exact model?" she teased.

"As exact as can be made with crumbs."

"And where is your cathedral?"

He tore off a larger piece of bread, carefully pulled and squeezed it into a small building with a steeple, and placed it in the semicircle. "Here is St. Paul's."

"Is it as beautiful as Notre-Dame?"

"Yes," he said, "and larger."

Her eyebrows flicked to dismiss the importance of size. "And here?" She pointed. "South of your river."

"Well, it is not part of London. On the south bank is Southwark. There are a few bishops' palaces there, but many..." He stopped, remembering his experiences at the bear baiting pits and one unfortunate evening at a brothel. "...many amusements."

After a moment, her green eyes lit up. "You mean houses of pleasures are there?"

"Yes"

"This proves the superiority of Paris," she asserted. "We have the best university in Europe south of our river; you have whorehouses."

As she laughed, he was suddenly aware of the rise and fall of her bosom, of the flush on her cheeks, of the candlelight on her hair. As if sensing his thought, she stopped laughing, smiled, and stood. "Well, we have settled our contest for one night. I must manage my inn, and you must also have things to do."

Hunter stood as well. Was she embarrassed? She did not appear so. He attempted to conclude their conversation with gallantry. "Thank you for taking time to talk with me."

"It was my pleasure," she smiled. "We shall speak again tomorrow."

Saturday, 12 April 1572

"We shall begin our tour of the Left Bank here, in the Place Maubert," Crespin declared.

Hunter nodded towards the gallows. "With a recurring theme of your tours."

"And I foresaw your objection," said Crespin, "and prepared my defense."

"Well, how do you plead?"

"To enriching my tours by telling stories of violent deaths instead of merely reciting names and dates?"

"No. To emphasizing blood and gore and death."

"If that is your choice of words, I plead not guilty," Crespin said. "And I have a strong defense."

"Let me hear it." Hunter folded his arms.

"First, people are fascinated by death. Look at the crowds at any execution. Second, death gives birth to art." Crespin squared his shoulders. "Of what does Virgil sing? Of arms and a man. What would the *Aeneid* and the *Iliad* be without violent death?"

"But the *Iliad* is a story of war. It must contain violent death; and the *Aeneid* also tells of Dido's love."

"And her suicide when abandoned."

"Surely there is as much literature devoted to the subject of love," Hunter said.

"Love! It is always mixed with death. Do people choose to read of loving couples, who marry, peacefully raise their children, and grow old together? No. We prefer love that is tragic—Troilus and Cressida, Tristan and Isolde, Lancelot and Guinevere..."

"But some stories of love end happily," Hunter protested, searching for examples as he spoke. "What about Perseus and Andromeda?"

"Their love endures, but Perseus hacks off Medusa's head."

"But Medusa was a monster."

"Those pushing to get a better view at an execution would argue that a heretic is a monster, too."

"You are straying from literature."

"Only to my first point, that people are fascinated by death. Look at church altarpieces," Crespin pressed on. "What event of the saints' lives do you see? Their martyrdoms. Torture and gruesome death are preached and carved and painted."

"Well, I will grant myself an adjournment in this debate," Hunter said. "I do not concede your gory stories are justified, but I will no longer prosecute the case at this time."

Crespin smiled. "I count that a victory, if only temporary, against an English lawyer."

Hunter extended his arms. "The celebrated University of Paris is all around us. Must we linger in the shadow of the gallows? Tell me stories of sublime scholarship and virtuous living."

"Scholarship, yes. Virtuous living is hard to find on the Left Bank, even inside monasteries. Nevertheless, I will spare you the stories of the Huguenots who were hanged or burned here..."

Hunter fixed him with a stare that accused him of already doing so.

"Since you ask for scholarship, I can give you—not exactly stories, but at least names. Down that street at the Abbey of Saint-Victor Thomas Becket was a student. The librarian has a collection of English books, so some of your English Catholic friends visit him from time to time."

"I have no English Catholic friends as yet," Hunter said. "You said you will show me where they gather. The Antelope, is it not?"

"Yes. Let us work our way in that direction."

They wandered the streets of the Latin Quarter, Crespin telling stories of the famed scholars who had walked there, and naming each college they passed. After two hours, they paused at the end of the rue de la Serpent. "Down there, you will see the sign of *L'Antilope*. That is where the English Catholics are wont to gather."

"It is appropriate that those planning the overthrow of their queen meet on the street of the serpent," Hunter said. "Might we take our midday meal there?"

"I imagine they serve food, but I have never heard it recommended. I plan to take you to a place in Saint-Germain-des-Prés. Let us continue our tour. Ahead is the Church of Saint-Cosme-et-Damien. Many English Catholic students worship there. There are seven colleges further along the rue de la Harpe."

"My head swims already," said Hunter.

"It is too soon for swimming; we have but waded up to our knees into the Latin Quarter." Crespin turned the corner and abruptly halted.

Advancing towards them were two men. The shorter, about thirty, wore gray hose and doublet, and carried several sheets of paper. The taller looked past forty, his beard and hair speckled gray, with a thin sharp nose and menacing eyes. He recognized Crespin and his small mouth curled in a cold smile. "Master Crespin, you have another gullible Englishman in tow, I see."

"Good day, Master Izard." He glanced at the shorter man. "Master Martin." He gestured to Hunter. "Gentlemen, this is Master Paul Adams, from London. Master Adams, meet Antoine Izard and François Martin."

"Good day, Master Adams," Izard said. Martin nodded.

"What brings you two to the Left Bank?" Crespin asked, then explained to Hunter, "Master Izard is a drawer of gold wire in our quarter."

"I am here as a captain of militia."

"Of course," Crespin nodded. "And Master Martin accompanies you as your ensign, although,"—he looked up—"he has forgotten his ensign."

"You are as full of quips as always." Izard threw him a hostile look.

"I was simply trying to cheer your day," Crespin said. "But I am still confused on two points. You are the captain of a militia in the parish of Saint-Jean-en-Grève, not here, and the militia was disbanded over a year ago."

"Not that it is any of your business," Izard tilted up his thin nose, "but Captain Girard, of this quarter, asked for our assistance. The militia may be officially disbanded, but those of us most concerned with the security of the city have continued to meet. One cannot expect this peace to last much longer, and when our king needs us again, we must be ready."

"So you update your list of Huguenots?" Crespin nodded towards the papers Martin held.

"We do. Not only Huguenots, all Protestants." Izard looked at Hunter for a moment. "For example, we know an Englishman recently took lodgings at L'Échiquier. Is that you, Master Adams?"

"Yes."

"It is relatively easy to keep track in the town, but here in the university students come from all over Europe. They change their lodgings more often than they change their linen." He laughed dryly at his own joke. "So Captain Girard asked for our help." His face darkened. "As you are so curious, perhaps you should be helping us, Master Crespin. But then, I have never noted your deep desire to rid our city of heresy."

"No one can compare with your fervor, Captain Izard." Crespin turned to Hunter. "During the last war, Captain Izard arrested over forty Huguenots himself."

"More than any other militia captain," Martin beamed. Izard allowed himself a brief smile of satisfaction.

"But now the king bids us live in peace with the Huguenots," Crespin said.

Izard's smile faded. "As I say, this peace will not last. Did you not hear Simon Vigor's Lenten sermons? The king must answer to God for the heresy in his realm. If he says the heretics are to be spared, for now I must spare them; but if he says they must be killed, it will be a sin to disobey him."

"He has never given such an order against peaceful Protestants, only those in rebellion," Crespin said.

Izard fixed him with an ominous stare. "You are half English yourself, and you spend much time at the English Embassy and in the company of Englishmen."

"As you know, that is how I make my living."

"If you spend too much time with Protestants, some of the stain of heresy might rub off," Izard said.

Hunter subdued his irritation at Izard's remarks, and affected a confused face, as though he had not understood the French.

"I attend Mass at Saint-Merri every Sunday," Crespin said.

"But you are not a member of the Confraternity of the Blessed Sacrament," Izard said.

"Such an honor is for those of a higher station," Crespin said, with a convincing show of humility.

Izard snorted. "It takes courage to attack heresy and make this kingdom one body again. It is easier to hide in a corner and leave that work to others. If you will excuse us, we must see to that task." He turned to Martin.

"Have you the paper for these lodging on the left?" As they passed, Izard added, "I hope you enjoy your little tour, Master Adams."

"Tell me more of this Captain Izard," Hunter asked when they were out of earshot.

"He draws gold into thread to make the lace and braids the nobles love. He has become rich. He was one of those who approached Madame Moreau when her husband died, but she rejected his advances. Then he offered to buy L'Échiquier, so perhaps he wanted her inn more than her."

"And the militia?"

"In the first civil war, he was chosen as captain of one company of the Paris militia. There are almost a hundred in the city and faubourgs, but, because many captains did not want to lead patrols or stand sentinel all night, those captains who were most active, like Izard, made big names for themselves. To some, he became a hero. He was equally zealous when the Huguenot armies drew near Paris during the second war. Now he and a dozen other captains think of themselves as the saviors of Paris and the Catholic Church. They range far and wide 'helping' the more reluctant companies."

"He threatened you."

'He has threatened me before," Crespin said. "I think you are the one who could be in danger if Izard took it into his mind. You are the foreigner here."

"So, he and other militia captains know where every Huguenot lives?"

"They know where most live, and, as you see, they try to keep track of newcomers. But here we are at the Collège de Bourgogne."

As Hunter entered L'Échiquier, Marguerite Moreau approached him. "Well, now you have had four days here. How does our Paris compare with your London, Monsieur Adams?" Behind her smile, he recognized the defiance he had seen the day he arrived.

"You live in a truly fascinating city."

"Thank you," she said, "but that does not answer my question. Can London match Paris in any way?"

A point had occurred to him during the day. "Yesterday you spoke of the University of Paris, and today I saw—it seemed—all of its colleges.

Although London has no university, at Oxford and Cambridge we have two of the greatest universities in Europe."

"So you will need two universities to match Paris?"

"No small town like Oxford or Cambridge could support a university as large as Paris."

"But we have universities at Toulouse, Orléans, Montpellier, and a new one at Reims. If you can add Oxford and Cambridge, I must be able to count them as well."

Hunter was stuck for an answer.

"And how many colleges does Oxford have?" she pressed.

"Oxford? I am not so sure. I know Cambridge has fourteen colleges, and Oxford has more. Maybe thirty together."

"Ha! Here in Paris we have over fifty. You could put your universities together and Paris alone would have more colleges."

"But greater numbers do not mean greater quality."

"And how shall one measure that?"

"I grant you, that is harder."

"Did you go to Cambridge? You know the count of its colleges."

"I was a student at St. John's."

"For how long?"

"Two years."

She raised her eyebrows and pursed her lips. "If it had such great quality, why did you not stay longer?"

He did not want to explain his mother's wish that he become a clergyman, nor his disillusion with the religious rancor at St. John's. "The fault was mine, not the university's."

"But I understand that you are learned in the law. You learned that in two years? England must have few laws."

"No. One does not learn law at university, but at the Inns of Court."

"Inns of Court," she struggled with the English words. "What is that?"

How could he explain? "They are a combination of a school and a gentleman's club," he began. "You take your dinners at the hall, you attend readings, you observe trials at the Queen's Courts, you argue at the moots..." He stopped when her face clouded with confusion. "The Inns of Court are a peculiar English institution," he concluded.

"If you do not understand them, neither can I," she said. "But, as you are a lawyer, I can present you a case for the superiority of Paris, and you will see if you can argue against me."

"I agree." He feared he would lose, but enjoyed matching wits with Madame Moreau.

"First, Paris has more people."

"More does not mean better," Hunter countered. "If Paris is bigger, it has more thieves and beggars and prostitutes."

"And more priests and virtuous women. And I know we have more monks and friars, because you condemned all yours."

"They were not killed, but pensioned," he corrected. "And are all your monks virtuous?"

"Look, sir. As we cannot measure the virtue or evil of each person, let us agree half the people are bad and half are good."

"All right."

"So, if Paris has more people, it has more goodness than London." She concluded with a satisfied smile and sparkling eyes.

Hunter smiled in return. "Well argued, madame. But it also has more evil."

"So virtue and evil will always be equal, not matter how many people. But more people is still one point for Paris. Our university is two. We have already established that."

Hunter started to protest, but she hurried on. "Hercules, a demi-god, founded Paris. Who founded London?"

"Brutus of Troy, so they say."

"A mere mortal," she sneered.

"But it was probably the Romans, or some tribe they conquered."

"And the Romans were here too, but they were here *before* London. As Paris is closer to Rome, we became civilized before you." She raised a third finger. "The palace of our king and the houses of our nobles are more modern." A fourth finger. "We have more bridges—four. London has only one bridge." Her thumb popped up. "And our cuisine is much superior." She challenged him with a look.

Hunter was trapped. He could not insult the innkeeper who was providing him with such excellent meals.

"*Voila!*" she exclaimed, waving six fingers. "Have I bested the English lawyer?"

"You have, my good lady," Hunter said. "And you did not even mention how welcoming and accommodating the hostellers of Paris are."

She laughed. "Not all. Just the best. But you try to flatter your way out of a forfeit."

"What?"

"I have won the debate, so you must pay a forfeit."

"What would you have of me, madame?" he asked with false shock.

"Some secret of yours." Her eyes danced.

"And what is that?"

"I would know if you have a girl you love in England."

The pleasure of bantering with Marguerite Moreau vanished. She saw it in his face. "I am sorry." She reached as if to console him, but pulled back.

"Do not apologize," he said. "Yes, there is a girl who is special to me."

"In London?"

"No."

"Is that why you look so sad?"

"Yes. She is far away now. She was even far away when I was in London. And her father does not approve of me."

"I am sorry." Again she stepped towards him, then back. "You must forgive my asking. I meant only to jest with you."

"It is all right," he assured her. "I lost the argument today, but beware the next time."

"Tonight, to make it up, I shall serve you myself. Auguste is preparing a lamb ragout, and I will give you a superior wine with it."

"Though I lost the case, I will win at supper."

Tuesday, 15 April 1572

Treaty negotiations dragged on. As Hunter could not approach merchants or court officials yet, he decided to explore the bookshops on the Left Bank. The first shop was crowded with students, buying inexpensive Aldine Press editions of Greek and Latin authors. Nearby was a shop stocked with religious texts—no pagans or Protestants here. At the next shop, under the sign of the Unicorn, he picked up Rabelais's *Gargantua and Pantagruel*, opened it at random, and read a few pages that mocked the Parisians and told how Gargantua drowned them in piss.

"You appear to enjoy Master Rabelais," the shopkeeper said. "Would you care to buy the book?"

"How much is it?"

"Five sols."

"That is a fair price, but I have other errands. I shall return for it in the afternoon."

The shopkeeper gave a doubtful look, but extended his hand. "If you pay now and give me your name and lodging, I will have my boy deliver it." Hunter agreed.

Further along, he wandered into a shop displaying a pentangle, catering to customers interested in the occult. He found works by Agrippa and Trithemius, and the prophecies of Nostradamus. On a line hung broadsheets reporting sensations: a celestial serpent appearing over Lyon, the birth of a monstrous half cow and half sheep, a list of twelve signs the Apocalypse was near.

The bookstore next door, under the sign of a cardinal's hat, had a political slant. Here, too, papers were clipped to a line, but instead of sensational stories of miracles or demonic possession, Hunter found octavo pamphlets recounting the siege of Poitiers and the funeral orations for François, Duke of Guise. On a table lay volumes of sermons and the decrees of the Council of Trent. From the back came sounds of a press. This was not merely a bookseller stocking aggressively Catholic books, but a printer as well, just the sort of man he was looking for.

He remembered Beale's warning to progress slowly, but he felt he could establish a contact by purchasing some item. His eye caught the word *Angleterre* on a pamphlet. He read "*Discours des troubles nouvellement advenez au royaume d'Angleterre, au mois d'octobre 1569.*" Here was an account of the Northern Rebellion, an event he had participated in himself. How accurate would a French Catholic writer's account be? He asked the apprentice the price in his worst French accent.

The boy stated the price. Hunter reached for his purse and pretended to puzzle over the coins. Handing some to the boy, he asked, "Is this enough?"

"Too much, sir." The boy sorted through the cash box, gave Hunter his change, and then hesitantly asked, "Are you English?"

I overacted dreadfully to make that obvious, Hunter thought, but he said only, "Yes."

They stared awkwardly at one another, then Hunter asked, "Who is your master here?"

"Nicolas Colin."

"Did he print this?" Hunter held up the pamphlet.

"No, sir. But these are ours." He indicated the funeral orations and siege reports.

Hunter wanted to ask if they printed in English, but remembered Pickering's disappearance. "Do you have any English books?"

"No, sir. You might try the rue Jehan de Beauvais at the sign of the lion."

"Indeed, you will find some there," came a nasal voice from behind him, speaking English.

Hunter turned to find a blond gentleman, slightly taller than himself, dressed in a green suit with cream silk showing through its slashed sleeves and between the panes of the trunk hose. "Forgive me, sir. I could not help overhearing your conversation. I am Roger Barnes."

"Paul Adams," Hunter said. He recognized the name from Pickering's notes. Barnes came from a wealthy Worcestershire family, divided in terms of religion. His older brother was a Protestant, but provided him financial support.

"You are new in Paris?" Barnes asked.

"Yes."

"Where are you from?"

"London."

Barnes's eyebrows twitched. He had hoped for a better clue in order to place Adams geographically and socially. He bowed his head slightly. "Forgive my asking, but what brings you to Paris."

"I am here to speak on behalf of a syndicate of London merchants who wish to increase trade with France."

Barnes pondered for a moment. "You did not find a treatise on trade here, did you?"

Hunter saw an opening. "No, but I purchased this"—he held up his tract—"hoping to read of French support for the Queen of Scots."

A smile spread across Barnes's face. "You will find it there. I have read that. Am I correct that you also are favorably disposed towards Queen Mary?"

Hunter stepped close and whispered, "My masters do not know my loyalty. To keep my position, I must conform to the established religion."

Barnes gave him a long look. "We must all weigh our duty carefully. I have many friends in England who are in your situation."

Hunter nodded.

"But you are in Paris now," Barnes pressed. "There are no laws demanding you attend English services, or fining you if you do not."

"True, but I hear that one is always watched in Paris."

"You must be careful, but no one is watched all the time." He appeared to consider an idea. "Will your London merchants be angry if you happen to meet a fellow countryman in Paris and accompany him to a tavern."

Hunter smiled. "How could they possible object?"

Barnes smiled back. "I have several friends you might like to meet."

CHAPTER 5

Expatriates

THE OUTER ROOM OF THE ANTELOPE WAS EMPTY, SAVE FOR A MAN SLEEP-ing on a table. As Hunter and Barnes approached the door of a side room, loud guffaws erupted.

Barnes opened the door. The laughter died as the men inside turned to look. "Gentlemen," Barnes said, "I apologize for interrupting what sounds like a lively discussion. I encountered a compatriot at the Cardinal's Hat. May I introduce Paul Adams, recently come to Paris to negotiate for London merchants. He is a man sympathetic to our cause."

Barnes gestured to the men sitting at the table to his left, "Sir James Kempson, of Griffin Hall, Gloucestershire." A short stout man in a brown silk doublet nodded. "And Sir Gregory Wilkes, of the Willows, Norfolk." A taller, thinner man with an aquiline nose gave a condescending nod. Pickering's notes called Kempson a jaded émigré, who had lived in Paris since early in Elizabeth's reign. Wilkes, a client of the Duke of Norfolk, fell along with his patron when his plans to marry Mary, Queen of Scots were discovered.

Barnes gestured to the three men sitting at a table to his right. "Simon Lodge of Oak Hall, Lancashire." A gentleman in black, with a stylish beard and a serious expression rose and nodded. Pickering's accounts painted him as a firebrand, in favor of a Spanish invasion to restore Catholicism.

"Barnaby Timmons from Yorkshire." A young man with a thin beard in a gray woolen suit stepped forward. "Barnaby is a student at Collège Mignon," Barnes said. Pickering called him devout. From the West Riding, he was unlikely to know the Spranklins.

Behind Timmons another plainly dressed young man, the only one in the room without a beard, smiled at Hunter. "Timothy Heath," he announced, "from Berwick-on-Tweed. I am also a student at Mignon. Grateful to make your acquaintance."

Leaning against the mantelpiece stood a thin man, dark hair falling across his face. His faded green doublet was worn around the cuffs and collar. "This is Thomas Fisher, from County Durham," Barnes announced. Fisher nodded, a bemused smile on his face. Pickering had reported he was usually drunk and revealed little of his background.

All the men sat quietly looking at him. Hunter realized he needed to speak. "It pleases me to meet you all. I am but newly come to Paris, and I feel fortunate to have encountered Master Barnes. As he has told you, officially I represent a syndicate of London merchants who hope for increased trade agreements with merchants of France." He paused, weighing how best to present his religious and political views. "He said I was sympathetic to your cause, yet I am unaccustomed to explain my views candidly. As you know, stating opinions about the status of the Queen or the authority of the Pope are dangerous in England."

"Indeed, we know it," Lodge snorted.

"But you are no longer in England," Sir Gregory said.

"And I can already feel that I will be freer to follow my conscience here than in London," Hunter said. He hesitated. Whereas these men had chosen to live abroad, Paul Adams had to return to England. He must show fear that his words might be reported, yet demonstrate enough trust in them to encourage them to trust him. "I pray you all not to repeat my words to those who sent me here. They do not know my private thoughts. I intend to negotiate trade honestly for them, and if I continue to hold their trust I may be able to travel freely between France and England. I hope in that capacity I might do some service to our cause." He had not actually made any treasonous statements, only hinted at his Catholicism and opposition to Elizabeth.

"Exactly what that cause is, we were discussing as you entered," Sir James Kempson stated. "Come, sit with Sir Gregory and me, and have some wine." Hunter and Barnes joined their table. Lodge strode to the door and called for more glasses and jugs of wine.

Kempson began a recapitulation of the interrupted conversation. "Simon, who I thank for seeing to the supply of liquid refreshment, advocated all-out war on Protestant heretics, and named the Duke of

Anjou as a chevalier in that crusade. Sir Gregory here is not so sanguine, believing with Erasmus that the written word has more power than weapons, but he admires Anjou's steadfastness of faith, which led him to reject marriage with Queen Elizabeth. He believes his example will inspire similar firmness in others, and benefit Catholicism throughout Europe."

Sir Gregory nodded. "A slight exaggeration, but basically correct."

"Master Timmons countered with the suggestion that Anjou could have better served the Catholic cause by marrying the Queen and begetting an heir." A smile played around the corners of Kempson's mouth. "Fisher reduced that argument to a succinct but memorable phrase." The men around him chuckled in anticipation. "He said Anjou might have done more for Catholicism with his prick than with his sword." They guffawed again.

"Marriage has worked better for the Habsburgs than conquest," Timmons said over their laughter.

"When they married fertile stock," Barnes said. "But when King Philip tried to conquer England by marrying Queen Mary, they had no heir."

"Alas," said Timmons.

A servant entered with a tray of glasses and two jugs of wine, placing one on each table.

"Master Timmons," Sir Gregory said, "your argument rests on several unlikely eventualities: that Elizabeth and Anjou produce a boy, that Elizabeth conveniently die shortly thereafter, and that Anjou by then will have developed such a following in England to be named regent and permitted to raise the boy in communion with Rome."

Simon Lodge snorted. "This conversation is idle air. Anjou has already decided he will not marry the heretic queen. But, God willing, she may die soon, and Mary of Scots will inherit her crown."

"Many labor to that end," Fisher chimed in from the fireplace.

"And may God speed their work," Lodge said.

Hunter's blood chilled to hear the death of the Queen so bluntly desired. Playing his part, he forced himself to smile and nod.

"So you again advocate the sword, Master Lodge?" Kempson asked.

"But his position has improved," Timmons piped up. "Last week Simon argued for war against all heretics, or at least for an invasion of England; but now he speaks of an assassin. Instead of advocating the death of thousands, now he would only kill one."

"Friends," Kempson said, "you will frighten Master Adams on two counts. First, he will quake to hear that we even contemplate the assassination of an anointed queen..." Noisy objections erupted.

"A bastard usurper." Lodge banged the table.

"She has been excommunicated; she is no longer an anointed queen," Heath said. Timmons nodded in agreement.

Kempson raised his hand, and continued in a sardonic tone, "Second, he might believe that we are a united party actually able to undertake some bold act."

A few brief chuckles, but Hunter noted silent, humorless smiles around him.

"You mock us again, Sir James," Wilkes said. "And you are justified to point out that we often disagree, that we repeat the same arguments, and that we often take no action. But this does not mean none of us *ever* does anything."

"Sir Gregory, I did not mean to slight your travels, your letters, your petitions ... I can only hope your efforts lead to more results than a decade of mine did." Bitterness mixed with regret in Kempson's tone.

Kempson said Wilkes believed the written word more powerful than the sword. Could Sir Gregory be connected with the smuggled Catholic tracts?

"But tell us more about yourself. Were you born in London?"

Kempson's words recalled Hunter. His heart beat faster. Had his thoughts shown in his face? He took a breath to calm himself and recited the history that he had constructed for Paul Adams during his time at Glasswell Manor. "I was born on a small estate in Hertfordshire. My father is a gentleman, but we are not well-to-do. As the second son, I was sent to Gray's Inn to learn enough law to offer my skills to the merchants of the City of London. My father is a close friend of the draper Frances Reddan. He shares our religion and was instrumental in my appointment as agent for the syndicate."

"Regarding matters of religion, Master Adams," Lodge interrupted, "can you speak more candidly? By your earlier remarks, I gather your family conforms."

"That is correct," Hunter said. "As I said, we were not wealthy enough to have our own chapel or priest, nor to pay fines for not attending the parish church. My father suffered with guilt, and he read to us daily from his breviary to compensate. As so many in England, we were forced to lead a double life."

"You are a church papist, then?" Fisher said.

"Yes." Hunter feigned shame.

"Must one also swear the Oath of Supremacy to practice law?" Lodge asked.

"No. Not to practice law. A barrister or judge must swear, though."

"Do you think that a lawyer would have a problem taking an oath?" Fisher interrupted. "They are paid to lie and have much practice in it." Hunter considered for an instant whether Adams would take offense, then laughed with the others.

"Where in Hertfordshire does your family live?" Wilkes asked.

"Our estate, barely more than a farm, is between Hertford and Ware." Hunter prayed Wilkes was not well acquainted with the area.

Wilkes shook his head. "I have never heard of an Adams of Hertfordshire. But, as you yourself say, your family is of a humble station, though your father may style himself a gentleman."

Hunter looked down. It would be wise to allow this man his snub and simulate shame.

"And Master Reddan, can you tell me more of him?" Wilkes continued.

Hunter felt on firmer ground. "His shop is on Fish Hill Street. He is a draper who deals primarily in trade with Spain and Portugal. He imports currants, raisins, and lemons, and exports kerseys. He is now seeking, with a syndicate of others, to trade with France as well."

Wilkes raised an eyebrow. "But did you not say you must hide your beliefs from those who sent you?"

"Yes. Francis Reddan is but one among many in the Rouen Syndicate. His Catholic faith is not known to his peers."

"Have you been to Mass since you came to Paris?" Lodge returned to his probing.

"I arrived but last week." Hunter sensed this was a weak response.

"From what you say, it must have been some time since you gave confession and received the Host from a priest," Lodge pressed.

"Yes, it has." Hunter saw where his questions were leading and decided to leap ahead of his interrogator. "I feel the lack of absolution sorely. I would that I had had the strength, but I felt such a stranger in the city. I feared that my masters at the syndicate might learn of it. But having met you, I take heart. Your courage is greater than mine. You have left your lands and possessions for the sake of religion. Might one of you introduce me to a priest, that I might make confession and be shrived?"

Lodge exchanged looks with Timmons. "Father Philippe at Saint-Cosme-et-Damien speaks a little English, does he not?"

Timmons nodded. "He counsels the English and Scots students." He turned to Hunter. "I can take you to Father Philippe to hear your confession before vespers, or you can meet me at Saint-Cosme tomorrow morning. Father says Mass at nine."

Hunter grasped at the chance to delay. "I will come to you tomorrow morning at half eight."

Lodge said, "I, for one, will join you. Should we not all attend? Will it not be pleasing to see the joy on Master Adams's face at receiving once again the Body of Christ?" Did Lodge suspect him of being a spy?

"Surely," Kempson said, "if we all come at half eight and confess our sins, Mass might be delayed be several hours." The others chuckled.

"We do not want you to rise earlier than usual, Sir James," Wilkes said. His companions laughed again.

"I am content that Masters Timmons and Lodge bear him company," Kempson said.

"I shall join them," Wilkes announced with an upward tilt of his head.

"And I," Heath added.

"I shall worship as usual at Saint-André at eight," Barnes said.

The men glanced at Fisher, draining a glass of wine. He became aware of their attention and said, "I shall worship as usual here at the Antelope, starting at noon." The laughter rippled around the room again, and Hunter hoped his promise of attending Mass had dampened any suspicions about him.

As if in answer to his wish for less attention, a short gentleman with sandy hair and a pointed beard charged through the door. "Have you heard the news of the wedding?" he asked the room in general.

Several voices asked, "What wedding?" while others simply said, "No."

"Marguerite of Valois is to marry Henri of Navarre," the stranger announced. His words confirmed what many hoped for and others feared. Ever since Jeanne d'Albret had arrived at the Château of Blois in February, news had leaked out that she and Catherine de Medici were discussing a union between the houses of Valois and Bourbon. Hunter glanced around the room to note the reactions of the expatriates.

"God's blood!" Lodge exclaimed through clenched teeth. "No," Heath said in disbelief. Timmons looked disappointed, but silently resigned. Fisher laughed aloud for his own reasons. Kempson turned to a frowning Wilkes and said, "That is the reason your recent petitions were ignored."

Barnes asked, "The rumor is true, then? You are sure?"

"I have seen a copy of the official proclamation," the newcomer said.

"When will it be?" Heath asked.

"August."

"Richard," Kempson said, "excuse our lack of hospitality. Sit and join us. There is an extra glass there. And I should introduce you to Master Paul Adams, newly come to Paris from London. Master Adams, this is Richard Chandler, from Somerton, Somerset."

They exchanged greetings, and Chandler took his seat near Timmons.

Lodge was railing to his companions about the match. "Only two years ago, the king was at war with the Huguenots; now he will marry his sister to one of them!"

"It will make them bolder," Heath agreed.

Fisher stumbled over to the table, "Yes. They will demand more privileges." He laughed. "They will knock the saints off Notre-Dame."

Lodge turned on him. "How can you laugh at this matter?"

"Do you suggest I cry?" Fisher asked. "Why should I shed tears over this French marriage? I am a foreigner here."

"You know as well as I that the king's toleration of Protestants hurts the Catholic cause throughout Europe. The Huguenots even now itch to ride to aid the Flemish rebels. And after this marriage to the House of Bourbon, Elizabeth will sit ever more securely on her throne."

"Well, I am well and truly chastised by my schoolmaster," Fisher made a mock bow to Lodge and refilled his glass. "But pray tell me what *I* can do about Queen Catherine's decision—for it is hers rather than the king's—to marry her daughter with Henri of Navarre? You may vent your spleen as loud as you wish, Simon, but it will not make a damned bit of difference to the decisions of the mighty. Realizing that, I choose to laugh and drink." He tipped his glass and took a long draught of wine.

Chandler spoke. "Do you hold, Thomas, that only kings and queens may influence affairs?"

"They have an easier time than I," Fisher replied.

"That is because they are sober more often," Kempson said.

After the laughter died, Lodge said, "Brutus did not believe that only the mighty could determine matters."

"There you are again with your assassins," Kempson said.

"Neither did Martin Luther," said Wilkes. Silence descended at the mention of the reformer. "You may be surprised to hear me name him, but you cannot deny that, although no monarch, nor even a gentleman, he certainly influenced affairs."

"So, you return again to the power of the book," Kempson said.

"Indeed I do," said Wilkes. "If Luther and Calvin can write and alter affairs, so can Laurence Vaux and William Allen."

Hunter's ears pricked up. Vaux was the author of the Catholic *Catechism* that he had read at Glasswell Manor. Allen had written the *Defense of the Catholic Church,* and recently founded the college for English Catholics at Douai. If Wilkes was convinced of the efficacy of printed tracts, could he be organizing their production? Could his elegant hands be stained with Pickering's blood?

Timmons was animated. "Father Allen does not only write; he prepares priests to re-establish the Church in England." He looked expectantly at Wilkes.

"Yes," Wilkes said. "You may come with me when next I go there. Have you written your father?"

"Yes," Timmons replied. "I have not received his reply, but I am sure he will give his permission."

Wilkes turned to Hunter. "Master Timmons wishes to end his studies in Paris and join Father Allen at Douai."

Lodge reached over to pat Timmons on the shoulder. "We are all proud of you, Barnaby." He turned towards Wilkes, "But it takes time to write books, and smuggle them in, and for people to read them. Even Allen's new priests must wait for Elizabeth to die before they can return."

"Perhaps," Wilkes admitted.

"And time is not on our side," Lodge stated. "Every year that passes more Englishmen settle into comfort with the so-called reformed church. Boys at university have never known anything else."

"I have thought of someone who decided to change affairs in our country," Thomas Fisher announced, eyes shining. "Anne Boleyn." The expatriates turned puzzled expressions towards him. "Using her as my example, I intend to seduce the fat Queen Catherine. She will be so grateful for my skillful fucking that she will persecute the Huguenots and send an army to free Mary, Queen of Scots." Fisher roared with laughter at his own joke, but the others glanced uncomfortably at one another. Lodge groaned.

"You are drunk again, Thomas," Chandler said, standing. "Sir James, let us take him home."

"I have never confessed to a priest," Hunter explained to Crespin that night.

"It's not hard," Crespin said. "You cannot get through a day without sinning, so there is always something to say. I will play your confessor."

"How do I begin?"

"You say, 'Father bless me, for I have sinned.'" Crespin prompted.

"All right. Father, bless me, for I have sinned."

"Yes, my son," Crespin intoned, playing the priest.

Hunter stared at him for a long moment. "That's not much help."

"Well, he's just waiting for you to get on with it."

"But that is just the problem. I don't know how to go on."

"Well, you know—pride, lust, envy, gluttony, sloth…"

"Yes, I know the seven deadly sins. If I say I have been proud, is that good enough, or will the priest ask for details?"

Crespin shrugged, "In my experience, he is more likely to ask for details of lust."

"I will not confess lust."

"No? I have seen the way you look at Madame Moreau."

Mary Spranklin's image sprang to Hunter's mind, and he felt a twinge of guilt. "I said I will not confess that. I will concentrate on my attendance at English services. According to Vaux, the Pope has said that is a sin."

"Ah, I forgot. First the priest will ask you when you last confessed."

"I cannot tell him I never confessed." Hunter paused a moment. "I imagine it is not easy to find a Catholic priest in London. Perhaps I should say nine months, or a year."

"That might help. If you have not confessed for a whole year, he cannot expect you to give him all the details. But you *should* mention lust. No priest will believe you have gone a year without lust."

"All right. Let us try again." Hunter cleared his throat. "Father, bless me, for I have sinned."

"When was your last confession, my son?"

"Almost a year ago, Father. There are few priests in London."

Crespin sat silently, waiting.

Hunter broke the silence. "I have spent time in gambling, and lusted after women in taverns."

"How many?"

"Will the priest ask that?" Hunter said.

"I don't know," Crespin said. "I would if I were a priest. I would want to know how many, how often, and what they looked like."

"Fine. If he asks, I can describe Joan at the Red Lion. But let me go on."

Crespin looked disappointed. "You will have to tell me about Joan later."

"I have been weak, Father. To avoid paying fines, I have attended English church services often."

"That is very serious," Crespin said. "You imperil your immortal soul by worshipping with heretics."

"I know. I truly repent my weakness. In Paris I will attend Mass every week."

"Every day would be better," Crespin said, "and drop an écu in the collection plate each time."

"He will say that?" Hunter asked.

"He will think it," Crespin said. "But I jump to the penance too soon." He resumed his clerical character. "Unburden yourself, my son. Do not hold back."

"I have been guilty of pride, Father," Hunter began. "I have looked down on those of equal rank in the law courts, in my lodgings, in the markets."

"Hmmm," Crespin said.

"And I have envied my betters: the rich merchants who employ me and the gentlemen and nobles I see."

"Envy will destroy you, my son. Do not question those whom God has seen fit to bless. What else?"

"Too often I have been moved to anger."

"You speak in general of sins in your mind, my son. Have you no sinful acts to confess?"

"I have spoken harsh words to friends and servants over small matters."

Crespin gave Hunter a dismissive glance. "Have you killed?"

"No."

"Stolen?"

"No."

"Fornicated?"

"No."

"Really?"

Hunter looked down. "In truth, I am a virgin."

"Easily corrected, but let us continue. Have you lied?"

Hunter sat in silent. He had lied to his parents and Mary about going to Emden, but he could not confess that. He realized he had drifted into thinking and answering as Edward Hunter, not Paul Adams. As Adams, *he* was a lie. His confession tomorrow would be a lie.

"Have you lied, my son?" Crespin repeated.

Hunter improvised. "Once when a pie seller gave me too much change, I kept the coins."

Crespin rolled his eyes.

"When I was late to an appointment in Finsbury Fields, I said my horse had gone lame, though I had started out too late."

"Have you lied about your faith, my son?" Crespin prompted.

"Oh, yes," Hunter said. "I have led others to believe I was a Protestant. I have hidden and denied my true faith."

"That is better," Crespin said, breaking out of character. "Do not mention the petty lies. He will want to hear about lies of religion."

"I told you I needed to practice," Hunter said.

"Well, you must practice alone," Crespin said. "I have another appointment."

Hunter raised his eyebrows.

"You are not the only one who needs to prepare for confession," Crespin said. "In a few hours, I hope to collect some excellent details of lust for my next one."

Hunter added notes on each English expatriate. Which ones might be connected with Pickering's disappearance? None had mentioned Pickering, and he had not asked, as Paul Adams would know nothing of him. If Beale was right, and Pickering's disappearance was the result of enquiries into the printing and transportation of Catholic tracts bound for England, then he had to suspect Wilkes. If Wilkes were not involved in producing and shipping tracts, he would know who was. But Lodge seemed most likely to use violence. Fisher was large enough to overpower another man, if he were sober. He was imagining an attack on Pickering, but that was uncertain. He might, as Crespin suggested, have left suddenly to avoid his debts.

His mind drifted back to his confession. He must keep himself and Adams separate. His mother would believe that confessing to a priest and attending a popish service endangered his soul. She despised those French Protestants who attended Catholic services to avoid legal and social penalties, calling them Nicodemites. Likewise, the Pope called on Catholics in England to confess their faith and suffer the penalties rather than conform. Both faiths held up martyrdom as an ideal. As paintings of martyred saints adorned the altarpieces of Parisian churches, so a copy of Foxe's *Book of Martyrs* sat next to the Bible in each of his relatives' houses.

But he was no Nicodemite. He was not lying about his beliefs to make his life easier. His lies made his life more difficult and put him in danger. His entire mission was based on a lie. Every spy lived a lie. In his mother's eyes, would his service to the Queen balance his lies and idolatry? How did God judge spies? Did the ends of thwarting treason and protecting Her Majesty justify the means of deceit?

It was too late to ponder theological questions and far too late to change his role. He had accepted this position to serve his queen, and more importantly, to raise his position to be worthy of Mary Spranklin. He lay down and drifted to memories of her washing his chest and back, of her soft lips, of her body pressing against his.

Philip, King of Spain, Naples, Jerusalem, and the New World, Prince of Sicily, Duke of Milan, Burgundy, and Brabant, Count of Habsburg, Flanders, and Luxembourg, sat at his desk in the Alcázar in Madrid. It was late at night. As usual, council meetings, audiences, and conferences had eaten up his day, and only after supper had he been able to turn his attention to the mountain of correspondence on his desk.

He placed de Spes's letter to one side. He had little confidence in the former ambassador's judgment. He had been proved wrong so often: over-estimating the numbers of Catholics who would take up arms during the Northern Rebellion, letting John Hawkyns convince him he would trans-port Spanish soldiers from Flanders to England, putting faith in Ridolfi to coordinate a plot against Elizabeth. He should have left Brussels by now, and would be in Madrid soon enough. He would speak with Guerau de Spes in person then. Most of the letter was his complaining about how the English had treated him. Yes, it was against diplomatic conventions, but when a diplomat had spent as much time plotting the overthrow Elizabeth's government as de Spes had, he should not be surprised to get short shrift. Of course, he would instruct a secretary to lodge a complaint at Whitehall, but nothing would come of it.

There was one paragraph about Secretary Cecil sending a spy to Paris. He should relay that to ambassador Zuñiga soon, but just now there were more urgent matters. A report from Constantinople said the Turks had completely rebuilt their fleet, so that their naval strength was as great as before the Battle of Lepanto. Would they choose to raid the Italian coast? Make another attempt on Malta? He must write demanding more information from the Eastern Mediterranean. And the news from the Low Countries. Although de Spes did not mention it, a faster messenger from Alva arrived with the news that the Sea Beggars had seized the town of Brill on the first day of April. Had Alva succeeded in recapturing the port by now? Were the troubles in the Low Countries going to become even worse and more expensive?

CHAPTER 6

Death of an Englishman

Wednesday, 16 April 1572

THE CONFESSION PROVED TO BE SURPRISINGLY EASY AFTER ALL HUNTER'S worrying. His sincerity as he genuflected, knelt, bowed, and prayed his way through the Mass must have been convincing to both Lodge and Wilkes. They congratulated him afterward and excused themselves on other business. Hunter stood outside Saint-Cosme with the students Heath and Timmons.

Barnaby Timmons fixed him with excited eyes. "Do you now feel whole again?"

Hunter put on his most devout face. "Yes, it is a great relief to be in true communion with the Lord again."

"I do not know how you endure living a lie," Timmons said.

Hunter was instantly on his guard. Had this earnest young man seen through his acting? Had he spoken ironically a moment ago?

"It pains me to think of all the faithful at home who must dissemble each Sabbath." Timmons was thinking of Catholics in England.

Hunter relaxed. "Must your family in Yorkshire do so?"

"Before last year, our Justice of the Peace was lax about enforcing church attendance," Timmons explained. "But now my father pays the fines."

"As does mine," Heath said.

"Do not think we are wealthy," Timmons said, "but my father asks what price a man can put on his soul."

Hunter hung his head. In Timmons's eyes, Paul Adams and his family had chosen gold over salvation. But Adams would not think so. "We believe that, though we may perform other rites, God knows what is in our hearts." He remembered the argument now. "Elisha allowed Naaman the Syrian to bow before idols because God was in his heart."

"I know many think as you do." Timmons looked at him with pity. "But I fear they are in error. How can you have salvation without a priest to forgive your sins, to bless the Host, to administer last rites?"

Hunter recognized Timmons's assumption that salvation came only at the hands of a priest, but this way of thinking was so far from the spiritual framework he had grown up with that he was unable to present an adequate answer. "We can only pray God will understand."

"That is why I want to go to Douai," Timmons continued. "I cannot tell someone he is in error without offering hope. When I become a priest, I can go to England to give comfort to those whose souls are in danger."

"Will you not be in danger of your life, if you are caught saying Mass?" Hunter asked.

"I must weigh my danger against the souls of those I can help to salvation. And what is my life worth sitting safely in Paris, knowing I am too cowardly to do what I know is right?"

"I believe Barnaby is right in his resolve," Timothy Heath said.

"Will you study at Douai as well?" Hunter asked.

Heath shook his head. "I regret I do not feel the call to God's service as Barnaby does."

"Then to what does He inspire you?"

"Barnaby will work to keep the faith of Catholics alive until the Church can be restored in England; I will fight to bring that time about." Heath squared his shoulders.

"How?"

"I used to think I would offer my service to the Duke of Alva. If Elizabeth's forces are to be overthrown, it will be his soldiers that do it, and meanwhile I could fight Dutch rebels."

Hunter nodded. Many Catholic Englishmen who had fought in the Northern Rebellion were now in the Low Countries with Alva.

Heath continued, "But I have spoken recently with Archbishop Beaton."

Hunter recognized the name, the French ambassador of Mary, Queen of Scots and the Archbishop of Glasgow. "He commands no army."

"True. But he convinced me that I can serve Her Majesty by returning to Berwick."

This made sense. Heath was from Berwick, England's stronghold on the Scottish border for almost a hundred years. The Marian party would want men inside such an important town.

"What would he have you do?"

"He said we would speak of that later. It is too soon to return now, but at the end of the summer I can perform the Queen of Scotland a great service."

Hunter filed the information away and pursued another line of questioning. "Yesterday, Sir Gregory Wilkes defended the use of the printed word to promote Catholicism in England. Do you agree with him?"

"Yes," Timmons said. "William Allen's writings refute false doctrine. They have kept many faithful, and even converted some."

Heath looked more dubious. "It is no doubt the books and pamphlets help sway minds, but words without action will change nothing."

"I agree," Timmons said. "That is why, when my father gives his approval, I will go to Douai."

"Has Sir Gregory written anything himself?" Hunter asked.

"I do not think so," Heath said. "But he has contacts with printers in Paris, Louvain, and Antwerp."

Hunter feigned confusion. "If he does not write, why does he contact printers?"

"To ensure that the output from their presses reaches his friends in England," Heath said. "He knows merchants who regularly cross the Narrow Seas."

Hunter compressed his lips to keep from smiling. Ambassador Walsingham would be impressed that he had convinced the expatriates of his Catholicism and discovered Wilkes's part in exporting Catholic tracts. He was about to bid Heath and Timmons goodbye, when Roger Barnes sprinted toward them, looking distraught.

"Pickering has been murdered," he blurted. "I have just seen him."

"No!" Timmons responded.

"Where? How?" Heath asked.

"At a tannery on the River Bièvre," Barnes said. "Some workmen found him yesterday behind a mound of hides. He had been stabbed several times."

Hunter, remembering that Adams knew nothing of Pickering, asked, "Of whom do you speak?"

"George Pickering was a gentleman from Herefordshire," Barnes explained. "He came about a year and a half ago and studied for some time at,"—he turned to Timmons—"at your college, was it not?"

"Yes," Timmons agreed. "He was at Collège Mignon for perhaps six months, but he was not cut out to be a scholar."

"You were at the tannery?" Heath asked.

"No," Barnes said, "The Châtelet. The tanner sent for the authorities yesterday. As they moved the body last night, someone said it looked like an Englishman who lived near Place Maubert. At Saint-André this morning an officer sought me out and asked me to come identify a dead Englishman." He shuddered. "I saw at once it was Pickering."

"Stabbed?" Timmons asked.

"At least four times. You could see the gashes."

"Who would kill him?" Hunter asked.

"The officer said it was likely robbery. His purse was missing."

Hunter knew Pickering had missed a meeting the Monday after Easter, but when had the expatriates noticed? "When did you last see him?"

The three exchanged looks. "About a week ago, was it not?" Barnes said. "Yes. I saw him speaking to Sir Gregory after Easter Mass."

"I have not seen him this past week," Timmons said.

"Nor have I," Heath said.

"When I said I knew Pickering, they asked me if I would make arrangements for burial," Barnes said. "Is Father Philippe inside? Pickering worshiped here when he was a student."

"He said Mass a quarter of an hour ago," Timmons said.

Hunter wanted to hear what might be said about Pickering. "I will assist in any way I can," he offered.

"I will speak to Father Philippe," Barnes said, "but Sir James and Sir Gregory must be notified." He exchanged embarrassed looks with Timmons and Heath, then added in a lower tone, "We must depend on them to manage the costs of a funeral."

Timmons nodded. "I shall go inform Sir James."

"Then I will go to Sir Gregory's lodging," Heath said.

"I will come with you, Timothy." Hunter seized the chance to witness Wilkes's reaction to the news of Pickering's death.

As they walked, Hunter probed further. "Timmons said that Pickering was not cut out to be a student."

"One should not speak ill of the dead," Heath said, "but he spent more time looking in his mirror than in any book. He bought several silk suits when he first arrived. He did not lodge at the college, but with a lawyer near Saint-André-des-Arts."

"He withdrew from the university?" Hunter prompted.

"Barnaby said he attended few lectures. He argued with his family about continuing at the university, and they stopped supporting him. He moved from Saint-André parish to a small room near Place Maubert." His tone made it clear that this was a step down. "He dreamt King Charles might appoint him as a special advisor on English affairs, if he could gain an audience."

"A man with grandiose ambitions," Hunter said. "How did he support himself?" Might the expatriates suspect he had received money for spying?

"I spent little time with him after he left the university, but I gather Sir James and Sir Gregory helped him. He spoke of doing Sir Gregory valuable services, but never said exactly what those were. He liked to foster an air of mystery and importance when he spoke of it."

"Then both Sir James and Sir Gregory trusted and valued him?"

"They tolerated him. And I think each of them gave him money at some time. But neither one recommended him."

'Recommended?" Hunter asked.

"Both Sir Gregory and Sir James have acquaintances at the French Court," Heath explained. "Somehow, Pickering got the idea that one of them would recommend him for a place or a pension."

"But they did not?"

"The idea was folly." Heath counted off the points on his fingers. "First, King Charles has no money to give to Englishmen. He is in debt to the Italian bankers. Second, neither Sir Gregory nor Sir James has any influence in Court patronage. And third, even if they had, neither would recommend Pickering. But here we are." Timothy Heath knocked on the door of a four-story building across from the Hôtel de Saint-Denis.

A tall, burly servant answered his knock and, recognizing Heath, ushered them upstairs. As they entered a paneled room, Sir Gregory Wilkes rose from his chair. "Timothy, Master Adams, I saw you scarce an hour ago at Saint-Cosme. What brings you here?"

"George Pickering's body has been found," Heath said. "He was murdered."

Sir Gregory's eyes opened wide, then shifted down. Hunter detected shock, then guilt. "I had begun to fear as much. Where was he found?"

"He was discovered by workers at a tannery on the Bièvre yesterday evening," Heath said.

"Was the body in the river?"

Hunter heard no note of pretense in his questions, but Wilkes could have ordered the murder and still not know where the body would be found.

"No," Heath said. "He was discovered behind a pile of cowhides."

"How was he killed?'

"Barnes saw several stab wounds."

Wilkes looked down again, as though in thought. "Thieves?"

"They think so."

"And where is the body now?"

"At the Châtelet. Barnes is asking Father Philippe for permission to inter Pickering at Saint-Cosme. I am come to request that you meet him there at your earliest convenience."

"Robert," Sir Gregory said loudly, "my cloak." His servant appeared and helped him secure a black cloak with a satin border.

They had scarcely begun their walk back to Saint-Cosme when Heath stopped abruptly. "There is Simon Lodge." He pointed to a figure walking away from them down the rue Pavée. "You two proceed to the church. I must tell him the news." He turned and shouted, "Simon!"

"We will not wait for them," Sir Gregory announced. They walked eastward in silence for a minute.

Except for the flash of guilt upon hearing of Pickering's murder, Sir Gregory had asked all the questions one would expect of an innocent man. However, if he were deeply involved in the publishing of Catholic pamphlets bound for England and Pickering enquired too closely, he might have killed him. It was impossible to imagine Sir Gregory, with his silk doublet and starched ruff, stabbing anyone. But his servant Robert looked strong enough to overpower most men, or he might have hired others. "I did not know Master Pickering," Hunter began. "What sort of a man was he?"

Sir Gregory walked a few moments in silence, as though deciding what was proper to say of this dead man. "He seemed to have a background like your own."

Hunter understood. Pickering's family styled themselves members of the gentry, but had limited income and no family history.

"But Master Heath said he wore expensive clothing."

Wilkes gave him a stern look. "I am not the first you have asked about Pickering."

"I was with Timmons and Heath when Master Barnes brought us the news. They described his character somewhat."

"I expect I will have little to add."

Despite Sir Gregory's reluctance, Hunter ventured another question. "They said Pickering asked your assistance in certain matters."

"Did they?" Wilkes snorted. "I would have thought that was a private matter between Pickering and myself."

"I am sure it is," Hunter said quickly. Better not press too hard. "I imagine that Pickering told them."

Wilkes sniffed. "They heard nothing from me, you can be sure. And as for imagining, I would do as little of that as possible. A man has been killed, and imagining can lead to conclusions that might prove dangerous to the one who imagines, as well as those about him."

His tone implied that their conversation was at an end. Was his warning about imagining sage advice, or a threat? Wilkes was the one who had mentioned theft as a motive. It seemed that some had license to imagine, but others must beware.

Hunter listened in the background while the expatriates spoke with Father Philippe. Heads were shaken in disbelief. Sighs were sighed. Wilkes and Kempson, who would be paying the costs, wanted a respectable burial, but not an elaborate one. George would have a coffin, an evensong that night, and a funeral Mass with candles and a tolling bell tomorrow morning, but he would not have paid mourners and he would be placed in a churchyard grave, not a *charnier*.

"I must return soon to the Châtelet," Barnes announced, "or the sisters of Sainte-Catherine's hospital will arrange for burial at Holy Innocents. Michiel, the gravedigger, can collect the body in an hour."

Heath and Timmons volunteered to accompany him. Eager to see the body, Hunter asked if he might come too. After a moment, Sir Gregory said he would as well. Sir James asked to be excused, as he had business to attend to, and Simon Lodge, uncharacteristically quiet, also declined to join them.

Although Pickering had been missing over a week, his body had just been found. Barnes did not say he had begun to rot, so he must have been killed recently. Where had he been in the meantime? Walking along the rue de la Harpe, Hunter fell in alongside Timothy Heath. "You last saw Pickering at Easter, but his body was found last night. Where do you think he has been?"

"I do not know, but I was not surprised at his absence. Sometimes a man with debts may want to disappear."

Wilkes's head snapped around. "A man may come and go without explaining himself to everyone. And a man's finances are his own affair."

"True," Heath said, "but we all knew about Pickering's affairs. He complained often of his debts."

"A man may properly choose to speak of his own affairs, but not those of another man," Wilkes said.

They crossed the pont Saint-Michel in silence after Sir Gregory's reproof. Hunter hazarded another question as they stepped onto the Île de la Cité. "Did no one visit his lodgings during the past week?" His companions muttered they had not. Trying another tack, Hunter asked Barnes, "Will we be able to see George Pickering's body?"

"I don't know. The sisters of Sainte-Catherine's were due to come and shroud the bodies this morning."

Heath spoke from behind him. "I hope to look again upon his face."

"And I," Timmons said. "By looking on the face of the dead, they say, one may discover the state of his soul at death."

"But the body may tell us more than the face," Hunter continued.

"Have you some desire to see his wounds?" Sir Gregory sneered.

Hunter explained. "As you know, I am trained in the law and have observed trials. Wounds can show how a victim was attacked, the state of mind of the killer, and the ferocity of the struggle. Such details have led to the discovery of a murderer."

Heath and Timmons nodded at Hunter's words.

"Surely the investigating officers of the Châtelet know these things," Sir Gregory snarled.

"Anything that may lead to the capture of his killer is to be commended," Timmons said, "but I am concerned that he died unprepared. Surely we should care about his soul now more than his body."

"He had confessed at Easter, Barnaby," Heath said. "He could not have many sins since then to answer for."

Their conversation stopped at the end of the Pont au Change, and Barnes led them down the foul-smelling vaulted passage through the center of the Châtelet, to the morgue entrance. There a tall officer led them down a flight of stairs. On one side, several naked bodies lay on waist-high tables. Beyond, two nuns were washing down one of last night's anonymous victims.

"Over here," the officer gestured. "The sisters were just about to wrap him in a shroud."

In life, Pickering would have stood about five feet, five inches, slightly built. He wore a thin moustache, but no beard. The stubble on his face suggested he had not shaved for several days. His light brown hair was cut short, in the usual fashion. His closed eyes gave him a peaceful appearance, but his mouth was slightly ajar.

"Poor George." Timmons bowed his head and muttered a prayer.

Heath put a hand on Timmons's shoulder. "He looks peaceful enough."

Wilkes shook his head slowly; Hunter thought he detected guilt again in his eyes.

Four wounds gaped, all on the left side of the chest near the heart. Any one of them might have killed him. "These wounds are from two different assailants," Hunter pointed, speaking French for the benefit of the Châtelet officer. "These two were made by a thin-bladed dagger stabbing upwards, the other two by a larger blade stabbing from above, over his shoulder while holding him from behind. See, his collar bone is bruised here."

"Well read," said the officer. "We reached the same conclusion. There were two attackers, one taller than the victim."

Hunter glanced at Wilkes. His servant Robert would have been tall enough to tower over Pickering, grabbing him around the neck and stabbing down. Did he have another servant? Wilkes glared back, but said nothing.

Hunter squatted and examined Pickering's legs. "There are scrapes and tears on the feet and shins."

"The body was dragged after he was killed," the officer said. "The scrapes on the shins mean he was loaded on a cart. He was not at the tannery one day, but was found the next."

"You are experienced in these matters," Hunter addressed the officer. "How long has our friend been dead?"

"Perhaps two days."

"And do you have any idea who killed him?"

"We questioned the tanner, his journeymen, and his apprentices. They found the body yesterday evening. None of the men could identify it, and none showed any emotion other than surprise and confusion. We have no reason to suspect them. In all likelihood, it was two thieves."

"Is it not unusual for a thief to hide a body, instead of leaving it in the street and running away?" Hunter asked.

"Somewhat," the officer admitted.

"What have we seen that the Châtelet did not already know?" Wilkes said. "Two thieves attacked Pickering somewhere near the tannery, then took his body there and hid it."

"When I was here this morning, he was still dressed." Barnes said. "Where are his clothes?"

"In a bag over there." The officer pointed. "A shirt, a doublet, nether stocks, venetians, shoes. No jewelry, no purse."

"So everything points to robbery," Wilkes said.

"Except for hiding the body," Hunter said.

"Tell me, officer," Wilkes said, "do thieves never hide the bodies of their victims?"

"Sometimes they do; more usually they do not."

Wilkes looked at Hunter, challenge in his face, then addressed the others. "We have done what we can do here, gentlemen. The grave-digger will soon come to bear away his body and his clothes. Tonight, the evensong for the dead will be read. Tomorrow morning will be Pickering's funeral and burial. But I feel I owe him more. Tomorrow I will go to his lodgings and gather his belongings. We must settle his debts, notify his relatives in Hereford, and arrange to ship his effects back to them."

Hunter's jaw tightened. If Sir Gregory sorted through Pickering's rooms, he could find and dispose of any evidence that might implicate him or his servants in the murder. He would have to visit Pickering's lodgings that night with Crespin, while the expatriates were at evensong.

Barnes pressed a silver coin into the hand of the sister waiting to shroud the body. Timmons asked Sir Gregory how much it would cost to have extra masses said for Pickering's soul. Heath asked the Châtelet officer, "What chance is there of finding the thieves who killed our friend?"

The officer sighed. "Unless a murderer is discovered in the act, he is seldom caught. Sometimes one thief will betray another, but more likely he will lie and say they were in some alehouse, instead of at the scene of the murder." He shrugged. "And we do not even know where the murder was committed."

Another officer announced that Michiel from Saint-Cosme-et-Damien had arrived with a barrow to carry away a body.

"Gentlemen," Hunter said. "I must return to my lodgings now. I will see you tomorrow morning at Pickering's funeral."

"You again," the landlady snarled as she opened the door. Her gray hair stuck out at odd angles from under her black coif, giving her the appearance of an unkempt monk whose shaved head had been painted black. "It didn't take long for you vultures to come, but you didn't beat me."

"My good lady, what do you mean?" Crespin asked.

"I remember you. You come after Pickering last week. Said he owed you money. Well, you're too late. I heard today he'd been found dead out in Saint-Marcel. I carried down a chest of the best clothes to cover the rent he owed me. Gaston from the Antelope come by just an hour ago. Said he'd run up quite a reckoning for food and drink, so I let him have a look. He made off with a hat and some hose. If you give me three sols, I'll unlock the door and you can get third best."

Hunter's spirits sank as he stepped into the hall. Two others had already rummaged through Pickering's belongings. "Madame, an English gentleman will come tomorrow to inventory Pickering's possessions and send them to his family. He intends to pay your tenant's debts."

"He won't have much to list, I reckon. And he needn't worry about paying his debts. Most o' those he owes money to will have come after what they can find by then, like you. Afore I let you go up, though, I should ask you for some papers. Gaston showed me a whole stack of bills with Pickering's name signed on 'em. I don't want to be accused by your English gentleman of letting thieves in just on their say-so."

Hunter and Crespin exchanged looks. "Well, madame," Hunter said, "you may be in trouble already. This English gentleman I spoke of will not look kindly on what you have done. He'll have the law on you for sure."

Her eyes bugged out. "But he owed me for the rent!"

"Relax, madame." Crespin held up his hands. "Have you sold any of the clothes?"

"No, sir," she whimpered.

"Good, then we may be able to help you." Crespin exchanged looks with Hunter again. "We can help you carry the clothes and the chest back upstairs."

"But when will I get my rent?"

Hunter spoke slowly. "Well, this English gent will want to do it properly. He'll want to list all of Pickering's things. He'll put up posters asking for creditors to bring their papers. Then he'll pay the debts and recover his money either by selling the possessions or from the family."

The landlady's shoulders collapsed. "That'll take weeks."

Hunter made a show of weighing an idea, then asked, "How much did he owe you?"

"Fifty sols."

"We will pay you fifty sols now," Hunter said. 'But you must send to the Antelope for the hat and hose. When the gentleman comes tomorrow, there should be no sign that anything was taken. You should say nothing about what you did, or about Gaston, or about us. We are taking a risk to help you, you realize."

The landlady nodded. "Oh, thank you, sirs."

"Did you keep the bills from the Antelope?"

"Yes. Gaston left them."

"Well, quickly, madame," Crespin said. "Go to the Antelope with them, or send a boy, and fetch back that hat and hose."

The landlady nodded again and turned to her room.

"If you give us the key, we will carry the chest up while you do that," Crespin prodded.

The landlady lifted a key from a nail with a shaking hand and gave it to Hunter. "There's his chest—the smaller one. I swear I haven't taken a thing out of it."

Crespin picked up the chest. "Take care to get those bills to the Antelope, now, before Gaston sells something."

"Right, sir." She scurried to a box on a table and began to sort through it.

"Will she leave us alone in her house?" Hunter asked as he climbed.

"I don't think she is that foolish," Crespin said, "but we should have a few minutes to search Pickering's chamber."

Hunter unlocked the door. On one side stood an unmade bed with a gray blanket. On the other side sat a large chest with the lid open and a pile of clothes on the floor. Near the door was a small table with papers and a wooden box next to it. Hunter began to examine the papers. "Pray examine the chest, Jacques."

A letter to Secretary Beale requesting an advance of funds. An unfinished begging letter to Kempson, with sections crossed out. Beneath it were undated letters in French to the duc de Guise, the duc de Nevers, the duc de Retz, and other noblemen—eight letters with almost identical wording. Pickering promised his eternal gratitude, offered to provide "valuable advice on how to win the allegiance of those Catholics who make up the majority of Englishmen," and requested a private meeting. Pickering was working both sides. Were these copies of letters sent, or unsent drafts? Was he planning to try each aristocrat in turn?

Hunter opened the wooden box next to the table. Here was a list of expatriates, without any notes. Under that were three copies of a pamphlet entitled "A Treatise on the Duty of All True Catholics." Were these the pamphlets Sir Gregory Wilkes was involved in shipping to England? Had Pickering intended to pass them on to Walsingham? He tucked all three inside his doublet and dug further.

Another draft of a letter, this time to Wilkes, dated April 5, the day before Easter. He scanned it. "Beg pardon...sorry to have given offense... swear I will not reveal all that is privy between us...can keep a secret... would not knowingly disclose anything to your disadvantage." The language was general, but it was clear Pickering knew something Wilkes wished to keep secret. Deeper still, he found letters from Kempson and Wilkes from previous months. It was clear one or the other had lent him money several times.

A rustling below and a door closed. The landlady was back. "Have you found anything?"

"No, just clothes." Crespin jerked his head towards the staircase to indicate he too had heard the landlady. "I'll put them all back in the chest. What do you have?"

"A box of letters." Hunter made an instant decision. He would take Pickering's draft letters of recent date, but leave those he had received. Wilkes might expect to find letters he had sent Pickering, but no one would know whether or not Pickering had kept copies of those he wrote. He swore silently, stuffing some up his doublet and others down his trunk hose. What valuable evidence might he be leaving behind in the letters Pickering had received? But the landlady's tread was loud on the steps.

He shoved a handful of letters back in the box, replaced it on the floor, and stood as she opened the door.

"Look, madame, I have returned those garments you took. They are in his chest with the others." Crespin wafted her away from Hunter and pointed vigorously at the bottom of his doublet. A paper jutted out. He quickly poked it in, hoping the landlady would not notice the crinkling. "Did you send a lad to the Antelope?"

"Oh, yes, sir," the landlady bobbed. "Thank you, sir.

"We made what order we could of Master Pickering's room," Hunter said. "If Gaston sends back the apparel he took, your English gentleman will think that his room has not been touched." He began to reach in his doublet for his purse, but his hand froze. He looked at Crespin. "Can you pay this fine lady the fifty sols that Pickering owed her?"

Crespin stared back with surprise. "My friend, you know I do not carry so much as that." Then he guffawed. "Madame, I believe my friend has lost his purse in his trunk hose. Pray walk down the staircase with me, and allow him to find it with modesty."

The landlady threw back her head with a howl. "Search carefully," she said with a lascivious glint. "I'll wait at the bottom of the stairs so you can give me whatever you find." She howled again and Crespin joined her.

Hunter glared as they left, but had to admire Crespin's quick thinking. He removed the hastily stuffed letters, arranged them more compactly, then reinserted them in doublet and trunk hose. He extracted the fifty sols from his purse, added ten more to ensure the landlady's silence, and descended towards the laughter with as much dignity as he could.

CHAPTER 7

Getting to Work

Thursday, 17 April 1572

HUNTER STACKED THE PAPERS NEATLY. GEORGE PICKERING HAD CERTAINLY played a complex, contradictory game. A sheet of accounts showed he had received money from both Kempson and Wilkes, starting almost a year ago. Then funds from Kempson ceased. Those from Wilkes increased for a time, but diminished sharply three months ago. It was hard to see what recompense Sir James had expected from Pickering, other than fawning attendance and immediate agreement with his cynical opinions. Sir Gregory was a different matter. If he had been deeply involved in the publishing and distribution of Catholic tracts, Pickering could have transported messages, manuscripts, even the pamphlets themselves. The letter in which Pickering apologized and assured Wilkes he could keep a secret hinted at such activities. Had Wilkes discovered he was passing information to the English Embassy? Had he revealed some secret that led to his death?

The "Treatise on the Duty of All True Catholics" counseled its readers to absent themselves from "heretic services" and to remain steadfast in the faith. It painted the noblemen and gentry who supported Catholic priests as heroes, and advised those "of the lesser sort" to approach them to gain access to absolution and the sacraments. As an act of Parliament had forbid the circulation of the papal bull of excommunication, the pamphlet paraphrased it, assuring the readers that they were not immediately excommunicated if they continued to obey the laws and recognize Elizabeth's authority. But loyal Catholics were to be ready to join the struggle against heresy at any time. Once any Catholic power proclaimed its authority in England, they were obliged to attach their loyalty to that power under threat of excommunication. He wondered if the phrase "Catholic power" was purposely vague, to cover a domestic rising in favor of Mary, Queen of Scots as well as a French or Spanish army. Unsurprisingly, the pamphlets were anonymous.

At the same time Pickering accepted money from Wilkes and Kempson, he was offering information about them to Walsingham. Were the pamphlets being delivered for Wilkes, or evidence he planned to present to the embassy? If his expatriate patrons had learned of his dealings with the embassy, would they have considered that sufficient reason to murder him?

As a third design, Pickering was offering his services to French aristocrats. The man wanted to sell himself to everyone. If Walsingham had discovered he was offering himself to the French, could the ambassador himself have arranged his killing? Unlikely. Pickering could have justified any involvement with the French Court to Walsingham as a ruse to cover his spying. According to Heath, those offers to French courtiers had never led to a meeting, and might never have been delivered.

During the funeral service that morning, no expatriate had behaved in a way to suggest he was involved in Pickering's murder. But what would a murderer act like at a funeral? Many a spouse or friend had wept prodigiously, after arranging for the demise of the one he pretended to mourn. Wilkes had displayed no hint of guilt, only grief. Kempson appeared stoic rather than cynical. Lodge, combining philosophy with a call to action, said Pickering had been full of plans, which had come to naught. His death was a reminder they must act while they could. Timmons and Heath had served as pallbearers, the former praying and weeping most of the time, the latter comforting him as best he could. Fisher was uncharacteristically sober. Only Barnes had asked if Hunter had any ideas that might lead to Pickering's killer. Everyone else, it seemed, had accepted that he had met his end at the hands of anonymous footpads, who would never be caught.

A tap at the door. Hunter quickly dropped the papers into the chest next to his stool and closed it. "Come in."

Madame Moreau wore a brown kirtle with ivory sleeves. A transparent partlet with white embroidery rose to a delicate ruff at her neck. She held a package. "I did not see you when you returned from the," she paused, "the funeral of that Englishman, was it not?"

"Yes."

"A horrible murder. But unfortunately, quite common. I advise my guests to be very careful where they venture out after dark."

"That is good advice in London, as well."

"A boy brought this for you."

The parcel must contain the book he had purchased two days before. "I thank you, but you need not have come yourself to deliver it."

"Laurent was busy cleaning the kitchen, and besides," she smiled, "I am curious what you are reading." She handed him the parcel.

He began to blush. "I am not sure it is a book I can share with a lady."

"Oh, you are one week in Paris, and you have found already our naughty books?"

"I gave way to curiosity. I heard in England of the works of François Rabelais, but I have not read him."

"Oh, Rabelais," she laughed. "There are worse than he. Let us see what you have."

Hunter cut the string and unwrapped his book.

"Ah," Marguerite said, "this edition has the first two books. They have many clever conceits."

"You have read them?"

"Yes, and books three and four also. Do not look surprised. Did you think me illiterate?"

"No, indeed."

"Shy and innocent?"

"Well," he stammered. "I am sure you are a woman of honor."

"Indeed I am," she drew herself up and looked at him with defiant eyes. "But I *have* been married." She paused. "And I run an inn. I see life as it is lived every day, not only its honor and loyalty, but its betrayals as well, its pretensions and lusts, its farts and folly. Monsieur Rabelais describes the world I see better than the authors of romances do."

Hunter did not know what to say.

Marguerite Moreau laughed. "Do I frighten you?"

"You certainly surprise me. I see a new side of you each day."

Her eyes sparkled. "That is the way we women are. We are weaker, so we must keep you men off balance."

"You are succeeding wonderfully well with me."

"I almost forgot, I have a message from Jacques Crespin." She pulled a note from her sleeve.

As she handed it to him, their hands touched, and immediately their eyes met. "I will leave you now. Enjoy Monsieur Rabelais." With a swish she was gone.

Hunter read. "Walsingham, Smith, and Beale at Blois with French commissioners. They may return next week."

His report of Pickering's murder, and his discoveries and suspicions regarding the expatriates, would have to wait. He need not spend the evening writing a report for Walsingham. He had examined Pickering's documents. He could write more false letters from Emden, to his parents and Richard and Mary Spranklin. He could dig out the French pamphlet on the Northern Rebellion he had found no time to read. Or he could read Rabelais until dinnertime. Madame Moreau might serve him tonight.

~~~

Monday, 21 April 1572

Hunter sat across the table from the ambassador and Secretary Beale in Walsingham's oak-paneled study. Walsingham pursed his lips and nodded "Your observations show Pickering in a different light. He certainly knew more than he revealed to us." His eyes clouded for a moment with what might have been regret.

"As for the activities of the expatriates, their talk could be judged treasonous," he paused, "in England. But we are in Paris. I might bring the matter up with King Charles, but he takes little interest in English expatriates. He does not support their plans, at least not openly, and certainly not with any money. If I describe what these men have said, it would raise the question of where I had obtained such intelligence. That might put you in great danger. Or if not danger, the English Catholics would surely banish you, and your mission would come to naught. No, we can do nothing against the expatriates. If Heath actually does leave Paris for Berwick, we can send word there ahead of him."

"What about Wilkes?" Hunter asked.

"Your suspicions that he might be responsible for Pickering's murder are only suspicions. You said your visit to the tannery with Crespin produced no further clues. We must let the officers of the Châtelet do their job."

Hunter's shoulders sank.

"But I shall send a copy of the Catholic pamphlet you recovered to agents in English ports, that they may keep watch for its arrival."

"That is, if it has not already arrived," Beale put in.

"Yes. We may be too late. But discovering the printer would be something. I could object to the king that a French printer is producing pamphlets to stir up sedition in England. The Crown and Parlement are both eager to control the presses, though they do a miserable job of it. They might be willing to act against a printer, not because of what he printed, but because he did not obtain a license to print it."

"To tell the truth," Beale added, "Solving Pickering's murder is less important to the security of the realm than discovering those who receive and spread Catholic books."

"Am I no longer to investigate what happened to Pickering?" Hunter asked. Did the ambassador really not care about finding the murderer?

"Only so far as it might connect to the production of these seditious books and pamphlets," Walsingham said.

"May I ask Wilkes to help me with the publication of the manuscript I brought?"

Walsingham pursed his lips. "I would prefer that you not meet the same end as Pickering. His death may not be connected. It might have been at the hands of robbers..." Hunter opened his mouth to object, but Walsingham raised a hand. "Despite your belief that he must have trusted those who attacked him, he may have been taken by surprise, or have been set upon by those he had been drinking with all night." He paused. "Nevertheless, I would prefer you not approach Wilkes, but instead ask printers directly, find one willing to take on printing in English, and ask for samples of his work. If we find a printer, that is another piece to the puzzle. We are keeping an eye on Reddan in London, and we are watching the captains of the two ships where Catholic writings were found. Soon we may see the whole picture."

"We will send your 'letters from Emden' today, with our dispatches concerning the treaty," Beale said.

"As regards the treaty," Walsingham said, "Sir Thomas Smith remains at Blois, making arrangements for the ratification. Her Majesty will send a delegation here next month, and King Charles will send a delegation to London. The treaty will be officially signed and ratified on the same day in both capitals. Both monarchs will pledge to support one another if attacked, even if the alleged reason for attack is religion. There we did well."

Yes, both Elizabeth and Charles feared the power of Spain.

"But the defensive portions of the treaty need not concern you. The section you need to read is the one promising the establishment of a staple for English merchants in France." Here Beale pushed a copy of the text towards Hunter. "Although Rouen is not mentioned specifically, the treaty states the merchants may build their own house, and may worship there according to the rites of the English Church. Other important matters, however, such as tolls and customs duties, are to be decided within four months of the official signing. Those matters will be decided at Court in Paris, and in due course I hope you will be able to speak with the officials who will decide them. In the meantime, you are to meet with various civic officials and merchants, explaining the advantages of the treaty, so that we may get as favorable terms as possible without arousing resistance from French merchants."

"Plan to attend a dinner here Wednesday," Beale said. "We are arranging for you to meet Justin Lepage, and, if he is free, Estienne Thibaudoux, Lord of Prideaux. Master Lepage is a lawyer who has been a great help to us at the embassy. He saw to the lease of this house during Ambassador Norris's time, and drew up the contracts to supply our food, candles, paper, and so forth. He found some of our staff. He arranges the laundering of our linen and, when necessary, the hiring of extra horses. He has agreed to introduce you to his contacts at the Hôtel de Ville, and to those merchants whose favor would promote the Rouen Syndicate.

"The Sieur de Prideaux is secretary to the Viscount de Beaulieu, a *maître des requêtes*, a judge in the court of appeals, we would say. Beaulieu was one of the main promoters of the Treaty of Blois. He hopes to see Rouen replace Antwerp as a commercial center, and has convinced the king that the resulting revenue will help solve his financial problems."

Wednesday, 23 April 1572

"Sieur de Prideaux," Walsingham said, "It pleases me to introduce Master Paul Adams, an agent for the Rouen Syndicate I hope will secure the staple granted in the treaty." Prideaux's round face smiled back, his mouth framed by a graying moustache and goatee. He was dressed in a black satin suit with silver embroidery. His matching bonnet was set off with a peacock feather.

"I am delighted to meet the representative of such a distinguished group as the Syndicate de Rouen," Prideaux began.

"Thank you," Hunter said. "I am sure that the members of the syndicate would be flattered to hear themselves described as distinguished."

"But I understood many noblemen were partners, even some members of Her Majesty's Privy Council," Prideaux said.

Walsingham cleared his throat loudly.

"Ah, I beg your pardon," Prideaux exclaimed. "You have your secrets, you English." His eyes twinkled.

"Monsieur Justin Lepage," Walsingham said, moving on, "Master Paul Adams."

"I look forward to working with you, Master Adams," Lepage said. In contrast to Prideaux's round face, Lepage's was fashionably narrow, emphasized by a pointed goatee. He stood only a few inches shorter than Prideaux, and he wore a suit of gray velvet edged with black piping.

"Gentlemen, our supper is almost ready," Walsingham said. "If you will come to table, I believe we can conduct our business and fill our bellies at the same time."

Jean, the usher, guided them to the formal dining room and seated them around one end of its large table. Ned Howell, Beale's servant's son, passed among the guests with a ewer, basin, and towel. André, the butler, began to pour wine as Jean retired to bring in the first course.

Prideaux spoke. "I apologize for my indiscretion about those involved in your syndicate, but I do not understand their reluctance to be known. His Majesty and the Queen Mother are both extremely positive about this venture, and not shy to say so. There are many at Court who may be interested in being part of such a promising trading arrangement. Of course, one might be struck from the rolls of nobility by taking part directly in commerce, but *investment* is a different matter."

"My masters hope that an English staple at Rouen will benefit merchants and investors, both English and French," Hunter said.

At that moment, Jonas and Étienne entered with platters of sliced beef tongue, boiled capons in white sauce, and small pastries filled with spiced chicken. Walsingham said a brief prayer and each diner was served. When Prideaux complimented the food, Walsingham said the praise should go to Gilbert, the French cook whom Lepage had engaged.

Lepage asked, "When the staple is established, will the English import more playing cards, paper, and linen?"

"The treaty makes no mention of French imports to England," Beale said.

"True," Lepage replied, "but when Master Adams speaks with merchants, or investors, they will raise such issues as I do now. They will ask what more the English will buy from France. They will ask if the staple will export hides to France."

"I believe the syndicate will be able to deal in all products, subject to the laws of each realm," Hunter said.

"But it is of the laws I speak," Lepage said, leaning forward to emphasize his words. "If the English ban on exporting hides were lifted, it would be of great benefit to the leatherworkers of France."

"It is reasonable that each French merchant will enquire how an English staple will benefit him," Walsingham conceded. "Although Master Adams cannot speak to matters of policy, I might write Her Majesty's Council with suggestions."

"Thank you, ambassador." Moving on, he said, "French woolen merchants fear that if the English are given trade concessions, English cloth will drive down the price of French cloth."

"I believe Master Adams will have an answer for them," Walsingham said.

"I have with me a large chest with cloth samples produced throughout England," Hunter said. "The merchants of Rouen who saw them found many fabrics that are not woven here. Our worsteds and gabardines are of longer fibers than can be cut from any sheep in France. I would be happy to show you the cloth."

"I am no expert," Lepage said, "but I will be happy to see your samples. I am glad you have real cloth to show the merchants, and not mere words and promises."

Prideaux cast a sharp look at Lepage. "The Viscount de Beaulieu is convinced that, once an English staple is established, Rouen will become a new Antwerp."

"Many hope," Lepage said, "that Rouen will not have the same problems as Antwerp. Protestants there felt compelled to destroy beautiful statues and church ornaments."

"But we are not here to discuss politics or religion," Prideaux cut him off. "Our purpose is trade."

"All trade, like religion, is mixed with politics," Lepage said.

Prideaux looked stern. "Master Lepage is fortunate. He benefits from the patronage of both those in trade and in politics."

"Indeed I do." Lepage met his look. "And I do my best to promote the interests of my patrons."

The Englishmen sat uncomfortably. Jonas and Étienne emerged from the kitchen with the second course. "Ah," Walsingham seized the arrival of food, "We have for your pleasure roast pork, lamb, and duck."

Again, the conversation veered to the quality of the dishes. After some moments, Walsingham said, "Master Lepage, on behalf of the Rouen Syndicate, I ask if you will be kind enough to introduce Master Adams to those merchants and city officials who might assist their enterprise."

"And I require the same on behalf of the most esteemed members of His Majesty's Court," Prideaux added.

Lepage's smile appeared permanently fixed to his face, concealing any thoughts. "I will be delighted to do so. As I said before, I always do my best to promote the interests of my patrons. Should I provide Master Adams with letters of introduction or arrange personal introductions?"

"Both," Walsingham said. "In consultation with Sieur de Prideaux, Master Beale has prepared a list of the men that Master Adams might speak with. We would ask you personally introduce Master Adams to those marked with a cross; letters will suffice for the others."

Beale passed a sheet to Lepage, who ran his eye down the names. "It may take me some time. Pardon my asking, but will the embassy provide the usual fees agreed for my services, or will the Rouen Syndicate?"

Walsingham looked at Hunter. Although he had received no instructions regarding this from his uncle, he risked an answer. "I am sure that the syndicate will cover such fees for service as the embassy has customarily agreed to." He hoped he was right.

Lepage smiled. "I must enquire as to the engagements of these men. When I am finished, shall I notify Master Adams or Master Beale?"

"You may contact me directly," Hunter said.

Monday, 28 April 1572

Lepage was as good as his word. Saturday a package of letters of introduction had arrived at L'Échiquier. Today he met Hunter at the Hôtel de Ville and accompanied him to a formal meeting with the *prévôt des marchands* and the *échévins*. There the mayor and aldermen of Paris, as Hunter chose to think of them, all expressed their official pleasure that a treaty had been agreed. They made predictable speeches about the benefits of peaceful relations and trade between their two countries. They asked Hunter to outline the plans of the Rouen Syndicate, which he did in vague terms. The *prévôt*, a stocky man with a proud face, handed him a scroll authorizing his discussions with municipal officials and the merchant community of Paris, asking those who read it to show him respect and courtesy. As they left the Hôtel de Ville, Hunter thanked Lepage.

"I am always happy to assist Ambassador Walsingham," Lepage replied, "and your syndicate will pay me for it."

Hunter smiled back. He hoped the syndicate would agree to Lepage's fees. "Should I present this scroll at each interview?" he asked, unsure of Parisian custom.

"Not to everyone. I can tell you which of those on your list are most impressed by formal documents. Some may ask to see it, so they can say their meeting with you was commanded by the Bureau de la Ville."

"Will they be criticized for merely speaking with me?"

"Paris is a city full of fear, Master Adams. We have lived through a dozen years of war. Five years ago, a Huguenot army was at our doorstep. Last winter, many saw a Protestant plot in the shortage of wheat. Here you are, suggesting a change in what our merchants buy. Some will see a plot in that, too. And there are always those who are against any change."

"But I am merely trying to promote trade, not change religion," Hunter objected.

Lepage raised an eyebrow. "Trade, religion, politics"—he placed three fingers of his right hand into his left palm and moved them in a circle—"all mixed together." He raised a forefinger. "But I might put a word in the ears of some that would make things easier for you."

"And what is that?"

"I understand you have made the acquaintance of some Englishmen abiding in Paris and that you attended Catholic services with them."

Hunter was on his guard. "Yes, I have." Where had Lepage obtained this information?

"Should I make this known to some on the list? Do the members of the syndicate know your religious sympathies?"

Hunter chose his words carefully. "In England, I conform."

"A prudent policy," Lepage said, showing his smile-as-mask face. "What would they say if they learned you had attended Mass here?"

Was that a threat? "I hope they do not."

"So, you are either a Catholic pretending to be a Protestant or a Protestant pretending to be a Catholic."

Lepage was getting too close. Taking offense might deflect him. "Do you doubt my integrity?"

"Master Adams," Lepage said, "we are both lawyers. We must, as a matter of professional necessity, doubt everyone's integrity."

The man was damnably disarming.

"Is it not ironic that a Catholic, assuming that is *your* true faith, is working to promote an alliance between France and Protestant England?" Lepage asked.

Hunter saw an opening. "Is that not what you, presumably a good Catholic, are doing as well?"

"*Touché,*" Lepage said with a genuine smile. "I said before that I promote the interests of those who pay me."

"Then we both march to the same drum," Hunter said, "but let us do so with no religious banner over our heads. I hope the syndicate will value my work as an agent, and not enquire too deeply about my faith. You had best not introduce me to your contacts as a Catholic."

"Then I would advise you not to attend Mass too often," Lepage said, "lest that be reported to your masters. If you become labeled a papist, they would recall you to England, would they not?"

What was Lepage playing at? Was this level-headed advice, or was the man threatening to reveal Adams's Catholicism to his masters? What would be his motive for doing so? Of course, a report of his Catholicism would not lead to his recall, but his role demanded that he fear it. "I am sure they would," he said. "I will heed your warning."

Saturday, 10 *May* 1572

May had erupted as a whirring wheel of activity, one interview following hard upon another. Hunter had met first with an alderman who had requested a meeting to discuss how an English staple might benefit him. Soon invitations arrived from other aldermen. It seemed that, if Master Adams had met individually with one *échévin*, it would be considered an insult if he did not pay his respects individually to each of them. Each one, it seemed, had relatives or colleagues in the cloth trade, or who were *avocats* or *procurers* at one of the sovereign courts. Failing to contact those mentioned, Lepage informed him, would be considered offensive. Thus, Hunter had found himself waiting in many antechambers, and smiling at many officials, some of whom took a genuine interest in the proposed Rouen Syndicate, and others who acted as if they had no idea why he had come to their offices. Prideaux arranged for Hunter to present a pair of silver goblets to the Viscount de Beaulieu, in return for an interview with a royal councilor at a later date.

` As well as officials, Hunter spoke to many merchants: cloth wholesalers, who hoped to trade French linen or Italian silks for English woolens; manufacturers who controlled networks of weavers, fullers, dyers, and trimmers; retail drapers with large shops near Les Halles or on the rue Saint-Denis. Crespin had dutifully accompanied him, pushing a barrow with the samples chest through the streets of Paris. Hunter noted which merchants were attracted by the fine Worcesters, and which wanted lower quality kerseys to sell to the Italian market. He recorded the objections as well: several drapers claimed that French weavers already supplied cloth as good or better; another thought the merino wool imported from Spain of finer quality than any grown in England. One mercer tore up his letter of introduction and swore no cloth woven by English heretics would ever contaminate his shop. One wholesaler promised to buy a shipload of English broadcloth if in turn he could send a ship full of linens to England. The dyer Gobelin, on the Bièvre River, wanted to see how well each sample would take his scarlet dye.

Today he spoke with his first Huguenot merchant, Pierre Merlet. "When an English Staple is established," Merlet said, "you can rely on me as a customer for your bays, serges, and flannels—any fabric we can use for linings. I supply over a dozen tailors who marry wool linings to Italian silks to produce garments beautiful but durable."

Hunter smiled. "You have said 'beautiful but durable' several times."

"Well, if a man will not promote his own products, who will? I make sure all who deal with me know my motto." He opened a door into a courtyard bordered with flowers, which separated his office and showroom from the domestic part of his house. "Anna."

A young woman wearing a cream apron over a brown kirtle emerged from the door opposite. She led two girls, who looked at one another and giggled nervously. An older woman, dressed in black silk, followed and stood slightly behind the children and their nurse.

"Master Adams, may I introduce my family. My wife Sarah." The older woman curtsied to him. "My daughters, Rachel and Rebecca." The girls curtsied, giggled again, then said in English, "Good day, sir."

Hunter laughed at the unexpected greeting, and the family laughed at his surprise. Rachel and Rebecca beamed, proud of their accomplishment. "Very good," he said to them. "Do you study English?" Their faces immediately clouded over.

"They have only learned a few words, in honor of your coming," Merlet explained.

"It is my honor to meet such lovely young ladies," Hunter said in French.

The girls laughed, at ease again.

"And their nurse, Anna," Merlet said. Her blue eyes met Hunter's briefly as she bent her knee to him. "Ladies, this is Master Paul Adams."

Rebecca's eyes lit up. "Adam!" she said, and turned to say something to her nurse.

"She says your name is that of the first man," Anna said.

The mother leaned over and explained, "His name is Adams, not Adam. It is his family's name—short for 'son of Adam.'"

Rebecca looked up, confused. "But he is not that old."

The others laughed at her confusion. She turned her face away, and her lower lip began to tremble. Her father knelt. "Rebecca, my sweet, he is not the son of Adam. There have been many, many men since the Garden of Eden named Adam, and one of those Adams was an ancestor of Master Paul."

Rachel, not content to see her sister have all the attention, piped up, "His other name is in the Bible, too. Paul, like the Paul who wrote the letters."

"That is right, Rachel," her father said. "You are my little scholar." He stood. "Let us dine."

They all seated themselves around a table, Hunter at Merlet's right hand, his wife at his left, and Anna between the two girls at the foot of the table. Two servants brought in loaves of bread, meat pies, pottage, pike in a sauce, a salad, and a plate of dried fruits. Pierre Merlet read a psalm, then blessed the meal. The servants moved from their places behind Merlet and began to cut and serve the dishes. The girls quickly finished their bread and pottage. Their mother allowed each one two candied fruits and dismissed them with Anna to the courtyard.

"Madame Merlet, I must thank you again for the dinner," Hunter said.

"You are welcome."

"And I must again thank your husband for his enthusiasm for my mission."

"Why should I not be enthusiastic?" Merlet said. "I have told you how I hope to prosper myself from this opportunity, but it will help all of us of the Reformed Church."

"It must have been difficult for Protestants in Paris," Hunter said.

"We have had to leave the city twice," Merlet said. "But praise be to God, with each peace we who have not borne arms have been restored to our property."

Sarah's face tightened, and her elbows drew in.

"Where did you go?" Hunter asked.

"Sarah has a sister near Cambrai. If the English staple is established in Rouen, I hope many from Flanders will move to northern France. There will be more need for cloth workers of all kinds."

"One of the merchants I spoke with was against the treaty for just that reason."

"They fear the truth," Merlet said. "God is working his will on earth. Mark you, how events flow in favor of the righteous. The Dutch rebels gain against their Spanish tyrants, town by town. The Princess Marguerite will marry Henri of Navarre. Admiral Coligny is at Court and the Guises are not. King Charles agrees a treaty with your queen. And just yesterday, news that the Pope died."

"What you say is true, but the cardinals will elect another pope."

"Let us hope the next one will not be so quick to hunt down heretics and excommunicate queens."

"We may, but I doubt King Philip hopes as we do."

"We can do more than hope," Merlet said. "We can pray God will give strength to those working to do His will."

"Amen," said Sarah.

"Amen," Hunter echoed. Could he include himself in those working to do God's will?

Anna entered with Rebecca and Rachel, each bearing a handful of lilacs. They marched up to Hunter and thrust out their flowers. "For you," Rachel said in English.

Hunter looked into their beaming faces, moved by their kindness to this English stranger.

"Master Adams, you deign to sup with us tonight. You are lucky I have saved you a place in the dining room."

Hunter smiled at Marguerite Moreau. "You must forgive me for my absence. I have been obliged to grace the tables of your city councilors and rich bourgeoisie."

"So I understand from your messages. 'I regret I will not be dining at L'Échiquier today.' 'Pray excuse my absence this evening.' 'I will be attending a banquet at the Hôtel de Ville.' By your favor, tell me the luminaries whose company you keep."

Hunter named the officials and merchants. Madame Moreau nodded, then raised her eyebrows, and finally let out a gasp. "Those are very important men."

"They may have wealth and position, and serve mountains of food, but they cannot provide such delightful company as the Chessboard Inn."

Madame Moreau smiled. "I hope those important men did not expose their wives to that flattering tongue of yours. You might charm their virtue from them."

Hunter was aware again that Marguerite Moreau had beautiful green eyes, set off by long dark lashes. "I must use any charm I possess to talk trade. I smile so much that my cheeks ache."

"You waste your smiles then. They should be used when you talk of love, not buying and selling."

"I have seen only glimpses of wives," he said, "save for today. A Huguenot merchant, Merlet, had me to dine with his family, his wife and two daughters."

"What a foolish man, to let you near his daughters."

"You may say so. Each one gave me a flower to remember her by."

"You made a conquest of both?"

"And both made a conquest of me."

"And you accomplished this in the presence of their father?"

"I might say he encouraged it. He taught his daughters to say words to win my affection."

"The more fool he," she said

"Not so. They had but six and eight years," he said.

Both laughed. "But the wife?" She arched an eyebrow.

"Meek and demure. She said little except an amen after the blessing and some admonitions to the children."

"And you prefer a woman who is more lively?"

"Definitely," he said.

She laughed in her throat, and asked, "Have you read any more Rabelais?"

"I have neglected him lately. I am reading a pamphlet about our Northern Rising written by a Frenchman."

"Your Northern Rising? I know it not."

"Some earls in the north of England rebelled some three years ago," he said concisely, though complex memories of his part in that affair raced through his mind.

"Is it interesting?" she asked.

"The author says little of the Rising, and that often in error. He mostly presents a defense of Mary of Scotland and the Duke of Norfolk."

"I know of them. She was our queen for a year. But now Elizabeth holds her prisoner. And the Duke of Norfolk is to be executed for writing love letters to her, is he not?"

"What he wrote about who should rule England was more stressed at his trial than his protestations of love."

"That might count more at his trial," she said, "but when your queen thinks of pardoning him, she will remember the duke's vows of love. A woman without a lover tastes bitter gall when she thinks of a rival who has one."

Was she speaking from personal experience? Her husband had been dead three years. Had she had lovers? "You may be right," he said. "The chance of a pardon for the Duke of Norfolk looks dim."

"This doleful talk comes from your reading politics rather than Rabelais. His stories are better for the spirit. Now tonight we have garlic soup, carp in English sauce, pigeon stew, and roast lamb."

"I retract what I said before. Both the food and the company are better here than in the halls of Paris officials."

Tuesday, 13 May 1572

Hunter and Crespin were headed down the rue de la Verrerie, late for a meeting with a mercer and his brother, a dyer. Puddles stood in the street from an overnight rain, and the ordure smell of "Paris mud" lingered in the air. Around the corner ahead of them came the tall thin figure of Captain Izard, with three men in his wake.

"Master Adams," he called, "where are you and Crespin hurrying?"

"To Les Halles, where I have an appointment with the Messieurs Vizet."

"What do you have in that chest?" Izard asked.

"I have samples of English yarn and cloth," Hunter replied, resisting the urge to tell him it was none of his affair.

"Open it."

"Captain," Hunter said in what he hoped was a conciliatory tone, "if we delay, we will be late for our appointment. Why do you need to see our cloth?"

Izard's eyes narrowed. "Do you question my authority? I have responsibility for the security of the people of this quarter. Do you expect me to allow foreign Protestants go about freely, carting God knows what?" Two or three passersby stopped to watch.

The mention of authority led Hunter to open the chest a crack and pull out the authorization the *prévôt des marchands* had given him. "Here is my authority from the Bureau de la Ville to meet with merchants and officials."

Two porters set down their baskets to watch the drama before them.

Izard unrolled the parchment with a distasteful expression. He eyed it and blew air out his nose. "I wonder what the spinners' and weavers' guilds will say when they know the *prévôt* endorses the selling of English cloth in our markets."

"It is a part of the treaty between your king and our queen, to the mutual advantage of English and French merchants." Hunter repeated the words he had used in all his meetings.

"Ah, yes. It will be such an advantage to work together in harmony. That is what we were told at the Peace of Amboise, then the Peace of Longjumeau, and now,"—he spat on the ground—"the damned Peace of Saint-Germain. When will His Majesty learn that there will be peace only when the heretics have been destroyed?" As the crowd gathering around them muttered their agreement, Izard demanded again, "Let me see what is in your chest?"

Hunter checked his urge to push past the man. He may as well let him see the cloth samples and go on to his appointment. He opened the chest. "You see, no weapons, nothing suspicious, just cloth."

Izard felt along the sides of the chest. He pulled a spool of thread up from the bottom. "What is this?"

"Fine stammet yarn from Norwich."

"Fine yarn indeed." Izard's voice grew louder. "This is yarn which will bind King Charles to Elizabeth of England, just as the Queen Mother will bind Princess Marguerite to Henri of Navarre." He spat again. "One may as well bind the Virgin Mary to a leper." As the crowd behind him shouted approval, he dropped the spool back into the chest and pulled out a piece of satin worsted with a floral pattern woven into it, one of the most expensive samples Hunter had brought.

Hunter looked at the three serious-faced men standing behind Izard, and the crowd beyond them, and held his tongue.

"We do not need more attachments to heretics!" Izard was playing to the crowd. "No." He pulled his bread knife from its scabbard. "We need to cut ourselves free." He plunged his knife into the worsted and ripped outward, slicing it in two.

Hunter leapt forward to grasp Izard, but a militiaman intercepted him. As they struggled, Crespin reached across the barrow to help. The two other militiamen lunged at him. The crowd erupted in shouts. In the confusion of pushing and shouting, Crespin and one of his assailants fell against the barrow. It tipped, and the contents of the sample chest tumbled into the muddy street. Dark stains spread over the white broadcloth. A barrage of laughter and catcalls echoed around them.

"Robert! Gaston! René" Izard called to his men. They stopped struggling, but the man who held Hunter did not let go. Izard looked at the pieces of cloth on the ground. "Master Adams," he said in a voice dripping with insincerity, "I must apologize for this unfortunate accident. Gaston, help Crespin and René up, and gather their cloths." He turned to Hunter. "You are fortunate that Robert stopped you, a foreigner and a Protestant, from laying hands on a captain of the militia in the process of his duties." They stared silently at one another for a moment, then Izard turned his head with a gesture that included the watching crowd. "I think you may release him now, Robert."

Robert loosened his grip; Hunter shook his shoulders and stepped away. He resisted the urge to reach for his dagger, realizing his position. "I shall report this incident to the Bureau de la Ville, and I trust they will fine you for the damages done."

Izard extracted a coin from his purse. "I apologize that my emotion overcame me. Perhaps I need a surgeon to bleed me. But I believe this teston will pay for the sewing of the cloth I cut." Behind him, the crowd muttered a commendation of his generosity. He looked down. "As for those, Crespin is as much to blame for their soiling as René. The laundresses of Paris can help repair any damage at little expense." He dropped the slashed cloth into the now upright chest.

Robert and Gaston were gathering up the samples, mingling those that were soiled with the clean pieces on top. "Ask your men to stop," Hunter said. "We will take care of our samples."

Izard shrugged. "Drop them," he said. His men did, spreading the samples further about the muddy street. The crowd laughed again. Hunter stared at Izard with hatred, mixed with anger at himself for making things worse.

"If we can be of no further service," Izard said, "we will continue with our duties." He jerked his head. Smiling, his men backed away from the barrow and the piles of dirty cloth. "About your business, all of you," he said to the crowd. They began to disperse with laughter as Izard and his men walked towards the Place de Grève.

"I never felt more thwarted and helpless," Hunter concluded.

"You did well to restrain yourself," Lepage said. "Izard is highly respected in the city. Some would say he is a law unto himself. His militiamen consider him a hero. Even the Bureau de la Ville would hesitate to cross him. They remember how he whipped the crowd up during the cross of Gastines riots."

Was there a trace of admiration in Lepage's voice? "At the embassy when I first met you, you expressed some views that seemed similar to Captain Izard. You said you feared more Protestants would come to France."

"Come now, Master Adams. We are both trained in the law. I did not state my views on the matter that evening. I merely stated some of the opinions you needed to know were abroad in the city. Sieur Prideaux was telling you only one side, that everyone would welcome the treaty. I submit that Captain Izard has proved my wisdom in warning you of the opposition you might encounter."

"He is a strong piece of evidence, to be sure."

"I deem it wise to keep my political views to myself," Lepage continued. "On the one hand, many of my clients are allied with the House of

Guise, but on the other, I serve Ambassador Walsingham. A lawyer must remain neutral."

He flashed his glued-on, opaque-window smile. Hunter noted that, although he mentioned Walsingham, he did not list any Huguenots among his clients.

"Tell me," Lepage asked, "is Ambassador Walsingham looked on with more favor by Lord Burghley or by the Earl of Leicester?"

Hunter was surprised by the question, and with Lepage's knowledge of the divisions within the Queen's Council. "I do not know. I am not privy to the workings of Her Majesty's Council."

"One hears that Burghley and Leicester struggle to control the Queen," Lepage said.

"No one controls Her Majesty," Hunter said, "though many try."

"But will you not hazard a guess as to which lord has more affection for the ambassador?"

"An acquaintance of mine once said a lawyer must remain neutral," Hunter said, "so I must say that both esteem him equally."

Lepage laughed.

"What led you to ask such a question?" Hunter asked.

Lepage stroked his pointed beard. "News of the company who will come from England to sign the treaty arrived at the embassy today. Your queen is to make Baron Clinton an earl, to increase the prestige of her envoy. And with him will come Philip Sidney, the nephew of the Earl of Leicester. I wondered if Master Sidney, young as he is, is coming to look after the interests of his uncle."

"You are better informed of English affairs than I," Hunter said.

"Well," Lepage said, changing the subject, "I will arrange that the laundresses who serve the embassy take special care of your samples. I advise you to reschedule any appointments that would involve your samples until next week."

CHAPTER 8

Discoveries

Thursday, 15 May 1572

HUNTER PLACED THE MANUSCRIPT HE HAD RECEIVED AT GLASSWELL House in his satchel and headed for the Cardinal's Hat bookshop. The same young man stood by the cash box. "Do you print many of the wares you stock?" Hunter asked him.

"Yes, sir." He pointed to the cardinal's hat colophon in the corner of a broadsheet.

Hunter scanned the sheet. Elizabeth of England was a monarch no one could trust. She had insulted the Spanish by seizing their treasure ships, turned against the Dutch Protestants by banishing them from her ports, and betrayed her cousin by supporting rebellious lords in Scotland. It warned Huguenots that she betrayed them before and counseled the king not to ally himself with such an unreliable witch.

"Is your master both the bookseller and the printer?"

"He is," the boy said with pride.

"I would like a word with him, if I may."

The boy disappeared through a curtain, then reemerged. "He will see you in the back."

Hunter followed down a narrow passage stacked with boxes and books on either side. They entered a workshop with a large printing press at its center, and sheets of paper hanging on lines drying. Two men were cleaning the press, while another sorted type into trays. He looked up and wiped his hands on a rag. "Nicolas Colin, at your service."

"I am Paul Adams," Hunter said. "I am looking for someone who could print a small pamphlet in English."

"English, French, Latin—it's all the same letters," the printer said. "We need not understand it to set the type."

"Have you printed any English works before?" Hunter tried to appear calm as he asked the crucial question.

"Yes."

"If you do not read English, how do you make sure there are no errors?"

"The man who ordered the work read the first pressing and corrected it."

Hunter resisted the temptation to ask who had commissioned the printing, and instead asked, "Do you have a sample of your printing in English?"

Colin rummaged through a pile of papers. "Here." He held up a copy of the "Treatise on the Duty of All True Catholics," the very pamphlet they had found in Pickering's room.

Hunter pretended to look it over. What luck that he had discovered the printer of at least one of the Catholic tracts destined for England. "Have you done others?"

"Only one other English job. A broadsheet. But I have no copies."

Now that he had discovered his Parisian printer, he needed to play out his role. "How much would you charge for something like this?"

"Quarto size, like that?"

"Yes."

"How many pages?"

"Between sixteen and twenty, I would guess."

"May I see the manuscript?"

Hunter extracted the sheets from his satchel.

Colin looked them over and nodded. "Sixteen is about right. How many copies?"

"Let us say five hundred."

"Sixteen pages. Five hundred copies." Colin paused for a moment as though calculating, but looked carefully at Hunter's clothing as he did so. "Three livres, ten sols."

Hunter frowned. "So much? Perhaps I should show this to another printer."

"You may if you can find another who will print English works in Paris. You may have to travel to Louvain."

"Can you in honesty say no one else in Paris prints in English?"

"I will not swear to it, but I know of no one who does," Colin said. Then he handed Hunter the prize he had been fishing for. "If you do not believe me, ask an Englishman who lives here. Ask for Sir Gregory Wilkes at the Antelope on the rue de la Serpent. If there are other printers, he will know."

Hunter could hardly contain his excitement. "You printed this pamphlet for him?"

A worried look crossed the printer's face. He had promised to keep Wilkes's name a secret.

"Do not worry," Hunter said. "I will not reveal what you said. It is good to know that you will keep my identity to yourself if you print my pamphlet." He exchanged the "Treatise" for his manuscript. "If Sir Gregory recommends you, I will return."

Hunter left the bookshop with a spring in his step. It had been so easy. At his first enquiry, he had chanced upon the printer who had produced the treatise that Pickering held, and he identified Wilkes as the one who ordered its printing. Walsingham would be impressed with his information. In a little over a month, he had raised an interest in English cloth among the merchants of Paris and discovered the source of seditious pamphlets. Accomplishing his mission for the syndicate and Lord Burghley in less time than expected might bring him to the notice of the Privy Council. Would he be called to Her Majesty's service? Such a position would allow him to ask Sir Lawrence Spranklin for Mary's hand, with excellent prospects for approval.

He stopped, suddenly aware that his feet had taken him to the Antelope without a conscious decision. It had been over two weeks since he had spoken to any expatriate. He had been heeding Lepage's advice to avoid attending Mass, but now might be the time to renew his connection. Wilkes might be there. Was it time to confront him with the evidence: Pickering's possession of pamphlets he had had printed, his payments to Pickering, his clear desire to avoid any discussion of Pickering on the day his body was discovered? Should he ask him directly whether Pickering threatened to reveal his seditious writings to Walsingham and why Pickering apologized and swore he could keep a secret? Would such questions lead Wilkes to confess to Pickering's murder?

He imagined Wilkes's calm face and bland replies. Yes, Pickering was moving pamphlets for him. He had paid for his services. There had been no threats. Of course, he and Pickering both had to keep the printing and transporting of literature a secret, as much for Pickering's sake as his. A slip of Pickering's tongue had for a moment endangered him, but the danger had passed, and Pickering wrote to excuse his slip. How did Adams come to know of Pickering's private affairs? Had he somehow broken into Pickering's lodgings, even before his body was discovered? Clearly Adams was not who he claimed to be! Was he a fanatic Protestant, who had undertaken to murder Pickering for his actions in defense of the Holy Mother Church? Was Adams a mortal danger to them all?

Even in his own mind, his evidence could be blown away like leaves by a sudden breeze, and he might be exposed as the agent he was, foolish and useless rather than successful. No, he would have to wait. He entered the room habitually used by the expatriates, but Wilkes was not there. Roger Barnes and Sir James Kempson sat alone at a table.

Barnes's eyes lit up. "Master Adams, we have not seen you for a long time."

"Come join us," Sir James offered. "Antoine! A cup of wine!" To Hunter he said, "I hear you are provoking the interest of Paris mercers in the products of English looms."

"Where do you hear such sunny news?" Hunter asked.

"Sieur de Prideaux says you are convincing merchants that trade in Rouen will be more advantageous than Antwerp."

"I hope I am. You know Prideaux?"

"Yes. He serves the Viscount de Beaulieu, a man of great influence."

"Perhaps it is the influence of such men that leads the merchants to see an advantage in a new English staple at Rouen," Hunter ventured.

"Perhaps, but you should take credit while you can," Sir James said. "Opinions can change quickly."

"What do you mean?" Had Kempson heard of his encounter with Captain Izard?

"Not everyone at Court wants closer ties with England," Kempson said. "The Duke of Anjou and the Guises will do what they can to obstruct this new treaty."

"So I gathered. Some of the officers I spoke with, who were cool towards English trade, stated their respect for Anjou."

"Whom have you spoken with?" Barnes asked.

The wine arrived, and Hunter listed the officials and merchants he had seen. Barnes and Kempson responded with their own observations regarding them. Then Hunter asked their news.

"Lodge has disappeared," Barnes said.

"Disappeared? I hope he has not come to harm," Hunter said. The last time an expatriate had gone missing he had turned up dead.

Kempson shook his head. "I suspect that he finally acted on his words and went to fight for the Duke of Alva against the Dutch rebels. He blew at everyone just before he disappeared. Said all we did was sit and moan about how the tide was flowing against us, but that he would not stand idle while the Queen Mother led France to ally with heretics."

Barnes said, "You were thinking of Pickering, weren't you, when you said you hoped Lodge had come to no harm."

"Yes," Hunter admitted.

"I am still troubled by the questions you raised at his death." Barnes said. "Why was the body hidden? Did he know his killer? And his landlady said she had not seen him for a week. Where was he during the week after Easter?"

"You still think his death some mystery, rather than an unfortunate encounter with footpads?" Sir James asked.

"I am still uneasy," Barnes said.

"After the funeral, Sir Gregory was to examine his belongings, see to his affairs, and notify his family," Hunter prompted.

"He did," Kempson said. "He collected such possessions as he found at his lodgings. He asked any creditors to make a claim. His landlady, two tailors, a hatter, a wine merchant, Wilkes himself, and the proprietor here at the Antelope came forward. He sold items to clear the debts, then sent the little money that was left to his father."

Hunter reported his own investigations. "I spoke to the tanner and his men, and looked around where his body was found, but I found no clue. Did you hear any report from the Châtelet?"

"They have set his death down as a robbery," Barnes replied. "But your mention of the tannery reminds me of a thought I had yesterday. If he were killed near the tannery, he might have been staying nearby. There are many inns in the faubourg Saint-Marcel."

He should have thought of that at the time. But if Pickering were so near the embassy, why had he not gone there? "You are right," Hunter said. "We might go even now and enquire."

"Do not encourage him," Kempson said. "Will you both play officers of the Châtelet?"

Hunter could not appear too eager.

Barnes answered. "The Châtelet has washed their hands of this matter. And if am still disquieted, then like Lodge, I may as well act as sit and moan." He stood and downed the last of his wine, and Hunter stood with him.

At the first inn, the proprietor said no Englishmen had stayed there in over a year. "But someone else came asking if I had an English guest. Just after Easter."

"Was he English?" Hunter asked.

"No, sir. Definitely a Parisian."

"What did he look like?"

"I can't recall. That was a month ago, and he was here only a minute."

As they left, Barnes asked, "Could the person looking for him be the reason Pickering left his lodgings?"

"I am thinking as you are. He left in fear and went into hiding somewhere, but whoever he was hiding from came to look for him."

The next innkeeper made a show of his haste, snapping a "No" when Barnes asked about an English guest, and "I don't know" when asked if others had sought such a guest. At a third inn, the story was the same as the first innkeeper's. No Englishman had lodged there, but a Frenchman had come asking the week following Easter. He could not recall what he looked like.

As they walked farther from Paris, the quality of the inns dropped and the pungency of the tanneries and slaughterhouses along the Bièvre increased. At their fourth stop, a small building under a peeling sign of a lamb, an old man with a wizened face opened the door. He wore a leather apron over faded brown clothes. Although the weather was mild, he wore a cap with flaps that came down over his ears and tied under his chin. "An Englishman? Yes. One was here a month ago. Stayed a week, then went out one night with a friend and didn't come back." Hunter and Barnes exchanged glances. "A few days later, it turns out he was robbed and murdered, and his body dumped just a few furlongs yonder, at Gaston's tannery. Course he hadn't paid me, so I was out for his bed and board."

"May we come in and talk with you?" Barnes asked. The old man led them into an entrance hall. To their left was a room where several laborers from the slaughterhouses and tanneries of Saint-Marcel stood drinking at a bar.

"Would you like to sit in here and have some refreshment?" the old man gestured to a vacant table.

"Some place more private would be better." Noticing the innkeeper's disappointed face, Hunter added, "We may take some refreshment afterward."

The innkeeper ushered them into a small room that served as combination office and storage closet. Two casks stood near the door. Beyond them a table covered with papers was pushed against one wall. Shelves next to it held a hodge-podge of bound papers, folded gray cloths, candle-ends, and broken crockery. Strings of onions hung from a nail on one side. The old man squeezed past the barrels, repositioned a basket of mugs from a bench to the floor, and invited Barnes and Hunter to sit on it. They sat, hams pressed together, neither completely on the bench. The innkeeper perched on a stool.

"This friend the Englishman left with," Hunter began, "was he English too?"

"Oh, no. A Frenchman."

Could Wilkes pass as a Frenchman? "What did he look like?"

"Hard to say. Well dressed, but he had a long cloak with the hood pulled up around his face, so I couldn't see."

"How tall was he?"

"A little shorter than you."

"Can you remember anything about him?"

"Like I say, well dressed. I think he had a beard."

"What color? What shape?"

The man shrugged. "I could see only the end of it. Dark. Brushed to a point."

Three-quarters of the men in Paris had such beards. "What did he say to you?"

"Said he understood there was an Englishman lodging here, and asked me to describe him. When I did, he claimed he was an old friend who wanted to surprise him."

"Did you not tell Pickering someone had come asking for him?" Barnes asked.

"Pickering?" The old man screwed up his face. "That weren't his name. It was Simpson."

"But you're sure your guest was the same man they found at the tannery?" Hunter asked.

"I didn't see the body myself, but Gaston himself described his face and clothes to me. It was that same Simpson who was lodging here. You're telling me he gave me a false name?"

"I am afraid he did," Hunter said. "He may have come here to hide from someone. You are sure the man who came asking for him was not an Englishman?"

"I am indeed. No offense to you gentlemen—I hear you can speak French—but you will never sound like a born Frenchman. The man he left with that night was definitely French."

"But I want to ask again," Barnes said, "did you send up a message to your Simpson that someone had come asking for him?"

The old man looked down and exhaled. "No. The gentleman swore he was an old friend. 'Don't tell him,' says he. 'Just point out the door to me and I will surprise him.' And he handed me two testons."

A little silver overcomes any caution. Hunter asked, "Did you see how your guest reacted when he saw the gentleman at his door?"

"I didn't see, but I heard. He gave a gasp and then some sort of cry, like he recognized him. It was as you might expect."

"That cry of recognition—did he speak a name?" Hunter asked.

"Maybe." The old man scratched his stubble chin with dirt-caked nails. "But I can't remember." He shook his head.

"What happened then?"

"They spoke a bit at the door, then the gentleman went in to Simpson's room."

"And did he stay long?"

"Oh, yes. Over an hour."

"Have you any idea what passed between them?"

"I could hear them talking, but I couldn't make out what they were saying."

"Then they left together?"

"Yes."

"Did you see them leave? Was the gentleman still hooded?"

"Yes, he was. They came down together, laughing. Simpson said he was going for a drink and would be back later."

"And that was the last time you saw him?"

"Yes."

Hunter started a new line of questions. "Did anyone else ask for an Englishman before the gentleman in the hood turned up?"

"Yes. A man came the day before, asking for an Englishman. When I said I had one, then he described Simpson—or whoever he was—and I said yes, that was him. Said his master had lost track of a friend who was an Englishman in Paris, and would be glad to learn he was at the Lamb. And the day after, the gentleman appears. You see, it all made sense."

It made sense to Hunter, but in a different way. "Did the servant return with his master?"

"No."

"Could he have been outside that night?"

"I suppose so."

"You talked for some time with the servant. What did he look like?"

"Oh," the old man sucked at his teeth, "an ordinary looking man. Average height. Burly. Dark brown hair. Nothing particular 'cept his ear."

"His ear?"

"Yes. Had a piece out of it, like he'd been in a knife fight. The top of it was chopped at a slant, like this." He drew the index finger of his left hand across the top of his left ear.

"It was his left ear?" Hunter asked.

"Yes," the man said. "This side."

"Can you remember anything else about him?"

"No."

"When did the Englishman who called himself Simpson come to you?" Barnes asked.

"He was here near a week." He reached behind him and picked up a small black book. He leafed through a few pages. "Here. Here's his mark." He turned the notebook around and showed it to Barnes, pointing to a signature. Next to "J. Simpson" were eight straight lines. "This here," his grimy fingernail hovered over the seventh line, "was the night he left with the gentleman. The next day he didn't come back, but I marked it down against his reckoning. That was the day we heard they'd found a dead body at the tannery and sent word to the Châtelet."

"What are these marks?" Barnes pointed to checks and squiggles beneath the lines.

"Those are the victuals he ate and the beer he drank. He paid his way the first few days, but then he asked me to put it on his account." He replaced the book on the table.

"Did he eat in there?" Hunter pointed through the wall to the bar.

"No. Kept to his room. Asked us to bring up his food and drink."

"He never went out?"

"No."

"Can we see the room where he lodged?" Hunter asked.

"Why are you gents so interested in Simpson?" The old man was suddenly cautious.

"We are friends of his," Barnes replied.

"You are? You don't seem to know his other friend, the gent that he left with that night, and you've been a whole month before you come here asking what happened to him."

"Look, sir," Barnes explained, "we did not neglect our friend. In fact, I arranged his funeral. It is only that we did not know he was lodging here under a different name until now."

The innkeeper looked dubious.

Barnes continued, "As for the gentleman who came that night, I doubt he was truly a friend of Simpson."

"If he wasn't, why did Simpson leave with him?"

"I don't know," Barnes admitted, "but have you not considered that that gentleman, who took such pains not to be seen, might have lured him to his death?"

"I reckoned after he had a drink with his friend, he had the bad luck to meet some thieves. They said his purse was gone. I particularly asked Gaston about that."

Hunter spoke slowly. "One man asks you about an English guest. The next day someone comes to talk with that guest and leads him out, and he is killed. Do you not see that these two men might have something to do with your guest's murder?"

The old man sat silent for a moment, then blurted out, "There are innkeepers who listen at doors and spy on guests and demand money to keep secrets, but I am not one of them. No. I stay out of it. Who a lodger has to his room and what he does there is not my affair. If one man talks with another in his room and leaves with him—that is nothing strange."

"But when that man is murdered on the same night..." Hunter said.

The innkeeper's defense collapsed with his shoulders. "Even if I did think afterward that the gentleman might have led him to the robbers, what could I do?"

"Did you not tell the Châtelet when they enquired?" Hunter asked.

The old man laughed. "The Châtelet did not ask me, and I stay as far from them as I can."

Hunter fished a douzaine from his purse. "Would you be so kind as to show us the room?"

The innkeeper rose and took the coin. "Follow me." He picked up a candlestick and led them up the staircase.

"You cleared his room?" Hunter asked as they climbed.

"Of course. Can't let a room sit empty, full of some dead man's clothes. Especially a single room that can be rented by the hour. He owed me a week's rent, so I wanted to sell them right away. But the missus said to hold on to his things, that his friend would come back and we could ask him to pay for the lodging and some extra for the clothes."

"But you didn't see his gentleman friend again, I gather," said Barnes.

"No. So last week I sold the clothes."

Hunter sighed. Whatever clues they might have held were now lost. The innkeeper stopped before a door at the end of the hall and fumbled for a key.

"He insisted on a room alone. Said he didn't want to share with anyone. This is the only chamber for one man." The innkeeper opened the door.

Hunter stepped into the tiny room. A single bed took up almost all one side. A small clothes chest sat at its foot. A stool and a small desk near the head of the bed were the only other pieces of furniture. The innkeeper opened the shutters of the window above the desk to let in the evening light. What fear would lead a man to spend a week in such a cramped room, Hunter wondered. He and Barnes squeezed past one another. Barnes looked out the window. Hunter opened the chest and found it empty. Although the innkeeper had cleared the room, he could not say he had cleaned it. Hunter knelt on one knee. "Hand me the candle," he said to the innkeeper.

There was a clear boundary, a foot under the bed, where the mop reached its limit and the dust and grime began. Beyond it lay an encrusted spoon and a few sticks that might have broken off a broom. At the bottom, crushed between the chest and a leg of the bed, was a piece of paper without a layer of dust. Hunter pushed the chest to one side and retrieved the crumpled paper.

"What have you found?" Barnes asked.

Hunter handed him the candle and straightened the printed broadsheet damning Queen Elizabeth, with the emblem of the cardinal's hat at the bottom.

"Did Simpson bring this with him?" Barnes asked.

"He might have," the innkeeper said. "He had other such papers in with his clothes."

"What became of them?" Hunter asked.

"We threw them away."

Hunter looked at Barnes and rolled his eyes. "Did he leave anything else behind but his clothes and the papers you threw out?"

"Only the ink and quill."

"He wrote letters then?' Hunter asked.

"Yes. He sent out letters."

"To whom?"

"I don't know."

Hunter let another sigh escape.

"But Nicolas will know," the innkeeper said. "He delivered them."

They traipsed back downstairs and waited while the innkeeper found Nicolas, a lanky, sandy-haired boy of about fourteen, whose face was marred with smallpox scars.

"The first message I took to a gentleman's lodgings across from the Hôtel Saint-Denis," he said. Barnes's eyes met Hunter's. Both recognized the description of Sir Gregory Wilkes's house. "Two days after that, he sent me to the English ambassador's house." They exchanged another look.

"And did you deliver both messages?" Barnes asked.

"Yes, sir."

"Did you wait for an answer?"

"No, sir. The gentleman didn't say I was to wait."

"Thank you, Nicolas." Hunter reached in his purse again and gave the boy a dixaine. He had no more questions for the innkeeper, but handed him a double sol as an alternative to tasting his beer. "This is for your cooperation. We may be back with further questions."

The old man looked down at the coin and smiled. "You will always be welcome at the Lamb."

Outside, they turned to one another. Hunter asked, "Who was the Frenchman?" at the same time Barnes said, "He was sending for help." After a second, Hunter said, "Do not tell Wilkes," as Barnes said, "He must have known the man."

Both paused a moment. "Let us go over Pickering's actions in order, as we walk," Hunter suggested.

They started towards the Porte Bordelle, and Barnes began, "Let us count backwards. Pickering was buried on the seventeenth of April. The morning of the sixteenth, a Châtelet officer asked me to identify his body, which had been found the evening before."

"At the tannery the evening of the fifteenth," Hunter said.

"Yes. That was a Tuesday. So Pickering left the Lamb with the Frenchman the night before, Monday the fourteenth."

"And was stabbed and dumped at the tannery that night," Hunter said.

"That was his seventh night at the inn," Barnes said. He held up his fingers and chanted, "Monday, Sunday, Saturday, Friday, Thursday, Wednesday, Tuesday. He came to the Lamb on the Tuesday after Easter. That more or less agrees with what his landlady said, that he had been missing a week. And none of us saw him after Easter."

Hunter was unwilling to share that Pickering had been scheduled to report to the embassy on the afternoon of the Monday before he went to the Lamb. "What happened between Easter Mass and Tuesday to cause him to leave Place Maubert and engage a chamber at the Lamb under a false name?"

"If he were escaping debts, Saint-Marcel is too close, even with a new name." Barnes paused. "He talked about returning to England. Perhaps he wrote to Wilkes for money and to the embassy for permission to return without facing arrest."

"Your explanation accounts for the messages, but why leave his lodging so abruptly?"

"To avoid a creditor," Barnes said without much conviction.

"What of the Hooded Gentleman? Was he only a creditor?" Hunter frowned. "Would a creditor spend an hour talking, then take his debtor out for a drink? I would expect a brief, angry encounter."

Barnes nodded. "You are right. But hold. What if a creditor engaged some mutual acquaintance? He asks this mutual friend to locate Pickering and to talk to him sympathetically about his debt. Encourage him to pay a modicum each week. Take him out for a drink to seal the arrangement."

"And the murder?" Hunter asked.

"It may be as everyone assumes, just a chance meeting with thieves."

Hunter scowled.

"Have you a better explanation?"

"Not entirely," Hunter admitted. "Let me try, however. Let us suppose that Pickering went into hiding, not because he suddenly felt worse about his debts, but because someone had threatened him. I admit I do not know the reason for that threat. Perhaps someone discovered

Pickering had betrayed him." Wilkes discovering Pickering's approach to the embassy would fit, but then who was the Frenchman? Barnes's explanation offered an answer. "That someone engages the servant with the chopped ear to find him, then a mutual friend to speak with him and convince him there is no danger. When the mutual friend, the Hooded Gentleman, lures him from the Lamb, two men hired by the Betrayed Someone murder Pickering to punish him or keep him from further betrayal."

"I grant that you have a possible explanation," Barnes said.

"Alas, both our cases have weak spots," Hunter said. "Yours supposes a sudden decision to depart on the Tuesday after Easter without an immediate cause and an unfortunate and unconnected meeting with thieves. My case supposes an unknown Someone who threatens, hunts down, and murders Pickering for an unknown reason. Neither identifies the Hooded French Gentleman."

"And your explanation does not account for Pickering's letters to Wilkes and Walsingham," Barnes said.

Hunter's did account for them. Pickering's letter to Wilkes had been the one apologizing and swearing he could keep a secret. The letter to the embassy might have been saying he was in danger from Wilkes, and asking for help. But how could he explain this to Barnes? "You are right," he said, "it does not."

"We must ask Sir Gregory about Pickering's letter," Barnes said.

Hunter's muscles tightened. He should have seen this coming; from Barnes's point of view, it was a logical next step. "I must ask you not to tell Sir Gregory of our mission today."

Barnes turned to him with a face of total surprise. "Why not?"

There was no help for it. "What do you know of Pickering's part in Sir Gregory's efforts to send books and pamphlets to England?"

"I know Pickering assisted Wilkes. Several times he went to Louvain and Antwerp. Whether he carried messages, manuscripts, or money, I don't know. Pickering intimated that his service to Sir Gregory was extremely important, but secret. He never explained exactly what he was doing."

"You would agree then," Hunter said, "that Pickering knew more than the rest of you about Wilkes's publishing and export of Catholic tracts."

"Yes."

"And you said he wanted to return to England."

"Yes."

"It might be possible that he offered information about printers, transporters, even Sir Gregory himself to Walsingham, in return for a safe return to England," Hunter said. There, he had stated the facts, but only as a supposition.

Barnes was silent a moment. "That is possible."

"Then suppose Sir Gregory found out that he offered, perhaps even gave, such information to Walsingham."

"So, you are suggesting Sir Gregory Wilkes is the Someone Betrayed?" Barnes was incredulous.

"Is that impossible?"

"It is not impossible," Barnes said, "but Sir Gregory would never order a murder!"

"I hope you are right," Hunter said. "But if there is the possibility that Pickering informed on him and Sir Gregory discovered it, then there is a possibility Sir Gregory might be involved in his killing."

"But he took charge of Pickering's affairs. Even paid some of his debts so that he could send some money to his father."

"And if Sir Gregory were trying to be sure no evidence of his activities was in Pickering's lodgings?" Hunter suggested.

"Yes," Barnes said. "I see. But you make a generous deed appear wicked." He was silent for a moment. "I cannot believe your explanation."

"All I ask is that you delay telling him what we have discovered, or asking him about Pickering's letter, for a few days. I must report to the embassy on my business with the merchants. Let me discreetly enquire about Pickering. Perhaps I can discover if he was providing information and what was in the letter he sent them from the Lamb."

"And what am I to say of our expedition today?" Barnes asked. "Kempson knows we were looking for a trace of Pickering."

"Say we found nothing. It is that simple."

"I am deeply troubled at your suggestion that Sir Gregory is involved," Barnes said, "and I am sure that if we ask him about Pickering's letter, your suspicions will prove baseless."

"If you ask, Sir Gregory needs only say he received no letter. That could be the truth, or a lie. Your question will reveal you know Pickering stayed at the Lamb, and may know of those who came for him. That could put you in danger."

Barnes struggled with himself. "All right. I will not ask him now."

They had reached the Place Maubert. "I must cross to the Right Bank now," Hunter said. "I will tell you what I learn in a few days."

As he walked, Hunter pondered. If Pickering's letter to Wilkes had revealed his location to Wilkes, then why had a servant trudged from inn to inn asking for an Englishman? Did Wilkes have a servant with half his ear missing? And who was the Hooded French Gentleman? The facts did not fit neatly into his explanation of Pickering's murder.

Marguerite Moreau's smile greeted Hunter as he entered L'Échiquier. "You are late for supper, Monsieur Adams. And tonight Auguste prepared one of your favorites—roast lamb with mint."

"Then I am glad I did not tarry longer."

"What business kept you so late?" she asked as he seated himself. "Didn't you tell me you canceled appointments because that meddler Izard soiled your samples?"

"That is true." What could he tell her of his discoveries that day? "But I had other interests to pursue."

"Ah, ha! And what was her name?" she teased.

He felt his face flush. "I assure you, it was not a woman."

She pursed her lips and gave a knowing nod. "Oh, of course not." Her eyes danced.

He shook his head and laughed. "You account me a more formidable lover than I am."

"Are you still doting on that girl in the cold north of England, then?"

Doting? Was that what she thought about his love for Mary? "Yes," he said, "I remain true to her."

The smile faded from Madame Moreau's face. Laurent arrived with a jug of water, towel, and basin. "Well," she said, "I am sure you are hungry and anxious to begin your supper. I shall send Martin with it in a moment." She turned and walked away. Hunter watched her go, concerned that he had offended her in some way, until Laurent cleared his throat. He held out his hands over the basin.

He scarcely noticed the flavor of the lamb. He resented Madame Moreau calling Mary "that girl in the cold north." Mary was not cold, but warm and full of love. Images of her smiling face drifted into her head.

He regretted the pleasure he had found in Madame Moreau's company. She could not compare to Mary.

He must report the day's events at the embassy tomorrow. His investigations had not found Pickering's killer, but Walsingham and Beale would surely welcome the information that Nicolas Colin, at the Cardinal's Hat, was printing Catholic pamphlets at the behest of Sir Gregory Wilkes. Beale had said that was of more value to the security of England. They would see his value as an information gatherer. When favorable reports reached Lord Burghley, he could hope for more assignments, perhaps even for royal favor, and for status that would allow him to ask Mary's father for her hand. Again he pictured Mary's laughing face and remembered their last embrace.

"Master Adams," Madame Moreau was at his shoulder, clutching a packet, "I hope you enjoyed the lamb."

"It was excellent."

"I forgot to tell you when you came in, but Jacques Crespin brought these from the embassy this afternoon." She handed him letters tied with a thin white ribbon.

Hunter's heart raced. In front of several letters from his uncle was a smaller one in Richard Spranklin's hand. Finally, he would have word from Mary. "I thank you, Madame Moreau, both for the supper and for these letters. It has been some time since I have heard from England."

"May all your letters contain good news," she smiled.

In his chamber, Hunter restrained the impulse to open Richard's letter first. He would deny himself the joy of seeing Mary's handwriting until he had dealt with the duty of reading the letters from his uncle and parents. His father wrote about the crops and animals at Bradhurst Hall and expressed their pleasure he had agreed to work for his Uncle George. He closed with one paragraph of warnings about avoiding illness and bad company, and another full of pious advice. Hunter could almost hear his mother dictating.

Three letters from his uncle bore different dates. In the first, Uncle George expressed his pleasure that Edward had done well during his tuition at Glasswell Manor and had reached France safely. He reiterated the points the syndicate considered important. The second was delighted that the Treaty of Blois had been signed. The third letter was dated a week ago. Uncle George was sorry to report that some Merchant Adventurers had raised objections to a syndicate conducting trade through Rouen. They argued that, with Flushing now in the hands of the Sea Beggars, it could serve as the new Antwerp. He cursed them for small-mindedness, but they had friends in Her Majesty's Privy Council. Edward was to proceed cautiously. Above all, he was to limit his expenses. Uncle George was unable to send the draft on the Biondi bank he had promised, but hoped to do so in a week.

Wonderful. He had assured Lepage that the syndicate would pay his fees, but the letter to his uncle seeking approval for this had crossed the one he was reading. The coins in his purse would not cover his expenses at the Chessboard Inn and Lepage's fees. If his uncle did not send the promised draft soon, he would be in trouble. He would erase this worry by reading Mary's letter, enclosed in her brother's.

He broke the seal and unfolded Richard's letter. Sure enough, a small piece of paper fluttered onto the desk. He turned it over and read.

My dearest Edward,

I am sorry. Forgive me.

Mary

Was that all? He turned the paper over. It was blank. What was she talking about? Why was she sorry? He smoothed out Richard's letter. As he read, his throat dried.

Richard began with the usual greetings and wishes for Edward's good health. He was now devoting his whole attention to the management of Coverton and the Spranklin estates, as his father had grown weaker and could no longer move his right hand or leg. His condition had made him anxious about his children's future. As a result, Richard had been betrothed to Alice Kittering of County Durham. Mary had been betrothed to Andrew Blankenship, the son of a landowner in the West Riding. Both families, as the Spranklins, were Roman Catholic.

CHAPTER 9

Adjustments

HUNTER SAT IN SHOCK. MARY, BETROTHED. AN IRON BAR LODGED IN HIS chest. He read Richard's letter again, then Mary's brief note. Was she truly sorry? Could she only spare five words for him? Could she not defy her father's wishes? Others turned their backs on their families to be with their lovers. Only five words! If she felt the pain he did now, she would have poured out page after page of anguish.

But perhaps she was being closely watched. He pictured a grim-faced Mistress Jane hovering about Mary's chamber, ensuring that she bow to her father's wishes. She had written, "Forgive me." What agony Mary must have suffered, unable to unburden herself beyond dashing off a few words on a scrap of paper. How unfair he had been to think ill of her. He was not truly worthy of her.

She may be betrothed, but she was not yet married. He could beg her to delay. He would promise to rush to her. How long would it take a letter to reach Coverton? The calculation lowered his spirits. Richard's letter had been written a fortnight ago, and both betrothals had taken place before that. Mary had been promised for over a month, but they would have to allow enough time for the banns to be read on three successive Sundays. Surely she was not yet wed. Could he arrive in time, if he started at dawn?

Tears streamed down his face. This plan of rushing to Yorkshire was a fantasy. If he abandoned the mission, he could never look to either Lord Burghley or his uncle for favor. He would arrive at Sir Lawrence

Spranklin's door, a man without prospects, who had betrayed the trust of his family and the most powerful statesman in England. He would be less of a suitor than he had been two years before.

And how could he expect Mary to abandon her family? She had given her promise to wed—he searched the letter—one Andrew Blankenship. He hated the man, though he had never met him. His mind reverted for a moment to a legal question. Had the marriage contract with Blankenship been *de futuro* or *de preasenti*—that is, had Mary said, "I shall take thee as my husband" or "I take thee as my husband?" But he was grasping at straws. A marriage contract had been made. Even if he rode day and night to Yorkshire, and Mary did agree to defy her father, that contract would stand as an impediment to their marriage.

If they did run away, how would they live? In some hovel, she disinherited and he in disgrace? But the only alternative was to lose her forever. How could he do either? He must write to Mary, to let her know his love, his pain, his willingness to fly to her side, despite all, if that is what she wished. He took out pen, ink, and paper, and began.

Friday, 16 May 1572

Hunter sat exhausted before Ambassador Walsingham and Secretary Beale, hardly hearing their praise. His information regarding Nicolas Colin was invaluable. They would take no action against the printer, but use him instead. When he produced an English pamphlet, it could be tracked from Paris. The English authorities could discover and apprehend those who received and distributed it. The entire network could then be shut down. Hunter must drag out the negotiations for the printing while they set up watch in England.

Hunter nodded. He glanced at his letter to Mary, sitting in the pile of papers at Beale's elbow. As he lay restless in bed last night, variations of the words he had first written churned through his head. His mind had found better phrases to use, reconstructed sentences, discovered thoughts he had left out that must be included. He had risen once in the middle of the night to rewrite the letter, then again before dawn, to pen a third draft. He composed letters to his uncle and parents, then he wrote a fourth draft before coming to the embassy. Had he struck the right balance of expressing sympathy for Mary's plight and revealing his own anguish? He could still ask Beale to give back the letter.

"I congratulate you on what you were able to discover about Pickering," Walsingham interrupted his thoughts. "I have been thinking of all you reported, and I am troubled."

"Yes." Hunter struggled to attend to his words.

"We received no messages from Pickering after he failed to keep his last appointment. You must be correct that he abandoned his lodgings in fear. But why go to a disreputable inn here in Saint-Marcel? It would make sense for him to come to us for help and protection. He said he desired to return to England, and we had promised assistance once he finished providing information."

"He could have provided information about Catholic publications and Sir Gregory Wilkes at any time," Beale said. "His only reason for delivering it drop by drop must have been to extract the greatest payment from us over time. If he were frightened enough to go into hiding, the need to withhold information and spin out the time was gone. He could have come at once, and offered all his information for safety."

"Perhaps he was afraid someone would intercept him before he reached the embassy," Hunter suggested.

Beale shook his head. "I cannot believe that there was not one instant in the course of a week when he felt safe to walk to the embassy."

"Are we overlooking the fact that Pickering was trying to insinuate himself with the French?" Walsingham asked. "Could he have received encouragement from a French courtier? Would a letter from someone like the Duke of Guise cause him to miss his appointment with us, go into hiding, and avoid the embassy?"

"But the boy at the Lamb said he sent a letter to the embassy," Hunter said.

"That may have been some excuse for missing our meeting, and the letter to Sir Gregory may have presented an excuse for his disappearance as well," Walsingham said.

"Assuming Pickering was responding to a French offer might explain the Hooded Gentleman, but it does not explain why that Gentleman's servant had to search him out, nor why he was murdered," Beale said.

"Unless an offer to employ him came from one French courtier, and the Hooded Gentleman is an enemy of that courtier. Suppose one was aligned with the Guises and the other was a client of the Montmorencys," Walsingham suggested.

"Would that be enough to get Pickering killed?" Hunter asked.

Walsingham sighed. "It is a difficult to keep up with the latest permutation of Court rivalries. Last week the Duke of Guise agreed to be reconciled with Admiral Coligny. At least he went through the formula of agreeing to it."

Hunter had been fitting Pickering's actions into his idea that Sir Gregory was responsible for his murder. His tired mind could not sort out the possibility of French courtiers.

"Pray continue your investigations," Walsingham said. "Talk to that lad from the Lamb again. Be sure he is telling the truth. Ask who at the embassy received the letter."

"I will."

"We must ask some further service of you." Walsingham looked at Hunter's tired face and laughed. "Do not worry. I think you will find this easier than extolling the virtues of English cloth."

But Walsingham could not know what was draining his energy.

"The Treaty of Blois will be formally ratified in a month, with ceremonies in London and in Paris. King Charles is sending the Duke of Montmorency to London; Her Majesty is sending a delegation headed by the Earl of Lincoln, formerly Lord Clinton."

"Yes, sir." Hunter had heard this from Lepage.

"Lord Lincoln's retinue will include Philip Sidney, who intends to stay after the delegation returns to England, as part of a tour of Europe. Much of their time will be taken by ceremonies surrounding the treaty ratification, of course, but Lord Lincoln feels that he and the other young gentlemen might wish to see some of the sights of the city. You are close to Philip Sidney in age. I hope you and Jacques Crespin might undertake to entertain the younger members of the delegation during their stay here."

"Of course," Hunter agreed. Here was another opportunity to gain favor among those who had the power to improve his position. But the rush of elation was immediately followed by a stab of pain. What use was any elevation in rank now? It would be too late. Mary would be wed to another.

Hunter walked mechanically from the embassy, passing through the streets without registering his surroundings, searching a focus for his pain. He could not be angry with Mary. She had written, "I am sorry." Was that not evidence she was marrying against her will? Why had Richard not argued against the betrothal? Perhaps he, too, was marrying against his will from a sense of filial duty. Could he be angry with Mary's father? If Sir Lawrence had not suffered a stroke of palsy, would he have pressed Mary to wed? If God had struck down Sir Lawrence, was Mary's betrothal to another the will of God? If he could not be angry with any of the Spranklins, how could he question God, whose purposes no mortal could fathom? Perhaps the stroke resulted from an inauspicious alignment of planets.

To feed his melancholy, he walked along the banks of the Seine. In the river, a bouquet of flowers slowly revolved and drifted downstream. Like Mary. Like his purpose.

Tomorrow the laundered samples were to be returned. Monday he was scheduled to meet a dyer. How could he smile and extol the virtues of English cloth? What did it matter? He turned from the river. He must move through each day moment by moment. He did not have to believe in what he did, but he had promised others he would perform a duty.

"English, good day."

Half a dozen adolescent boys blocked his way. The face of the largest boy was a contrast. The right side was almost cherubic; the left was deformed by a large, swollen strawberry-colored birthmark that started beneath his eye and extended to his neck. The smile on the angelic side changed to a frown. "Don't Englishmen have any manners?" he growled. "I said good day."

Behind him, a tall boy with unruly hair smirked at Hunter's discomfort. A shorter lad, cudgel in hand, laughed. Was that the same boy who had held his horse's bridle the day he arrived? Who were these rude urchins who dared block his way? He could draw his dagger and slash through these young ruffians. As soon as his anger swelled, it drained away. No honor would attach to injuring or killing any of these boys. No, he would answer the young man civilly.

"Good day to you." Hunter recognized where he was—the street he had passed with Crespin his first week in Paris, where boys amused themselves by lying in wait for Protestants. "Pray, what do you call yourself?"

The strawberry-faced spokesman was caught off guard. He hesitated a moment, then said, "Robert. And you?"

"Paul Adams."

"Well, Monsieur Paul Adams," Robert returned to his script, "My friends here tell me you have been in Paris some time. How do you like our city?" His gang strained forward, eager to find some word at which to take offense.

"I like it quite well, Robert. It is a fair city with many fine monuments."

"And our customs?" His voice edged towards insolence. "Have you learned our customs?"

"Some of them," Hunter said. "For example, I do not stand blocking the way of men who are going about their business."

"Oh, I hope we are not in your way," Robert said, with exaggerated surprise. Guffaws broke out behind him. "My friends and I merely invite some of those passing to take part in a custom I understand the English have discarded—paying homage to Our Lady." He gestured to the shire on the wall to his right.

The statue of the Virgin Mary stood in a niche with an expression of peaceful sadness. The column of hot air rising from the candles at her feet made her hand, raised in blessing, seem to waver from side to side. Hunter remembered the statue of the Virgin in the Spranklins' chapel in Yorkshire, a candle burning before it in memory of Mary's mother. Mary had knelt before it almost every day. The boys' eyes gleamed in anticipation of his refusal to kneel. Their bodies tensed to strike at him and pursue him.

Disregarding the Paris mud, Hunter dropped to one knee and began to recite the words he had learned at Glasswell Manor. "*Ave Maria, gratia plena...*" The young men stood, surprise mixed with disappointment, as he finished the prayer. "*...nunc et in hora mortis nostrae. Amen.*" He sprang to his feet before any could move to strike him, but none had raised a hand. Mud stained his right knee. "Not all Englishmen have forgotten," he said. To his astonishment, the gang broke into a cheer.

Robert stated the obvious. "You surprised us."

"You should buy him a drink," the tall unkempt lad said.

Robert looked at the shorter boy with the cudgel. Evidently he was the gang's treasurer. "Do we have enough, Armond?"

"Keep your money," Hunter reached into his pocket and handed the lad a douzaine. "And this is for a candle for Our Lady."

While the boys crowded around to see how much this unpredictable Englishman had given them, Robert asked, a challenge in his eye, "Will you not drink with me?"

"I will," Hunter said.

Robert smiled a lopsided smile, one half lost in his birthmark. "Stay," he ordered his band. "I am going to share a drink with the Englishman." He turned back with pride. "I know the barman at the Horn. Follow me."

On his guard, Hunter followed him down an alleyway. Robert must have considerable strength of body and character, not only to survive a childhood of abuse and mockery caused by his appearance, but also to have risen to the leadership of this gang of street urchins. His age was hard to gauge, perhaps fifteen—young enough that drinking in a tavern was an act that impressed him and his companions. He entered a side door.

The small room smelled of smoke from cheap tallow candles. There were no tables or chairs, only a small portion of a bar, where two men stood. The bar curved beyond them into a separate, larger room where Hunter could hear the chatter of a crowd of patrons. Robert exchanged nods of greeting, and the two men slid to the left to make room.

"Pierre," Robert called to the barman. "Two cups of wine." He indicated a broad-faced man with bushy eyebrows and a chin covered with gray stubble. "This is Georges Landon." He pointed beyond. "And Gilbert Vasse." A taller man with a well-trimmed black beard and a light blue cap nodded a hello. "Sirs, this is Paul Adams, the Englishman who is staying at the Chessboard Inn."

"Ah, yes," said Landon. "The one with Crespin. What's in that great chest of yours?"

Is this how the people of his quarter saw him, the Englishman at the Chessboard who goes about with a mysterious chest? "I have examples of English cloth in the chest. I hope to interest some of your merchants in buying them."

Landon turned to Vasse. "See, I told you there was nothing evil."

"I didn't say there was anything bad in it," Vasse retorted. "I said I didn't feel comfortable, not knowing what was in it."

"You acted like it was full of magic potions or Protestant Bibles."

Vasse ignored the comment and addressed Robert. "Why are you bringing this gentleman to the Horn for a drink?"

Robert smiled his lopsided smile. "Shouldn't I be polite to our foreign guests?"

"See," Landon said, "his mother raised him well, God rest her soul."

"If you say so." Vasse evidently held reservations about Robert's mother. "But I haven't noticed you spending all your time welcoming foreigners, Robert. Are you turning over light-finger work to be a greeter for the Hôtel de Ville?" They all laughed, and Pierre arrived with the cups of wine.

"Master Adams just honored Our Lady with a prayer and a donation," Robert said.

Landon raised his eyebrows. "Then you're an English Catholic?"

Hunter tasted the wine. It was sharp and watered. "I am free to say so in Paris."

Vasse leaned forward with interest. "I hear that you are forced to go to English church services and forbidden to attend Mass."

"That is right," Hunter said. "We are fined twelve pence for not attending."

"How much is that?" Landon asked.

"About thirty deniers."

"Each time?"

"Yes."

"That could add up," Landon rubbed his chin.

"So, you go to the English service each Sunday?" Vasse asked.

"I cannot afford to do otherwise," Hunter said.

"But you know the Latin prayers." Robert looked confused.

"You may pray in private all you want," Hunter said.

"Well," Landon mused, "if you're forced to go by the law, maybe you'll only spend centuries in purgatory instead of burning in hell."

"Then he can bear you company." Vasse chuckled. "Master Adams, you wince with each sip. Did that bastard Pierre give you some of that sour cask he tried to pass off on us?"

"It tastes all right to me," Robert said.

"You wouldn't know the difference, boy," Vasse said. Robert bristled. Vasse reached for his cup, sniffed at it, and curled his lip. He took the smallest of sips and ran his tongue between his teeth to scrape off the taste. "Pierre, you rascal!" he called. "Take back this pig's piss and give us two cups of your burgundy."

Pierre appeared, a bit sheepish. As he took the cups, Vasse cuffed at his head. "Rogue!" Pierre ducked the blow. "I've ordered you a cup that you may know the difference," he said to Robert. "I'll bet he gives you that vinegar every time you come in. Taking advantage of a boy."

"I feel sorry for all Englishmen." Landon followed his own train of thought.

"Because they don't know good wine from bad?" Vasse asked.

"No," Landon said. "Because they will all burn for eternity because their old king burned with lust. His appetite for cunny made him break from the Church and cut his subjects off from salvation. They aren't baptized in the faith, they don't receive the sacraments, and they will all be damned, not for their own sins, but because of their king."

Hunter thought his theology lacked subtlety, but said only, "I hope God's judgment is not so harsh."

"Georges here thinks deeply on such matters," Vasse smiled. "Here's Pierre with some decent wine. 'Friar' Georges and I will have two more as well, Pierre. And do not charge Robert and the Englishman for that vomit you gave them before."

The wine rolled rich and fruity on Hunter's tongue. "I thank you, Monsieur Vasse."

"It is the best this hole has to offer," Vasse said. "Now this, Robert, is what wine tastes like. Not like that rancid pond water Pierre has been fobbing off on you."

Robert's eyes smoked with resentment. "I will be sure he does not do it again."

"Now our Huguenots," Landon intoned, "they *should* rot in hell. Brought up in France, subjects of His Most Christian Majesty, they have every chance at redemption. But after listening to a sermon, or reading their French Bible, they suddenly are convinced they know more than all the popes and church fathers have learned for a thousand years. They will burn for their own folly, not their king's."

"Still worrying about eternity when you have a good cup of wine in your hand?" Vasse said. "But if you want to talk religion, how can you praise King Charles? He lets Huguenots hold services, even after his armies defeat them."

As they squabbled, Hunter's thoughts returned to Mary. With each image, the emptiness in his heart grew. It was not only memories of Mary that hurt, incidents that had never occurred wounded him: his anticipated reunion; the words of love he would say, which he had rehearsed over and over; the sweet embraces he imagined so vividly that his body had shivered and swollen with desire—these must all be discarded now. No, it was not only the loss of Mary; it was the death of a dream.

Robert thanked Vasse for his drink and turned towards the door. Hunter intercepted him. "I must thank you, Robert, for inviting me to share a drink—of whatever pedigree." Robert smiled his uneven smile. "Here is another pittance to buy candles for Mary."

"A good lad." Landon said after Robert left. "You have to watch your purse when he is about, but he has done much with little."

Hunter raised an eyebrow in question.

"His mother ran off with a tinker when he was seven," Landon explained. "And of course he had that ugly mark on him. The whores where his mother worked looked after him for a bit, but mostly he survived with a quick tongue and quick fists."

"Perhaps I should be going, too," Hunter said, but he faced a lonely chamber and a long night, filled with memories of Mary and the pain of loss.

"Why not share another cup with us?" Landon said. "Gilbert just got paid for finishing a leather doublet, so he's buying tonight."

"But I am already in your debt," Hunter protested. "Allow me to buy you both a cup."

Landon smiled. Vasse nodded and called, "Pierre, three more cups of burgundy."

"My master knows this treaty is aimed against him," Don Diego de Zuñiga said. "His Majesty is paying a great deal in pensions to those who claim to be his friends. Can they do nothing to stop it?"

The man in the hooded cloak understood the rebuke. He had been receiving money for over a year from Spain. Zuñiga had no doubt read the previous ambassador's records. Although it was their first meeting, as Don Diego had spoken directly to him, he felt he could speak candidly of the tensions between the two countries.

"As I am sure others have pointed out to you, it is hard to overcome almost a century of conflict between the Valois and Habsburg," the man said. "And the naval victory over the Turk at Lepanto"—he saw Ambassador Zuñiga's head snap up and quickly added—"for which every Christian gives thanks—nevertheless increased the considerable power of Spain. Finally, there are many at Court who continually remind King

Charles of the nine thousand Spanish troops in the Low Countries, on his northern border."

Don Diego snorted. "Those troops are needed to suppress the rebels there."

"My point is that it is easy for some advisors to make His Majesty fear the power of Spain."

"Some advisors? You mean Admiral Coligny and his heretic friends."

"The Queen Mother has labored for an alliance with England as much as the Huguenots. She was disappointed in Anjou, and still hopes for a royal marriage, but she will settle for this treaty just now."

"And you think this treaty cannot be prevented."

"Prevented? No. But some events may serve to annul it."

"I pray you, explain more clearly."

"The arrival of Lord Lincoln's party in Paris may present an opportunity," the man said. "Three important representatives of Queen Elizabeth will be in Paris: Lord Lincoln, Ambassador Walsingham, and Sir Thomas Smith."

"Yes, I know. What opportunity do you see in that?"

"Suppose Lord Lincoln, or he and Walsingham, or all three Englishmen, were to die during the ceremonies that will accompany the ratification?"

Zuñiga smiled. "A crisis would result. There would be outrage in London. Montmorency would be detained, perhaps held in the Tower. The treaty would be a dead letter, at the least. It might even provoke a war between France and England."

"That was my thinking," the man said. "I had spoken with your predecessor Don Francisco about disposing of only Walsingham, which he thought would please your king. I even have a man in the embassy who might assist with that, but," he paused a moment, as though recalling an unpleasant incident, "we were overheard by someone and forced to abandon the project for the moment."

Don Diego's eyes registered alarm.

"Do not worry. The eavesdropper was dealt with, and I am still in contact with my man in the embassy."

"A successful attack on all three at one time will not be easy to manage," Don Diego pressed his outstretched fingers together and brought them to his lips. "Suspicion would need to fall on King Charles or the Queen Catherine to provoke the response we desire. What means did you consider using?"

"I have given it some thought: poison, an accident, a direct assault..."

"Poison seems easy, but often proves difficult. If only one man becomes ill and dies, it may be deemed a natural death. And Walsingham was ill all last winter. That would not rupture the alliance."

"I agree that poison has its difficulties. But if the three most important Englishmen in Paris fall ill after a royal banquet, Queen Elizabeth would surely hold King Charles responsible, no matter what he said in denial."

"More likely the Queen Mother would be blamed, given the Italian reputation for poison," Zuñiga said. "But you mention an accident. What type? Three men do not trip down a staircase at once."

"I was considering a coach accident."

Zuñiga frowned. "They may ride in different coaches. All three might not die, and, even if they did, it might indeed be construed as an accident, and no offense taken. Have you ruled out a direct assault?"

"No, but direct assault would be most difficult. The ambassadors will be surrounded by their followers, and hosted by the king. It would take a company of men to dispose of all three."

Zuñiga shook his head. "No. Too complicated. And too many mouths that might talk before the deed...or afterward. And no one of rank would risk displeasing the king."

"Agreed. I am searching for an individual of lowly rank: someone more easily influenced by gold or hope of reward. A single assassin acting swiftly might succeed, but he would immediately be seized and probably killed. It would be a suicidal act."

"And naturally, you expect I will supply the gold."

"Your Master, King Philip, is known for his generosity."

Don Diego smiled. "So he is, by every plotter and expatriate in Europe."

The man decided not to take offense. "May I count on His Majesty to support the enterprise?"

"In principle, yes," Zuñiga said, "but you cannot expect me to provide funds until you have decided on the means and the agents who will carry it out."

"I shall make discreet enquiries during the next week." The man hesitated. "I may need some small amounts to help convince someone to act as an agent."

"You have the sums His Majesty grants you each quarter to cover such expenses as that," Zuñiga said.

The man's shoulders gave an almost imperceptible drop. "Very well. Shall we arrange to meet again, at the same time?"

Zuñiga frowned. "Need you come at such a late hour?"

"If I am seen coming to your embassy, I cannot work effectively for you and His Majesty. I deem it unwise to come before midnight."

"Very well." Don Diego sighed and rose from his chair. "I will let you out myself, rather than wake Juan."

The man also rose, wrapped himself in a black cloak, and drew its hood up over his head.

Saturday, 17 May 1572

Hunter sat up in bed. His head spun. His gorge rose. Pulling the curtains aside, he leaned over the edge of the bed, desperate for the chamber pot. He lunged towards its handle, too late. Vomit spewed onto the floor, his arm, and the bedcovers. His head and belly ached. He grabbed the chamber pot as a second wave of nausea hit. Most of this lot went into the pot, but the damage had been done.

He lay back, his whole body throbbing in complaint. He remembered drinking wine with two men—a leather worker and a stone carver. They sent for some meat pies, then moved on from wine to *aqua vitae*. Crespin had tracked him down, helped him stagger home, and put him to bed. God, how his head ached!

He had to clean up. Apologize to Madame Moreau. Ask for fresh linen. He lowered himself out of bed, trying to avoid his own vomit. There was the jug of water and the basin. He could wash off his right hand and his face. Then another wave of nausea hit, and he turned again to the chamber pot.

"Master Adams." The door creaked, and Laurent entered. "Madame Moreau thought you would be needing help this morning." He carried two buckets.

"I am sorry, Laurent."

"Do not worry. Just sit by your desk, if it please you. I have cleaned up worse than this."

Hunter stood up slowly, cradling the chamber pot in his arms.

Laurent lifted an ash shovel out of one bucket. "You can empty the pot into this, if you wish."

Hunter looked into the malodorous foam of vomit and urine he was embracing, and poured it into the pail. "I'm sorry," he said again, and edged towards the stool.

Laurent scraped vomit from the floorboards with the shovel. He took a wet cloth from the other bucket and wiped off the bedclothes, then scrubbed the floor. "Mistress was worried about you last night. Sent me to get Crespin to look for you after ten o'clock."

He must apologize to Crespin, too.

"Some visitors get drunk when they first come to Paris," Laurent mused. "But you left it a long time." He wrung out the cloth, then scrubbed again. "Surprised us."

He had surprised himself. Another spasm caused him to bow to the chamber pot. This time, only a thin stream of bile burned his throat and dripped from his lips.

"Be back in a minute with a clean bedspread." Laurent swayed away with both buckets.

Hunter sat, wearing only his fouled shirt. His doublet and hose were folded on the chest. Bless Jacques Crespin. Digging a clean shirt out of his chest seemed a monumental task, requiring more energy than he could muster. He closed his eyes. Why did he drink that fourth *aqua vitae*?

Laurent returned with a new bedspread.

"What a sight you are!" came Madame Moreau's voice.

Hunter looked up. A stab of pain reminded him not to move his head quickly. "Madame Moreau, pray forgive me."

"Oh, I forgive you," she said. "Laurent, be careful folding that coverlet. I shall add a fee to your reckoning, to help me forgive." She and Laurent smoothed the new coverlet.

"I am sorry," Hunter said. It sounded insufficient. He closed his eyes.

"Indeed you *are* a sorry-looking piece." She approached with a basin of water and a towel. "Put down that chamber pot and let me clean you up."

Hunter started to object, but the effort was too great. He lowered the pot to the floor.

"Laurent, replace that," Madame Moreau said. Laurent picked up the slimy chamber pot and the balled-up coverlet and left.

"Look at me," Madame Moreau ordered. She wiped his face with the damp towel, then reached into the opening of his shirt and ran slowly over his collarbone and chest. "There. Now wash your hands in that basin." He did as ordered, aware of the contours of her body beneath the brown apron and the crimson kirtle. "You must change into a clean shirt." Was she offering to help him change his shirt?

"But Madame Moreau..." he protested.

"Madame?" she said. "If I can wipe vomit off your face, then you may safely call me Marguerite."

"Marguerite," he began. It sounded odd. "Marguerite, I thank you for your kindness, but..." He did not know how to go on. Surely it would be improper for her to help him off with his shirt, to see him naked. But she could not have meant to do that.

"I will find you some clean linen, if you will permit it." She turned. "You don't look as though you can find your way from your desk to your chest."

"I thank you," he said, still uncertain.

"Laurent can help you change when he comes back." She sorted through clothes in his chest. "Jacques Crespin said he found you at the Horn, in its back room with two artisans. What were you doing there?"

It would take too much effort to describe his confrontation with Robert's gang, his conversation with Landon and Vasse. "Drinking," he said.

She planted her hands on her hips and fixed him with an annoyed stare. "Obviously!" Hunter was aware of her flashing green eyes and full lips.

"Perhaps I can explain later. I feel very tired just now."

Marguerite snorted.

"I am sorry,' he said again, then added, "I made a mistake."

"Perhaps I made a mistake when I promised Monsieur Walsingham to take care of you."

Laurent entered with a clean chamber pot. Marguerite extracted a linen shirt and handed it to him. "Pray help Monsieur Adams change shirts and freshen up." She addressed Hunter, "Could you take a little broth now?"

At the idea of ingesting anything, Hunter's stomach turned. "No." He reached towards the pot Laurent carried.

Hunter spent most of the day in bed, sometimes sleeping, but more often lying awake, his whole body aching. He could pray, but it was not right to ask God for relief. His suffering was just punishment. Twice his stomach convulsed, but there was nothing left to throw up. At times the physical pain overwhelmed him; at other times, the anguish of losing Mary blotted out the pain in his body. How long would it take for his letter to reach her? How would she react? Perhaps her father would find the letter and destroy it. Perhaps Richard would keep it from her. Would Richard continue to tell him of Mary in his letters? Did he want him to? Reports of Mary's happiness, of the children she would bear, of her life apart from him, would only be torture. Would his friendship with Richard, once so important, continue?

He drifted into strange dreams. Sir Gregory and Robert stood over him as he said the *Ave Maria*, judging whether he was sincere or only acting. He stood in his vomit-covered shirt while Marguerite Moreau, voluptuous in a transparent nightshirt, shook her head in disgust. Now Mary stood beside her, and both laughed at him. Landon and Vasse joined them. The bartender Pierre served them all cups of wine and laughed with them.

After noon, Crespin entered, carrying a bowl of broth. "Madame Moreau thought you might be able to hold this down by now."

The odor of the broth did not make him nauseous, so Hunter agreed to try some.

"The laundresses brought your chest of samples back this morning," Crespin said. "Madame Moreau paid them so you would not be disturbed."

"So I am in her debt even more."

"Indeed, you are. If she hadn't sent me in search of you, you might be lying robbed in the alley outside the Horn."

"Thank you for caring for me when I could not care for myself." He sipped the broth.

"We thought it was most uncharacteristic. What happened?"

Hunter did not want to explain choosing drink over the prospect of an evening mourning the loss of Mary. He described his meeting with Robert and his gang of boys, and how that had led him to the Horn.

"I have found them a good source of information. They know everything that is going on in Saint-Gervais parish. But I see you are tired. I will leave you." Crespin took up the bowl.

Sunday, 18 May 1572

Hunter awoke to the sound of church bells. His head was clear, thank God, and he was hungry. He had lost a day to drink. He needed to tell Barnes that Pickering's letter had not reached the embassy. If he hurried, he could walk to Saint-André-des-Arts in time for Mass. He dressed quickly and sprinted towards the front door, hoping to avoid Marguerite's questions. He was almost at the door when she called out behind him.

"Monsieur Adams, I am glad to see you up. How are you feeling?"

"I am well, Madame Moreau. Thank you."

She stepped close. "You are much better dressed that when last I saw you." Her eyes flashed, and a smile played about her lips.

Hunter felt himself flush. "I am grateful to you and Laurent for your kind attention when I was ill."

Madame Moreau's smile broadened. "It was nothing. But you must be hungry. Will you not break your fast?"

"No, thank you. I must meet someone at Saint-André. I will eat when I return."

"Oh," she said, as though she understood his plans to act the good English Catholic. "I will see you afterward, then."

"Yes, father," Hunter said, "besides gluttony, I felt hatred for a young woman whom I loved, who is now betrothed to another, hatred to her brother, who was my friend, even hatred to the man to whom she is betrothed, though I do not know him." He found himself speaking about his own faults, as if this papist on the other side of the screen could actually forgive his sins. The priest asked if his confession was complete. Did he truly repent of his folly, his gluttony, his ire? "Yes." Then he must speak to the young woman and her brother, the priest said, even her betrothed, offering his blessing and asking their forgiveness. Assigned twelve Pater Nosters and twelve Ave Marias, he slipped out of the confessional booth.

Was it the shock of Mary's betrothal, the excess drink his body had expelled, or the lightheadedness from fasting, that led him to confuse himself and his role? He saw Barnes standing near the entrance, and caught his eye. After greeting one another, Hunter said, "The embassy said they had not received Pickering's letter."

"But the boy said he delivered one."

"I know. I intend to ask him who received it."

"Now there is even more reason to ask Sir Gregory about Pickering's letter to him."

Hunter could see the logic of Barnes's intention, but it would allow Wilkes to hide any evidence of his part in Pickering's murder. "You have said nothing to him?"

"No. And I told Sir James we had found nothing."

Barnes would not be content to hold his peace for long. Hunter formulated a possible solution to keep his own role from being exposed. "Would you be willing to go to Saint-Marcel again?"

"Yes. When can we go?"

"Not we." Hunter said, "You."

The priest began, "*In nominee Patris, et Filii...* Hunter recognized the voice; it was the same priest who had taken his confession.

Barnes looked enquiringly at him. Hunter explained. "Sir James saw us both set off the other day. So far as he knows, we found nothing. If you return to Saint-Marcel alone, you can question the boy and innkeeper again, then report all of what we discovered as your own."

"What's the advantage?"

"Sir Gregory trusts you, but not me. He is more likely to be honest with you."

"And you think he would be dishonest if you told what we discovered?"

"Not necessarily dishonest, but more wary."

Barnes nodded in agreement.

"Whether he will be honest or dishonest depends on whether he was involved in Pickering's murder," Hunter said. "I do not expect he will admit that to either of us."

"You still believe he conspired to murder Pickering?"

"I hope I am wrong, but I remind you of what I said before. By revealing what you know about Pickering, you may be putting yourself in danger."

"I do not think so." Barnes looked ahead.

"Just watch Sir Gregory carefully as you tell him the facts..." A woman standing next to Hunter glanced up from her beads and shushed him. "If he looks guilty, you need not tell him all—about the Hooded Gentleman, for example," he concluded in a whisper.

The priest and his servers droned their way through the Mass, and Hunter struggled to concentrate on those portions of the ritual he was able to hear. The Gospel contained the familiar verse warning the disciples to beware of false prophets—wolves in sheep's clothing—and was followed by a sermon making clear that the heretic Huguenots of France were just such false prophets. "We know them by their fruits," the priest declared. "Secret nocturnal services, lascivious excesses, blasphemies, sacrilege, rebellion, and war." He changed metaphors. The heretics were cancers on the body of Christendom that must be cut out and thrown into the fire. Those who sought to be reconciled with heretics might be well intentioned, but they were misled. He quoted from Saint Paul, "Who can touch pitch and not be defiled by it?" When he spoke of King Ahab provoking God's anger by marrying Jezebel and worshipping Baal, it was obvious he was criticizing King Charles and Queen Catherine for arranging Princess Margot's marriage to Henri of Navarre.

As the priest censed the altar, Hunter reflected that forgiving another seventy times seven had become null and void in the Paris of 1572. He had been a fool to imagine that his love for Mary could bridge the chasm that divided their religions. The Spranklins had publicly conformed, but heard Mass in private. Such accommodations had grown more difficult in England after the pope's bull excommunicating Queen Elizabeth. Judging from this sermon, they would be impossible in France. He remembered the terrified face of the naked monk as the sailors' swords pierced his body. Perhaps Sir Lawrence had been wise to ensure Mary was joined with someone of her own faith.

A ringing bell recalled him to the service. The priest was elevating the Host. The Host? He was thinking like a Catholic now. The man is lifting a chunk of unleavened bread in the air. As the priest recited, he remembered a French voice from his childhood in Geneva. The Calvinist preacher asked in a mocking tone, "If bread can be turned to the body of Our Lord, what part is it turned to? His ear lobe? His toenail? His nostril?" Why had that stuck in his memory? The vividness of the images? The fact he had recently learned his French vocabulary for parts of the body, and so understood that part of the sermon? Or did it spring to mind now because the disdain of that preacher for Catholics echoed the disdain of this priest for Protestants?

Hunter shuffled forward as the congregation received the Eucharist. The priest placed a wafer on his tongue. The Body of Christ. Its nourishment would have to be spiritual; there was not enough of it to nourish the physical body. But spiritual nourishment could be obtained at any time. God was omnipresent. The mocking voice of the Genevan preacher was an irritating burr. He was wrong to speak of transubstantiation in such gross physical terms. The men and women around him did not think like that. If Catholics such as they chose to think of this wafer as a spiritual link to God, what harm did that do? If this was superstition or servitude to priests, how did those follies harm the reformed followers of the Gospel? Why did it so infuriate them if their Catholic brothers chose to be deluded? Were they concerned that these brothers might burn in hell for eternity, as Landon had been, or were they motivated by that greatest of deadly sins, pride, to prove that they were right?

The priest intoned the words of the first chapter of John's gospel, and the congregation began to chatter. "Paul," Barnes said, "what are you thinking?"

Hunter surfaced. "Sorry, I was debating religion."

"With yourself?" Barnes asked. "I usually debate religion with my brother."

Hunter smiled. "Then you might win or lose. If I argue with myself, I am always sure to win."

"And to lose at the same time," Barnes said. "But let us go. I will follow your advice and return to Saint-Marcel tomorrow. I will leave you out of it when I tell Sir Gregory what I have discovered about Pickering—no, I will not give him every detail before asking him about the letter. How much I reveal will depend on how he responds."

"I thank you," Hunter said. "When shall we meet again?"

"The Swan bookshop on the rue Saint-Jacques, at ten of the clock on Wednesday."

As soon as Hunter returned to L'Échiquier, Laurent led him to a table and lifted a towel to reveal a plate of bread and cheese. "Madame Moreau prepared this and ordered me to bring you here as soon as you returned."

"Where is she?"

"Gone to Mass at Saint-Jean-en-Grève."

Hunter stared at the plate. Although his stomach was empty, the ache of loss had returned to eclipse his appetite. Mary's face drifted through his head. Her eyes, the deep blue of a cloudless sky; the curve of her nose; the lines of her soft lips—each brought him pain. He broke off a piece of bread and chewed it slowly.

With burst of giggles, Marie and Jeanne entered the dining room, the former with a broom and pan and the latter with a pail and rag.

"Good day, Master Adams," Jeanne said. "Will we disturb you if we get on with our cleaning?"

"No."

Marie swayed to the far end of the room to begin sweeping, but Jeanne wiped the tables near Hunter. "We do not see much of you. You have been out most days."

"I have had many meetings."

"Yes," she said. "Madame Moreau tells us you must meet with important people."

"I have talked with some."

"For us," Marie laid aside her broom and stepped nearer, "you are a man of mystery." She looked at Jeanne and both sniggered.

"Why is that?" he asked.

"Madame Moreau has forbid us to clean your chamber, until she first examines it," Jeanne said.

"I have sensitive papers relating to a trade agreement," he said. "She is ensuring I am not careless with them."

The girls exchanged glances. "I told you she didn't trust us," Marie said.

"I think she just wants to keep Master Adams for herself." Jeanne's brown eyes stared at him boldly. Marie tittered.

Hunter was in no mood for silly chambermaids. "I will not keep you from your work." He rose and headed for his chamber.

"Come in," Hunter called in response to the knock.

Marguerite's eyes widened at finding him in bed. She entered, followed by Crespin. "Are you ill?"

"No, no." He sat up. "I am merely tired."

She placed her hand on his brow. "You do not have a fever." The concern left her face. "But I am not surprised you are weak. You ate little of the meal I left for you."

"I am sorry. It was no fault of the food. I find I have little appetite."

"You should not have pushed yourself to attend Mass this morning."

"Did I not need to ask forgiveness for my sins?" he smiled.

"Ah, your spirit is not sunk so low as I feared," she said.

"Master Adams," Crespin said, "will you be strong enough to keep your appointments tomorrow? You are to meet Messieurs Tibreghein and Brocquart."

Better to busy himself with meetings that forced him to smile and speak of trade, than to lie in misery, pining his loss. "Yes. What time are the meetings?"

"Tibreghein is at ten; Brocquart at three."

Hunter nodded. Crespin and Marguerite exchanged uncertain looks.

"Well, we will leave you to rest, then," she said.

"I will be here at nine o'clock tomorrow, to help you with the samples," Crespin said.

At the door, Madame Moreau turned. "Your dinner will be ready at seven, as usual. Appetite or no, you must eat to build your strength."

When the door closed, Hunter regretted their departure. Why had he not said more? But what was there to talk about? He could not explain Mary's beauty, the promises of love he had given and received, the images that haunted his waking hours, the grief that was tearing him in two. No, he must bear these himself. He closed his eyes.

Monday, 19 May 1572

Business helped the day pass. Hunter repeated by rote the fine points of his samples and the advantages of importing them. A voice in his head kept whispering that this did not really matter. Uncle George's letter had cast the future of the syndicate itself in doubt; his success at promoting English textiles might come to nothing. These discussions did not matter personally, either. No matter what notice or rank his mission brought him, he had lost Mary.

At supper that night, Marguerite led him to a small table and sat down across from him with a stern look. "Jacques Crespin reports you only picked at your pottage at midday."

"If Jacques had chosen a better ordinary, I might have eaten more," he said.

She fixed him with her gaze. "He said you had dined there before."

He hesitated a moment. "They must have altered the seasoning this time."

She rolled her eyes. "And you left most of the sage butter I gave you at breakfast to clear your mind. Today Auguste has prepared something to warm your blood and balance the cold, dry melancholy that is oppressing you." As if on cue, Martin appeared, carrying a bowl and a small loaf of bread. "Stewed capon with carrots and cabbage. Now I will see you eat this, if I must sit here and feed you spoonfuls myself." She tried to look serious, but the sides of her mouth curled.

"It would be rude to Auguste, and to you, if I did not eat this all." Hunter inhaled. "And it smells delicious."

"I have already tasted it, to be sure it was good enough for you."

"You are too kind a hostess."

"Thank you." She folded her arms dramatically. "All right now. Eat up."

"Did you ever consider being a mother superior?"

She gave no answer, but nodded at the bowl. "Go on, then."

Hunter tasted the soup. "Delicious."

"Of course." She held her posture as a demanding taskmaster.

For a few moments, he ate in silence. When he glanced at Marguerite, he detected a tender look of concern. She was really worried about him. "I feel stronger with each bite."

"Good. A second course will follow, also specially prepared by Auguste."

"I am obliged to him for his attentions. Did he prepare any dishes for the other residents of L'Échiquier?"

"After picking out the tenderest, most digestible pieces of the capon for your stew, he had to do something with all the tough, stringy meat," she said.

He feigned shock.

"Have you finished?" She leaned towards him.

Hunter tilted his empty bowl towards her. "Is this satisfactory?"

Marguerite gave a curt nod and took the bowl. "Do not move."

Hunter's appetite and his good humor grew. It felt good to spar again with Marguerite.

She returned with a tray containing a plate of thin-sliced roasted beef, sprinkled with pepper and galangal, and a cup of red wine. She set both before him and resumed her seat.

"Thank you. I am feeling better." After a few bites, he said, "I fear I am keeping you from your duties to your other guests."

She snorted and sat watching him.

He finished a second slice of beef. "You can trust me to finish. I swear."

"Mother superior," she snapped. "Do you think I am someone likely to take vows of poverty, chastity, and obedience?"

"Certainly not obedience," Hunter said. They both laughed.

"Very well, I will leave you for a while, but I will return to see you keep your promise, and to bring you some preserved plum to finish."

Yes, he must enjoy the pleasures of the moment: well-prepared food, rich wine, and the pleasant conversation of a beautiful woman. A letter from Mary saying she was fleeing her family was an idle dream. He must not dwell on the past, but take what solace he could from the present.

CHAPTER 10

New Relationships

HUNTER WAS SEARCHING FOR HIS CHEST OF NOTES. HE NEEDED THEM TO report to Walsingham. He was sure he had left it at one of the bookshops, but he couldn't remember which one. He rummaged desperately in the back rooms of one shop after another. He ran outside, but saw only taverns and churches, whichever way he looked. At a crossroads, he spotted the Hooded Gentleman and his servant, an enormous half ear protruding from his head, pulling Pickering's corpse away from him. He ran forward, calling, "Stop! Stop!" But for all his effort, he came no closer. They disappeared into a door. When he arrived, it was the entrance to the Spranklins' parlor. Confused, he opened the door. Yes, their tapestries were on the walls, and before him stood Mary. She stepped forward and his heart swelled. She still loved him! They would meld together in an embrace. But she shook her head and turned her back. She wore a nightdress and walked towards a large bed. Beside it stood a tall man in a nightshirt, his face out of focus. "No!" Edward cried. The warm glow of Mary's love, palpable a moment ago, had been ripped from him. "No!" He stood paralyzed as Mary wrapped her arms around the man and kissed him. "No!"

"Paul! Paul!" An anxious whisper in his ear. A hand grasped his shoulder. He opened his eyes to see Marguerite Moreau. Was he still dreaming? She stood beside his bed in a nightdress like Mary's, a small lantern in her left hand. Her right hand loosened its grip on his shoulder and she pressed it against his chest. "You were crying out and your heart is racing. Are you ill?"

"It was a nightmare."

She shushed him. "Speak quietly. Your shouts may have awakened others."

"I am sorry."

"You don't need to apologize." Her hand reached out to touch his cheek. "Your dream has gone. It is all right."

Hunter stared into the curtains at the bottom of the bed, where the last images from his dream flickered away. The gap torn in his heart as Mary kissed her fiancé still ached.

Marguerite studied the forlorn expression on his face. "It is that girl." Her tone was bitter. "She has broken your heart."

Hunter focused on Marguerite's face, framed by loose black hair. "I..." He looked down. "Why do you say that?"

"It began with those letters last Thursday." She raised one finger for each day as she explained. "The next day you didn't come back for supper, and Jacques pulled you out of that low tavern. I had never seen you even tipsy before, let along falling-down drunk. And on Saturday, you were sick, but not only with too much wine. Your spirit suffered too. Yesterday you hardly touched your food. You said you were tired, but I saw you were heartbroken. Even at supper tonight, though you finally ate, there was a cloud over your head. And now you have a nightmare." She raised a forefinger to issue a challenge. "Tell me all this was not about her."

"Not entirely," he groaned.

She set the lantern on the table, took both his hands in hers, pulled him towards her, and looked into his eyes. "Paul, you are an attractive and, until now, a healthy young man. There are many women in the world who could love you and whom you could love." A new spark flared in her dark green eyes. "Do not decide to waste away because one girl has bid you farewell."

She was looking at him differently. Moisture gleamed on the edges of her lips, and her hardened nipples pressed against her nightshirt as she leaned towards him. His heart beat faster. "I...It is very painful, that is all."

She cupped his head in her hands and guided it onto his shoulder. "We can make the pain go away." She kissed his forehead.

His heart pounded, and his breath came quick and shallow. Excitement mingled with fear. She had cared for his welfare and enjoyed jesting with him, but could this woman actually desire him? He looked into her eyes with the question. Her eyes answered and she smiled. "Marguerite," he breathed, wrapping his arms around her. Their lips met in a kiss, tentative at first, then hungry.

Hunter broke away for a moment and slipped from the bed to stand beside Marguerite, so that his whole body pressed against hers when they renewed their embrace. Her tongue probed his mouth and his penis swelled. She pressed harder against him. Her hand dropped to his buttocks and began to pull up his linen shirt. He did the same, tugging at her shift, eager to feel her naked flesh against his.

She broke away. "Let me." She pulled her shift over her head and let it fall to the floor. Hunter was paralyzed for a moment as the lantern light played softly over the curves of her body. "Now you," she prompted. He hesitated a moment, then pulled off his shirt. They stood naked before one another. Her eyes fixed on his erect penis, then she looked up and smiled with open lips. "Paul," she whispered. Their bodies met, her nipples hard against his chest, her soft belly pressing against his swollen member. A torrent of excitement flowed through his body; he began to groan. She shushed him and pressed her lips to his mouth. His loins shuttered, and his semen shot out and flowed between their pressed bellies.

She stepped away, a surprised look on her face. Then she smiled as she understood. "Paul, is this your first time?"

He turned his face away. His penis grew limp. "Yes," he admitted.

She placed a hand under his chin and turned his face back to her. "Then I am honored." She glanced down. "Do not worry." She embraced him again, kissing him gently. "We will climb into bed and it will not take long." She bent to retrieve her shift, and for a moment he was afraid she would put it on again, but she wiped her belly, then knelt and wiped the ejaculate from his stomach and pubic hair. He felt himself stir anew at her touch, and knew that she was right. It would not be long.

She led him to the bed. As she raised one leg to climb in, he took in her full but firm buttocks and caught a glimpse of her pudenda. Disbelief at his good fortune mingled with desire. He hoisted himself beside her. "I have admired you since I came to Paris."

"And you have not escaped my attention." She threw her leg over his and placed a hand on his chest.

"But I never thought you would favor me with your love."

"Hush. I cannot stay all night."

"If anyone saw you come in..." He was suddenly aware of the risk she was taking for him. "Your reputation."

"No one saw me come here."

"Can you be sure?"

"I will show you afterward." She looked towards the fireplace. "But now we must be quiet, even when we reach the peak of pleasure."

"I am sorry," he said, thinking of his groan of pleasure and premature ejaculation.

"No more apologies." She stroked his penis. "No more worries." She rubbed her pubic mound against his leg. "No more talk."

He nodded, speechless.

She kissed him deeply and rolled him on top of her. "Let me guide you." And she did.

But he exploded again when he first entered her. This time, he buried his face in the bolster next to her head to muffle his cry. "Stay still a moment," she whispered, "and support yourself." He hovered close above her, her tongue tracing a pattern on his lips, and darting into his mouth, her breasts rising and falling beneath him. Then, as he grew stiff again, she slowly rocked her pelvis, gradually increasing the rhythm until finally she was the one who had to bite her hand to stifle her gasps.

When both were spent, they lay beside one another, basking in the warmth of one another's bodies. "Marguerite," he said, "you have opened a new world to me."

She kissed him. "Like the New World in the west, there are many things we may explore."

She had given him such bliss; how could he ask for more? Yet he wanted more. "But how can we love again without being discovered?"

She sighed. "You remind me I may not stay long, though I would lie beside you all night." She kissed him again and rolled away. "We must dress ourselves."

He embraced her again, not wanting to let her go, but she slipped off the bed and retrieved her shift. He fumbled into his nightshirt. Holding the lantern, she walked to the paneled wall beside the fireplace. She pushed against the fourth panel from the mantelpiece, and it opened. "Look inside," she said, stepping through.

He followed her into a narrow passage, about two and a half feet wide. To his left were the cracked plaster walls of the original room. To his right, a wooden framework filled with wattle and daub formed a new wall, on which the wooden paneling of his current chamber was mounted. In front of him a set of narrow, steep steps, almost a ladder, descended.

"The man who built this inn must have had a large family. He and his wife lived in the rooms below, now my parlor and bedchamber, and used this room for their nursery. That staircase," she flashed a conspiratorial smile, "leads to my bedchamber. It goes down to the cellar, as well. A later owner, before my husband bought it, built walls which cut down the size of the rooms, but he kept the staircases."

Surprise after delightful surprise! Hunter stood dumbfounded.

"I do not know why he kept it. Perhaps for secret amours." She smiled at him again. "There is a latch on the inside so that the panel stays firmly shut, unless this mechanism,"—she pointed to a series of levers beside the door—"is engaged. When it is, someone in your room who knows the proper places to push..." she paused and giggled. "...can enter."

"Margot," he whispered.

She tensed. "I beseech you, do not call me that."

"I am sorry. I thought..."

"I know you meant no harm, but my husband called me that."

"Marguerite," Hunter dropped to his knees and grasped her hand, "I offer you my service. I am not worthy of your love, but I will try to earn..."

"Shhhh," she warned. "We must speak no more tonight." She pulled him to his feet and kissed him. "Good night. If any ask you, tell them of your nightmare and say you talk in your sleep." Another kiss. "Again, goodnight." She pushed him out through the hidden panel door and turned the latch.

Tuesday, 20 May 1572

Hunter slept little, overcome with the thrill of his first sexual consummation. This is what older boys had whispered, laughed, and bragged about. Despite their advice on choosing a whore and how to treat one, he had always held back. Any visit to a Bankside brothel held the possibility of being seen by someone who knew him, and the news reaching his parents. And he had seen sores on the faces of whores. He knew Geoffrey Stringer, of Lincoln's Inn, had gone mad of the pox. Men's purses had been stolen as they lay next to their strumpets. Others had been attacked and robbed by a whore's bawd. Yes, fear was one reason he had never had a woman. Now he was sure that purchased sex, with a disinterested drab in a cramped room, his mind full of doubts and fears, would have been nothing like the encompassing bliss that he had found in Marguerite's arms.

He remembered Marguerite's face as she said, "Do not decide to waste away…" and the joy of their flesh melting together, of being engulfed by her. He had been a fool to wait so long.

He had been waiting for Mary Spranklin. Had he betrayed his vow of love to her? How could he think so? She was to marry another. His promises to her were surely canceled, and he was foolish to feel bound to her. His letter, full of professions of love, was now on its way to Yorkshire. What if she wrote and begged him to come and carry her away? To his surprise, he hoped she would not.

Yes, he had endured the taunts of more experienced students when he admitted his virginity, but now he felt he had advanced to a new level, and not with some whore or a frightened virgin, but with a mature experienced woman. The three usual fears that keep one a virgin, he heard someone say: detection, infection, and conception.

Conception! How had he been so selfish as to overlook her risk! Oh, God, what if Marguerite were to become pregnant as a result of their copulation? He would not leave her to bear the shame and the child alone. He would do the right thing, and marry her. How would his family react to that? She was only an innkeeper, a widow, and an older woman—not the type of partner his mother imagined.

He pictured Mary's body, slim and girlish compared to Marguerite's mature, voluptuous curves. Mary had given him her heart, but not her body; Marguerite had given her body, but what was in her heart? Doubt fluttered through his mind. She had said, "There are many women in the world who could love you and whom you could love." She had said, "You are an attractive man." She had said, "We can make the pain go away." But she had not said she loved him.

He must talk to her earnestly at breakfast. No, they must act as usual in public: conventional greetings and brief conversations. The serious talking must wait until night. But was he assuming too much? He hoped that this night—for it was now near dawn—would be a repeat of last night. But would she come to him again or expect him to come to her? She had not shown him how to open the panel from his room. Perhaps she already thought better of her actions, fearing detection or pregnancy, and would tell him that they could not meet again. How could he stand it if she were to say so? He must speak with her again, swear his love for her, and express his gratitude that she had given herself to him, despite his clumsiness and inexperience.

Sieur Prideaux was upset. "Not with you, mind you. Everyone tells me you are charming, informative, encouraging." Hunter could list several merchants who would disagree, but why contradict? "But convey my disappointment to the ambassador. I hear enthusiasm for the Rouen staple is less in London than in Paris."

"I apologize for my countrymen."

"I understand they yearn to resurrect the Antwerp trade."

"Many have strong ties there."

"They look backwards, not forward. Have they not heard of the fighting in the Low Countries—Brill, Flushing, Walcheren, Veere? How do your merchants imagine they can carry on trade in a land that is tearing itself apart?"

Hunter had no answer. He had little attention to spare as Prideaux chattered on, listing the advantages that he himself had presented to Parisian merchants for the past month. His mind slipped to the evening ahead and Marguerite. When Laurent told him at breakfast that she was feeling ill, his body tightened with fear. Throughout the morning appointment with a draper, he had worried that she was avoiding him and regretting the night before. Crespin had seemed to push his barrow irritatingly slowly on the way back to dinner at L'Échiquier. But, thank God, Marguerite had been there, welcoming him with a broad smile that melted his fears. He was the luckiest man alive.

He had had to restrain his desire to run to her, but instead walked over calmly. When he had whispered, "I need to talk with you," she had raised one saucy eyebrow and asked, "Talk?" Joy flooded his heart.

"I cannot believe that there is a problem with your bed hangings," she had said loud enough for all to hear. "I must see for myself." On the second stair she had turned with her finger on her lips. In his room, she had slipped out of his attempted embrace, with, "You are too hot," and walked to the fireplace. "We are here only so I can show you how to open the panel." After indicating the loose brick beneath the mantelpiece and the molding above the panel that hid the levers to release the hidden door, she had allowed him a brief embrace and a kiss, then pushed him away and said, "Tonight at eleven, come to my bedchamber. Be careful. The step before the last one creaks."

"...uncertain of the attitude of your queen," Prideaux was saying. He looked at Hunter as though he expected a response.

"It is difficult to predict what Her Majesty wishes" Hunter hoped this generality would hide his lack of attention.

"So I hear," Prideaux said. "She blew hot then cold towards the Duke of Anjou, but perhaps Alençon will have more success." He gave a shrug that suggested there was no accounting for taste. Although Catherine de Medici was said to be trying her best to substitute one son for another, the general opinion was that the short stature and smallpox-scarred face of the Duke of Alençon was unlikely to please Elizabeth of England, and that a woman of thirty-eight, although a queen, would be unlikely to appeal to a seventeen-year-old prince. "I know policy should always override personal preferences, but the examples of Henry of England and Mary of Scotland show otherwise." He leaned forward again. "But a royal marriage may have little to do with trade. Does Her Majesty favor a new staple in Rouen or does she, too, yearn for Antwerp?"

She yearns for the restoration of Calais, Hunter thought, but said, "In her way, she is a respecter of tradition."

"Well, we may know more soon. In a few weeks, Montmorency will go to London, and Lord Lincoln will come here. Those who go will talk with your queen's councilors; those who come, I will speak with."

"Lord Lincoln's party will certainly have more recent information than I," Hunter said.

"I have spoken to the viscount. As you have worked so diligently for the success of the treaty, he will ask the king that you be allowed to attend some of the ceremonies and celebrations." Prideaux beamed with the air of a patron who had just presented a generous gift.

Hunter took his cue. "I am greatly indebted to you and Viscount Beaulieu for such an honor."

"As I say, you have worked hard for the treaty." He leaned back in his chair. "Till now you have spoken mainly to the merchants of Paris and the city dignitaries, but you must now reinforce my efforts, and explain to the Officers of the Crown, and of the Household, how the Rouen staple will benefit them."

If he had successfully flattered merchants and city councilors; he imagined he could now spread an even thicker layer of flattery in his dealings with the officers of the king. He thought again of Marguerite and believed for a moment that he could do anything. Before, fulfilling his mission had been mixed with the desperate need to prove himself worthy of Mary. Now he must perform well to meet his own expectations.

In his chamber, Hunter found it difficult to write notes of his meetings that day. Although he had watched for Marguerite throughout supper, he had caught no glimpse of her, and his doubts grew. Finally, the bell at Saint-Gervais chimed eleven. He picked up his candle and walked purposefully to the hearth, wearing only his linen shirt tucked into venetians. He seized the brick on the right side of the fireplace, carefully removed it, reached inside, felt the metal hook, and pulled. The mechanism released the lock with a soft clink. Replacing the brick, he moved to the paneling, grasped the piece of molding she had shown him, and twisted it. With a push, the door opened. His breathing quickened as he climbed down the staircase. He found the panel door in her bedchamber, lifted the lever, raised the crossbar, took a deep breath, and pushed it open.

Marguerite sat across the room at a table covered in pots and small jars, running a brush through her hair. Their eyes met in her mirror, and she turned with a wide smile. He crossed, placed his candle on the table, and embraced her. The warmth and pressure of her body against his, separated by only shirt and shift, excited him. He kissed her hungrily, but after a moment she pushed him away. "You said you wanted to talk," she teased.

Following a script he had been composing in his head all evening, he fell to his knees and said, "Last night you gave yourself to me, but you stopped me from pledging my love and service. I have longed all day to swear to you that I will do anything..."

"I shall stop you again, Paul." She pulled him up. "Pray sit by me and let us talk sense."

"How can I talk sense when I am out of my mind with love for you?" But he did sit, his arms around her.

She held his face in her hands, kissed him lightly on his nose, and gazed into his eyes. "Paul, we are not in a romance. I am not your lady fair, nor are you my knight. We are two modern lovers. We owe one another discretion, consideration, trust..."

"Not love?" he asked.

Her hands slid behind his head and she kissed him deeply. "We shared love last night, and we will again tonight."

"I was afraid this morning that you regretted what we did."

"I regret nothing."

"I do not want my love to harm you."

"We will not be discovered," she said. "No servant knows of the secret staircase. If we speak as softly as this, we will be safe. Laurent and Martin sleep downstairs, near the doors."

"But if you should conceive..." he began.

She raised her hand to his chest. Her face clouded over. After a moment, she said, "I am barren."

"Are you certain?" Oh, why had he said that?

She stared beyond him, her face like a statue of the Madonna Dolorosa. "I did conceive once, but miscarried. After that, I was infertile. I know it was me. My husband fathered a child by another."

He embraced her. "I am sorry," he said, knowing it was inadequate.

After a moment, she pulled away. "Even though you are new to love, I trust you will not brag to others, as young men often do."

"I would never do so."

"So I thought. As you were faithful to your cold northern girl—what was her name?"

He hesitated. Was? Yes, she was in his past now. Surely it was no betrayal to tell her name. "Mary."

"Marie," she repeated. "As you were faithful to her, I judged you would be faithful to me."

"But you said I could not pledge you my love."

"No pledge of eternal love, to be sure, because you will leave in some months." She delivered a blunt truth he did not want to hear.

"But I care for you. I do not want to leave you."

"Did you think we pledged to marry last night? that that one act can bridge differences of station? age? nativity?" Her words stung, but he recognized their truth. "But for the time you are here, we will share our love. I am trusting you with my reputation."

He embraced her again. "And I will honor that trust. I said I do not want my love to harm you."

"It does not bring me harm, but joy." She returned his embrace. "What joy it is for me to be able to love again."

How long had her marriage been loveless? Had she had other lovers in the three years since her husband had died? No, that was an unworthy thought. He would never ask her that. No more questions now. She was giving herself to him again. He was eager to do the same. "Then let us give one another joy." He kissed her.

Wednesday, 21 May 1572

Hunter was leafing through a French translation of Castiglione's *Il Fortepiano* at the Swan. Barnes arrived punctually and greeted him. Although he attempted a relaxed idleness, his body was tense. "Have you heard that Louis of Nassau left Paris last Thursday to aid the rebels in the Low Countries?"

"Some merchants at the Chessboard Inn said King Charles approved his going, and Admiral Coligny will follow with thousands more," Hunter said.

"Are you not concerned that France might soon be at war with Spain?" Barnes asked.

Marguerite Moreau had erased all cares about the affairs of kings and their wars, but Hunter said only, "I hope it will not come to that. At any rate, I can do little about the Lowlanders' conflicts with the Duke of Alva. What did you find out when you visited the Lamb?"

"The boy says he delivered the letter to a big, tall doorman at embassy," Barnes reported.

"Pierre. I must question him. What about a letter to Wilkes?"

"He described Wilkes's servant Robert as the man who received it."

"Have you confronted Sir Gregory? What did he say?"

"He looked grief stricken. When I asked him about the letter, he first refused to speak. I pressed him. I asked him why he had not mentioned it the morning we learned of Pickering's death. All he would say was it was a private matter."

"Do you still think he had nothing to do with Pickering's murder?"

"I'm not sure," Barnes said, "but I did not read guilt in him. He sat there, his face a picture of regret, repeating it was a matter between Pickering and himself."

"I suppose you could call murder a private matter. Did you mention the Hooded Gentleman?"

"No. Nor his servant, nor the letter to the embassy."

"Good."

"And what do you propose now?" Barnes asked.

"I would like to go with you to speak with Sir Gregory," Hunter said.

"But you said he mistrusts you."

"I think I may have a way to alter his opinion if I speak with him first alone. I will leave a message for him at the Antelope."

Saturday, 24 May 1572

Hunter arrived at Sir Gregory's at the appointed time and eyed Robert closely as he was ushered in. He had two complete ears, as Barnes had said, but he was of formidable height and breadth, someone who could easily have overcome Pickering.

Sir Gregory greeted him politely. "You wrote that you needed to speak with me privately about a matter that would give heart to the Catholics of England. That is a very general claim. May I ask for details?"

"I have a mission I have not revealed before," Hunter answered. "You know I agree with you, that our faith is better served by writing that confirms the faith than by armed conflict."

Wilkes nodded. "So you have said."

"One of the London gentlemen who sent me to promote trade with France gave me a commission. He had written a pamphlet encouraging Catholics to remain faithful, but could not find an English printer willing to take the risk. He asked me to find a printer in Paris."

Wilkes raised an eyebrow as if to say Hunter had taken his time doing so.

"I know I have neglected my commission," he said. "But I did not forget it. I spoke recently to the printer at the Cardinal's Hat, Nicolas Colin." Sir Gregory's jaw tightened. "He said he had printed works in English, and—well, I tricked him into mentioning your name."

Wilkes scowled.

"I asked if there were other printers in Paris who had printed in English. He said you would know."

"I believe there may be."

"I would appreciate their names, so that I might approach them as well."

Wilkes appeared to weigh the advisability of revealing their names. "You could ask at the Quill on the rue Saint-Jacques and the Lion in the rue Jehan de Beauvais."

"And would you recommend Nicolas Colin? Is his work good? Does he charge too much?"

"His printing and his fees are good," Wilkes replied, "but I cannot now say much for his discretion."

"But you found him reliable?"

"Within the bounds of all printers. They sometimes finish when they promise, but presses break down, a chance to make quick money by printing a broadside may come up.... He is perhaps more reliable than the others."

"Thank you."

"Do you have the manuscript of this pamphlet?" Wilkes asked.

Hunter pulled the papers from his doublet.

Wilkes skimmed it, pausing to read sections. "Nothing particularly new here, but it may hearten some of the more timid." He handed it back.

"I had thought to take it back myself," Hunter ventured. "I believed I would be traveling between London and Paris frequently, but now it seems I may stay here until next year. I need a way to transport the pamphlets to England."

Sir Gregory's face tightened. "I cannot help you until I consult with others. We must be wary. Cecil and Walsingham have spies everywhere."

"So I understand," Hunter said. "I do not wish to endanger you."

"How many pamphlets will you have printed?"

"Five hundred."

"That is not so many. They may be easily hidden. I will speak with my friends."

"I thank you for your help," Hunter shook his hand.

Tuesday, 27 May 1572

Lucky, lucky, lucky. He was the most fortunate man in the world. Marguerite had given herself to him, and continued to do so, forgiving his inexperience. Wilkes had taken a step towards trusting him, and he had just discovered two more printers who were willing to print pamphlets bound for England. He stood now at the Cardinal's Hat, awaiting Nicolas Colin. If only a letter from his uncle would arrive with a note of credit he could take to the Biondi bank. His eyes rested on a book of hours. He should be thanking God for his blessings, instead of counting himself lucky. But was it right to see carnal relations with Marguerite, and deluding Wilkes and the printers, as gifts from God?

Colin was at his side. "Good day. I was hoping to see you again, master, but I did not ask your name when you came before."

"Adams. Paul Adams."

"It is a pleasure, Monsieur Adams. I remember your face and your English printing job."

"That is why I am here. I have spoken with the gentleman you mentioned, who said the quality of your work is fine, but your price is high." A lie. Another sin to adhere to his soul like the mud of Paris on the hem of a white gown. But as he needed to pay both Marguerite and Lepage at the end of the month, he had to squeeze the most out of every dernier. "I have visited some other printers who have quoted better prices. Can you print my five hundred pamphlets for four livres and five sols?"

The printer frowned. "May I see your manuscript again?"

Hunter handed him the pages. He looked them over, although how that helped him determine whether he would accept a lower price, Hunter could not tell.

"If you pay me half now, I will undertake it," he said.

"That should be satisfactory, but if I might have my pages again, I want to make a few changes." Hunter needed to drag out this printing project, as Beale had advised.

"And when will you finish?" the printer asked.

"I should return to you within a week."

Colin sighed. "Very well. Remember to bring forty-five sols."

Hunter noticed he had rounded in his favor, but he agreed. A few steps took him to the Pentacle, where he found Pierre, the embassy doorman, squinting at a broadsheet hanging on a line. He was in luck again. Without seeking him out, he had found Pierre and could ask about the letter from Pickering. "Pierre," he called.

"Good afternoon, Master Adams." He touched his cap.

"What brings you here?" He had assumed Pierre couldn't read.

"I look at these papers, looking for signs."

"Signs?"

"The End is coming."

Hunter followed his gaze to a woodcut print of a scaly seven-headed beast crawling towards the reader, its teeth and claws bared. "Oh, the End of the World."

"This time was foretold in the Bible. Saint John had a vision."

"Yes. I have read it. It is difficult to interpret."

"It is clear for some."

Who, he wondered, was Pierre listening to? But he did not want to engage in a discussion of Revelation with this doorman. "I must ask you about a letter that was delivered to the embassy a few days after Easter."

Pierre wrinkled his forehead. "That is some time ago."

"It was delivered by a boy, thin, about fourteen, sandy hair, a face scarred by smallpox."

"We have many letters every day," Pierre said.

"But you might remember this boy's face, because of the scars."

Pierre shook his head.

"He might have said it was from Master Pickering."

A slight movement of Pierre's head. "Was that the man who was murdered?"

"Yes. It might have been the last letter he wrote." He looked into Pierre's eyes. "You see why it is important."

Pierre looked away. "No. I can't remember anyone like that."

"I beseech you, if you do remember, tell me." Hunter decided to go directly to the embassy. Pierre evidently had the afternoon off, so he judged the time propitious to inform Walsingham of the disparity between the statements of Nicholas of the Lamb and Pierre.

Jack, Walsingham's English valet, answered the door. "Come in, sir. They are busy talking in the study, but I will tell the ambassador you are here."

Hunter followed him up the stairs. In a moment, Beale peered out the door. "Yes?" Behind him, Walsingham, Smith, and Lepage stood around a table filled with papers.

"May I have a word with you?"

"I have a moment." Beale closed the door behind him. "We have a great deal of work to prepare for the arrival of Lord Lincoln's party. They may number sixty souls."

"I will be brief then," Hunter said. The glimpse of Lepage reminded him of the money he owed. "First I will ask if you have received any letters for me. I expect one from my uncle."

"No. Not yet."

Hunter spared only a moment for his disappointment. "I have discovered two more printers who agreed to produce Catholic works for the English market."

Beale smiled. "Excellent. Include details in your next report. Perhaps we can provide some work for them."

"I wish to ask you about Pierre, your doorman. Are you sure he is trustworthy?"

"He has served here since before I arrived. He came when Sir Henry Norris was ambassador. Why?"

"I continue to look into the death of George Pickering. He sent a letter to the embassy shortly after Easter. The boy at the inn where he was hiding said he delivered it to Pierre, but Pierre says he does not remember such a letter, and you never received it."

"Hmm. Could the boy be lying?"

"To what purpose? I see no motive for him to lie."

"Well, it is over a month ago. Pierre may well not remember."

"Can you ask him about it?"

"I will." He glanced back at the door. "Is that all?"

"I have one more thing. I may use the threat of an embassy investigation into Pickering's death to wring some information from Sir Gregory Wilkes. Will you countenance such action?"

Beale considered a moment. "Yes, but keep your threats general." Another glance at the door. "We are counting on you to entertain Philip Sidney and the younger men in the company."

Hunter nodded. "It will be an honor."

"When we have details arranged, I will send you a message." Beale disappeared through the door

~~~~~

"You may to bed now, Juan." Ambassador Zuñiga addressed his yawning servant.

When Juan had slumped down the hall and disappeared into a room, the man said, "I had hoped you would allow your servants to retire before our meeting time, Your Excellency."

"What, and open the door myself to whomever should knock at midnight?" Don Diego asked. "Besides, your hood prevented him seeing your face. Come in and sit."

The man took off his black cloak and seated himself across from the ambassador, who had provided a glass of wine on a small table.

"The news that Nassau has captured Mons increases the danger that England and France may be persuaded to take advantage of His Majesty's troubles in the Low Countries," Zuñiga began. "Although King Charles issues proclamations forbidding Frenchmen to join with Louis of Nassau, he winks as he does so, and Walsingham applauds such winks. In short, your plan grows in importance. So tell me, monsieur, what progress?"

"I have learned the plans for the visit of Lord Lincoln's party. They are to be housed at the Louvre, which will separate Lincoln from Walsingham and Smith for much of the time. However, there should be many events when they will be together—receptions, banquets, ceremonies."

"And have you selected one as a proper time to act?" Zuñiga asked.

"Several possibilities suggest themselves, but the final plans will not be made until the Court returns," the man said.

"We spoke last time of poison."

"So we did, but when my contacts enquired, they found that it was impossible to predict which server would be assigned to which diner at the formal banquets."

Don Diego nodded and lifted his glass to his lips.

"In addition, I was unable to locate anyone in the royal household skilled in poisons."

Don Diego raised his eyebrows. "I am surprised to hear that."

"Oh," the man said, "I am sure that the Queen Mother has such a person in her entourage, but he does not bear a title such as "Royal Poisoner." He is likely 'Valet of the Secretary of the Queen's Physician' or some such designation. He is well hidden and not likely to be pliable to any offer I might make."

"So, you have no agent yet, and no plan?" The ambassador's voice held an icy edge.

"To remove some possibilities is to move towards a plan," the man said. "I have a man in the royal stables gathering information about the transportation to and from the banquets and ceremonies. He is to report to my servant by next Tuesday. I need to find a moment when Walsingham, Smith, and Lord Lincoln might be traveling together in one of the king's coaches. That would be an ideal occasion for an accident."

"Accidents are not always fatal," Zuñiga objected.

"I know, but I will do my best to ensure this one will be."

"I am also wary of this stableman. You are paying him for the information?"

"Of course," the man said, "but not in person. Through my servant's friend. He only knows that he is giving *La Hache* information in exchange for payment."

"You are *La Hache*, eh? The Axe."

"I think that sounds suitably mysterious and aggressive."

"Let us assume you find a coachman to cooperate. What will he say when they torture him? After the accident, what is to prevent them tracing the payments given the stableman and coachman, through your servant's friend, through your servant, to you, and to me?"

"The easiest method is to remove one of the people in that chain."

Don Diego raised an eyebrow. "You would kill your own servant?"

"If necessary," the man said.

Wednesday, 28 May 1572

Days had passed in an agreeable rhythm for Hunter: meetings by day, Marguerite by night. She was giving him lessons in love. He was still too quick to spill his seed, but she patiently reassured him. "What is the most important part of your body in making love?" she had asked.

He had blushed.

"No, not that," she laughed.

"Lips? Hands? Fingers?" he guessed.

"No, no, no."

When he gave up, she answered, "Your mind. Control your mind and you will control your prick." And that was the lesson they practiced.

Later, they lay together in the dark. "You give me such pleasure," he said.

"You give *me* such pleasure," she said, "that I shall have to go to confession."

Hunter was suddenly tense. Her words stirred a debate he had had with himself. "I hope you do not count our love a sin."

She laughed. "You are so serious. I do but jest. It was a compliment."

"I thank you. But we are not wed. The Church counts love such as ours sin."

She rolled towards him. "You are trained in the law; I will give you two cases. First is the coupling I did with my husband for years—cold and mechanical; he dismally doing what he felt was his duty, while his passion was elsewhere; I, filled with anger and lying still beneath him. Second is the love we just shared. Which, lawyer, is the greater offense to God? Which is sin?"

He took her in his arms and kissed her. "I am not trained in canon law, but I know which case can truly be called love."

Thursday, 29 May 1572

"Gentlemen," Sir Gregory Wilkes waved them to chairs as he sat. "Your note said you wished to discuss something of the utmost importance." His expression showed he doubted that their business could be accurately classified in that way.

Barnes began. "I spoke to you before of the death of George Pickering."

"So you did," Wilkes's tone was irritated and impatient.

"Sir Gregory, you must have seen my disappointment when you deigned not to tell me what Pickering wrote to you."

"As I told you, it was a private matter."

"Sir, it may be a private matter, but it was the last letter written before Pickering was killed. Its contents might contain some clue as to his killer. Do you want a guilty man to go free because you insist on privacy?"

Wilkes's eyes flashed. "This is no way to speak to me in my own house."

Hunter spoke up. "You should know Roger is not alone in investigating Pickering's death. When I was at Ambassador Walsingham's recently,

Secretary Beale told me that they had discovered Pickering hid at an inn in Saint-Marcel before he was killed."

"How did they discover that?" Wilkes asked.

"As you yourself said, they have spies everywhere." Wilkes looked uneasy. Was he remembering Pickering's threats to tell the embassy? Hunter decided to tighten the screw. "I am not sure why they are so interested in Pickering."

Hunter detected fear on Wilkes's face. He leaned forward and adopted a soft tone. "Roger and I are here to warn you. The ambassador now knows what we know: Pickering left his lodgings, took a false name, and hid at an inn in Saint-Marcel. It will not be long before he discovers he wrote you a few days before he was killed. The ambassador may ask you the contents of the letter."

Wilkes snorted as if to say, "Let him."

"He may go to the Châtelet with this new information and ask them to investigate further." Hunter watched closely as he spun out his story. "By keeping the contents of his letter private, you allow others to imagine the worst."

"What?" Wilkes's tone remained defiant.

"They might think Pickering's letter threatened to reveal a secret, and that you arranged his killing to silence him."

"Me?" Wilkes's face showed surprise, not guilt. "To think that I would do such a thing! No matter how indiscreet or untrustworthy he might have been, I would never consider that." He paused. His gaze shifted from his guests to some spot outside the wall of the room, and his expression changed to one of regret. "Yet I bear some responsibility for his death."

Hunter started to speak, but stopped himself. If Wilkes was considering a confession, best not to distract him.

"I might have been able to prevent it," Wilkes said.

After the silence stretched for some moments, Hunter almost whispered, "I beseech you, tell us. If I know the truth, perhaps I can dissuade Walsingham."

Wilkes fixed Hunter with a frightened stare. "He cannot know the whole truth, either." He turned to Barnes. "Nor those at the Antelope."

Hunter knew he expected a promise of secrecy, which he could not give if Wilkes confessed to having a part in Pickering's death. "I will do all I can to prevent anyone falsely accusing you."

"And I," Barnes said.

Wilkes looked from one to the other; his body relaxed slightly. "Roger, you may know that I employed George Pickering in the past. He sometimes bragged of it to others, which was one point of contention between us."

"He frequently boasted that he was engaged in some vital secret business on your behalf," Barnes said, "that he must journey here or there, doing something important that you only entrusted to his hands."

"That sounds like George," Wilkes said. "And I chastised him for it many times. In his attempt to impress others, I feared he might reveal information that would endanger those working for the reclamation of England."

"He always spoke in general terms, and made a great deal of the fact he could not reveal identities," Barnes said.

"Yes," Wilkes said. "Concealing secrets made him feel more important than telling them. That is why I continued to use him." He looked at Hunter. "Pickering served as a courier between Paris and the Low Countries. He carried letters, funds, manuscripts, contracts. But at the end of last year, the situation changed when I found reliable Parisian printers. Working with them was simpler and less expensive. I still kept Pickering on, but he felt less important walking across the city, and of course I paid him less."

"That was when he began to complain about his poverty," Barnes said.

"Yes. Another bone of dissention between us. He kept asking for loans, for letters of recommendation to the French Court. One day he hinted that there were those in England that would pay well for what he knew."

He is drawing close to a confession, Hunter thought. "So he did threaten you."

"It was less a threat than a hint, but we quarreled, and I told him to leave, that I had no need of his services."

"When was that?"

"Just before Easter."

Several weeks after he had begun selling information to the embassy.

"Is that the reason he left Place Maubert?" Barnes asked.

"I had no knowledge that he left, nor why," Wilkes's face clouded over. "When he came, Robert turned him away."

"He came to see you?" Barnes asked. "After Easter?"

"Yes." Wilkes looked truly miserable. "He had written me a letter of apology, but I told Robert not to admit him if he came." Hunter remembered the letter in Pickering's chest, assuring Wilkes he could keep a secret. "If he had awakened me, if I had listened to what Pickering had to say, perhaps he would not have died."

"But the letter," Barnes prompted. "The one he sent you. Was that after he tried to see you?"

"Yes. That was a second chance I had to prevent his murder."

"What did it say?" Barnes asked.

"That he was in great need of my help. He must see me immediately. He was desperate and afraid. Would I meet him at Porte Bordelle at noon the next day? I dismissed it as more of his exaggeration, more of his begging for money." Wilkes gripped his head with both hands. "But this time he was actually in trouble."

This was not the confession Hunter had hoped for. "He didn't say where he was?"

"No." Wilkes continued to hold his head. "I thought, there is Pickering again, being mysterious with his 'meet me at Porte Bordelle.' After his death, I realized he was being cautious. I tried to do all I could for him— paying for his burial, seeing to his effects, writing his family—but it cannot atone for my hard heart when he needed me."

Hunter and Barnes exchanged looks. It was clear Barnes believed Wilkes, and Hunter did as well, despite himself. If Wilkes was indeed innocent, where could he look now? To the labyrinthine jealousies of the French Court? Or should he analyze again the attitude of Beale and Walsingham? Finding Pickering's killer was of less importance that discovering those importing Catholic tracts, Beale had said. Perhaps they did not want him to discover who had murdered Pickering.

CHAPTER 11

Preparations

Friday, 30 May 1572

MARGUERITE MOREAU'S EMERALD GOWN SWAYED GRACEFULLY AS SHE walked past Hunter into the dining room. She leaned over a table to speak with four gentlemen from Lyon. The man with his back to Hunter said something, and they all laughed. Never mind that he had no good reason for jealousy—he was sharing her bed each night; these men were only sharing a jest—he still envied them at that moment. As she had made her way around the room, stopping for a few words at each table, he tried to catch her eye. She flashed him a smile, but turned instead towards the kitchen.

Her hips thrust up against him more urgently. Hunter willed himself to hold on. He pictured the streets between Gray's Inn and Westminster Hall. Other mind experiments had failed. Imagining the rooms in his childhood home had made him go limp. Visualizing the churches of London had not helped him withhold his seed. Perhaps too many steeples. Now, the image of a Fleet Street pie shop competed with the pulsating friction on his penis.

An anguished, animal noise erupted in Marguerite's throat. She buried her face in the bedcovers to muffle her cries. Yes! He had held himself in check until Marguerite had first reached consummation. His self-satisfaction dissolved in an orgasm, and he was the one burying his head in covers.

She wrapped her legs and arms around him. Both lay breathing hard. "You become a better lover each day," she said.

"I have an excellent teacher." He kissed her. "But now I must correct you, my teacher. I do not become a better lover each day, but each night."

"And you also become a more pedantic scholar," she chided.

"Well, during the day, I scarcely see you," he said. "And when I do, you are dallying with other men at the inn."

"Oh?" she said. "Dallying? Am I to ignore my clients and neglect my business because you are so unsure?"

"Unsure?"

"Should I say jealous?" She sat up and thrust out her breasts. "I know I drive you so wild with desire that you cannot endure being far from me."

"In sooth, you do," he reached for her breasts, but she dodged away and laughed.

"Yet you tamed your wild desire tonight," she smiled, "for just long enough."

"Practice makes perfect, they say. Shall we practice again?" He reached for her.

"Tomorrow." She intercepted his hands.

"Then I must endure again the agony of seeing you laugh with others and neglect me."

"Did you feel neglected just now?"

"Not at all, but you speak to me less in the dining room than you used to."

"Perhaps you are right. To keep down suspicion, I will remind you publicly that you are weeks behind in your account."

"But I explained that my uncle..."

She held up her hand. "We are not discussing business now. I do understand. But if I am too friendly with you in public, you might attack me and couple with me on a dining table, scandalizing all, and provoking the Hôtel de Ville to shut me down."

His hands slipped onto her breasts. "I have thought about doing that," he said. "But my developing self-control has kept me from acting." He pulled her down and kissed her.

Father Antoine became aware of a figure standing in the shadows in the Carmone Chapel, a man of medium height, enveloped in a black cloak with a large hood. He could not make out his face. "Can I help you, my son?"

"I believe you can, Father." The man stepped into the feeble light of flickering candles. "May I speak with you in private in the sacristy?"

The priest of Saint-Gervais paused a moment, staring where the man's face was hidden by the shadow of his hood. The quality of the cloak and shoes, the man's bearing, argued he was a gentleman. He turned and led the way to the sacristy. As he closed the door, the stranger passed him and stood with his back to the two candles on the vestments cabinet.

"You can remove your cloak now," the priest said, irked that he still could not see the man clearly.

"It is better I do not."

"Do I know you?" Father Antoine asked.

"Again," the man said from the depths of his hood, "it is better you do not."

"If you are plagued with guilt, my son, I will hear your confession."

"No, father. I have not come to confess, but to help you, and to ask your help."

Father Antoine wrinkled his forehead. "You speak in riddles, my son. What precisely do you want?"

"I understand you meet regularly with those members of the Confraternity of the Holy Name of Jesus who have a particular interest in prophecies."

"That is correct."

"I, too, am a student of prophecies. I believe our troubled times were foretold by the Hebrew prophets, Saint Paul, and Our Savior himself.

Father Antoine's eyes grew brighter. "Then you, too, see evidence that we are living in the End of Days."

"Certainly the Four Horsemen of war, famine, disease, and death have been riding across France for a decade," the man intoned.

"My thoughts exactly," the priest said. "And the false prophets—there are so many that you may say they are a plague of locust. And the ten heretic kings of the Apocalypse; I make those England, Denmark, Sweden, Saxony, Brandenburg..."

The visitor interrupted. "Yes. My friend says you instruct them well, and show them how prophecies are fulfilled in our time." He paused and spoke in a softer, deeper tone. "He says you prepare them for the battle to come."

Father Antoine bowed his head humbly. "I try."

"In the struggle to come, we will need those who are strong in the faith and will fight to preserve the Church. I come to you because I wish to support such men."

Father Antoine's face was a mixture of hope and wariness. "What do you mean?"

"First, I wish to make a donation to the confraternity. Then, by your leave, I would hope to speak with some of the members and encourage their faith."

"You are generous, sir, and I am grateful on behalf of the confraternity for any gift you see fit to bestow, but I am troubled that you hide your face and keep your identity secret."

"I am in a delicate position," the stranger said. "I have a connection at Court who is charged with enforcing the abominable Edict of Saint-Germain. Officially he must uphold the privileges of the Huguenots; but in private he may, through me, work to combat the heretics. Under these circumstances, I must remain anonymous. But if you could accept this..." He drew a bag heavy with coins from the folds of his cloak and handed it to Father Antoine.

The priest felt its weight. "Bless you, sir, and bless your patron. I regret that I cannot personally thank him for such kindness and generosity."

The man paused only a moment to demur, then said, "I should be obliged, Father, if you could show me the names of the members of the confraternity."

"The membership of the Confraternity of the Holy Name of Jesus is no secret." He lifted a book down from a shelf. "In fact, they will all march proudly in the Corpus Christi procession next week."

"And would you be so kind as to point out the names of those who take a special interest in interpreting the prophecies?"

Father Antoine did so.

Saturday, 31 May 1572

"Yes, I agree that Sir Gregory's story makes sense," Hunter said. He walked beside Roger Barnes towards the Antelope. The mystery of the Pickering's disappearance irritated him like a pebble in his shoe.

"And I have found no support for my idea of an angry creditor," Barnes admitted.

"Then we must pin any hope for a solution on my enquiries at the French Court."

"How are you to make enquiries there?" Barnes looked perplexed. "And what about?"

"Did I not tell you?" What a poor spy he was. It was important to keep track of what information he had given to whom. "Sieur de Prideaux has arranged that I attend some of the official treaty ceremonies with Lord Lincoln's party."

"Ah, then I must treat you with more deference," Barnes said, as they reached the Antelope. They joined Kempson, Heath, Fisher, and Chandler. Barnes announced that Hunter was to attend ceremonies along with Lord Lincoln's party.

"So, you are going to Court." Kempson's tone showed he was impressed.

"That was not really my aim," Hunter replied, "but it appears that those I serve believe that if I flatter the king's ministers, it will ensure favorable terms for the Rouen Staple."

"This proves again that *any* man can have an influence on affairs." Chandler looked at Fisher.

"Yes, yes." Fisher raised both hands. "I have already conceded your point. You need not offer another example."

Hunter considered whether he should be offended. Chandler's intonation had suggested that "*any* man" might encompass the most untalented and lowly.

Barnes came to his defense. "Paul has spent much time talking with city officials, merchants, and members of Parlement. It seems just that he should be included."

"If you feel that a treaty between France and England should be celebrated," Heath said. "It bodes no good for the Queen of Scots. Archbishop Beaton lamented its provisions just the other day."

So, Heath was continuing to meet regularly with Queen Mary's ambassador.

"I grant it is not to Queen Mary's advantage," Barnes said, "but do you not feel that it may be of some aid to English Catholics?"

"Wherefore?" Kempson asked.

"If Queen Elizabeth follows the example of King Charles's policy towards Huguenots, she will allow English Catholics at least limited freedom of worship," Barnes said.

"I know you long to return to England, but you should not put your hope in such miracles," Kempson said. "Is Elizabeth likely to follow the lead of Charles IX or of Burghley?"

Barnes's shoulders slumped.

Fisher spoke up. "If the Northern Earls had raised an army that fought Elizabeth's forces as fiercely as the Huguenots fought the king's armies, then English Catholics might be celebrating Mass throughout the North, at least. Lodge was right that you have to fight, not just talk."

"Thomas," Kempson held up a hand, "let us not fight old battles again: 'If Northumberland had done this, if Norfolk had done that, if Westmoreland had moved earlier or later.' We all know the reason the Rising in the North failed was because you had left Durham the spring before, and were not there to advise the earls."

The others laughed, but Fisher aimed a sour glance at Kempson.

"Let us instead focus on the news that Master Adams is to attend the Court." Kempson turned to Hunter. "When is Lord Lincoln due to arrive?"

"The Sunday after Corpus Christi."

"Just over a week." Kempson grasped his chin in his hand and appeared to ponder. "Can you speak Italian?"

"No." Hunter was confused at the question.

"That's a pity. You won't have time to learn it in a week."

Fisher, Heath, and Chandler guffawed.

"Why should I learn Italian?" Hunter asked.

"So you can speak with the rulers of France: de Medici, Gondi, Gonzaga, Ruggieri."

Hunter joined their laughter, recognizing the Queen Mother, the Baron of Retz, the Duke of Nevers, and the queen's famous astrologer. "I have heard they all speak excellent French," he said.

"They might to you," Kempson said, "but when they speak among themselves to decide what the king's policy will be, they speak only Italian."

The laughter turned half-hearted.

"Your analysis is amusing, but out of date," Fisher said.

Now it was Kempson's turn to aim a harsh look at Fisher.

"The last time you were at Court was four months ago. Now Admiral Coligny has the king's ear. Nassau has captured Valenciennes and Mons, and the king winks at the Huguenots who have gone with him."

"Nassau may have some success for a time, but King Charles can never openly support him. The Queen Mother will put a stop to that. She is not so foolish as to start a war with Spain," Kempson argued.

"Suppose the chick is finally ready to leave the nest and fly on his own?" Chandler asked, supporting Fisher.

"He might flail and flap about, but a Spanish falcon would soon swoop down and destroy him."

"He has relied on his brother to do the fighting till now," Heath said, "and Anjou will not aid heretics in the Low Countries, no matter how much glory or land he might win."

"But Anjou's glory already rankles the king," Chandler persisted. "That argues that Charles will send support to Nassau's forces, to win glory for himself."

"What man wants to hear his *younger* brother praised as a warrior?" Barnes asked. Hunter wondered if Barnes's Protestant brother in England was younger or older.

"Therefore, allowing Huguenot 'volunteers' to capture Hainault shows Anjou who is the better man," Chandler concluded.

Kempson turned to Hunter. "Now you see our interest in your invitation to Court. You will be able to see what we only hear by rumor. Who sits closer to the king, Coligny or Anjou? To whom does he speak? Smile at? Laugh with? Those are the signs all watch to predict affairs in the Netherlands."

"You also need to notice who speaks to the Queen Mother," Chandler added.

"But don't spend all your time watching the royals," Fisher put in, "when the ladies-in-waiting to the Queen Mother go to such great lengths to be seen and admired."

"Even Sir James, old as he is, was taken by the court beauties," Heath said.

"I may be old," Kempson said, "but I am not dead."

They all laughed.

"Though they did not approach Sir James, the ladies of the court seduce men to learn secrets for the Queen Mother," Fisher said.

"Trust you to bring our discussion back to lechery," Kempson said.

"If Fisher speaks true, pray provide me some secrets before I go to Court, so I may be seduced," Hunter said.

Amid the laughter, Heath looked at him seriously. "Your faith will remain a secret, will it not? While you are with Lord Lincoln's party, you will have to play the faithful Protestant."

"Indeed I will," Hunter said. "In fact, I explained to Roger that I have stayed away from Mass on good advice, to avoid upsetting my masters. A recent syndicate letter," he improvised, "warned me I should be careful of speaking with 'those treacherous Englishmen who have abandoned their homeland for religion's sake and hatch plots in Paris.'" His melodramatic tone produced smiles. "Nevertheless, they may have received some reports of my visits with you, so I must take care."

"Has your coming here put you in danger?" Heath's face was serious.

"Stopping by a tavern for a drink cannot be judged too suspect, I hope," Hunter said, "though I cannot come often. What grieves me more is that I dare not attend Mass openly." He turned to Kempson. "Sir James, are there those at Court to whom I might offer your respects?"

Kempson was caught between the desire to brag about his connections and the fear that a lowly lawyer working for merchants might approach them. He mentioned the *maître de la chapelle* and the *Grand Panetier*, but said their duties and rank make it unlikely that Hunter would meet them.

Thursday, 5 June 1572, Corpus Christi

Hunter started down the staircase in the morning, then backed upwards. Martin and Laurent were climbing towards him, with what appeared a rolled-up carpet on their shoulders. "What is that?"

"It's the tapestry for Corpus Christi," Martin replied. The boys headed to Marguerite Moreau's chamber.

"Set it down by the windows," she said.

Hunter looked in. "You hang a tapestry for Corpus Christi? You are not even on the procession route."

"And good morning to you, Master Adams. Yes, I hang a tapestry. Captain Izard looks for any tiny reason to harass me. He has complained that I rent a room to a heretic Englishman. I do not want a crowd throwing mud or worse at L'Échiquier because I do not honor the Eucharist on Corpus Christi."

"I had not realized you were under pressure from Captain Izard," Hunter said.

"He is the darling of the most zealous Catholics. I am a woman who rejected his advances. He revenges himself as he can." She turned to the boys, maneuvering one end of the tapestry towards a window. "Be careful not to snag it on that hook." She turned back to Hunter. "By the way, you owe me three weeks' rent."

Was this the same woman he had shared a bed with last night? This morning she had transformed into a no-nonsense businesswoman. "I can but repeat that I expect a letter from the syndicate any day."

"Yes," she said. "You have sung that song before. But I do not have time to argue now. I must superintend these clumsy lads before they knock over that vase. Take care!"

Guillaume carried his long candle with pride, carefully balancing it to keep it from swaying and walking slowly so that it would stay lit. Although the Confraternity of the Holy Name of Jesus was not as ancient as those of the wine merchants and the tanners, it had been granted a more prestigious place in the procession, just behind the clergy of Saint-Gervais. From his position, he could see the red velvet canopy that the churchwardens held over Father Antoine and the Holy Eucharist. Whenever Father Antoine raised the jeweled monstrance for the crowd to see, he caught a glimpse of the Host, the Body of the Lord Jesus, the focus of all devotion this day, miraculously present in all the sacred vessels carried in all the processions that wound their ways towards Notre-Dame de Paris.

His candle flickered when a wanton draft of air hit it, and he held his breath as though doing so would calm the air and ensure the flame did not go out. It continued to burn, and he breathed again. He chided himself for being afraid. It was foolish, his notion that the success of his mission depended on carrying the candle all the way to the cathedral without letting it go out. It was in God's hands, not his. God knew of the vow he had taken before the Hooded Man, of the trust that had been placed in him, a lowly groom of the coach, to speed the coming of His Son in glory. He looked to his left where Charles marched beside him. "Will you pray for me when I am in need, Charles?"

Charles wrinkled his brow. "Of course. We pray for one another all the time, Guillaume. We are brothers, and we are always in need of God's mercy."

Behind him, another confraternity member shushed them.

Guillaume felt a moment of shame. Asking Charles for reassurance had shown his weaknesses: selfish fear and self-doubt when he should be concentrating on Christ's Body, broken for his salvation and honored today throughout Christendom. No, he corrected himself, not by the heretics who called themselves Reformed. He burned with anger towards those, some even here in Paris, who would deny the Real Presence, who would so insult their God and the Savior of Mankind. But the time of vengeance was coming, and he was to be a humble instrument of God. That's what the Hooded Man had said. He had explained how the death of Guillaume's wife and children in the last visitation of the plague had been part of God's plan to free him, in order that he could serve Him completely with his whole being. He must not be afraid of his approaching trial. He must focus today on the Eucharist. Then he must pray and fast for the next week to prepare himself.

As the procession passed, men and women on either side knelt and crossed themselves. Guillaume swelled with joy to see the people of Paris united in their faith. For a moment he could imagine the glorious future, how all the peoples and creatures of earth would sing the praises of the Lamb when He appeared. He prayed for strength to play his humble part to bring His coming nearer.

"I have changed my opinion on methods," the Hooded Man said.

"You no longer favor an accident?" Zuñiga asked.

"As you said, all may survive an accident. The first time we met I said that a direct assault would be suicidal."

"You did. Very few would be eager to undertake such an act."

"Yes, very few," the Hooded Man repeated. He smiled. "But if you found a man in the royal household, who believes the end of the world is close at hand, who knows it will involve a holy war between the Catholic Church and heretics, and who is certain that any man who starts such a war will bring the Kingdom of God to the world and become a martyr for Christ,"—he ticked off the clauses on his fingers—"such a man might be the man we seek."

"And I judge by your expression that you have found him," Zuñiga said.

"*La Hache* has."

"Does he have the skill to successfully assault three men?" the ambassador asked.

"He was a soldier in the last civil war. And if the three men are cramped inside a coach, unable to mount a defense, it might not take superior skill."

"And where will this apocalyptic assassin be?" Zuñiga said doubtfully. "Surely the English will not invite him to share their coach."

"The man works in the royal stables. We have a plan to enlist him as a guard of the English ambassadors."

"And he could kill all three?"

"There is no surety of that, but even one or two deaths might have the required effect. The King's Court is gathering now. The final plans will be made within a few days. But I have no doubt there will be at least one opportunity when all three will travel by coach."

"Have you spoken to the man?"

"*La Hache* has. He does not know me, nor did he see my face."

"You owe a lot to the deep hood of your cloak."

"And a mask. The attacker is only one part of the plan. I told you *La Hache* has other contacts in the royal household. I think I can promise that, whether this man successfully dispatches one or all three, he will not survive the attempt."

Zuñiga looked into space, silently.

The man sensed his hesitation. "Do you wish that I cancel the plan?"

"You have been fortunate to find an agent so well placed. Such a favorable opportunity may not arise again soon." He bit his lip. "You are sure your man will not be able to identify you, if by chance he survives after his assault?"

"I am certain."

"Then let your plan go forward."

Hunter lay in Marguerite's arms. "I have a question for you. When I first came, you led me to the chamber above you that connects to your bed-chamber by the secret staircase."

"Yes. What is your question?"

"Did you place me in my chamber by chance," he teased, "or because you were impressed with my beauty and overcome with lust."

Marguerite snorted. "You flatter yourself, Paul. I said upon your arrival that Walsingham had charged me to take good care of you."

"And you have certainly done that." He caressed her leg.

She removed his hand from her thigh. "So it was your ambassador, not me, who determined your lodging."

"Does he know of your hidden stairs?"

"Only you and I know of that staircase," she said, "but the Ambassador warned that you might need a place to hide or a way out in a time of danger."

The existence of the secret staircase ate away at him. "You have placed other lodgers in my room in the past..." he began.

She held a finger to his lips. "Do not ask."

"What..."

"I know what you are thinking," she said. "All men want to know their lover's history. They all want assurance they are special, the only one, the best."

He could not deny it.

"You have my body. And though I have tried to stop myself, you have my heart now as well. But you cannot have my soul, Paul."

Had she had other lovers? She had said things to make him believe she had not had another man since her husband, but he could not be sure.

"You want to know everything about me, but I do not even know your real name."

"I am sorry," he said. Why, other than pride, should it matter to him if he had not been her only lover? "You are right that I want too much. I should be grateful for the love you give me now. I know that should be enough."

"It must be enough," she said. "We know this is only for a time. We know you will leave and return to England."

Every time she reminded him, a heaviness filled him. "All right. No questions about the past. No thoughts of the future. Kiss me now."

Sunday, 8 June 1572

Hunter felt honored clattering towards the Louvre in the ambassador's coach, the only non-embassy member of the party. He sat next to Robert Beale, opposite Francis Walsingham and Sir Thomas Smith, wearing the gray suit tailored for him after his arrival in Paris.

Throughout the drive, Walsingham had addressed himself to Smith, mostly bemoaning the expenses connected with the visit of Lord Lincoln's party. "My new suit cost twelve livres. And to host the Admiral's delegation tomorrow for dinner, I had to engage eight additional men, four in the kitchen and four serving. The food alone will cost as much as three weeks' supply for the embassy. I am sending another letter to Her Majesty explaining that the allowance for the Paris Embassy is far too little, and asking that she appoint someone else. Even if I could return home now, I should be over six hundred pounds in debt."

Lord Lincoln and his entourage had arrived in Paris that afternoon, where suites of rooms in the Louvre had been prepared to accommodate them. The King and his Court, who had gathered in the capital only a few days before, after a month entertaining and hunting at their châteaux, were ensconced at the Château de Madrid in the Bois de Boulogne, some miles to the west.

At the gateway to the courtyard, Swiss guards halted the carriage with crossed halberds, then, after inspecting the note Beale handed them, allowed the party to proceed. One servant sprinted into the entrance of the old northern wing of the palace as soon as the carriage appeared, while others rushed forward to open the doors and hold the reins of the horses. As the passengers clambered from the carriage, a stream of English servants from Lincoln's delegation ran to meet them.

They followed the servants towards the central entrance of the west wing, built some twenty years before in the Italian style. To the south, a second wing in the same style was under construction. To their right and behind them stood the towers and turrets of the old palace, built during the wars with England and Burgundy two centuries before, and now ironically housing the visiting Englishmen. Goujon's massive figures sat heavily on either side of the west wing's top window. To Hunter they appeared to be brooding, appropriately, for a country divided by religion, a ruling family divided by jealousy, and a Court rife with faction.

Walsingham's party entered a large hall. At the north end, four tall statues of armless women in Greek chitons supported a gallery. Servants stood awkwardly shifting their weight from foot to foot, glancing over their shoulders at the door behind the caryatids.

The door opened. The servants stepped aside as Lord Lincoln, the Lord High Admiral of England, led a group of perhaps twenty gentlemen into the room. His mouth was mostly hidden by a graying beard and a large, bushy moustache. He had a long, hooked nose. Above his dark eyes, his eyebrows rose diagonally, giving him the look of someone who was slightly surprised. He strode forward and greeted Smith and Walsingham.

Lincoln introduced his party: Lord Dacre, his cousin; Lord Talbot, Shrewsbury's heir; Lord Sandys; Sir Arthur Champernowne. Sir Henry Borough... Hunter strove to remember names and faces, but he had already spotted a tall, beardless man in a beige suit with a long face, thin, pale lips, and eyebrows arching over intelligent eyes. This was Philip Sidney, although now a gentleman without a title and so, according to the rules of precedence, to be introduced after the noblemen and knights, he was the nephew of Robert Dudley, the Earl of Leicester, Ambrose Dudley, the Earl of Warwick, Thomas Radcliffe, the Earl of Sussex, and Henry Hastings, the Earl of Huntingdon. Hunter considered mentioning that he had served Sussex as a spy and a messenger to Huntingdon during the Northern Rebellion, but at once realized that then he had been Edward Hunter (or John Edwards when in the rebel camp), but now he was Paul Adams. He bit his lip. Entertaining Sidney was a great opportunity, but also a frightening responsibility

Now it was Walsingham's turn to introduce his smaller party. "Of course, you all know Sir Thomas Smith, his scholarly achievements and the long service he has rendered to Her Majesty." The heads nodded. "What little I might have achieved as Ambassador to France I owe to Sir Thomas, or to my secretary, Master Robert Beale." Beale bowed as the men in Lord Lincoln's group murmured their recognition. "This is my clerk, Henry Roberts, without whom the embassy would not function." Roberts walked forward, eyes on the ground, and bowed. "The last member of our party is not a member of the embassy, but for two months has represented the Rouen Syndicate and worked daily for the benefit of our English merchants, Master Paul Adams."

Hunter felt the eyes of all on him as he bowed. "Master Adams has agreed to help Master Sidney and the younger members of your party enjoy Paris." Laughter revealed that some members of the delegation had definite ideas of what young men might wish to do in Paris. "Gentlemen," Walsingham said, "I have promised young Sidney's uncle that I will look out for his welfare here. Be sure I shall." He looked sharply at Hunter.

Did Walsingham think he would lead him directly to the brothels of Paris?

"I apologize that our meeting today will be brief and filled with business," Walsingham said, "but I invite you all to the embassy tomorrow for dinner, where there will be more time for discussion and good cheer." Murmurs of approval. "But we are now eager to hear news from England and to receive any messages you bear for us."

Lord Lincoln cleared his throat. "We bring greetings from Her Majesty and Her Privy Council. I can tell you more of their counsel when we adjourn to my rooms, where I have letters for you. We also bear the chest with fine fabrics that Master Adams requested. Alas, I also bear regrettable news. The Duke of Norfolk was executed six days ago on Tower Hill. Word arrived just as we set sail from Dover."

The noblemen and ambassadors shifted uncomfortably. These men had talked, dined, and worked with Thomas Howard, Duke of Norfolk. Privately, they had to regret the death of a colleague, but publicly they could not show grief over the death of a peer found guilty of treason. In fact, some of them might have judged his case and rendered the verdict.

The formal greetings over, the men broke into smaller groups. Philip Sidney made his way towards Hunter, smiling. "I understand you have the misfortune of looking after me in Paris, Master Adams."

"It is an honor, rather than a misfortune, sir."

"I hope you will think so at the end of a week," Sidney said. "But let me introduce you." He motioned to a man of equal height who had followed him forward. "This is Lodowick Bryskett, who has given good service to my father, and is now my traveling companion for the next two years, as I tour the chief cities of Europe."

Bryskett was a few years older. His eyes were friendly, he wore a closely trimmed beard, and curly black hair extruded from his cap.

"So you are not here only as a member of the Earl of Lincoln's delegation?" Hunter asked.

"No. It is rather a case of my following along with His Lordship, as I planned to start my travels in Paris this month."

"How long do you intend to stay in Paris?"

"Two months at the least," Sidney said. "I hope to meet some scholars and gentlemen of note here. We plan to stay long enough to witness the royal wedding and improve my spoken French."

Picking up his cue, Bryskett said, "If you will accompany us to our chamber, we have some letters for you."

Hunter followed them through the door behind the caryatids, up a broad staircase, and down a corridor into the older part of the Louvre. As they entered the chamber, two servants turned to greet them. A third glanced up, but continued to brush a traveling cloak vigorously.

Sidney made brief introductions. "Master Adams, Henry White, my valet, Griffin Madox, my secretary, and John Fisher, who looks after all of us and our horses."

Bryskett pulled a packet from a chest and handed it to Hunter. At a glance, he could see two letters from his uncle, several from his mother, one from his sister Jane, and one in Richard Spranklin's hand. His heart quickened. Had Mary written? No. The letter was thin. He was surprised at his own relief. Marguerite Moreau had made it easy to forget Mary Spranklin and regard his thoughts of carrying her away as extreme folly. He hoped one of his uncle's letters contained the bank draft that would allow him to pay his debts.

Bryskett nodded, as though he could read his thoughts. "I have a cousin who works at the Biondi bank." He pulled a sealed envelope from his doublet. "He asked me to hand this directly to you."

"I am grateful to you, your cousin, and Master Sidney" Hunter said. "I am in your debt."

"And we shall make you pay it," Sidney said. "I have a list of sights I wish to see, and another of books I intend to buy here or in Venice."

"You said you will travel for two years," Hunter said. "Where will you visit?"

"Heidelberg, Frankfurt, Vienna—Italy, of course: Venice, Padua, Rome."

Bryskett clicked his tongue.

"Or perhaps not," Sidney said. "Some members of my family deem it too risky to travel to the Papal States, despite the works of art I might see in Rome."

"They simply believe the threat of the Inquisition outweighs the beauty of any objects or architecture you might see," Bryskett said.

"The Bible says we should not covet the possessions of others," Hunter said. "I hope the commandment does not extend to coveting the experiences of others."

"I am no theologian," Sidney said, "and I do not blame anyone envying me my travels, but others might equally envy you your time in Paris."

"That may be true."

"And you are here alone, while, as you see," he gestured to Bryskett and his servants, "my family feels I need a great deal of support."

"Which you said only yesterday you would welcome when we arrived in Italy," Bryskett said.

"I said that I would rely on you and your Italian, and be greatly in your debt," Sidney said, "but I know my mother and Uncle Robert have given you instructions to watch over me." He turned to Hunter. "They believe I am but a green spring bud, so delicate it must be protected from any frost."

"I am sure your family only wants to keep you safe from harm. It is the constraining jerkin of filial love which chafes all young men," Hunter said.

Sidney smiled. "You match me metaphor for metaphor. I think we will enjoy one another's company. But you have me at a disadvantage. It seems everyone I meet knows a great deal about me, but I do not know much about you."

Yes. It was hard not to know about someone who was the heir of two earls and counted two more as uncles by marriage. Yet Sidney had not mentioned his noble relatives, or flourished their titles to impress. Robert Dudley was not the Earl of Leicester, but Uncle Robert. Perhaps they would enjoy one another's company.

"My family are modest landowners in Hertfordshire," Hunter began, carefully separating the shared truth of Paul Adams's life from Edward Hunter's. "I attended St. John's College, Cambridge, and studied at Gray's Inn. I am in Paris representing a syndicate of London merchants..."

He broke off at a knock at the door. A servant poked his head in. "Pardon me, sirs, but the ambassadors are ready to leave now, and I was told to fetch Master Adams."

"Well," Sidney said, "we will be at the embassy tomorrow, and you can continue."

"It will not take long," Hunter said. "I pray you bring more interesting topics."

"I shall try," Sidney said, with what could almost be described as a shy smile.

Monday evening, 9 June 1572

The political situation had changed. The embassy had received the news of the death of Jeanne D'Albret, Queen of Navarre. Members of Lord Lincoln's delegation all agreed that her death was a blow to the

Protestant cause. Although she had arranged the marriage of her son Henri to Marguerite de Valois, Henri was only eighteen, boorish, and naïve. He could not provide the leadership and wisdom of his mother. There would be one less voice urging action in the Netherlands.

Parisian reactions reflected the religious divisions of the city. Huguenots mourned and spoke of the gloves Catherine de Medici had sent Queen Jeanne a few days before. Given the wiles of the Italians, those gloves had no doubt been poisoned. Catholics rejoiced and speculated. Perhaps after Henri married Marguerite, he would come to his senses and reject the Protestant heresies forced on him by his mother.

Hunter's personal outlook had changed as well. The bank draft Bryskett delivered allowed him to pay his debts. Richard Spranklin's letter had lifted a burden. Mary had married on the fifth of June. What a relief that she had not appealed to him to rescue her from a forced marriage. Marguerite's loving attention had cured him of any heartbreak over Mary. He no longer connected success in Paris with his chances to court Mary. Now his ambition to prove a competent agent was personal. He sought to rise for his own sake.

After mingling with men of quality in the great chamber of the embassy, Hunter felt as though he, too, were an accepted member of this governing group. Lord Lincoln and his cousin Baron Dacre were backers of the Rouen Syndicate, and had heard good reports of his efforts in Paris. Lincoln invited him to accompany the delegation the following Sunday to witness King Charles swear to uphold the treaty. A new black suit in the French style would be justified—no, necessary. He hoped the tailor could include silver braid trim and finish it in a week. Five banquets would follow the ratification. Details would be worked out tomorrow, but Philip was certain Hunter would be included.

Philip. Yes, Sidney had said, near the end of the embassy reception, "If we are to spend weeks together in Paris, you cannot continue to call me 'sir' and 'Master Sidney.'" They had spoken at length of their mutual appreciation of Ovid. Philip had spoken of his own interest in astronomy, including the new ideas of the Polish astronomer Nicolai Copernici. He planned to explore the bookshops of the rue Saint-Jacques, and Hunter related his own discoveries there. He longed to see the Italian style of the new hôtels of the nobility. Hunter promised that Crespin could supply details of each builder and date of construction. His uncles had advised him to keep a journal noting the manners and conversation of men as he traveled, so he was eager to observe the customs of the French court. They agreed to compare notes after each reception.

Philip Sidney had made him feel an equal, but he knew this was an illusion. Although he had smiled and jested with lords and knights, he knew his social position, and they knew it, too. Sir Henry Borough, although only a knight, acted haughtier than any earl. Hunter overheard him say, "A lawyer may do an excellent job, but he is still a lawyer." Worse, Sidney had invited Borough to join them touring Paris. Hunter would have to endure his snubs for the rest of the week.

Guillaume could not take his eyes off the man's left ear. It looked as if it had been cut cleanly with a sword blow. He would wager that beneath his cap the man had a straight scar across his temple.

"The *premier écuyer* will receive an anonymous message within the hour, warning him that the English ambassadors are in danger Friday," the half-eared man said.

Guillaume froze. "Has someone found out the plan?"

"No," the man said. "This is part of the plan. You must find the *écuyer* after you leave me and stay near him. When he receives the note, it is your chance. Ask what troubles him. Volunteer to ride on the steps of the coach, clinging to the door, as a close guard on the ambassadors."

A smile spread on Guillaume's face. "I can say I consider it a holy mission to be near them."

"Yes." The man placed a teston in Guillaume's hand. "This is from my master, *La Hache*." Guillaume knew he meant the Hooded Man who had spoken to him at Saint-Gervais.

Thursday, 12 June 1572

Crespin began the third day of his Paris tour at the Place de Grève. Borough and Bowes again asked for details of executions, and throughout the day Crespin provided gory stories of the struggles between Armagnacs and Burgundians. Hunter had suffered through two days of Sir Henry Borough: his praise of the hôtels of the highest nobility, no matter what the style; his disparaging remarks about lawyers at the Cemetery of the Innocents; his impatience as Sidney lingered in the bookshops on the rue Saint-Jacques. At least, as they took their dinner at L'Échiquier, he saw in Madame Moreau's eye that she shared his disdain for Borough.

Late in the afternoon, the party finished their tour near the abandoned Palace of Tournelles. There, Crespin pointed out the new hôtels of judges and officials. Each elicited a caustic remark from Borough.

"Presidents of Parlement. Counselors of Parlement. Do none of these houses belong to noblemen?" he asked.

"I believe some of them have purchased titles since they built their hôtels," Crespin said.

"The French," Borough sniffed, "have contrary brains. They cling to superstition when offered reformed religion, yet they abandon respect for breeding, sell honor, and allow anyone to set himself up as nobility."

An uncomfortable silence floated over the group.

"Now, if you gentlemen are not too tired, we will walk to see the Bastille, then return across Paris to the Louvre," Crespin said.

All agreed, and Crespin turned west. "We had best go this way."

"Dear Guide, you are the one who is supposed to know Paris best. Surely the shortest way to the Bastille would be by this road." Borough pointed east. "Does it not go through to the rue Saint-Antoine?"

"Yes, but I would advise you not to take that route."

"As the bourgeois builders of mansions do, you presume too much." Borough looked down his nose. "A gentleman does not need the advice of a street guide."

"Perhaps, sir..." Crespin began.

"I will see the Bastille and pass you as you make your roundabout way there," Borough announced. "And I can make my own way back to the Louvre. I have paid careful attention and have a good sense of direction."

Borough spun on his heel and headed off on his chosen road. Crespin opened his mouth to speak, but Hunter placed a hand on his arm. "Does that road lead past the Virgin's statue?" Crespin nodded. "Who are you to question the wisdom of an English knight?" Hunter said aloud.

Crespin turned to the group. "I promise you my way will not inconvenience you."

"Pray excuse Sir Henry," Sidney said. "He sometimes takes a notion into his head and will not be gainsaid. You have led us well for three days. I see no reason to leave you now."

A few moments later they emerged onto the rue Saint-Antoine and turned east towards the Bastille. "Built during the war with the English and Burgundians in the last century," Crespin began, "it has eight towers..."

Ahead of them shouts erupted. Crespin smiled at Hunter. Around the corner at a run came Sir Henry Borough, holding his hat with one hand as he sprinted towards them. Behind him ran a crowd of boys, hurling insults and stones. When Borough dodged into a crowd, they stopped throwing stones, but continued to shout "Infidel! Heretic! EEEEnglisssh!" The crowd added their curses and laughter.

Sir Henry stood before his countrymen out of breath. "What happened?" Sidney asked,

"Those street urchins tried to extort money from me for their idol," Borough said.

Hunter and Crespin stood with lips bit shut.

Sidney looked him over. "Come, Sir Henry, you have not suffered any harm."

"They insulted me," Borough spat. "They should be taught a lesson."

"What honor would we gain battling with children?" Bowes asked, peering at the hooting boys.

Borough looked daggers at Crespin. "The ambassador shall hear of this."

"Sir Henry, it is you who demanded to take that lane when our guide warned you against it," Sidney said.

Borough looked from one to another of his companions, then pulled himself erect. "You are right, Sir Jerome. There can be no honor fighting boys." He turned to Crespin. "Nor inferiors." He stared defiantly. "Well, Master Street Guide, I intend to return to the Louvre on my own. Are there any dangers you feel you should warn me of?"

"Only the usual: pickpockets, runaway horses, dung on the road," Crespin said.

"Thank you so much," Borough said. "I could not have foreseen such dangers myself."

"I shall walk with you," Sir Jerome said. "Gentlemen, will you excuse us?"

Borough and Bowes made their way west, and the rest turned back towards the Bastille. A remnant of the boys stood on the corner.

"If we turn here," Crespin said, "we can see the hôtel of the Prévôt and the church of Saint Paul. And while we do so, the boys will lose interest and return to their statue."

Friday, 13 June 1572

Guillaume opened the door of the royal coach so the English ambassadors could climb in. As he bowed, he breathed a quiet prayer for strength. Lord Lincoln mounted first and sat with his back to the driver. Sir Thomas Smith, the oldest of the group, strained a bit reaching the coach steps, and turned to make some jest to Walsingham. Guillaume could not understand their English japery, but he was relieved to see they were relaxed, although they had been told of some vague threat against them. For that reason, Walsingham and Smith were leaving the embassy carriage here at the Louvre and riding in the royal coach to the Château de Madrid to meet the king. An escort of eight mounted cavalrymen would accompany them, to ensure their safety, as well as a guard standing on the carriage steps, armed with a sword and pistol. Guillaume smiled to himself, a devoted man who had volunteered immediately to serve as that guard when his master first mentioned the danger.

Other English gentlemen were climbing into their carriages to follow the ambassador. Guillaume prepared to close the door when he heard, "*Arrêtez!*" An English nobleman hurried towards him, cape billowing. A servant's call halted him. The nobleman leaned over, and the servant positioned his hat carefully on his red hair. With a nod, the lord turned and walked with self-conscious dignity towards the coach. Guillaume was dismayed. He had counted on only three riding in the coach. One of the passengers called the fourth man Dacre and said something that caused the others to laugh.

Guillaume closed the door and called up to his coachman. He hoisted himself onto the step, grasped the vertical bar beside the door, and looked inside. Lord Lincoln and this Dacre faced backwards; opposite them were Smith and Walsingham. As the coach jerked forward, he whispered another prayer, dedicating himself again to Jesus and swearing to bring about His return in glory, in the war that would destroy False Prophets and the Antichrist and establish His thousand-year reign. The warmth in his chest spread throughout his body. He knew that God had heard him. He felt surrounded by divine love, as during the rites of the confraternity. Although he had fasted, he felt strong. He was ready.

The coach jolted through the Porte Saint-Honoré. Ahead, the horse guards shooed the gawking crowds away from the road. Behind followed other coaches with their cargoes of English heretics and their escorts of horse guards. Guillaume's knees flexed, absorbing the shocks from the uneven road. Placing his left foot on the narrow ledge at the bottom of the door, he raised himself to eye level. He smiled and nodded to the ambassadors, and they nodded back and continued to talk in English. He calmly calculated the angles from where he stood to the chest of each man.

He lowered himself to the top step. This fourth man, Dacre, was a problem. To reach his first target, Lord Lincoln, he would have to reach across Dacre. Why was he here? So far as Guillaume knew, he had no importance. He would die simply because he was riding with the ambassadors. But if this act brought about the war with the heretics, it would not matter if this Dacre died now or in that war. Although Guillaume carried a pistol, he did not plan to use it. After several misfires, he did not trust it, and its loud report would attract attention and alert everyone. Better to rely on quick work with the sword. By the time anyone became aware, he would have delivered a dozen thrusts. He must be fast and accurate. God would guide his hand.

The coach picked up speed. The distance from the horse guards ahead and behind lengthened. Guillaume closed his eyes and uttered one last prayer. He glanced at the trailing riders. They would notice his next gesture, but he would have a minute at least before they were able to close with the coach. He crouched and drew his sword with his right hand, then planted his left foot on the door ledge and, in one motion, pulled himself up with his left arm and leg and thrust his sword into the coach.

CHAPTER 12

Attack

"The consort will entertain us all before dinner," Smith said. "The king's emissaries praised the skill of the musicians, especially the players of viols and crumhorns."

"Do they compare with the musicians at Whitehall?" Dacre asked.

"You may not tell Her Majesty I said so," Smith replied, "but I believe they are superior."

The guard appeared in the coach window, smiled, and nodded. The passengers nodded back. His head disappeared. "I will tolerate the entertainment," Lincoln said, "but the scrapings of viols and squeaking of crumhorns do not comfort my ears."

"Then the dinner will comfort your stomach," Walsingham said. "His Highness has excellent cooks and bakers."

"I am most curious to see Alençon," Dacre said. "Some say he is a scarred and deformed dwarf, yet Queen Catherine urges Her Majesty to wed the boy."

"I will allow you to make your own judgment," Walsingham said. "Did you receive instructions to report on him?"

"Of course," Lincoln replied. "We are each to report on young Francis, and Her Majesty will no doubt compare our reports. And she bid us note his brother Anjou."

"Ah, the one that got away," Smith smiled.

"Though his religious scruples doomed the match, Her Majesty is always interested in the appearance of a man, especially one she might have wed," Lincoln said.

"There will be no discussion of any matters of consequence today," Walsingham said. "It will be all smiles and formal compliments until after Sunday's ceremony. Next week, however, during the banquets and celebrations, be prepared for questions about Her Majesty's mind on marriage, religion, Scotland, and especially war in the Netherlands."

"I have no commission or authority to treat with the French on any of these matters," Lincoln said.

"You must be prepared to repeat that many times," Walsingham said. "The Queen Mother returns to the same topic again and again, hoping always for a more favorable reply, or the hint of a crack in your armor."

"Aye," Smith chimed in. "And if she perceives a chink, no matter how small, expect that every one of her creatures at Court will insert a blade and twist to wedge it open."

Dacre laughed. "From what I hear, she has some luscious creatures who are not difficult to wedge open—at least their legs."

Lincoln turned towards Dacre and reared back in a laugh. Suddenly a figure loomed before the coach's window, darkening the interior. The blade of a sword flashed towards him, pierced the left sleeve of his doublet, and, with a thunk, stuck in the wooden bench next to him.

"My God!" Smith exclaimed.

"Treachery!" Walsingham swiveled towards the window.

Dacre instinctively grasped the quivering blade. Guillaume jerked the point loose and pulled it back. Dacre cried out and stared at the blood dripping from his hands.

As Guillaume lunged again at Lincoln, Walsingham punched through the window and knocked the attacker sideways. The blade sliced past Lincoln's head.

"Stop! Stop!" Smith yelled, but the driver was already reining in as Guillaume thrust a third time. Off balance, his sword slashed across the roof of the coach.

The coach bounced to a stop. Guillaume fell awkwardly, sword flying from his hand, and landed hard on his back. He could hear the horse guards thundering towards him. Panic filled him, then resolve. He had marred his holy mission, may God forgive him, but the pistol gave him one last chance. He grasped it, sprang onto the coach's step, and pushed the door closed on the emerging Walsingham. He pressed his pistol into Walsingham's chest and pulled the trigger. The wheel whirred against the flint, sparks jumped, but the powder did not ignite. The flank of a horse pressed against Guillaume's back, then a hand clamped onto his shoulder and threw him to the ground. Two horsemen loomed above him, each with a drawn pistol.

"God will slay all heretics!" Guillaume shouted.

Both men fired.

"Slay them all," he choked, before his world went black.

Hunter breathed deeply, swaying with the rhythm of the coach, trying to calm himself, but doubts flew through his mind like swallows. No, like vultures circling a wounded man, but with the speed of a swallow. Damn! He could not even produce a satisfactory simile for his worries.

He had never attended Queen Elizabeth's Court. That would have been problem enough, but this was a foreign court. Who could be sure of the manners expected here? He took comfort in the fact that Sidney had invited him to ride in his coach. Philip did not know the etiquette of the French Court either, but had heard it was less formal than the English. But he had been to Whitehall and Greenwich many times. It was easy for him to say not to worry. "Just do as I do," he said. "Then at least we will make fools of ourselves together."

But he did not want to make a fool of himself. As an information gatherer, he should not draw attention to himself in any way. As an agent for the syndicate, he must be regarded as knowledgeable and refined by the officials he would meet. Any *faux pas* would impede him in both roles.

But if he worried too much, he would impede himself. He needed his wits about him to identify quickly who was who at Court, then to notice, as the expatriates had suggested, who spoke with whom. How could he do that if he were worried about his table manners? At least the tailor had finished his new black suit in time, with a silver lining that shone through the cuttes of the doublet and the panes of the trunk hose, and matched the silver braid.

"Why are we slowing?" Sidney asked.

Hunter came out of his reverie and leaned out the window. "All the coaches ahead are stopping." A crowd was forming around the ambassadors' coach. Fear gripped him. "Something has happened. Some accident."

Hunter, Sidney, and Bryskett scrambled out and ran forward. They saw only a throng of Englishmen. Someone said, "Attacked," and another cried, "Dead." Had an ambassador been killed? Hunter pushed his way through. Four dismounted guards stood over a servant in the uniform of the royal stables, blood flowing from two wounds in his chest. Near the coach stood Francis Walsingham and Sir Thomas Smith, their heads together. Lord Lincoln supported Baron Dacre, whose hands dripped blood. A servant began to wrap a sash around his left hand.

"What happened?" Sidney asked.

Henry Middelmore turned. "This guard attacked the ambassadors."

"We may all be in danger," a voice said. "This may be a trap." Hunter recognized Sir Henry Borough, his face pale.

In response to Borough's words, Walsingham spoke up. "Gentlemen, I ask you to return to your coaches."

Lord Talbot was at his side. "Sir, we fear for your safety. It may be...." He did not finish the sentence. To accuse the French King of treachery would be unwise and offensive.

"No," Walsingham silenced him. "Sir Thomas, Lord Lincoln, and I are in agreement. The king's horse guards protected us. They have killed this would-be assassin. He died crying that God would slay heretics. We believe he is a madman acting alone."

"I hope you are right." Talbot's eyes scanned the guards.

"He is not the only Frenchman who wants 'heretics' killed," Dacre said softly, then glanced at Walsingham and added, "but I am sure the king and his guards will protect us."

"But your hands," Middelmore said.

"It is not serious," Dacre said.

"And another slash on my sleeve," Lincoln said, "makes me more fashionable."

Nervous laughter ran through the crowd.

"By your leave, sirs," Walsingham spoke again. "We are not seriously harmed. We cannot let this mindless act interfere with the treaty ratification. Let us proceed to the Court." As though to preclude discussion, he turned and climbed the steps to his coach.

The news of the attack reached the Château de Madrid before the coaches. Nobles, officials, and servants swirled in buzzing crowds and descended upon the coaches as they arrived, asking for details, apologizing, and expressing horror. Despite the efforts of the ambassadors to downplay the attempt, the clamor continued. It took nearly an hour of confused shouting to get the courtiers into sufficient order to begin the formal ceremonies of welcome. Shaken, King Charles asked the ambassadors to dine alone with him and his brothers, and their small party disappeared into the Château de Madrid.

Everyone else ate in the building adjoining the château. Baron Dacre sat at the head table in the place of honor, to the right of Queen Catherine de Medici, who enquired frequently whether his hands pained him, and fed him herself. Several of her maids of honor, the same "creatures" he had been talking about when the attack began, approached him with doe-eyed concern that he appeared to enjoy.

As seating was by rank, Hunter found himself at the low end of the hall, with Charles and Isaac, members of Admiral Coligny's Huguenot retinue, to either side. Throughout the first course, they prodded him to recount what he had seen of the assault. He explained patiently and pointed out the members of the English delegation. In return, Charles volunteered his knowledge of the Frenchmen in the hall.

Although the head table was far away, the diners were easy to identify. Marguerite de Valois sat quietly near her mother, her face pale, her blonde hair arranged in curls under a French hood adorned with pearls. She had her mother's mouth. Admiral Coligny and his Protestant followers were on the queen's right with the highest ranked of the English delegation, while the Duke of Guise and his family sat to her left. The Frenchmen outranked their English guests. One earl, a baron, and two lords sat at a table with French dukes and princes of the blood. Now that Norfolk had been executed, England no longer had any dukes. As Queen Elizabeth was more niggardly with her honors than French monarchs, Hunter reckoned the number of titled Frenchmen would outnumber their English counterparts for some time.

At his elbow, Charles was describing Henri de Guise as the devil incarnate, second only to his uncle the Cardinal of Lorraine in plotting the extermination of those who followed the Gospel. Guise looked the part. His beard was trained to a spear point, his bearing was proud, and the looks of pure hatred he directed at Admiral Coligny made it clear that their formal reconciliation had been an empty gesture to appease the king.

The Huguenots, dressed in black out of respect for Jeanne d'Albret, were greatly outnumbered in the hall. Charles named the noblemen at the head table—Retz, Nevers, Montpensier—each seated next to his wife. These were the noblemen Pickering had written, trying to gain a foot in the door at Court. Isaac launched into a complex explanation of who was related to whom by blood or by marriage, and Hunter tried to remember the genealogical charts he had studied at Glasswell Manor.

Isaac, on his left, specialized in Court gossip. He added a scandalous counterpoint to Charles's melody of identification. "He keeps a mistress of extraordinary beauty at Fontainebleau...They say she has taken Count Coconato, another damned Italian, as a lover... Madame de Sardini sits there as though she were a virtuous matron, yet, as Isabel de Limeuil, she was one of the most notorious women of the Court."

Hunter had never heard of her.

"She was one of the first of the Queen Mother's flying squad. In her youth she played the whore to Guises. She caused a scandal when she bore the Prince of Condé a bastard."

Hunter looked at Henri of Condé, seated at the head table.

"No, not Prince Henri; his late father, Louis. She had to go to a convent for a while, but the poor baby died, and then she married one of the wealthiest bankers in Paris, so of course she has been washed clean in a bath of gold," Isaac concluded.

As the servants cleared the final course, Hunter noticed two young women near the head table wearing gowns of green velvet. They leaned together in amused conversation, their heads bobbing up as they looked in his direction, then across to Philip Sidney. "Who are those ladies?"

"The Viscountess of Tours and Madame de Challon. The Viscountess is on the left," Charles said. "Why?"

"They were looking our way."

"Perhaps they were speculating about the prowess of Englishmen as lovers," Isaac suggested.

"Your mind runs all in one channel," Charles said. "Don't let him corrupt you, Paul."

The nobility at the head table rose. "We are to follow," Isaac said. "Paul, if you do not want to approach those ladies, I will be glad to ask what interested them so much."

"And the Admiral will box your ears for it," Charles said.

"Only if my *friend* tells him," Isaac said.

"Someone has to keep at least a scrap of your virtue intact," Charles replied.

Sidney maneuvered to Hunter's side as the crowd flowed into the adjoining room. "Come with me. Henry Middelmore promised to introduce me to Admiral Coligny."

They carved their way through the guests, nodding and smiling. Intriguing snatches reached Hunter's ears: "...fixed on riding to war...cannot depend on the English...making a huge mistake..." Sidney maneuvered his way to Middelmore. Beside him, Admiral Coligny stood, dignified, his face determined, his mouth solemn, his blue-gray eyes tired. His body still proclaimed energy, but his face looked older than his fifty-three years.

"Ah, Sidney," Middelmore said. "Admiral, here is the gentleman I spoke of the other day, young Philip Sidney."

Sidney doffed his hat and bowed, "It is an honor to meet you, sir. All those in Europe who revere the Gospel are grateful to you."

"You are too kind in your praise, sir," Coligny said. "There are thousands who have done more for the cause than I. Many risk their lives even now."

"We pray for their success." Sidney stepped aside. "Let me introduce my friend Paul Adams. He represents the syndicate hoping to establish a staple at Rouen."

Hunter removed his hat and bowed. Coligny spoke a polite greeting, but his tone suggested trade agreements were of little importance. He said to Sidney. "I have spoken at length to Master Middelmore and Sir Arthur Champernowne of the importance of English support in the matter of the Netherlands. I hope you will write your uncle, urging this."

Sidney appeared unsurprised at Coligny's blunt request. "My Uncle Robert is a sincere friend of the Reformed religion. I am sure he always speaks in support of policies to advance it."

"Events have reached a point where we must do more than speak. Louis of Nassau and the Dutch burghers cannot stand alone against the might of Spain. France and England together could humble Spanish pride and ensure the survival, nay, the triumph of True Religion." Coligny put Hunter in mind of an Old Testament prophet.

Middelmore looked ill at ease. Perhaps he had heard this all before and, from his expression, had been unable to give the Admiral a satisfactory assurance of English help.

"I understand your queen's reluctance," Coligny continued, "but it is now too late. It has begun. Those who support the Gospel will triumph or they will be crushed."

"I cannot speak for Her Majesty," Sidney said, "but I can relay to my uncle whatever you wish."

"The attempt on the ambassadors today," Coligny said, "They say it was some madman, but I am sure the hand of Spain was behind it. It was aimed at breaking the treaty and preventing English participation in the Netherlands enterprise."

"The king has promised a thorough investigation," Sidney said.

Coligny said, "One cannot question the dead."

Beyond Middelmore, one of the women in green velvet turned in his direction. Dark brown curls escaped from a French hood and surrounded a pale face with an upturned nose and large brown eyes. Was this Madame Challon or the Viscountess of Tours?

Coligny launched into an assessment of the Spanish forces available to the Duke of Alva. While Sidney listened intently, Hunter's attention strayed to those large brown eyes. She smiled. Middelmore glanced over his shoulder and back at Hunter. He raised his eyebrows and stepped closer. "Do you know her?"

"No," Hunter said.

"She looks worth knowing." He looked sideways at Coligny and Sidney, fully engaged in analyzing the conflict in the Low Countries. "Go ahead. I'll make excuses for you whenever there's a pause."

Hunter uttered a *"Pardonnez moi,"* which Coligny acknowledged with a curt nod, and backed away. He caught the eye of the woman in the green gown, smiled, and approached her.

"Good afternoon, madame. Allow me to introduce myself. I am Paul Adams. I could not help noticing you and your lovely smile."

Her smile wavered. "Thank you, monsieur. I call myself Marie de Challon. Did you say you are Monsieur Adams? Then my friend, the viscountess, was mistaken. She assured me you were Monsieur Sidney."

"No," Hunter said. "That is Philip Sidney over there, speaking to Admiral Coligny."

"Then I was right," Madame Challon said. "I should have wagered with her. We argued about which of you was Sidney. She held that you looked the nobler."

"I am flattered."

"By the Viscountess of Tours, no less. So, you are of Lord Lincoln's company?"

"In truth, no."

"But you are an Englishman here with Lord Lincoln."

"True, but I did not come with His Lordship. I have been in Paris for some time, representing English merchants who seek trade in France."

"Oh!" Her face lit with recognition. "You are the one with the chest of clouts and rags." She giggled.

Clouts and rags! His shock must show on his face, as her giggling increased. After a moment, she regained control. "Forgive me. I am sure you have fine English cloth in your chest, but the ladies at Court, they make a joke that you are an English peddler, trundling through Paris with rags and patches."

"I cannot accuse *them* of flattery," Hunter said.

"They say worse about one another, believe me," Madame Challon said. "A woman is as likely to be cut to pieces at the Louvre as a man is on the battlefield."

He could detect no signs of serious injury in her large brown eyes. Perhaps she was only repeating a commonplace refrain of the Court. "What is your interest in Master Sidney?"

"The interest any lady might have in one who is said to be a model of courtesy, intellect, and gallantry." She flashed her eyes and her smile.

Was this a member of the Queen Mother's famous flying squad, assigned to seduce Sidney? Should he shield his friend or offer to introduce him? "Are all the ladies of the Court interested in my friend, or you especially? Or perhaps you enquire for your friend, the viscountess?"

"Ah-ha." She placed her hand dramatically on her collarbone. "You have seen through me. The viscountess sent me to confirm her guess, before she arranged an introduction. You are clever as well as noble of bearing."

"Now you turn from insult to flattery again," he said.

"The insult was not mine, but a jest of others at Court," she said. "And it was the Viscountess who said you had a noble bearing. My only judgment is that you are clever."

"I hope at least I can plead guilty to that." Hunter was aware of the Viscount of Beaulieu, Prideaux's patron, resplendent in a gray doublet, approaching.

"Madame Challon," Beaulieu began, "I hope I am not interrupting, but I must introduce Master Adams to Viscount Harduin, one of the king's Counselors of Finance."

His tone, and Madame Challon's intake of breath, told Hunter he should be impressed at the name Beaulieu had just uttered, but she recovered and announced her own connections. "I must speak with my friend the viscountess just now." She flashed her eyes at Hunter once again. "We might continue our conversation later."

"I look forward to it." He turned to Beaulieu. "I will be honored to meet the viscount."

"Indeed, you shall be." Beaulieu led him away. "He is one of the king's most important financial advisors. He has information that must be conveyed to the merchants of London. He wanted to speak with someone from Lord Lincoln's deputation, but I convinced him they speak for Her Majesty, not her merchants, and that you would be the best conduit for his message."

"Am I to speak with him now?"

"No," Beaulieu said. "You might attend him in a few days. But he wants to assure himself that you are the right man." He fixed Hunter with his gaze. "I trust you will not disappoint me."

Hunter's muscles tightened. He hoped Viscount Hardin had not heard him described as a peddler of rags. Or one who had drunk himself into a stupor at the Horn. Or one Captain Izard had humiliated. He took a deep breath. He could not let his inner voices of doubt hobble him. "I will not let you down, my lord."

"Good." Beaulieu smiled. They continued through the crowd. "Damned disturbing, this mad stableman."

"Who do you think was behind the attack?"

Beaulieu was silent a moment. Hunter judged he was ticking through possible suspects, but in the end he said, "Just a solitary madman, as I said. The king should not have madmen working for him, or near him."

Whatever his suspicions were, Beaulieu was politic enough not to make them public. He halted near a group of officials. A burly man, whose black padded doublet and trunk hose made him look even larger, turned and excused himself from his companions. His eyes raked over Hunter skeptically.

"Viscount Harduin," Beaulieu said, "This is Paul Adams, the agent I told you about."

Harduin nodded as Hunter bowed. "Master Adams, Viscount Beaulieu says you are the man to communicate my thoughts to those London merchants who make up the Rouen Syndicate. May I ask how you came to represent it here in Paris?"

"At Gray's Inn I became familiar with a son, and a son-in-law, of two of the principal merchants of the syndicate." Hunter mixed some truth with the story created for him.

"Why did these merchants not send their own relatives?"

"Master Blodgett's son was about to take over an important part of his business in London, and he speaks little French. Master Babcock's son-in-law is his agent in Hamburg."

This explanation seemed to satisfy the viscount. "How often do you communicate with the syndicate?"

"I write them weekly."

"And within the syndicate, who has the power to make decisions?"

"A governing board of seven merchants chosen from the three dozen who are active members," Hunter explained.

"Your answers are clear," Harduin turned to Beaulieu. "Very well, I will convey my thoughts to the syndicate through Master Adams." To Hunter, he said, "Pray come Monday, the day after the treaty is signed, at the Hôtel de la Chambre des Comptes, in the court of the Sainte-Chapelle. I want to be sure my letters go to England with yours when Lord Lincoln returns."

"It will be an honor to wait upon Your Lordship," Hunter said.

Whispers swept around the hall that the king's party was about to enter. Catherine de Medici and those nobles who had sat at the high table approached the door, as other guests drifted away. A team of servants opened it with exaggerated ceremony. First ambassador Walsingham entered alongside the Duke of Alençon, the king's younger brother, then Lord Lincoln and the Duke of Anjou. Finally, King Charles entered. With each entrance, the guests in the hall bowed, each bow lower than the previous.

Hunter was struck by the youth of the royal Valois brothers. King Charles was a year younger than he was. Although dressed impressively in a suit of cloth of gold, he appeared an uncertain, awkward adolescent. His expression as he engaged in a brief *tête-a-tête* with his mother revealed his eagerness for her approval. Henri, Duke of Anjou, though younger than his brother, had a confident air and eyes of keener intelligence. Francis, Duke of Alençon, was not the deformed hunchback Hunter had expected to see, but his face was marred with pits and scars, and he did not stand straight. Both brothers stood calmly beside their English guests, waiting for the king to speak. An attendant struck his staff on the floor and announced, "His Most Christian Majesty, Charles IX, King of France."

The king began by welcoming Lord Lincoln. He expressed shock that his English guests had experienced any danger in his realm, and promised an investigation and punishment of anyone connected with such a heinous act. He declared his esteem for Queen Elizabeth, "his dear sister," and respect for the English delegation.

As the king's predictable words rolled forth, Hunter scanned the hall. He spotted the Viscountess of Tours near Sidney. She had succeeded in finding her quarry. He did not see Madame Challon. Throughout the hall, ladies and gentlemen stood still, politely listening to the king. Along the far wall, servants slipped silently from the banqueting room to a small service door at the side of the hall. One carrying a tray above his shoulder brushed another man. The tray dislodged his cap, which fell to the floor. The man turned and snarled a comment to at the servant. Hunter froze. The uncapped man had only half an ear. For a moment, he doubted what he had seen. As the man bent to retrieve his cap, he vanished from view, then he stood up and carefully pulled it down on the left side to conceal his injury. Hunter tried to make out some detail of the man's face. It was broad, with high cheekbones and a dark beard, but at this distance he could not see the man well, as he proceeded towards the service door. Was he a servant of the king? A messenger who had been sent to Court? Hunter longed to push his way through the crowd and pursue him, yet he stood beside Viscounts Harduin and Beaulieu, surrounded by courtiers and officials. The king was speaking. He stood frozen by the bonds of propriety while the man with half an ear vanished out the door.

Upon his return to L'Échiquier, Hunter found Crespin and Marguerite anxious to hear his account of the attempted assassination. After answering all their questions, he asked Crespin to his chamber. "You remember that Barnes and I discovered on our visit to Saint-Marcel that the Hooded Man who came for Pickering had a servant with half an ear?"

"Yes."

"Well, I saw a half-eared man today, at the Château de Madrid."

"Why do you think this is the same one who looked for Pickering two months ago?" Crespin asked.

"I believe that whoever was behind Pickering's murder is connected to the French Court. My other suppositions have come to naught. The letters I found at Pickering's lodgings were addressed to Guise, Nevers, Retz, Montmorency, Tavannes, Saint-Suplice..."

"So many?" Crespin interrupted. "Among them they have hundreds of servants."

"And one of them could have half an ear. Can you not make enquiries?"

"Go about asking people if they have seen a half-eared man? And when they ask why, what do I say? And downstairs you asked me to find out what I can about Guillaume Nadeau, the coach guard. At least I have a name, an occupation, and a place to start. That's more than 'a man with half an ear.'"

Hunter sighed. Crespin was right. Identifying who had tried to assassinate Walsingham was more important than his quest for Pickering's murderer.

"I am sorry, sir, but I told you I have seen several men with such an injury. After the wars as we have had, you cannot be surprised. But I never saw one constantly in the same place."

"Just keep it in your mind, Jacques. If I had not been in the midst of courtiers, I would have pursued him myself."

"If he serves one of the nobles you mentioned, you are more apt to see him at Court than I am among all the men of Paris."

Saturday, 14 June 1572

Hunter was surprised when Monsieur Picard, an alderman, walked into the Chessboard Inn and sat down at his breakfast table. Casually, he said he had heard Adams was among the party who went to the Château de Madrid yesterday and had witnessed the attack on the English ambassadors. Hunter barely began to recount his experiences when a draper from the rue Saint-Martin approached them, his curiosity as apparent as if he had painted a question mark on his forehead. All morning merchants and minor officials dropped by "to make sure Master Adams was safe" and hear his account of the foiled attack. Hunter repeated the official explanation that this had been the work of a madman and feigned ignorance of the attacker's identity. His hearers pronounced that they knew who was really behind this attack. One man or another identified the Spanish, the Pope, the English expatriates, the Scots, the Guises, the Montmorencys, the Huguenots, and the king himself as the instigator. After a few hours of this, Hunter longed to escape, but felt obliged to stay. After all, he was an information gatherer, even if the 'information' was baseless speculation.

Near noon, a silk merchant arrived and announced the attacker was Guillaume Nadeau. Several men in the dining room claimed to know him, but not well. A quiet little man, often seen at Saint-Gervais, always at one altar or another. The death of Nadeau's wife and child had turned him into a saint. He stopped drinking, prayed incessantly, and asserted with a smile that God would set all things right.

Crespin arrive at noon, and Hunter excused himself. In Hunter's chamber, Crespin reported that Nadeau had joined the Confraternity of the Holy Name of Jesus two years ago, after his wife and child died of the plague. He met regularly with Father Antoine to read and interpret the scriptures. The promise that Christ would come again gave him consolation. The priest was surprised at Nadeau's act. He had never counseled him to violence.

"When I went to Nadeau's lodgings, the wives there opened their doors a crack and said the kings' men had taken their husbands for questioning. His Majesty acted more quickly than I could. I returned again, but those husbands who had returned would say nothing."

"So you learned little."

"Yes, but I am convinced there is more to learn. Gold and fear make men keep silence."

"Gold to the priest and fear for the men near his lodgings," Hunter said.

"Just so."

CHAPTER 13

Celebrations

Sunday, 15 June 1572

HUNTER SAT NEAR SIDNEY INSIDE THE CHURCH OF SAINT-GERMAIN l'Auxerrois as King Charles IX swore his oath to uphold the treaty. After the ceremony, the king hosted the English delegation at the new Tuileries Palace his mother had built west of the Louvre. In its gardens, the tent interiors were painted light blue and decorated with signs of the zodiac. Behind the royal party's platform were hangings with fleurs-de-lis and the English royal coat of arms. A consort of viols played. A chorus of boys sang. Hunter scanned the room for a servant with half an ear. He spotted Madame Challon, who smiled at him. As he smiled back, a servant directed Sir Henry Borough to a seat next to her. Disappointment and envy washed over him. But he should rather pity her, having to endure the evening next to that ass.

An usher directed him to a seat next to a middle-aged couple. The man rose. "Louis Moutonnet, and this is my wife Juliette."

Hunter introduced himself.

"I serve the Duke of Nevers," Moutonnet announced.

"And I am a servant of the London syndicate who may soon have a staple in Rouen." Hunter reviewed the information he had studied at Glasswell Manor. Nevers was Louis Gonzaga, of the family of the Dukes of Mantua, one of the Italians who had come to France with Catherine de Medici. Raised with her children at Court, he acquired his title and vast estates when he married Henrietta, the eldest of the de Clèves sisters.

He was a member of the King's Council. "It must be an honor to serve such an illustrious lord."

"My husband is too modest to say so, but His Grace places great trust in him. He keeps His Grace's personal accounts." Juliette Moutonnet held her head high.

"That is indeed great trust." Hunter silently thanked her for her information.

Discomfort crossed Moutonnet's face, but he said, "The heralds are about to begin." Trumpets sounded, and everyone rose while the royal party and the ambassadors entered and assumed their seats. After another fanfare, all sat and servants appeared, carrying trays piled high with the first course.

Moutonnet spoke across his wife. "Were you in the coaches when the ambassadors were attacked?"

Hunter sighed to himself and recounted his experiences again.

"His Grace has a high regard for Ambassador Walsingham," Madame Moutonnet said.

"Oh?" Hunter looked at her husband.

"I have heard him speak of the ambassador's loyalty and courage," Moutonnet said.

"His Grace does him great honor," Hunter said.

"And he does not say such things lightly," Moutonnet added. "Do you know His Grace's example of loyalty as a young captain in the Habsburg wars?"

"No."

"He was captured at the battle of Saint Quentin and taken before his uncle, the commander of the Spanish forces, who begged him to change sides. Yet His Grace, young as he was, put his oath of loyalty to King Henri above family and wealth. He was obliged to pay a ransom of 60,000 écus for his freedom."

"And he has proved his courage in arms," his wife added. "He was wounded and crippled by the Huguenots in the last war."

As a server set a platter of cold meats near them, Hunter ventured a question with wording vague enough to allow Moutonnet to interpret it as he wished. "As His Grace values loyalty, how does he regard those matters under debate at Court?"

The couple exchanged glances. The husband served his wife some venison, then turned. "Would you care for some meats?" Hunter feared his question might go unanswered, then Moutonnet continued, "As you know, His Grace's brother-in-law is the Duke of Guise, and within two months he will have the Prince of Condé as a brother-in-law as well. With relatives on both sides of the religious dispute, the duke hopes to see a united country, where all are loyal to their king."

A politic answer. Hunter transferred two slices of venison onto his plate. "Does he agree with Admiral Coligny, that a foreign war would unite all Frenchmen?"

Moutonnet chewed thoughtfully. "Although His Grace would fight if it were the king's will, I believe he will advise the king not to involve himself in the Netherlands."

Hunter launched a different probe. "Madame, you mentioned the duke suffered wounds. Many of your countrymen must have been maimed in combat, yet I see few serving men who bear any scars."

"I urge you to look more closely, sir," Madame Moutonnet said. "Those selected to serve the king on formal occasions are the most handsome and able. However, I know His Grace takes care of those who have been wounded in his command."

"I am glad to hear that. But how does he employ a man with only one arm or one leg?" Hunter employed his most naïve tone.

"One former soldier with one hand serves His Grace in the kitchen, making excellent sauces," Moutonnet said. "Another with one leg has such a way with horses that he is invaluable in the stables."

"Excuse me for misprizing those who have been wounded," Hunter said. "Yet something in your comment, madame, troubles me. Suppose a man's face has been disfigured, or his nose or ears lost in battle. Are such men kept hidden away, lest they offend?"

Madame Moutonnet looked at her husband.

"His Grace has several former soldiers about him who have scarred faces," Moutonnet said. "One serves him as a porter; another is his ewerer at banquets. He considers their wounds marks of honor."

"I have heard tell that a Danish nobleman who dabbles in astrology lost his nose in a duel and wears one of gold," Madame Moutonnet said.

"I have heard that as well," Hunter said, "but such a costly substitution is beyond most men. If they lose half an ear in a sword fight, they must live with half an ear." He watched the Moutonnets carefully for some reaction, but saw none.

Servants cleared the cold meats, and then paraded in with the roast meat course. Hunter spotted Madame Challon, laughing at some remark of Borough's. How could anyone be pleased with that popinjay?

"I would be pleased to hear more of your syndicate's plans," Moutonnet said.

Hunter launched into a brief version of usual speech. Mindful that Moutonnet kept accounts for the Duke of Nevers, he concluded by suggesting that a nobleman might invest with certain Rouen merchants.

Madame Moutonnet stifled a giggle.

Her husband gave her a sharp look. "I believe my wife is amused at the notion of noblemen having excess money to invest. If the merchants of Rouen grow richer as a result of this treaty, it is more likely a nobleman will ask them for a loan. Many are deeply in debt."

"Not His Grace, of course," Madame Moutonnet added. He husband gave her another stern look.

Hunter said, "I understood the Duke of Nevers is one of the richest men in the kingdom."

Moutonnet shifted uncomfortably. "With great position comes great responsibility."

And great expense, Hunter thought. This was as close as the loyal Moutonnet would come to admitting his master was in debt.

After the final course, the guests rose from the tables nearest the platform where the king and the ambassadors sat. Servants bustled about, adding trestles and boards to construct a sizeable stage. The inconvenienced guests were reseated on benches with a prime view of the entertainment.

A beautiful young woman in flowing robes entered and bowed to the king. She turned and announced in a loud voice, "*Pax sum.*" She recited a poem praising the wisdom of Carlos and Eliza, sovereigns of neighboring lands, for insuring the prosperity of both their realms. When she finished, a corps of shepherds and shepherdesses performed a rustic dance. The shepherds left the shepherdesses to execute a graceful variation of a *basse danse.* With a clash of cymbals, a group of satyrs appeared, and the shepherdesses fled. But the mood of peace was not to be ruined. A group of nymphs pranced coyly on and, after some flirtatious posturing, performed a vigorous dance with the satyrs.

After the applause, the nymphs and satyrs welcomed Ceres and Bacchus, then Apollo and Diana. Hunter reflected that the gods were chosen to accord with the interests of France—grain, wine, cattle, and the chase—rather than those of England. But he supposed that Pan, assuming he looked after the welfare of England's sheep, might be considered too primitive and bestial for an appearance at a royal court.

King Charles and his sister Marguerite joined Apollo and Diana; the Queen Mother and Lord Lincoln joined Bacchus and Ceres. They danced a slow pavane as Elizabeth of Austria, Charles's pregnant queen, sat watching. After that, the nymphs and satyrs returned and chose partners from those on or near the platform. Hunter noted the Viscountess of Tours dancing with Sidney and Madame Challon partnered with Borough. She moved with grace to slow tempos and with a lively vitality when the cadence increased.

Hunter sipped his wine and surveyed the crowd. He found no half-eared servants, but a brunette with a French hood and a light blue gown met his glance. As he walked towards her, another man approached and asked her to the floor. The music lasted until late, but neither Hunter's fortune nor his mood improved. Refusing Sidney's offer of a bed at the Louvre, he made his way back to the Chessboard Inn.

Marguerite opened one eye as he entered her chamber. "You are quite late. Could you not tear yourself away from the feasting and dancing?"

"I danced but little," he said, "and then only with plain women." This was no excuse, but at least it was true.

"Even less reason to linger." She rolled away from him.

"I could not be rude by leaving early."

She snorted. "You stink of wine."

"I drowned my sorrows at being apart from you."

She snorted again. "The more you say, the more the thread bearing your excuse stretches to the breaking point."

He stood next to her bed, forlorn. Why had he lingered? Hope that Madame Challon might be available for one dance? Hope that a half-eared serving man would materialize? A feeling that he might miss something? He had no good reason.

Marguerite turned her head. Their eyes met. She smiled. "I accept your apology." She patted the bed next to her.

Monday, 16 June 1572

Viscount Harduin sat majestically behind a huge desk covered with papers, a black cloak with a gray silk border over his shoulders.

"The primary point I must impress upon you is that His Majesty needs to increase his revenues. He hopes the trade resulting from the Rouen

Staple will contribute to them. The interest on loans and the cost of our internal wars weigh heavily on the kingdom. In addition, establishing the Staple itself has costs for the king. The merchants of Dieppe and Le Havre have protested, and those ports must be appeased. Church officials object to granting religious privileges to foreign traders. All His Majesty's officials that must approve and supervise the English Staple will expect compensation for their efforts." He glanced at the silver salt-cellars Hunter had presented to him. "Your masters in the syndicate must keep these points in mind as they consider the details of the Rouen Staple."

Yes, the merchants of the syndicate had not realized the layers of officials and courtiers, the counselors and magistrates and secretaries and assistant secretaries and notaries that expected bribes to approve the details of the Staple.

Harduin lifted some sheets of paper. "Master Middelmore gave me a copy of the syndicate's most recent position. I assume you have seen a copy."

"I have," Hunter said. "They expect terms similar to those the Merchant Adventurers enjoyed at Antwerp."

"They may expect what they wish," Harduin said, "but His Majesty is not in competition with Antwerp. Antwerp is closed to English shipping. London must compare the benefits of an agreement with His Majesty to those available in Germany."

Hunter nodded. "The Merchant Adventurers have agreements in Hamburg and Emden."

"We are both aware of that. We both also know that an agreement with His Majesty encompasses a kingdom, from the Channel to the Mediterranean. How many German princes and electors and bishops would you need to negotiate agreements with, in order to reach a market equal in size? How long would such negotiations take? And, given that every prince and elector and bishop would exact his price, how much would remain for your syndicate after such negotiations?"

Hunter had no ready answer. These were not arguments the Merchants of London were eager to hear.

"In return for access to such a large market, it is only reasonable the king would expect English merchants to pay duty on their cloth—duty sufficient to provide the treasury a steady stream of income."

There it was—the one royal demand that must be met. Yet Hunter was here to represent the interests of the syndicate. "But such a duty would surely be less than at present."

"Yes," Harduin said "We both expect a great increase in the amount of cloth shipped through Rouen. In my letter, I suggest the rate might fall if the annual amount increases."

"I am sure that idea would meet with favor among the syndicate members, if the initial duty is not set too high."

"That is yet to be determined," Harduin said. "I have prepared a letter I will send to England with Lord Lincoln. In it I have stated my arguments in Latin more politely and diplomatically, but for you I wish to be as plain as possible. I trust you will convey what I have told you clearly, in English. Both His Majesty and I want the Rouen Staple to be established as soon as possible, but it must be beneficial to both sides."

"The members of the syndicate wish that as well," Hunter said. But both sides of course want a little more benefit for themselves.

"There is another matter I have not included in the letter, which I trust you will convey." Harduin's brows furrowed. "His Majesty dreams of being a victorious general, laurels on his brow, admired by all of Christendom. He longs to outshine his brother. Admiral Coligny understands him and fans his martial ambitions. He and others, of a certain persuasion, work to convince His Majesty to invade the Netherlands, or at least to support those who are willing to do so on their own." He paused, fingered the silk border of his cloak, and sighed.

"I, and many others, fear the signing of this treaty will make him bolder. We fear it may lead him to ruin. He may appeal to Queen Elizabeth to join him in this enterprise of the Netherlands. I must tell you that a war with Spain would be disastrous. Even though some ill-advised alliance of France and England with the Dutch rebels might achieve a few victories in the Low Countries, in the long run, no other monarch has silver mines in the New World to finance a war.

"I am sure Admiral Coligny and those Huguenots who surround him at Court will urge everyone in Lord Lincoln's delegation to convince your queen to enter into a war, perhaps an undeclared one. English noblemen may dream of military glory as much as French noblemen, but I hope that the merchants of both countries agree that conflict is not good for trade. Pray tell your masters, in whatever cypher you use, what I have said about this talk of dividing the Netherlands. I will do my utmost to advise the king against such a calamitous course of action."

That evening Hunter heard the opposing case. Admiral Coligny hosted a feast for Lord Lincoln's party. The king and counselors were in attendance, but a much smaller number of courtiers than at the Tuileries feast. There was neither dancing nor masquing, whether due to the state of mourning for Jeanne d'Albret or because of the strict moral principles of the Huguenots was not clear. Hunter noticed that neither Madame Challon nor the Viscountess of Tours were there.

Coligny was speaking to Lord Lincoln of the Battle of Saint Quentin, when they fought on opposite sides. "You fought for Philip II then. His marriage with Queen Mary bound you to the House of Habsburg. Now France and England together can humble Spanish pride and ensure the survival, nay, the triumph of the Gospel. Alva cannot be allowed to crush the Dutch. I have pledged to aid William of Orange. Nassau holds Mons. The time is near…"

Hunter walked on to where Téligny, Coligny's son-in-law, pressed Sidney again to encourage England's participation. "I know your queen hungers for the return of Calais, but King Charles will never agree to that. If she seeks a base on the Continent, she might gain Brill or Flushing, or even all of Zeeland."

This was the division of the Low Countries others had alluded to. Who would control Antwerp, Hunter wondered. And Amsterdam. Would William of Orange be allowed an independent duchy, or a county?

Sidney was speaking. "That possible gain must be balanced against a considerable risk. If victory over Spain were so easy, King Charles would now rule much of Italy, but years of combat between Habsburg and Valois have gained little for the House of Valois."

"The past is not the present," Téligny protested. "This is the moment for action. The Netherlanders are in revolt. The Queen of Scots is a prisoner in England. King Charles is sympathetic to the advice of my father-in-law. I know one should not even whisper of the death of monarchs, but think how circumstances would change for the worse if either King Charles or Queen Elizabeth were to pass away. The Duke of Anjou is the darling of the Guises and Mary, Queen of Scots is their cousin."

"God forbid" Despite Sidney's objections, he agreed with Téligny's argument on timing.

Téligny turned to Hunter. "Noblemen are not the only ones who can whisper in the ear of their sovereign. Your masters must resent Alva's arrest of English merchants and his closure of Antwerp. Bid them consider the advantages of the Netherlands without Spanish overlords—Low Countries divided among England, France, and the Prince William of Orange."

"I am sure many of them would favor such an outcome," Hunter said, although he knew the Merchant Adventurers had done very well in their dealings with Antwerp under Spain.

Before Hunter could continue, Charles, Duke of Mayenne, a younger Guise brother, approached. Without skipping a beat, Téligny said, "His baker makes the most delectable raisin cakes." He turned to Mayenne. "Your Grace, I was just telling these English gentlemen the sweets they can look forward to at the Duke of Anjou's banquet tomorrow…"

On the night Coligny hosted the English delegation, the Hooded Man sat with Ambassador Zuñiga.

"Your plans came to naught." Zuñiga's eyes were cold. "The treaty is ratified, the English ambassadors are praised for their courage, and you are in danger of being discovered."

The Hooded Man sat unfazed. "I grant your first two points, but I feel in no danger."

"Can the man who spoke to this groom not identify you?"

"They would have to find him first," the Hooded Man said. "He left Paris late Saturday."

"But when he returns?"

"If by chance they are still investigating then, and they chance to find him, he has good reason to remain silent."

"Even if they put him to the question?"

"Even under torture, he will be mindful of his daughter," the Hooded Man said, "and I can guarantee her welfare. Should he prove unloyal, both he and his daughter would suffer."

"Odd," Zuñiga reflected, "how even those so base they will kill anyone for a price retain love for their families, while a nobleman might slay his brother for an inheritance."

"It is."

"I will accept your judgment regarding the risk of discovery, but as to my master's interests, we have been foiled."

"By your leave, I would judge it only the loss of a minor skirmish in King Philip's grand strategy," the Hooded Man said. "We both knew it had only a small chance of success, but the possible benefits made it worth trying. Compared with the battle that looms in the Low Countries, it is of little consequence. Other opportunities will present themselves, I am sure."

"And meanwhile you hope to continue to receive King Philip's largesse?"

"If it pleases him to so honor me," the Hooded Man said. "Some time must pass, and dust must settle, but I shall work to develop a plan."

"Contact me when you do," Zuñiga said, in what was clearly a dismissal.

Tuesday-Wednesday, 17-18 June 1572

The treaty celebrations continued throughout the week. Tuesday the Duke of Anjou hosted a banquet at the Hôtel de Bourbon. Wednesday the Duke of Alençon entertained at the house of the Duke of Retz. The royal brothers tried to outdo each other, each presenting a plethora of elaborately prepared courses, followed by singing, lute and viol music, a brief comedy, and a display of acrobatics.

At each banquet, Hunter kept his ears open for news of a French offensive in the Low Countries and his eyes out for a servant with half an ear. Varied predictions of events in the Netherlands rippled through each gathering. Coligny would lead an army of 6000 Huguenots to the Low Countries to join Nassau. France's religious strife would end, and both sides would unite to war with Spain. The Catholics of France would never fight in a war to support the Protestants of the *Pays Bas*. The English and the French would join in a successful assault on the Netherlands, and divide it between them. Elizabeth could not be trusted; she would sit amused in her island window and watch Charles and Philip battle one another in the courtyard of Europe. Alva would crush the rebels by August, and then turn his troops on anyone who had aided them.

Hunter was obliged to tell courtiers his version of the attack on the ambassadors. As the week wore on, it became old news, and everyone agreed it was the work of a solitary madman. Many ladies asked Hunter's opinion of a match between Queen Elizabeth and the seventeen-year-old

Duke of Alençon. They repeated the story of a conversation where Queen Catherine said, "I know your queen will be happy with my son," to which Walsingham replied, "I know nothing for certain where Her Majesty is concerned." Hunter laughed politely each time and explained he knew even less.

Under the melody of political speculation ran a steady rhythm of Court gossip. Birague could not fill the shoes of Morvillier as Chancellor. The Duke of Anjou, infatuated with Marie de Clèves, was ignoring his mistress Renée de Rieux. The astrologer Cosimo de Ruggieri had too much influence over Queen Catherine, and had tempted her to dabble in black magic. The cruel and arrogant Count Coconato was the lover of Baroness de Retz. Did the fact that Charles's queen, Elizabeth, was pregnant mean he would spend more or less time with his mistress, Marie Touchet?

At Alençon's feast, Hunter was introduced to Pierre de Bourdeille, seigneur de Brantôme, a deep well into which all Court scandal drained. He spoke of each nobleman's current and past mistresses and listed the lovers of each noblewoman. He mentioned both Madame Challon and the Viscountess of Tours as members of Queen Catherine's flying squad, but was interrupted and borne off before Hunter could ask him for details. Hunter's questions about the lot of soldiers wounded in the religious wars did not reap any information about a half-eared servant. Questions about English expatriates yielded a few courtiers who knew Kempson or Wilkes, but no one had heard of Pickering.

Thursday, 19 June 1572

It was after noon when Hunter returned to L'Échiquier after two nights sleeping at Sidney's lodgings. He crept to his chamber and found Marie cleaning. "Oh!" she exclaimed, twirling to face him, "Madame Moreau said she did not know where you were or when you were returning, and that I should clean your chamber."

"Go on." He plopped down on the stool near his desk. He would have to face Marguerite's displeasure soon.

She dusted the mantelpiece, glancing at him from the corner of her eye. "Madame Moreau says you are attending banquets with the king. Is that right?"

"Yes."

She sighed. "I would give anything to go to one. Do they last all night?"

"No. I spent the night with a friend."

Her eyes grew big and she blushed.

"No," he said. "It is not what you imagine. I was with Master Sidney. You have seen him. He was with the party you served at midday last week."

"I remember." She stepped closer and began to dust the bedposts. "You and he must attract the notice of the Court ladies."

"Not many of them."

Her look told him *she* had noticed him. "Do you think Jeanne is pretty?"

Startled, he replied, "She is a comely girl."

Marie dissolved in giggles. "I will go now," she blurted, rushing to the door.

After changing into his gray suit, Hunter faced Marguerite in her office and explained that he had felt obliged to stay at Sidney's in order to protect her reputation.

Her expression was dubious. "So after these nightly festivities, which you feel you *must* attend, you stay away from me for *my* benefit?"

"You know Walsingham wants me to observe what courtiers do and say at these banquets. It would be rude to decline an invitation to join such eminent gatherings."

"And rude to decline Master Sidney's invitations, too, I suppose," she said.

"Bryskett suggested that your embrace was the reason I wanted to return to L'Échiquier. I could not confirm his suspicions by returning. My love, pray grant me respite until these celebrations are over."

"Respite? Are our nightly meetings proving too tiring for a lusty young Englishman?" Her smile turned to a frown. "Or are you getting too much stimulation from the ladies of the flying squad to have energy for me?"

"No ladies of the court have flown near me," he protested. "These banquets with their speeches and gossip and talk of politics are proving dreary."

"Dreary?" she said. "That is the first time I have heard the revels of the Valois Court described as dreary. But I hope for you they will be. I can tolerate you sharing the beds of other Englishmen, but no French women."

"I swear I shall not."

Thursday the Duke of Nevers hosted yet another feast. A wise courtier, he chose not to compete with the royal family, so he arranged no acting or acrobatic displays. Instead, he set up tables among the trees in his ample park and arranged musicians strategically to serenade the diners. The usher escorted Hunter to a table in the shade of a sycamore, where the large brown eyes of Madame Challon flashed up at him. His pulse quickened.

"Good evening, Madame Challon. I am honored by your presence."

"The pleasure, Master Adams, I am sure will be mine."

"I will do my best to make it so."

"Have you enjoyed the banquets to honor the Treaty of Blois?" Madame Challon asked.

"The food has been excellent, the music delightful, and the acrobats at the Hôtel Bourbon were impressive, but I have not had the pleasure of such delightful company as tonight."

"Just a few nights at the French Court, and you have learned how to flatter with ease," she teased. "I am sure you have found plenty of fascinating ladies to converse with."

"A few," he said, "but many of the most attractive, like yourself, seem to attach themselves to one of Lord Lincoln's train for the entire evening. Sunday you were with Sir Henry Borough, Tuesday with Henry Middelmore, and yesterday with Sir Jerome Bowes."

"I am flattered you pay attention to my every move."

"I also noticed the Viscountess of Tours attached herself to certain noblemen of the delegation."

"Attached herself? You speak of her as though she were a limpet."

"I could never compare such a beautiful, accomplished woman to a limpet."

At that moment, two other couples arrived. Introductions were made, and the first course was served. They made small talk, comparing the dishes to those served on the previous evenings, complimenting one another's clothing, and commenting on the apparel of other guests. After some time, a bell rang as a signal that guests might wander about the Duke of Nevers's park between courses.

As they strolled, Madame Challon said, "You seem critical that the viscountess and I should entertain visiting Englishmen at the treaty celebrations."

"Not critical. I merely observed."

"It is only proper that the distinguished guests *your* queen has sent should be shown every courtesy. Queen Catherine wants to make sure each one receives the proper attention."

"Then is it true the queen has a group of ladies she assigns to *entertain* foreign guests?" he asked meaningfully.

Marie Challon's eyes locked with Hunter's. "Her ladies-in-waiting help entertain visitors, yes, as I am entertaining you."

"I have heard that a more select group exists, that does not include all her ladies-in-waiting."

She laughed. "Oh, the 'flying squad.' Who told you that?"

"Several people."

"Before, you could tell me in detail whom I, and Charlotte, spent time with. Now you become general and coy when I ask who spoke of a flying squad."

"Is it true?" Hunter asked.

"What?"

"The flying squad."

"Explain this 'flying squad' to me?"

Hunter felt trapped. He was sure she knew what was rumored, but propriety forbade him to state that ladies of the squad traded their bodies for secrets. "Well, according to many, the Queen Mother surrounds herself with a number of very attractive ladies. That I know to be true." He nodded towards her. "It is said she employs them to ferret out the secret plans of those at Court, or visiting foreigners. She uses the information to maintain her power."

"And how should they find out these secret plans?" Her eyes dared him.

Hunter's mouth was dry. "I have heard they, well, they have many charms they can use."

"Charms?" Marie raised her eyebrows in mock astonishment. "Do these anonymous gossips say the ladies-in-waiting use magic?"

"Not magic, my lady. Rather, their physical charms."

"Such as..."

Again he struggled to construct his response. "A beautiful face, or sparkling eyes."

"Is that all?" Another challenge.

"Would those not be enough?"

She smiled. "I am glad you did not think one of Her Majesty's ladies would use any more of what you call 'physical charms.' Her Majesty chooses her attendants for their intelligence and wit as well as their appearance." Her eyes danced with amusement. "I suppose a woman might use those to discover some secret plan."

He could not resist returning a challenge. "A woman might use her tongue."

She turned to one side and suppressed a laugh, then recovered. "I can see how all this story of a 'flying squad' may have started. Of course Queen Catherine wants her ladies to entertain the important men at Court. She wants a lively court, filled with witty conversation, with laughter, with singing and dancing. But she must also advise her royal sons and her daughter Margot. She has an obligation to them and to all France, especially in these troubled times. So, yes, she does expect her women to keep their ears and eyes open to everything, and to inform her. In the past ten years, one faction or another has plotted to capture the king. How could she not wish to gather information to prevent such a tragedy?"

"As one trained in the law, I must applaud your defense," Hunter said. "But you do not deny, then, that there is a flying squad, after all?"

"I have told you what Her Majesty expects of her ladies. I fear that there are many who ascribe wicked motives to the queen. And if they believe she is ruthless, they might also imagine her attendants are ruthless women. Scandal always make more sensational conversation that the truth. If one of the queen's ladies 'uses her tongue,' as you put it, it would only be to persuade someone into revealing his intentions, and not in any unchaste way."

"Do not think I could have considered such a thing," he said, but their eyes shared his joke.

"And if I am to be a lawyer, arguing a case," she went on, "I might call as witnesses those members of the English delegation to whom, as you say, the viscountess and I have 'attached' ourselves. Did they report anything dishonorable?"

"Those I talked with spoke only of the beauty and wit of the ladies they met."

"Then you know the truth of these rumors of a flying squad," she concluded with a nod.

At the interval between the second and third courses, Hunter and Madame Challon walked about the grounds again.

"While I have been in Paris," Hunter began, "I have met several Englishmen who left England because of their religion. I understand that such expatriates might be an embarrassment for the king at these celebrations, but do they regularly come to Court at other times?"

"Englishmen at Court?" she said. "I have heard of some of these expatriates that you mention, but I have not met any."

Walking clear of a hedge, they encountered Louis Moutonnet and his wife.

"Master Adams!" Moutonnet's face lit up, "I had hoped to see you tonight." Hunter introduced Madame Challon, then Moutonnet continued. "When the dining is finished, pray come to His Grace's table. I told him of your interest in those mutilated in battle, and he said he would like to meet you." He turned to Marie Challon. "You would be most welcome, too, my lady. I can introduce you both."

"Thank you," she said. "I already know the duke, but I will be interested to hear a conversation about the fate of maimed soldiers." She glanced sideways at Hunter.

"I am grateful that you mentioned me to the duke. I shall repair to his table after the last course," Hunter said.

Hunter and Marie Challon strolled on.

"You seem to have a wide range of interests, Master Adams."

"How so?"

"I thought you were promoting the sale of English cloth, yet you have said nothing about woolens," she said. "I am surprised at your concern for wounded French soldiers."

Had Marie detected he was more than a syndicate agent? Hunter took care to respond to only part of her comment. "To promote English cloth, I am working indirectly. The details of an English staple are to be negotiated in the next four months. I hope to influence those officials who will decide those details, and those merchants whom they might know. The more they desire English cloth, the better the terms of the agreement."

"I would have thought you would offer samples of cloth to ladies at Court, so they would become *la mode*," she said with a smile.

"Alas, I had not the pleasure of meeting you earlier," he said. "Several bales of cloth came with Lord Lincoln's delegation, as the result of requests from officials and merchants I spoke with in May. Perhaps some of that cloth will be made into gowns or petticoats for their wives."

"But the wives of merchants do not set fashion," she said.

"Would you deign to wear a gown from a rag peddler?" he asked.

"So that stings, does it? Surely some of your best cloth, worn by myself and the viscountess, would counter that slur well."

"Madame Challon, I will reserve some lengths of the finest cloths, which look as elegant as embossed silks, for you and the viscountess. But you must tell everyone that it is English cloth, and that when the staple is established at Rouen, more will be available."

"So, I am to be part of your indirect campaign, too."

"You seem talented at indirection."

"And at frontal assaults as well," she smiled. "But you have not explained your interest in mutilated soldiers."

Hunter decided an answer near the truth might serve. "I happened to glimpse a servant with half an ear at the Château de Madrid last Friday. Do you know whom he might serve?"

She knitted her brows. "No. Is that the only reason for your concern?"

"Seeing him set me thinking. Few of the servants here show any disfigurement, so I wondered if those men who were wounded in the recent conflicts in France had been dismissed by their masters or cared for in some way. Do you know of maimed soldiers well treated by noble masters?"

Madame Challon regarded him skeptically. "I admit I see those who have been mutilated begging in the street, but I do know of a crippled man who serves the Duke of Alençon."

Hunter was relieved when Lord Sandys of the Vine and the Viscountess of Tours approached and interrupted the discussion of maimed soldiers. They exchanged comments on the excellence of the Duke of Nevers's park. Madame Challon told her friend that Paul Adams had promised them fine English cloth for gowns.

As they walked on, Madame Challon said, "I wish to return to my examination regarding an alleged flying squad."

"Yes, Madame Avocat."

"When the Earl of Lincoln's party returns to London, will they not report to your queen all that they have heard and seen at the French Court?"

"I am sure they shall."

"So, Queen Elizabeth is using the gentlemen of this delegation as Queen Catherine uses her ladies-in-waiting. Are they not a male English 'flying squad'?"

"As I said. Madame, you would make an excellent lawyer."

"Is that a compliment?"

"I could only give compliments to one as lovely and clever as you."

"And what about you?" she asked.

Hunter was nonplussed. "Me?"

"Are you not using your 'physical charms' and your flattering tongue to find out secrets—of disfigured servants or English expatriates in Paris or how the Queen Mother discovers plots?" Her eyes were those of a hunter who had sprung a trap on her prey.

Hunter fought to hide his fear and show only surprise and innocence. "But I told you I represent London merchants."

"And your letters to them contain only reports of markets and trade?" she pressed.

"Of course."

"And your questions of maimed soldiers, of expatriates, of Court matters...?"

He forced a light tone. "You cannot expect me to spend all my time thinking of commerce, my lady. How would I then be worth the attention of a beautiful lady-in-waiting, even if only fourth rank attention?"

She laughed. A bell sounded, and the diners returned to their tables for a final course of fruit and sweets. Using information from Crespin's tours and taking advantage of the other couple's presence, Hunter guided the conversation into French history, the structure of the university, and modern trends in architecture. Madame Challon acquiesced to his lead, but when they had finished eating, said, "We must accept the invitation and pay our respects to His Grace."

"Master Moutonnet has told me you are interested in the lot of those wounded in our wars. That is laudable. I wish more were so concerned." The Duke of Nevers had a broad forehead, a large nose, and full lips below a thin moustache. A narrow beard followed his jaw line, but he had not brushed and waxed it into the modish point sported by so many others at Court. He wore a black suit, with a small ruff above the high collar.

"Your Grace is too kind," Hunter said. "It is your compassionate actions which are laudable. Master Moutonnet told me of your special care for those who were maimed."

"I have been crippled in action, as you can see," he gestured to his leg. "But, if you will allow me, I find it unusual that an Englishman should trouble himself over the fate of Frenchmen wounded while fighting one another." Hunter was aware of Marie Challon smiling. "Do you wish to compare France to the care England takes of her wounded?"

Was Nevers unaware that an Englishman wounded in battle could hope for little reward other than a swift discharge from service, or was this a subtle jab at his queen? The duke's face revealed nothing. Hunter recited the explanation he had given Marie Challon, that a chance glimpse of a servant with half an ear had led him to speculate.

"Half an ear," Nevers repeated. "I have seen such a man." Hunter tensed, but became aware Marie Challon was regarding him and willed himself to relax. Nevers shook his head. "I can't recall where." Hunter turned to Marie and shrugged to mask disappointment.

"Giles," Nevers called over his shoulder, "Come here. I wish to introduce you to another Englishman."

A thin man wearing Nevers's livery stepped forward. Marie's sharp intake of breath made Hunter steel himself before looking up. A diagonal scar ran from Giles's left forehead to his right chin. His left eyebrow, only half there, drooped down over his eyelid, his lips were split so that his mouth formed a cross rather than a line, and his grin revealed that he had lost several teeth from the sword blow. But the most arresting feature was his nose, or rather his lack of one. The blow that had split his face had sliced off the fleshy part, leaving only a bony ridge and two teardrop nostrils, giving his face the aspect of a skull.

"Master Adams, this is Giles, who fought well at Jarnac, and now serves me as ewerer." Giles gave a deformed smile and bowed towards Hunter. "Giles killed the man who wounded him so severely," Nevers added. Giles's smile grew larger.

"It is my honor to meet such a brave man and loyal servant," Hunter said.

"The honor is mine," Giles said. His speech was distorted and difficult to understand. "I have had the privilege of serving Lord Lincoln and the other noblemen of your party."

"We are all grateful for the hospitality your master has shown us," Hunter said. "Thank you for your part in making our evening so enjoyable."

At a nod from Nevers, Giles retired. Moutonnet likewise stepped away. Hunter sensed that he might also be expected to leave, but the duke addressed him, "Master Adams, I beg a word with you." He turned towards Madame Challon. "Will you excuse us, madame?"

Marie Challon smiled. "Of course. I promised a friend I would attend her."

Hunter watched her go, then looked towards Lord Lincoln and three other noblemen who were milling about near the table.

"Do not think me a poor host," Nevers said. "I have monopolized Lords Lincoln, Dacre, and Talbot all evening. At their request, my steward will guide them on a walk about the park." To Hunter's questioning look, he said, "After speaking with noblemen who represent Her Majesty, my mind, like yours, is led to speculation. I have few opportunities to speak with Englishmen of your station." He looked to see if he had given any offense. "Those of us with titles speak of honor and loyalty as though they were the exclusive possession of our class, yet, as Giles witnesses, these qualities are in all men's hearts."

Was he to explain what these abstractions meant for the common Englishman, Hunter wondered.

But the duke asked a different question. "Are you loyal to your queen or your God?"

"Both, I hope." Where was this leading?

"Then you and I are among the fortunate," Nevers said. "We do not feel the conflict so many do in these times." He took a few steps towards a chestnut tree, and Hunter followed, noticing his limp. "Perhaps the Germans have the solution."

"*Cuius regio, eius religio?*" Hunter asked.

"Yes," Nevers answered. "Let a man move to that place where his faith and that of his prince agree."

"That may be easier in a region as divided as the Empire," Hunter said.

"Yes," the duke agreed. "Far more difficult in France or England. Yet King Charles has unwisely granted Huguenots the privilege of worship in certain towns. Perhaps he believes he can be like the Emperor, and rule over subjects who pray differently in different regions. Would it not be better to exile them? Some Huguenot printers have moved to Geneva. Though I despise what they print, at least they are not printing in France. They do not say they are loyal subjects while demanding special privileges for what they claim is their consciences' sake."

Was this Lord Nevers's speculation, or was he trying to test this 'average Englishman's' sympathy towards the Huguenots? Hunter kept silent.

"Of course, it is easier for an artisan to move. A printer can take his skills when he moves, even if he must leave his press and blocks of type," Nevers said.

"But a landowner cannot take his land," Hunter said, following the duke's line of thought.

"I understand many German knights found it easier to convert than leave their estates," Nevers said. "Though history tells us many saints, born into noble families, gave up their inheritance to serve God."

"Such acts are so unusual that those who performed them are considered saints," Hunter observed.

Nevers smiled. "Yes. That is too great a sacrifice for our Huguenot noblemen."

"They claim they only want what was promised them in the Edict of Saint-Germain."

"So they say," the duke said, "but meanwhile hundreds of them slip over the frontier to join the Dutch rebels. They claimed their loyalty before they plotted to capture King François at Amboise. They swore it again before they tried to seize King Charles at Meaux. One minute they are loyal to the king, the next they are in arms against him, saying they must be loyal to their religion. If a man believes he alone knows God's will, could he only be listening to himself? Will the Huguenots' God ever reveal to them they are in error? I fear this kingdom shall have no peace until we return to *un roi, une loi, une foi*. Is that not your queen's goal, with her oaths of supremacy and uniformity?"

"She does require every loyal subject to recognize her as queen and governor of the church, and to attend the approved church services." Hunter chose his words carefully. "That, I suppose, amounts to *une reine, une loi, une foi*—though that does not work as well rhetorically."

Nevers granted him another fleeting smile. "She has not had a civil war—is that wise governance, good fortune, or God's favor?"

"Perhaps only God knows," Hunter replied. "The Rising in the North could have become a civil war, if Northumberland had been as strong a leader as Coligny."

"And at the end of that conflict, many of your Catholic noblemen ended up in Brussels, under the protection of a king whose religion they share," Nevers remarked. "Another example of the German solution."

"Some English Catholics have come to Paris as well."

"Yes, I have met a few of them," Nevers said. Before Hunter could proceed, he said, "Your Ambassador Walsingham is a loyal man. I could tell he was never keen on your queen's match with Anjou, yet he came to Court, day after day, to bargain with Queen Catherine in pursuit of the marriage. He knew his duty. And the courage he showed during the attack last Friday... He is the admiration of everyone."

A servant approached and whispered in the duke's ear. "I must leave you now to bid some of my guests farewell," he said. "It was a pleasure to speak with you."

As Nevers limped away, Hunter stood perplexed. He had expected to be questioned about his views, yet the duke had said much more than he. Had he fed Hunter information so that he would report it? Was he choosing to speculate aloud to a low-ranked stranger whose opinion held little sway with anyone? Hunter needed to think over all that had happened. If guests were leaving now, he could also excuse himself. He surveyed the park for Madame Challon. Should he spend more time looking into those brown eyes? Would she continue her probing questions? Would Marguerite's suspicions prove valid? He did not find her and resolved to leave early.

Monday, 23 June 1572, Saint John's Eve

"Lovely, is it not?" Walsingham gestured towards the silver ewer on his desk. "A gift from His Majesty." The departure of Lord Lincoln's party the day before had occasioned an elaborate exchange of gifts. "If only I could take it to a silversmith and use the proceeds to pay the debts these treaty celebrations have incurred." He sighed. "But word would make its way back to King Charles and the insult would undo all the treaty has established."

Hunter and Lepage smiled at the ambassador's words. Beale entered, nodded at everyone, and opened a file. "I have received a report from the king's *prévôt de l'hôtel*, his initial investigation of the attempt on Lord Lincoln." At a sound of doubt from Hunter's throat, he looked up. "We have agreed to state that the attack was directed only at Lord Lincoln, rather than against all three in the coach. It simplifies matters to assume officially he had only one target." He referred again to his papers. "There is little we do not know here: Guillaume Nadeau, thirty-five years old, in His Majesty's service for six years. Before that he served eight as a groom for the Duke de Retz. Before that, he was an apprentice to a livery stable owner in the faubourg Saint-Martin. He married one Marie, but there are no details of her parentage. She and a son died of plague two years ago. He was a member of the Confraternity of the Holy Name of Jesus at Saint-Gervais. He asked Father Antoine often about signs that the Apocalypse was at hand. Evidently there were a number of parishioners who met regularly with Father Antoine." He looked at Lepage. "I was surprised to find the name of our doorkeeper Pierre among those."

Hunter remembered his encounter with Pierre at the Pentagram bookshop, where the doorman had asked him to read the broadsheet predicting the end of days.

Lepage's mouth dropped. "Have you questioned him about this?"

"Not yet," Beale said. "The *Prévôt's* men are working their way through the members of the confraternity."

"That Pierre was so closely associated with Nadeau must give us concern," Lepage said. "I advise that you dismiss him immediately. I will tell him myself." He sighed. "I feel partly responsible. You continued to employ Pierre upon my recommendation when you arrived. That I had any part in placing so near to you one connected with this would-be assassin..."

"Should we not hear what Pierre has to say for himself?" Walsingham asked.

"I am certainly willing to hear what he has to say," Lepage answered, "but no matter how innocent his response may be, can you afford to take a chance? You are too tenderhearted, sir. If his association at Saint-Gervais seems innocent, I still say it is too great a risk to have him minding your door."

Beale voiced his agreement.

"I can find Pierre another place. He shall not go hungry, but he need not be here. Indeed, I had intended to recommend that you hire a second doorman after this attack. I can find two men for only a bit more than you pay Pierre. I will make up the difference from my fee, sir. Anything to guarantee your safety."

"Pierre has been a good servant," Walsingham said.

"That may be," Beale said, "but I agree with Lepage. We cannot take any chances."

"I am bold enough to offer an opinion as well," Hunter said. "I once encountered Pierre on the rue Saint-Jacques, looking over some broadsheets for signs of the end of time."

"He is scarcely the only man in Paris who looks for signs of the Second Coming," Walsingham said.

"Yes," Hunter said, "but if a belief in the Apocalypse led Nadeau to attack you—or Lord Lincoln—then there is risk employing a man who, like him, anticipates the end of days."

"Very well," Walsingham said. "But I trust you, Master Lepage, to be sure he does not suffer unjustly. Be sure you can find him a place."

"I assure you I will."

"There is little else here." Beale returned to his notes. "A churchwarden at Saint-Gervais saw Nadeau a month ago speaking with a man in a side chapel where it was dark. The man wore a long, dark cloak with a hood."

Lepage chuckled. "That helps us little. Many men wear such cloaks. Even I have one."

"Nor can we assume that that man urged him to his deed," Beale put in. "It may be that Nadeau took it into his head to kill Lord Lincoln, or all three in the coach, because in his eyes they were heretics. Those were his last words."

"Perhaps His Majesty's enquiries, or our own, will reveal more," Walsingham said. "Do either of you have anything further to report?"

For a moment, Hunter had considered that the Hooded Man behind Pickering's murder might be connected with Nadeau, but Lepage's comment and Beale's statement convinced him to hold his tongue. "No, sir," he said.

Lepage said, "As the failed attack is the talk of the town, I have asked some of my clients what they knew of Nadeau. Those in the service of the Guises, the Damvilles, Lord Tavannes, the de Thous, the Cossés, *et cetera*—no one reports any knowledge of the man."

Because Lepage had mentioned some of the French aristocrats Pickering had written, Hunter made a sudden decision as they left the embassy. "Master Lepage, I have a rather unusual question for you, but as you are well acquainted with many nobles of Paris..."

"You flatter me, Master Adams," he replied. "I am acquainted with the servants of noble families. Secretaries and stewards speak with a notary; not dukes and viscounts."

"It is of the servants I wish to ask," Hunter said. "Have you noted, in your dealings, a man with half an ear?"

"Half an ear? No, I have not. Is this a man who was wounded in battle? Someone punished at the Cross of Trahoir, and the executioner botched the job?"

"I do not know the origin of the deformity."

"Pray tell, what leads you to ask such a question?"

Hunter hesitated, unwilling to reveal all. "I have reason to believe that a man with half an ear—his left ear—is connected with George Pickering's death. He was asking for Pickering a few days before he was killed." He decided not to mention the Hooded Man, considering Lepage's previous comment. "On the day of the attack, I saw a half-eared man at the Château de Madrid."

"And you believe he may be the one who asked about Pickering?"

"I do not know what to think for certain. It could be that Pickering offended someone important. He seemed to have a knack for that. Or that someone who had entrusted him with a secret discovered he was speaking regularly with Ambassador Walsingham."

"And he was killed for that?" Lepage sounded doubtful. "It is difficult imagining anyone would trust Pickering with a secret so valuable that they would kill him for revealing it." It was the same objection Barnes had raised.

"If you would just keep your eyes open for a man with half an ear," Hunter said.

"Do you know any more about this man?" Lepage asked. "Tall or short? Dark or fair?"

"Dark hair and beard, a broad face, of average height, stout."

"Humph," Lepage exclaimed. "Your enquiry hangs by a very slender thread. But I will look out for such a man."

"Your handsome friend, Master Sidney, left you a message." Madame Moreau handed him a note to him. "And he sent one for me as well. He apologized for not taking lodgings here, but to make amends, he and his companions will dine here tonight."

Hunter read his message. Sidney had found lodgings nearby, in the rue Saint-Martin. After supper, he hoped Hunter would accompany him to the Place de Grève to witness the Feast of Saint John festivities.

"He spoke highly of Auguste's cooking," she smiled.

"As well he should."

"And afterward you will go to the Place de Grève?"

"You know as much about my movements as I do."

"That is a change from the last week." Her tone said that she had not yet forgiven him.

"I saw them stacking the wood for the bonfire in the Place," he steered the conversation away from his absence, "and gathering bags of stray cats."

"Each year they try to get more of them. How was your embassy conference?"

"No one has discovered the prime mover behind Nadeau. A servant at the embassy was a member of his confraternity and will be dismissed."

"A slender connection," she said. "Perhaps the man loses his position without cause."

"So Walsingham himself argued, but Beale and Lepage said it was better to be overcautious."

"Ah, Monsieur Lepage, the notary with a finger in every pie," she exclaimed.

"Why do you sneer every time I mention his name?"

"Just that he knows everyone's business, but where he stands is a mystery."

Hunter could not disagree.

"And what will you do with your time," she continued, "now that your celebrations are over and your reports are written?"

"Well, I must distribute the cloth that came with Lord Lincoln to those who can influence favorable terms for the syndicate." The smiling face of Madame Challon flashed in his mind. "Though I must await instructions from London before discussing details of the staple."

Marguerite arched one eyebrow. "Perhaps that will allow you to spend more time at your lodgings."

Spectators gathered at the Place de Grève several hours before darkness would fall on this Midsummer Eve. Smoke from many smaller bonfires about the city filled the air. The explosion of firecrackers punctuated the evening. After dining at L'Échiquier, Sidney's party arrived early enough to secure places near the bonfire logs, now piled as high as a man could reach, their crevices crammed with faggots and straw. Militiamen with halberds stood in a circle several yards from the stacked logs, keeping the crowds away. Izard strutted down the line of militiamen. As he passed, each man straightened up, adjusted his sash, or polished the blade of his halberd with an apologetic look. When Izard reached the young man standing before Hunter, he ordered him to adjust his hat. Izard glanced past the boy, recognized Hunter, and smiled. Was he thinking of the morning he dumped samples in the Paris mud? He nodded and continued along the line of militiamen.

Bryskett returned from a nearby shop with three bottles of wine. While waiting, they began to discuss the belief that fern seed was only visible for gathering on Saint John's Eve, and that it had the power to make one invisible. Sidney dismissed it as nonsense.

Hunter agreed, but speculated as to the effectiveness of such an herb. "Would it make you invisible for an hour? A day? How much fern seed would a person need to take?"

"A more important question is how one would use such a potent herb," Madox said.

"I would choose to visit the bowers of certain ladies each evening," Bryskett said.

"Ah, ha!" Sidney exclaimed.

"No," Bryskett objected. "Not to do the ladies any mischief, but only to see their full beauty."

"Do you believe that, Griffin?" Sidney asked.

"Not for a moment. Did you see the way he eyed Madame Moreau?" Madox said.

"Oh? Did you not examine her every limb yourself, Griffin?" Bryskett said.

"Even Sidney said she was pleasant to look at," Madox protested.

"I did," Sidney admitted. "Given her beauty and the quality of the food, I was a fool not to discard the lot of you and take a chamber at L'Échiquier."

"Your rejection strikes me to the heart." Bryskett thumped his chest dramatically. "Yet your true reason is to elude me and indulge in acts of folly that your father bid me prevent."

"It was folly for my father to select you as a traveling companion to watch my morals. I will put it to Griffin, whether it is more likely I will go astray myself or you will lead me astray."

"I dare take no side it this quarrel," Madox said.

"Your father's injunction to guard you against vice was not an instruction that I avoid all temptations," Bryskett said.

"So I must do as you say, not as you do," Sidney said.

"Precisely," Bryskett said. "But pray tell us what you would do with fern seed, Philip."

"I would use it to become the best of Her Majesty's intelligencers," Sidney said. "Imagine the secrets one could discover standing invisible in the closets of the Louvre or the Escorial."

The idea appealed to Hunter. "One might prevent a war."

"A much better use of invisibility than Bryskett's peeping," Madox said.

"I thought you were staying out of this," Bryskett said. "Do you believe using invisibility for intrigue is better than for observing beauty?"

"If that is what you call it," Sidney said.

Their banter continued, but Hunter imagined for a moment what an invisible spy could accomplish.

"English?" A tall, gangly man with a protuberant nose addressed him.

"I beg your pardon," Hunter said in French.

"Is that English you speak?"

"Yes."

"See." The man turned to his fat, ruddy-faced companion. "They are not Germans." He turned back to Hunter. "Are you visitors, come to see our celebrations of Saint John's Eve?"

"Yes."

"I am called Richard and my friend is Guillaume," the tall man said.

Hunter introduced himself and the members of Sidney's party. They engaged in small talk, though someone had to translate for Madox, who understood only a little French. Richard said they served a gentleman at a small farm beyond the faubourg Saint Martin. He explained how a crane had been moved from the river to stand beside the bonfire stack. "They will attach the bag of cats to the crane and swing it over the bonfire. Even above the noise of the crowd, you can hear them scream. It is good sport."

"This year they have captured a fox too," Guillaume added. "The cats and fox will fight until they feel the fire."

Although the servants were social inferiors, Sidney showed them every courtesy and even tolerated Guillaume's detailed description of how he would ravish virgins if he could become invisible. To interrupt his narrative, Sidney suggested Bryskett buy a bottle of wine for the Frenchmen.

After he returned through the considerable crowd, trumpets sounded, and everyone turned towards the coaches arriving from the Louvre. Hunter recognized the Dukes of Nevers, Guise, and Tavannes among the nobles who followed the king into the wooden gallery, festooned in gold and purple. He noticed Izard had positioned himself near the gallery. At a signal from the king, six city councilors with torches lit the bonfire stack. While it gained strength and dusk fell, a consort of crumhorns, shawms, and sackbuts played, and young men danced raucously around it. As the flames grew, they retreated, and four men marched forward, bearing a pole with a sack hanging beneath. The squirming bulges and yowls issuing from it made its contents clear. The men attached the bag to the crane. They cranked a wheel and the bag slowly rose in the air. The crowd cheered. As the fire reached its greatest intensity, the bag touched the top of the crane. Now the men transferred to a horizontal wheel, cranking it slowly to propel the bag out over the bonfire. The heat from the fire made Hunter's face flush, but the crowd behind him was too tightly packed for him to back away.

"Those are Protestant cats!" a voice called, and the crowd laughed its approval. The yowls from the bag rose in pitch and the squirming became more violent. The men lowered it a foot, and the cats began to scream. The crowd pressed forward and the militiaman, turned towards the spectacle with his halberd parallel to the ground, gave way a few paces. A spark caught on the bag's surface and its glowing infection spread over the trembling canvas. The bottom of the bag began to smolder.

Hunter realized it was damp from the animal's excretions. While those behind him shouted in excitement, his spirit rebelled. The street cats were pests, but to be enclosed in the dark, scratched and mauled by others, then suddenly to feel your flesh on fire…

The bag erupted in flames and the cats' screams blended with those of the crowd. One side ruptured, and the fox and cats, their fur ablaze, fell into the bonfire while the crowd roared its approval and surged forward.

A sudden blow in Hunter's back knocked him over the militiaman's halberd towards the bonfire. He twisted to his right, but his left forearm landed on a burning brand. His sleeve ignited. Heat seared his arm and forehead. He could smell his hair burning. The militiaman and Sidney leapt forward, pulled him back, and rolled him over. Sidney beat at the burning sleeve with his hat while Bryskett poured wine on his hair. Sidney peered into his face. "Are you all right?" Over his shoulder, the boy militiaman gaped in terror.

"My arm," Hunter said through gritted teeth. "Someone pushed me towards the fire." Beyond the pain, he was angry with himself. He had become too complacent, too confident that all those he had met believed his claims. The expatriates had accepted him as a secret Catholic; the officials and noblemen knew him as the syndicate agent; only Walsingham, Beale, Crespin, and Marguerite knew he was an intelligencer. And yet here he lay, in pain, his hair and eyebrows singed, and blisters rising on his arm and forehead.

Bryskett turned. Behind him Richard and Guillaume also turned, shouting, "You there, you bastard! You've injured a man! Stop, you rascal!" They pushed their way back through the crowd, provoking curses as they went. The young militiaman regained his composure and, facing the crowd with his halberd, ordered them to move back from the flames.

A woman who had been shouting in excitement at the cats' torment a moment ago gave Hunter her kerchief to bind his arm. A man handed him a wet cloth to wipe his face. Thanking these benefactors with some coins, Sidney helped his friend to his feet. Bryskett and Madox supporting Hunter on either side, they guided him through the crowd out of the Place. Behind them, they could hear Izard dressing down the young militiaman.

"I hope Richard and Guillaume catch the rascal who pushed them into Paul," Sidney said.

"I beg your pardon, sir," Madox said, "but I would swear there was no one behind those two shoving, though they turned to complain as soon as the tall one lunged into Paul's back. And though my French is poor, I am sure those behind denied pushing them."

"Then we were fools to let them run away chasing a phantom," Bryskett said.

"Events tumbled too fast for us to be nurses and watchmen at the same time," Sidney said. "Let us be sure Paul reaches his chamber safely."

CHAPTER 14

A Hot Summer

Tuesday, 24 June–Friday, 4 July 1572

F<small>OR THE NEXT WEEK AND A HALF</small>, H<small>UNTER STAYED AT</small> L'É<small>CHIQUIER</small>. His left forearm swelled with blisters and he could not bear that any cloth touch it. In his mirror, he was dismayed to see singed hair, discolored skin, and ugly blisters on the left side of his face. "I shall only approach you from the right," Marguerite teased, but she did not allow him out of bed the first two days after his accident. Sidney, Bryskett, and Madox visited often, usually, he noticed, at mealtimes. Although he tried not to flex his left arm, he was able to write with his right hand, so he set about condensing and sorting his papers.

When told of the incident on Saint John's Eve, Crespin assured them that Richard and Guillaume were known rogues.

"Why should they want to harm him?" Sydney asked.

"Because someone paid them." Crespin shrugged.

"Who?" Edward asked. Madame Challon's probing questions troubled him, but he could not connect her with the attack. More likely his questions about maimed soldiers had alerted someone who had hired the Hooded Frenchman.

"Someone who is against the English treaty?" Sidney said.

"The same someone who hired a groom to attack the ambassadors?" Bryskett offered.

"Surely no one considers me of equal importance with Lord Lincoln and Ambassador Walsingham," Hunter objected, "and the treaty is already signed."

"Could we report the incident to the Châtelet?" Sidney asked.

Again Crespin shook his head. "What can you report? That you think someone pushed you on purpose? They would laugh at you. Even if they did find the men, they would deny everything. Could we produce a witness?"

"I am sure I saw the tall man, Richard, lunge against Master Adams," Madox said.

Crespin and Bryskett regarded one another skeptically. Madox's word would scarcely be sufficient. Although they had stood in the middle of hundreds of people, they could not easily find a witness that would hold weight with the Châtelet.

"What have you done to offend someone?" Sidney asked.

"I may have committed a *faux pas* at one banquet or another," Hunter joked.

"Poor table manners would not be reason enough to roast you," Bryskett said.

"Had you cross words with anyone?" Sidney continued.

"No one."

Sidney rose. "Well, think on it. Someone wishes you ill. I must go now to Signore Coccitelli. As your right hand is whole, you should join me for next week's fencing lesson. And I'll arrange for a barber to attend you in a week as well. If the rest of your hair is cut short then, it will match what is growing."

Crespin rose, but Hunter signaled him to stay. After Sidney left, he said, "I may indeed have made errors at the banquets." He described his tangential questions about maimed servants. "If Pickering was murdered because of his involvement with some nobleman of the Court, then my questions may have alerted him to my interest in his half-eared servant."

"Whom did you ask about maimed serving men?" Crespin asked.

"I spoke to the Duke of Nevers, and to servants of the Duke of Retz and the Count of Cossé." He paused, "And one of Queen Catherine's maids of honor..."

"In short," Crespin said, "Half the Court may know of your curious enquiries by now."

Hunter sighed. "I suppose you are right."

"I fear neither you nor I can discover the actions of those of rank," Crespin said, "but I will keep *my* ear open for gossip." He smiled as Hunter winced.

Roger Barnes visited, with best wishes for his recovery from the expatriates and a warning that they would expect a full report of the banquets he had attended when he recovered.

Jeanne, the dark-haired chambermaid, contrived to visit his chamber frequently. Her forward manner when asking if she could do anything to make him feel better showed her interest too clearly. Uncomfortable, Hunter asked Marguerite to keep her away.

On the first of July, Sidney's barber trimmed his hair so that it looked somewhat more even. "Passable," was Marguerite's verdict. Although he could move his left arm with care, he asked Crespin to deliver the promised gifts of cloth to some Paris aldermen. After receiving a letter and two écus from Secretary Beale, he took the manuscript of the Catholic pamphlet and the payment to the printer Nicolas Colin.

On Friday the fourth of July, Hunter ventured out to observe Sidney's fencing lesson with Signore Coccitelli. He returned to find a letter from Uncle Babcock. The syndicate thanked him for his comments on Viscount Harduin's letter. Some felt the idea of a tariff that decreased was good, but most objected to the initial level of the tariff. Some wanted the Privy Council to send a commission to France, some argued Hunter could represent their interests more cheaply, and some felt that even maintaining Hunter in Paris was too expensive. This latter group also grumbled about the value of the cloth they had sent with Lord Lincoln. A faction of the Merchant Adventurers continued their pressure to delay establishing a Rouen Staple, hoping Antwerp would reopen to English merchants. His uncle could not guarantee how long the syndicate would underwrite his stay in Paris.

Marguerite was busy directing Marie, Jeanne, and Laurent to prepare rooms for gentlemen accompanying Henri of Navarre. "They will be staying for over a month. They say all the accommodations near the Louvre have been taken."

"You will do well on this Valois-Bourbon wedding," Hunter said.

"These gents are only the beginning. A couple from Troyes will arrive, and a gentleman from Bordeaux with his family. It is lucky for you you are such a good lover, otherwise I would throw you out and rent your room for double the price in August."

My room may be empty by then, he thought, remembering his uncle's letter, but he did not want to spoil the moment with Marguerite.

Tuesday, 8 July 1572

Hunter stood beside Philip Sidney in the Collège du Plessis, overlooking the rue Saint-Jacques. The crowds below cheered as the Dukes of Anjou, Alençon, and Guise led several hundred horsemen south, out the Porte Saint-Jacques. The mayor and aldermen in their scarlet robes, accompanied by archers, followed them as far as the city gate. The noise from the faubourg Saint-Jacques alerted all to the fact that Henri, King of Navarre, had arrived.

After a ceremony of welcome by the city officials, the combined retinues of Valois and Bourbon rode slowly into Paris. Although the riders had judiciously mingled, it was clear which party was which. All who accompanied Henri of Navarre were dressed in black, still mourning Queen Jeanne d'Albret. In contrast, the Court nobles shimmered in cloth of gold, cloth of silver, and rich hues of blue and scarlet. Henri himself, a sparse reddish beard emphasizing his youth, rode between Anjou and Alençon. The cheers might have seemed like a welcome, but Hunter heard calls of "Monsieur" and "Anjou," not "Navarre." A louder, more enthusiastic cry went up when the dark-clad Prince of Condé, riding next to the Duke of Guise, passed by.

"They are cheering the Duke," Sidney said.

"Yes," Hunter agreed. The Dukes of Nevers and Tavannes passed, then a group with Admiral Coligny and the Count La Rochefoucauld. "And now they become silent and as severe as the mourning clothes on the riders." The stern faces showed the citizens of Paris were not pleased to see hundreds of Huguenots enter their city. The cavalcade took over an hour, but once the more illustrious members had passed, the crowd began to dwindle, as did Sidney's interest.

Upon his return to L'Échiquier, Madame Moreau, in an effervescent mood, introduced Hunter to the guests from Pau and Béarn. Bernard Coran was a squat, dark man about thirty, his face set in a permanent frown, who spoke with a pronounced Béarnais accent. Vincent de Galion appeared to be the same age, but of opposite temperament, his face usually lit with a smile. Guillaume Poudampa was younger, with a military bearing and a serious expression. Guy Mongaston was the youngest, blond-haired, and visibly excited to be in Paris for the first time.

They told of their long journey from the south during June, each describing an inconvenience, delay, or accident greater than the one before. Coran's tale was all complaint, but de Galion chose to laugh at his own misfortunes. Poudampa summarized the trip as "Mud at the beginning; dust at the end." All had attended Jeanne d'Albret's funeral in Vendôme the previous week.

Coran complained Paris was too hot and stank. Mongaston said he expected to find enough pleasures to counteract the stink. Hunter described what he had observed that morning.

"I saw their sour faces," Coran snarled, his dark face as sour as any Hunter had seen earlier.

"We cannot expect the benighted Catholics of Paris to welcome those who follow the light of Reform," Poudampa said, "but the king's edicts forbidding the carrying of arms and the molestation of King Henri's followers should help maintain the peace."

"I imagine their humor will change next month," said de Galion. "After all, we have come to celebrate a wedding. The union of King Henri and Princess Marguerite promises a new era of peace."

Hunter said he hoped so.

"All those who attend a wedding can enjoy the wine," Mongaston said, "even if they do not like the bridegroom."

Thursday, 10 July 1572

Hunter's warm welcome at the Antelope revealed his increased esteem with the expatriates. Barnaby Timmons was the first to ask if he had recovered from his burns, but all expressed concern over his ordeal and gathered to examine the healing wounds on his face. Hunter thanked them for their concern and repeated that he believed the incident was an accident.

"I hope you are right, Master Adams," Sir James said. "Huguenots, Jews, Italians, even Englishmen—it doesn't matter to the rabble as long as they have someone to hate. But to move to more pleasant topics, we are anxious to hear more details of your rubbing elbows with kings and princes."

"I would not describe it thus," Hunter said, "but I can relate what little I observed."

"Come, come," Richard Chandler said, "Do not be modest. You did attend ceremonies and banquets with royalty."

"I did, but only as one of hundreds who gazed respectfully at his superiors."

"Then King Charles did not invite you to the head table?" Kempson asked with a smile.

"From where I sat, I could barely see the head table," Hunter said.

"Let us all sit," Sir Gregory led him to the table in the center of the room. "It has been over a month since you shared a drink with us, so here is a full bottle for you alone. Your throat may get dry as you tell us your experiences. Pray begin with your account of the attack on the English ambassadors."

Hunter again told his story of the assassination attempt, their royal welcome at the Château de Madrid, the ceremony of ratification, and the ensuing celebrations. He was frequently interrupted by questions.

"I heard that Walsingham showed no fear," Timothy Heath said, "and that he raised no protest with the king after he was almost killed. Is that true?"

"Yes."

"Did you speak with Walsingham yourself?" Wilkes asked.

Conscious that Wilkes might know of any visit he had made to the embassy, Hunter replied he had seen the ambassador on Saint John's Eve, to report on meetings with Viscount Harduin. Eyebrows rose at his mention of Harduin, but he begged to be excused from repeating any confidential treaty details.

When he described the ceremony of ratification, Barnaby Timmons lamented that English Catholics could now expect no help from King Charles, and Timothy Heath accused him of abandoning his sister-in-law Mary of Scotland. Kempson said they should not despair. "After all, any king's solemn oath lasts only so long as it is convenient—and any queen's as well."

When Hunter described the celebrations generally, Wilkes insisted that he recount each evening separately and in detail. Who had been seated where? What attention did the king give to Coligny? Anjou? the Duke of Guise? Which courtiers had not come to Coligny's affair?

Hunter answered as best he could, without revealing sensitive information. When he recounted the king's conferences with Coligny, Chandler interrupted with a diatribe against King Charles. "He has made a treaty with a Protestant queen, he takes advice from a Protestant general who has led an army against him, and now he prepares to fight for Protestant rebels in the Low Countries. Is this the way to keep his coronation oath to protect the Holy Catholic Church?"

Wilkes reminded him that a diplomatic reception obliged His Majesty to smile benevolently at all. Hunter confirmed that the king had meted out his time and attention among all the guests and that the entire Court feared a military expedition into the Low Countries. He described the speeches of congratulations and formal pledges of everlasting loyalty that had been made each evening.

Thomas Fisher interrupted. "All that is predictable tripe. I have listened patiently to the dissection of Court factions—who sat next to whom, who spoke with whom, and who smiled at whom. I want to know *who is sleeping with whom*! Did Master Adams hear no scandal during a week of banquets?"

Hunter was relieved to move from Court politics, where he had to be constantly aware of which facts to recount and which to conceal, to Court gossip. As he repeated what he had heard and described flirtations he had seen, the mood in the Antelope lightened. The expatriates exchanged ribald comments. When he stopped to sip his wine, Fisher asked if he had encountered any of the flying squad.

Remembering Madame Challon, he said, "I certainly saw many beautiful ladies, and was so fortunate as to speak to a few, but none identified herself as one of the flying squad."

"You could no more expect that, than that she would hike up her gown and invite you to board her," Fisher guffawed.

"Thomas," Wilkes said, "you have had your dose of Court tittle-tattle. Allow me to ask Master Adams about some matters of consequence."

Fisher scowled, but shrank into himself and gulped his wine.

"You spent some time with Lord Lincoln's party, particularly young Sidney, the Earl of Leicester's nephew," Wilkes began. "That should have allowed you to gain some knowledge of how matters stand at Whitehall."

Hunter had foreseen this. He had to give Wilkes some intelligence that could be used for the Catholic cause, without betraying any confidence. "The Queen Mother gave Lord Lincoln a letter for the Queen. No one read it, of course, but everyone said it urged Her Majesty to marry the Duke of Alençon."

"That much has been rumored for weeks," Kempson sniffed. "Surely you heard something more than that."

"Sidney was reluctant to say much about his uncle," Hunter said, "but he did mention that the Earl opposes the Alençon marriage and favors English intervention in the Netherlands."

"Leicester's opposition to Alençon is no surprise," Kempson said. "He opposes the Queen's marriage to anyone but himself. He has long dreamt of founding the House of Dudley."

"What is the Queen's opinion on the Netherlands?" Wilkes asked. "I have heard that a company of English 'volunteers' under Sir Humphrey Gilbert has landed in Flushing."

"I heard that as well only yesterday," Hunter admitted, "but no one in Lord Lincoln's party spoke of that."

"That is odd. Sir Arthur Champernowne, Gilbert's uncle, was one of the delegation."

"Perhaps I should say no one spoke of Sir Humphrey within my hearing."

"Did Gilbert not serve under Sidney's father in Ireland?" Wilkes pressed. "Was it not Sir Henry Sidney that knighted him for slaughtering Irish women and children?"

Hunter felt himself flush. The implication was clear. Gilbert was Sidney's client. Sidney must have promoted an English invasion of Holland, and his son must have had knowledge of it. "I believe Sir Henry did knight him—for defeating armed rebels. I too have heard Gilbert slaughtered women and children, which is a sin he will have to answer for." He paused, but Wilkes still gazed at him. "Sir Henry is no longer Lord Deputy. He is living on his estates in England, according to his son. Philip left England in early June."

"Well after Flushing had revolted. Probably about the time an expedition under Gilbert was being organized," Wilkes said.

Hunter struggled to disguise his discomfort. "However that may be, if he knew anything of this, he said nothing to me." Then he added to redeem himself, "But I shall mention Gilbert in conversation and try to draw him out on the subject."

"What matter is it whether this young Sidney knew of Gilbert's expedition?" Kempson asked. "Everyone expected that the more zealous English Protestants might sail to the Low Countries."

"Though everyone might repeat speculation," Wilkes replied, "precise information might allow an appropriate military response." A look of apprehension passed over his face. "That is, if one had means to relay such information to the Duke of Alva." Perhaps Kempson's objection had led Wilkes to reveal information he should have kept secret. Did he have a communication link with Alva?

"I doubt any exact information exists," Kempson said. "Coligny itches to ride into Flanders with a force of Huguenots, but has he concocted plans that could be classified as 'precise information'? He will not move while the king vacillates."

"Deciding the fate of kingdoms must be wearisome work for you two," Fisher said dryly.

"One need not be a councilor to consider affairs seriously," Wilkes snapped.

"Such consideration is more useful than taking refuge in wine," Kempson said.

Chandler added, "You seem to return again to your position that only the great can influence affairs. I thought you had conceded that disputation to me."

Fisher smiled, raised his glass, and said, "*Salut.*"

"Master Adams," Heath said, "you have not told us if you met those gentlemen at Court that Sir James mentioned." He turned to Kempson. "I apologize for not recalling their names."

"Father Grouard, the master of the chapel, and Sieur Charles Vinet, *Grand Panetier*," Kempson said.

"Unfortunately, I did not," Hunter said. "As you intimated, Sir James, I am sure both were occupied with arrangements necessary for the ceremonies."

Kempson smiled. "Then, aside from a few of the lovely ladies of the Court, you spoke only with lackeys?"

Hunter could not resist. "The Lord of Damville said to give Sir Gregory his regards, and the secretary of Bishop Gondi recalled meeting you, Sir James, but I would hardly call them lackeys."

"Indeed not," Kempson quickly agreed.

"And the Duke of Nevers said he had met with some Englishmen who were living in Paris," Hunter continued.

Surprise registered on the expatriates' faces.

"How did you happen to speak with His Grace the Duke?" Wilkes's voice held a hint of incredulity.

"I had the good fortune to be seated near one of his bookkeepers at a banquet, and he introduced me to His Grace." No need to mention his questions about maimed serving men.

"Of what did you speak?" Wilkes asked.

"Of honor and duty."

After a moment, Chandler asked, "You spoke only of abstractions?"

"No," Hunter said. "He commended a servant for bravery and praised Ambassador Walsingham for his loyalty to Queen Elizabeth." Chandler snorted his disapproval, but Hunter continued. "He speculated regarding the conflict some men feel between their duty to their sovereign and to God."

"Oh, ho!" Fisher exclaimed. "You did converse with the great! And on deep matters, as well."

"Did His Grace honor you with his solution to such a difficult conflict?" Wilkes asked.

"I do not believe he had a solution, but was grateful he felt no such conflict," Hunter said.

"And did you tell him your choice?" Wilkes pressed.

Hunter remembered his reply—that he hoped to be loyal to both his queen and his God—a truthful reply, but not one that Paul Adams, the secret Catholic, could give. "I am thankful he did not require my answer. You know that I must take great care to keep my beliefs secret. I remind you all of the trust I place in you."

"We will all be mindful of your situation," Sir James said, "but I would be curious to hear more of the duke's thoughts."

"He questioned the sincerity of the Huguenots' declarations of loyalty to King Charles," Hunter said.

"As well he should," Chandler interjected.

"And he seemed to favor the German solution of *cuius region, eius religio.*"

Timmons, long silent, spoke up. "That may be an admirable political solution, but it places the fate of subjects' souls in the hands of each ruler. Think how many may suffer from the error of one prince!"

"But one may move where his faith is that of the ruler, as we have," Barnes said.

"Not all have the means we do," Timmons replied. "Can a peasant leave his land? Will a cobbler be welcomed by a guild hundreds of leagues away?"

The conversation shifted from Hunter's experiences to the practical difficulties of relocating to a territory whose ruler believed as one did, then on to religious questions: Would a subject suffer eternal punishment for the sins of his ruler? Did God demand absolute obedience, or would His grace extend to those forced to participate in heretical ceremonies? Would outward conformity or inner faith weigh more in the Final Judgment? During the discussion, Hunter was aware of glances at him. Surely he was an example of one who hid his faith, and more for convenience than necessity.

When all rose to leave, Sir Gregory plucked him aside. He had received Hunter's note and asked him to come to his lodgings on Monday to discuss the transport of pamphlets. He would also have to arrive with some information from Philip Sidney.

"King Charles's proclamation recalling Frenchmen from Mons and forbidding others to go fools no one," Zuñiga said. "It is fiction, as bad as the rebel magistrates of Holland swearing fidelity to King Philip. William of Orange spouted the same equivocations when he crossed the Rhine with fifteen thousand foot. All this diplomatic double talk."

As a diplomat, you should know, the Hooded Man thought, but he said, "It would be too much to expect the French to admit they would love to seize Hainault and Artois. Honesty would result in a war King Charles would be bound to lose. Better to let Huguenot 'volunteers' aid their Reformed brethren. If the Dutch rebels should win and ask him to 'protect' the western provinces, he will graciously accept. If they are defeated, as in all probability they shall be, he can wash his hands of them."

"Ah, 'volunteers!' I hear English 'volunteers' have landed in Flushing. Elizabeth of England is a she-cat of the same stripe as Charles of France. She will wink at any mischief, so long as she may deny it later."

"Their fear argues King Philip's strength."

"I thank you for your optimism, but the tide of events appears to be flowing against us. No matter what they claim, towns in Holland and Zeeland have rebelled against His Majesty, Orangists control the northern provinces, and William is about to march on Brabant. France and England ratified their treaty a month ago, and both now have 'volunteers' in the Netherlands. A French army under Genlis marches to the frontier as we speak. And in one month Margot of Valois will marry a Protestant."

"But surely, in the long run..."

"In the long run, yes, King Philip can crush them all...at a cost." Zuñiga raised a forefinger. "But I had not finished my list. I was about to add that your own machinations have borne no fruit. The attack on the ambassadors failed. You are fortunate that no suspicion has fallen on you...yet."

Zuñiga's statement was a question. Had King Charles's agents found evidence beyond Nadeau? The Hooded Man knew they had not. But one man was moving towards a discovery. He had been injured on Saint John's Eve. Now he appeared to have abandoned his enquiries, but if he moved in the wrong direction, he must be dealt with. "No suspicion will fall upon me, or you, I assure you. The English Embassy remains penetrated; Walsingham might still meet with an accident."

"We have discussed that before. An accident is only an accident. To be truly effective, the manner of the ambassador's death must throw suspicion onto the French Crown."

"And neither of us has devised a way to do that yet." The Hooded Man was unwilling to take all the responsibility.

"No," Zuñiga said. "It is better to wait. An opportunity will present itself."

Monday, 14 July 1572

Hunter had decided to deliver the lengths of mockado and Worcester to the Louvre himself, on the chance that Madame Challon might accept them personally. Although his wounds were yet unsightly, and his hair had not grown back sufficiently, why should he care that she might recoil from his appearance? If he were true to Marguerite, he should not have such worries. But why was he thinking in terms of being true? He and Marguerite were lovers, but, as she frequently said, it was only temporary. He would leave.

Hunter crossed the pont Saint Michel and turned right. What had started him on this train of thought? Yes, Marguerite's joy when he presented her with fine English cloth. She had kissed him deeply. What bliss! Was it not enough to bask in the sunshine of the present moment, without questioning himself about his every thought? Best to clear his mind and to concentrate on the task ahead of him. Presently, he knocked on Sir Gregory's door.

Robert led him up. Sir Gregory bid him sit and asked Robert to bring them wine.

Hunter seized the initiative. "Master Colin informs me that I may collect my pamphlets at the Cardinal's Hat. I am grateful that you agreed to see me today, so that I might make arrangements to transport them to England as soon as possible. I fear that Francis Reddan will feel I have been too long about this business."

"Let us come to that in a moment," Wilkes said. "I wish to know first if you learned any more of Sir Humphrey Gilbert's plans from your friend Sidney."

"I did ask him. He was not surprised to hear Sir Humphrey had landed in the Low Countries. His father had spoken to him at Court, but he had never come to Penhurst. He did not know if his uncle Leicester had encouraged Sir Humphrey to go to the Netherlands."

"Did you think he was telling the truth?"

"I did. He was glad Englishman had sailed to aid the Hollanders, and hoped Protestants might prevail, but he said all was in God's hands."

"He knew nothing of plans to link these English 'volunteers' with an army of Huguenots?" Sir Gregory arched his brows.

"No," Hunter said. "He is less involved in matters of state than you believe. I know his Dudley and Sidney lineage makes him destined for high office, but just now his concerns are those of a scholar. He spoke of meeting Hubert Languet, the Ambassador of Saxony. At Languet's suggestion, he spends hours each day reading, and translates Latin passages into French and then back again. He buys books and attends public lectures. Paris is his first stop on a Continental tour."

Robert entered with the wine. "Perhaps you are right," Sir Gregory said, "but I daresay his discussions with Languet involve religion and politics as well as learning. And a man traveling through Europe might also gather information about a city's fortifications, the inclinations of foreign rulers...Thank you, Robert."

Hunter began a second attempt. "Sir Gregory, you believe the written word may do as much for one's cause as the sword, and I am in agreement. These conflicts in the Low Countries are less important to me than the conflict for the minds and souls of Englishmen. That is why I am eager to see my pamphlets on their way."

Sir Gregory sipped his wine. "I can arrange that."

"I am grateful for your assistance. As you know, I am in the process of distributing cloth samples to certain officials. It will be simple to collect the pamphlets, conceal them in a barrow, and bring them to your lodgings. Would that be agreeable, or should I transport them to a carter or a boatman?"

"How many copies?"

"Five hundred. They are sixteen pages only, so they do not take up much space."

"Then bring them here."

"When could they cross the Channel? I need to write Reddan when to expect the pamphlets in London." Hunter jerked back suddenly, as if stunned by a thought. "But I am ahead of myself. I imagine you will include my pamphlets with some of your projects. Though my pamphlets are to end up in London, I imagine the captain you employ more often lands in Kent or Sussex."

Wilkes's face tightened. Perhaps Hunter had asked for too much information at once. "Several ports could be used, and several ships. Perhaps your pamphlets might sail to London itself. The choice depends on information you might obtain."

This was another test. "What information?"

"You visit the embassy frequently, do you not?"

"Yes."

"Say you need to send expensive books to London, or some clothes you have purchased here—you can fabricate whatever tale you wish—but, as the shipment is important to you, say you fear it may be seized by pirates, and ask where Her Majesty's ships are likely to be, in order to send your packet by that route. Ask which ports are most watched and therefore are safest."

Hunter nodded. "Then we will arrange to send the pamphlets away from those sea lanes and ports."

"Exactly," Wilkes smiled. He sipped his wine again.

Hunter copied him and considered his next question. "Then it may be some time before the shipment can be arranged?"

"Not necessarily. One shipment is now ready. Once you obtain good information, we should move at once."

"But I might not have time to communicate with Master Reddan."

"If your letter goes off a few hours before the pamphlets, that should be enough time. Can they not remain with a trusted recipient until Reddan arranges collection?"

"I shall send a message as soon as I find out where they might be collected," Hunter said. "Would you have any idea what it will cost to ship them?"

"I would estimate three to four livres."

"So much?"

"Any captain landing Catholic pamphlets in England is running a risk, as is anyone holding them for collection, or carrying them to London. I will bear a greater cost than you."

Is that because you will be transporting books? Hunter might appear too curious if he asked. "Well, I will tend to first things first. I will visit the embassy to discover what I can of naval patrols, then I will collect the pamphlets and bring them here with the news."

Who am I becoming, Hunter asked himself, walking back from his meeting. I interrogate Sidney to feed information to Wilkes, so he will trust me with information I will turn over to Walsingham. So this is what it is to be a spy—betraying friends to enemies so that you can betray the enemies in their turn. Being berated by Captain Izard as a Protestant heretic and convincing the expatriates that you are a Catholic. What would happen if Wilkes told Sidney you were a secret papist? Is it only a matter of time before someone convinced Paul Adams is a Catholic speaks with someone who does not? The expatriates, he hoped, would keep his secret, but Robert and the urchins who guarded the statue of Our Lady believed he was a Catholic. So did Landon and Vasse at the Horn. How many had they told?

Yet it would do him little harm if other Parisians—the merchants, civic officeholders, Court officials—believed he was secretly a Catholic. It might even improve his influence. But if the Huguenots he had befriended heard that news, they would no longer trust him. Could he reveal his true mission to Sidney? No. If his own family was kept in the dark, how could he tell others?

Wednesday, 16 July 1572

A man Hunter had never seen opened the embassy door, a man of medium height with thinning sandy hair, who looked to be in his late thirties. "Is the ambassador expecting you?" he asked in French.

This was the new doorman Lepage had found to replace Pierre. "Yes. I am Paul Adams." Hunter pulled a note from his doublet. "Secretary Beale asked me to come at this hour. What is your name?"

"I call myself Alain Brune." He glanced uncertainly at the message. "Pray wait a moment while I check with the secretary."

It would not be easy to find a literate doorman, especially at low wages. Lepage had said he could hire two men to replace Pierre, for added security. Who was the second man, and where was he employed? Alain returned and asked him to follow.

Beale rose to greet him. "Ambassador Walsingham prays you will forgive him, but he is extremely busy just now. He hopes you are recovered from your injuries."

"Thank you, I have," Hunter said. "I understand why he may be busy. Many rumors about the Netherlands are flying through the city."

"What have you heard?"

"That an army of Huguenots crossed the frontier near Cambrai. Some say Coligny leads it, but others say he remains at Court. All think the force is to break the siege at Mons and relieve Nassau. I have heard Englishmen have landed at Flushing. English expatriates believe Sir Humphrey Gilbert is one of them. Are any of these rumors true?"

Beale smiled. "I can tell you Admiral Coligny is in Paris. Beyond that, I am not at liberty to say. But what of your progress with the Catholic pamphlets?"

"First, thank you for sending me funds. They will cover the cost of printing, but may not be enough for the transport. I have arranged to collect the pamphlets and take them to Sir Gregory Wilkes. He will send them with a shipment of his own."

"Have you discovered how he will transport them to England?"

"He said there are several ships and ports that might be used. He bid me, as a good Catholic, feign a need to transport something of great value, so I might enquire which sea routes are most secure, and which ports most closely watched."

"So, he employs you to pry information from us, as we employ you to pry information from him," Beale said.

"Yes," Hunter said. "He, of course, will use it to evade discovery."

"Well, he may be testing you." Beale glanced into the air above him. "Our knowledge is always stale. By the time we are informed of particular movements of the navy, the situation has changed. But hold a moment, let me speak to Ambassador Walsingham."

"Before you go," Hunter said, "let me tell you of Sir Gregory's particular interest in Gilbert's plans in the Netherlands, particularly if he might link with a Huguenot force. He spoke as though he might have means of communicating information to the Duke of Alva."

Beale nodded and left the room. He returned a few minutes later carrying a folder. "The ambassador thanks you for your information about Wilkes's possible connection with Alva. We have a plan." Beale opened the folder. "When you return to Sir Gregory, tell him the Channel to the west is being watched carefully, as England fears that ships from Spain may be bringing aid to Alva, so fewer vessels will be watching the Kent coast. That is at least partially true, should Wilkes have a way to confirm your information. At any rate, we do not want to intercept any papist pamphlets at sea. If we follow whatever texts Wilkes delivers, we may find an entire network of distribution in England, and identify those who are receiving this papist poison as well."

"So, I must discover where my pamphlets and his will land," Hunter said.

"We may be able to help." Beale said. "Say you have a contact at Sandwich who can arrange for one-third of the ship's cargo to evade customs. Say you are doing this in pious gratitude, for the captain's service to Catholicism. But not to seem suspiciously generous, ask that he cut his fee for transporting the pamphlets in return."

"I shall," Hunter said.

"As another enticement, you can say that Reddan has a contact in Sandwich who will collect the pamphlets. That will relieve Wilkes of the trouble of arranging delivery to London."

"Good. He asked if Reddan could not send someone to collect them," Hunter said, then added uneasily. "I am new to this, sir. I told Wilkes that once we determined the port, I would write Reddan to arrange collection. If he asks me who this man in Sandwich is, I do not know how to explain I instantly discovered him."

"I can supply you with a letter from Reddan to show Wilkes. In it, he will press you for the pamphlets, and ask to arrange delivery to one Thomas Miller at the Dolphin in Sandwich. Reddan will explain that he is the man who can arrange reduced customs as well. We can even include a password and reply he can pass on to the captain. Alas, we have no one who can encrypt it quickly."

"And if he should ask me to describe this Thomas Miller?" Hunter asked.

"Say you do not know the man personally. He works for Francis Reddan, who can inform Sandwich quickly once the shipping details are arranged."

"Your bait does sound tempting."

"I will send the 'letter from Reddan' to you tomorrow," Beale promised. "Good luck with your fishing."

Thursday, 17 July 1572

Hunter approached the Louvre, aware of the sweat running down his back. Crespin, dripping with perspiration, pushed the barrow behind him. This was not the appearance he had hoped to present, but he had not counted on such an abnormally hot day in July. He had dressed carefully that morning, in his gray suit with a newly starched ruff, to deliver the promised fabric to Madame Challon. His delay had been due to vanity, but his overheated state was a mix of vanity and folly. It was folly to wait for his burns to heal fully, to send her a letter apologizing for the delay and saying he would deliver it today, to take such pains to put himself in the presence of this fascinating but dangerous woman, and to imagine that she might receive the cloth directly from him.

The palace guard asked his business.

"I am Paul Adams of London, come to deliver a gift of cloth to Madame Challon."

The guard's eyebrows rose. "Wait a moment." He spoke with another guard, who nodded and headed away. "Our orders are to bid you wait inside." He looked at Crespin. "But your servant will have to stay outside."

Hunter was about to protest that Jacques was not his servant, but Crespin spoke up. "That's fine with me, master." He put an ironic twist on the last word. "Just give me a sol and I will wait in the ale house." He addressed the guard. "Shall I wheel these cloths in, or will you?"

"You may wheel the barrow inside the gate, then go back out."

Crespin did so with a smile and held out his hand. Hunter gave him a sol. "That should buy your silence as well as your drink." Crespin touched his cap and departed.

In response to Marguerite's enquiries, Hunter had explained that he was delivering samples requested months before to the mercers around Les Halles. He had not mentioned the destination of the two bolts in the bottom of the barrow. He had not told Crespin until those on top had been delivered. "No, they were not hidden. They were at the bottom because the Louvre was our furthest stop." Crespin had smiled. Hunter was aware again of his perspiration and wiped his brow with his handkerchief.

The second guard returned, followed by a boy. Hunter's spirits fell. He should have written a description of the two fabrics. How foolish he had been to expect he could describe their qualities to her. The boy said, "I serve Madame Challon. She bids you come speak with her. I will carry the parcels."

Hunter's pulse quickened, but he repressed a grin. "Thank you."

He followed the boy, who carried the large bolt of Worcester over his shoulder and the smaller bolt of mockado under his arm, across the court-yard, through a doorway, and up a winding staircase in the old part of the palace. He led Hunter down a corridor and stopped to knock on a door.

"Enter." Hunter did not recognize the voice. The boy opened the door and stood aside.

Hunter took a deep breath and stepped into the chamber to find Madame Challon and the Viscountess of Tours on settles, at right angles to one another. They smiled in amusement, and Hunter felt himself blush.

"Antoine, place the cloth on that bench," the viscountess said, "and fetch a jug of chilled water for us."

Madame Challon stood and stepped forward. "Master Adams, you remember Charlotte de Sauve, Viscountess of Tours, do you not?"

Charlotte de Sauve wore a light blue gown with tawny floral embroi-dery that matched her underskirt. From the low square-cut bodice a transparent ruff emerged to stand in a crescent behind her face. Her blue eyes gleamed beneath expressive eyebrows, her blonde hair had been arranged to form a heart-shaped frame for her high forehead, and her sensual mouth wavered between a smile and a smirk.

"How could I forget such a beautiful lady?" Hunter bowed.

"Marie told me you had a honeyed tongue," the viscountess said.

"I only speak the truth, but I thank you for your good opinion, Madame Challon."

"Opinions can change." Marie's large brown eyes danced. She wore a low-cut dark green bodice that pushed her breasts tight against her chest and complemented her light red gown. Unlike Charlotte de Sauve, she wore no collar, only a band around her neck. Her sleeves were transpar-ent silk. "You should have seen your expression when you entered. What did you expect to find?"

"As I had promised the cloth to you, Madame, I hoped to see you. I was surprised to find you both here—an honor unexpected but doubly delightful."

The women exchanged looks. "He says we are a double delight, Charlotte," Marie said.

"Another example of the honeyed tongue." The viscountess cut her eyes towards Hunter.

"To please us both, he must work twice as hard," Marie said. She giggled; Charlotte laughed deep in her throat.

"I hope my gift will please you," Hunter said. "And if you keep your part of the bargain, I will predict that in six months everyone at Court, even His Majesty, will be wearing English cloth."

"Let us see these fabulous fabrics, Marie." The viscountess rose.

"Allow me to describe them properly" Hunter crossed to the bench, untied the string, removed the paper, and picked up the smaller bolt. "This is a mockado from Norwich. The ground has a linen warp and a jersey weft. The pile is of silk and fine jersey wool. I am sure others at Court will take it for a piece of silk velvet. Feel it."

Both ladies handled the cloth. "It is very soft," Madame Challon said. The viscountess stroked her hand slowly beneath the fabric, her half-closed eyelids suggesting that every nerve was absorbing the sensation. "Yes," she exhaled, "one might stroke such a garment again and again." The ladies exchanged looks and smiles.

"I know that the mockadoes are impressive, and, as they are newly woven in England, they are much sought after, but you may have seen similar from the Low Countries." He unwrapped the larger packet and hoisted the larger bolt. "This is the finest traditional broadcloth of England—a Worcester long cloth, carded and spun from Leominster wool, seven quarters wide and thirty yards long. You may divide the two cloths as you wish. Both are white, so you may have them dyed any color you desire."

Marie held the mockado next to her light red gown. "I should imagine this dyed a deeper scarlet than my gown."

"Why not a deep murrey?" the viscountess asked.

"Perhaps. But there is not enough of this for us both to have a gown. I may leave this undyed and cut sleeves and a forepart from it, then dye the Worcester murrey and have my seamstress fashion the gown from that."

"The cloth wants adornment," the viscountess suggested. "Some embroidery with gold braid. You might line the sleeves with silk and slash them,"

The two ladies continued discussing fashion ideas as though Hunter were not there, then Charlotte caught her companion's eye, smiled, and turned to him. "And what cloth is in your fine gray doublet?" She fingered the shoulder roll.

"This is worsted russell, from Norwich. It was cut in the French style by a Parisian tailor only a month ago."

"You wore that to the Duke of Nevers's banquet," Madame Challon said.

Charlotte de Sauve looked him up and down slowly. "It fits you well." She met his glance boldly; her eyebrows seemed to ask a question.

A frisson of excitement mingled with fear surged through him. One of the most beautiful ladies of the French Court might actually be saying he was desirable. But why would such a courtly beauty pay attention to him? Perhaps she acted this way to every man she met, bestowing compliments to arouse hopes and desires. He was aware again of sweat running down his back.

Suddenly her eyebrows knit in concern. The viscountess touched his left temple. "But you have been injured here." Her lips opened slightly.

"Where?" Marie leaned in.

"I stumbled into a bonfire on Saint John's Eve," Hunter said, aware of little but the touch of the Viscountess and the closeness of both women.

"Does it give you much pain?" Marie asked.

"Not any more."

Charlotte glanced at Marie. "I shall give you a kiss of healing," She leaned forward and pressed moist lips against his left temple.

Hunter's heart beat faster. He sensed rather than saw Marie Challon tense. A knock at the door caused them all to spring apart.

"That doesn't count," Marie hissed under her breath.

The viscountess smiled. "Come in."

What didn't count? The kiss? What sort of game was this? Why not play along and enjoy it?

Antoine entered with a jug of water and three cups on a tray. "Place that on a stool near the settles," Marie said. The servant did so and bowed his way out. The women glided to the settles. Hunter eyed the bench that held the fabric, thinking to reposition it opposite the ladies.

"Come, sit next to me," Marie said. Hunter looked dubiously at the settle, mostly occupied by her gown. Was this another move in their game? "There is room enough." She shifted nearer the viscountess and pulled the hoops of her farthingale in the same direction.

Ignoring an inner warning voice, Hunter wedged himself next to Marie. The bottom half of her gown flowed back over his left leg. Her right thigh pressed against his. Charlotte de Sauve leaned forward with an annoyed expression and poured the water. Each took a cup. The water was unexpectedly cool.

"It flows pure from an underground spring in the palace," Marie explained.

"That is why it took so long," the viscountess said. "I must tell you, Master Adams, that Marie did not assess you well. Although she praised your appearance, after the Duke of Nevers's banquet she said you knew nothing of cloth, but today you have proved her wrong."

"I did not say he knew nothing of cloth," Marie corrected. "I said he spoke little about cloth that evening. My words were praise, not criticism. I said he was obviously much more than an agent of cloth merchants."

Hunter tensed.

The Viscountess of Tours appraised him again. "You may be right. I have heard he is seen with an important English visitor, Master Sidney. That both take fencing lessons from Signore Coccitelli."

"I had the good fortune to be chosen by our ambassador to introduce Philip Sidney to Paris," Hunter explained. "And he has been so kind as to invite me to accompany him on occasions. It is simply a case of two Englishmen together in a French city. In England, we would not move in the same circles at all."

"And you speak with the king's financier, with presidents of Parlement, with dukes!" Marie contradicted.

"My meetings with Viscount Harduin and members of Parlement were part of my task as the agent of the Rouen Syndicate, nothing more," he answered. "And you were there, my lady, when one of the Duke of Nevers's servants invited me to meet His Grace."

"Yes. It arose from your interest in maimed soldiers." Marie's eyes flashed. "An interest you never adequately explained."

Hunter reached for his cup and scrambled to change the subject. "I did explain that a man might be curious about many things, without hidden motives."

"Oh, yes," Marie exclaimed. "Master Adams was curious about some of Her Majesty's ladies-in-waiting. He seemed to believe that they could fly!"

The viscountess smiled and smirked simultaneously. "What an odd notion. How could any of us fly, weighed down as we must be with our gowns, petticoats, padded sleeves, and busks?" She looked up with mischievous eyes. "Perhaps if we stripped off our garments we might try. How much cooler we would be then."

Hunter pictured a naked Charlotte de Sauve, thinner, younger, and paler of complexion than Marguerite. He drained his cup.

"Charlotte," Marie chided, "we should help Master Adams to cool down. Your talk of shedding clothes might heat him further."

"It is not I, nestled next to him, covering his lap with my dress," she said. "But he does look as though he needs more water."

Marie Challon carefully pulled her gown from Hunter's leg and leaned forward to retrieve the jug. As she tipped it, the stream of water missed his cup and flowed onto his lap. He stood at once, frantically brushing off his trunk hose with his free hand as the cold liquid ran down his legs. Charlotte de Sauve's throaty laugh sounded.

"Oh, I am sorry," Marie giggled. She replaced the jug on the table, stood, and drew a handkerchief from her sleeve. Before he could stop her, she rubbed the handkerchief over his codpiece, then knelt before him. As he looked down at the swelling of her breasts, she ran the handkerchief up his right thigh.

"Thank you," Hunter choked out. "But do not trouble yourself. It will cool me now and soon dry."

Charlotte's laughter grew.

Marie tilted her head upward with a playful look and a smile, "But I must make amends for my clumsiness." She switched the handkerchief to her left hand and wiped slowly up his left leg from calf to scrotum.

Hunter's penis stirred. "Pray you, rise," he squeaked in panic, reaching down and pulling her up gently but firmly. For a few moments, he gazed into her roguish eyes, unable to speak. "I believe I had best pour myself a cup."

Both women laughed deeply as he did. Excited at Marie's touch, he was also embarrassed. He looked as though he had wet himself. He did not understand their game, but he felt somehow he had lost. He forced himself to join their laughter and drank his water. A point of etiquette offered him an opportunity to recover. "I beg your pardon, ladies, in my distress I was rude. May I pour you both a cup?"

Both stopped laughing aloud long enough to assent, but when they looked at one another their shoulders rocked in silent mirth. Hunter pretended not to notice and went about the business of pouring.

"Forgive me, Paul." Marie touched his hand gently as she took the cup from him.

Hunter felt a strange thrill; she had used his Christian name for the first time. "There is nothing to forgive," he said. "A trivial accident." As she held his gaze, it was clear she was aware her touch had aroused him. He turned and offered a cup to Charlotte de Sauve.

"Forgive my thoughtless laughter." Charlotte's eyes continued to dance in amusement.

Hunter continued to lean on manners. "You ladies have been so gracious, to share your time and refreshment with one of my station."

"You are the one who brought us gifts," Marie said, "and we have not been able to thank you adequately." Her eyes suggested more than polite words.

A knock sounded at the door. The viscountess bid the knocker enter, and Antoine quickly announced, "The Queen Mother requests that you ladies attend her at once."

From the women's faces, it was clear that they were disappointed, but that this command could not be ignored. "We must bid you farewell, Master Adams," Charlotte said. "Antoine can show you the way out."

"Alas, we may not see you again." Marie's regret seemed genuine. "I would that you might see us in the apparel we will make from your cloth."

"I wish that too," Hunter said, "though I know it is unlikely."

The women swept from the room, Marie looking over her shoulder and smiling. Antoine glanced at Hunter's wet crotch, then up at his face. Hunter assumed a stern expression and Antoine turned, suppressing a smile. Hunter followed him from the palace, picturing two cats playing with a terrified mouse.

Friday, 18 July 1572

"Your servant Robert stowed my pamphlets in a shed in your courtyard," Hunter said.

"Good," Wilkes said. "What did you discover at the embassy?"

Hunter relayed the news that the Queen's ships watched the western end of the Channel, with the caveat that such news was old. "But by a stroke of good fortune, we need not await an exchange of messages. Two days ago, I received a letter from Master Reddan urging haste and proposing a means of delivery in England." He pulled the forged letter from his doublet and handed it to Wilkes. "He seems to offer an advantage to any captain who can deliver the pamphlets as he wishes."

Wilkes read, occasionally hemming and grunting. He looked up and smiled. "This should work well. I know a captain in Boulogne with a cargo for Sandwich—paper and silk gloves, I believe, and a printing of Vaux's *Catechism* that should have arrived there from Louvain yesterday. Young Timmons might say that such a concurrence proves it is God's will." He chuckled. "Vaux's books were destined for Dover, but they may as well go with Baudin to Sandwich."

"Then the pamphlets will leave soon?" Hunter asked.

"They can leave Paris tomorrow. With a favorable wind, they should be in Sandwich within the week." Wilkes handed the letter back.

"If I may be so bold," Hunter said, "as the captain—what was his name?"

"Baudin."

"As Captain Baudin will avoid a portion of customs, I hope he might reduce the charges to both of us for the transport."

Wilkes smiled and nodded. "I shall suggest that. Will you join me in a glass of wine? We shall toast the success of our venture."

"I shall be happy to," Hunter said. He and Wilkes were thinking of different outcomes as successful.

As Robert fetched wine, Wilkes praised the effectiveness of Vaux's *Catechism*. "In the few years it has circulated, it has weaned hundreds of Catholics from the services of the Church in England. The more who refrain from a heretical rite, the more pressure builds for Queen Elizabeth to grant Catholics similar privileges as Huguenots have here."

Hunter could point out Huguenots had wrung those privileges from their monarch on the field of battle, but decided it was better to let Wilkes wax optimistic.

"Of course," Wilkes said as the wine arrived, "that is unlikely until Cecil—Lord Burghley now—falls from power. But he is old. The Queen herself may catch a fever at any time. If she dies, the nobility, even Robert Dudley, will trim their sails towards the House of Stewart. Let us drink to that." He raised his glass.

"To the House of Stewart." Hunter drank.

As he lowered his glass, a cloud passed over Sir Gregory's face. "I am surprised Francis Reddan did not write you in a cypher."

Hunter thought frantically. "He is not accustomed to. He sends his letters directly by messengers he trusts."

"I do have some knowledge of Catholic couriers," Wilkes said. "What is the name of this messenger?"

"Michael."

"Michael." Wilkes pondered a moment. "What does he look like?"

"A young man. Dark hair and eyes. A hooked nose. Thin. He wore simple clothes, like those of an apprentice," Hunter improvised.

Wilkes shook his head. "I will ask others if they know him."

Hunter knew no one would. "This was the first time I saw this Michael as a messenger."

"Reddan has used other men before?"

Hunter felt himself sinking deeper and deeper into a pit. "Yes, he has, but I have not seen them. Twice they left messages for me at my lodgings."

Wilkes's face turned incredulous. "Really? These messengers left unencrypted messages at your lodgings rather than waiting to give them directly to you? I wonder that Master Reddan trusts them."

"I cannot speak for him, but I did receive them safely," Hunter said with a tight throat.

"Well, let us hope this Thomas Miller of Sandwich takes greater care than the messengers. I shall tell Captain Baudin he must be careful," Wilkes said solemnly.

Monday, 21 July 1572

Walsingham's face was grim. "Alva's son, Fadrique de Toledo, defeated Genlis four days ago near Saint-Ghislain. Heavy losses. Over three thousand dead or wounded, many killed by the Hainault villagers. Over five hundred taken prisoner. It is a great blow to the Huguenots."

"The inn's taproom was buzzing yesterday after Mass with news of the Huguenots' defeat," Hunter said. "What about Mons?"

"Leonard Halston, an Englishman who was with Louis of Nassau, reached here yesterday. He is wounded and resting upstairs. He reports Mons can hold out for months. Orange may yet break the siege."

"Perhaps another attempt can be made from France."

"I doubt it. Halston heard horrifying tales. Soldiers who surrendered were slaughtered."

"That is contrary to the custom of war."

"When an officer protested, the Spanish captain said they were not soldiers following the commands of their prince, nor even mercenaries fighting for pay, but freebooters, outside the laws of war."

"Thus they justify their barbarity," Hunter said.

"Genlis's officers were tortured. Toledo sought evidence that King Charles had ordered the attack." Walsingham sighed and folded his hands. "But let us focus on the future. We received your message about the pamphlets and sent word to Sandwich. It is a pity you did not discover the ship's name. Has Sir Gregory given you any further news?"

"Yes. The pamphlets went on their way to Boulogne Saturday."

"Good. Our messenger will move faster than your pamphlets. Our men should be waiting to help Captain Baudin evade customs charges. They may help him unload Sir Gregory's *Catechisms* as well." Walsingham allowed himself a smile. "Any other news or rumors circulating among those you have given your lengths of cloth?"

"Monsieur Duelle, a draper near Les Halles, had news from Poland that their king had died. He predicted, as the Poles elect their king, that Queen Catherine will put forward the Duke of Anjou for the Polish Crown."

"Your draper's knowledge of Court affairs seems as thorough as ours," Walsingham said. "We believe the queen will angle for another throne for her offspring. She still urges Alençon as a match for our queen, despite his youth."

"That news is bruited in the streets with ribald comments. They say the duke must hurry to couple with the queen, ere she becomes too old to bear."

"I have heard those jests," Walsingham said. "Any other news?"

Hunter considered mentioning Madame Challon's suspicions that he was more than the syndicate's agent. Would Walsingham think he had been careless? He decided on an abridged version. "I delivered cloth to two ladies-in-waiting, who promised to have it made into gowns and promote the Court's taste for English cloth."

"Who?"

"The Viscountess of Tours and Madame Challon."

"I have heard of them. Both reputed able to turn heads. I hope your plan to stir up taste for English cloth succeeds."

Late July, 1572

As each day grew hotter, Hunter grew restive. All his cloth had been delivered. Although Harduin expected an official response by now, a letter from his uncle indicated a fierce battle within the Merchant Adventurers regarding Harduin's terms and warned him to say nothing.

The Huguenots from Gascony engaged him in conversation in the inn's taproom. They assumed him to be a Protestant, and shared anti-Catholic jokes with him. They spoke with sadness of friends who had followed Genlis into Flanders: four had died, and six had been captured. Coran wished he had gone, but his companions assuaged his guilt by pointing out that he would most likely be dead if he had.

Hunter spent more time in Sidney's company. They translated passages from Latin into French, and then back into Latin. They practiced fencing daily and took a lesson from Signore Coccitelli each Friday. Once, due to the heat, they stripped to their hose. Coccitelli encouraged them to drop their swords and practice wrestling and fist fighting as well, "as the king has forbid anyone to bear arms in Paris for now."

As the heat wave continued, Marguerite complained that it was too hot to sleep together each night. Hunter at first protested, fearing that he gave her less pleasure than before, then realized that he, too, would be satisfied with less frequent coupling. The ardor of their first encounters, the longing with which he had looked forward to each night, had given way to a routine arrival, performance, and departure. He was also aware that, as they made love, he often pictured Marie Challon or Charlotte de Sauve, their suggestive looks and throaty laughter, their bodies—younger, thinner, paler than Marguerite's.

CHAPTER 15

Royal Wedding

Monday, 4 August 1572

AMBASSADOR ZUÑIGA AND THE HOODED MAN AGAIN SAT OPPOSITE ONE another. "I demanded that King Charles withdraw Villars and his troops from the frontier or I would leave the kingdom. I listened to his feeble mutterings about necessary border security and his protestations of eternal amity." Zuñiga rolled his eyes, then smiled as he held his wine glass up and watched the dancing candle flame turn red. "The letters in our possession give His Majesty just cause to declare war on France. They show King Charles in collusion with the Prince of Orange, and that Genlis had his blessing, just as we thought."

"So his disavowal of Genlis, and his congratulations to Alva on his victory, are more posturing," the Hooded Man said. "Will King Philip label them the lies that they are?"

"You know the dance of diplomats better than that," Zuñiga said. "So long as Charles is unwilling to support Nassau and Orange publicly, His Majesty can focus all his energy on crushing the Dutch rebels. He does not need a war with France as well. But Alva has the letters, and King Philip can show them to the world when he needs to."

"Charles will surely claim they are forgeries," the Hooded Man said.

"Such claims will do him little good if the Army of Flanders marches into Picardy." Zuñiga sipped his wine. "But it may not come to that. After Genlis's defeat, Charles should be more cautious. He may pour cold water on Admiral Coligny."

The Hooded Man laughed. "A fitting fate for an Admiral who has never sailed the sea. I am pleased to see you in better spirits than our last meeting."

"The future looks brighter after the deaths of three thousand Huguenots. I hear the Prince of Orange cannot pay his soldiers. And, after the defeat of Genlis, is Elizabeth Tudor likely to send her 'volunteers' to the same fate, or order them home?"

"Yet the Treaty of Blois remains."

"Yes, but it is a defensive treaty—England and France are to support one another if attacked. That is another reason Philip will quietly accept Charles's false words." He took another swallow of wine. "But treaties are fragile things." He looked at the Hooded Man. "Cannot some incident be arranged? Is there no Englishman who can be bribed to insult a royal Valois?"

"The English Catholics who have fled here are not likely to insult those who provide them a haven. There are only a few English students at the University, and they seem less prone to riot than those of France." The Hooded Man paused a moment. "I had hoped that young Sidney might prove more of a reveler—so many young noblemen are—but he appears as virtuous and studious as he was rumored to be."

"Suppose something happened to him?" Zuñiga suggested.

"I have considered that. It would be easy to arrange for someone to kill him, but such killers are common criminals. King Charles and every nobleman in his court would express outrage, Sidney's body would be returned with great pomp and honor, French dukes would accompany it to London, some poor wretch would be executed here, and the treaty would be even stronger." The Hooded Man drank.

"Would that some French duke could be convinced to strike Sidney down," Zuñiga sighed.

"French dukes are more likely to strike one another down, I fear," the Hooded Man said. "No, Ambassador Walsingham must be the means by which we unfasten this bond."

"You tried that once," Zuñiga objected. "Yet even when a servant of the king fired a pistol at his heart, he did not demand an apology."

"It would have been far different if the pistol had not misfired," the Hooded Man said.

"Pray provide the next assassin a better pistol," Zuñiga said.

Wednesday, 6 August 1572

As Hunter sorted through a stack of papers, Laurent entered and handed him a packet of letters. Hunter thanked him and sighed. He did not need more pieces of paper.

On top, a message from Wilkes. Captain Baudin and the *Hippocampe*—now he revealed the name of the ship—had successfully delivered the pamphlets to Sandwich. As thanks for the reduced customs, Captain Baudin had charged Adams only two livres. Hunter smiled. Wilkes and his captain had taken the bait. Walsingham would be pleased.

His pulse quickened as he opened a small, square note from Madame Challon. She thanked him for the cloth and described in detail how she and the viscountess planned to transform it into gowns for the celebrations following the wedding of Princess Marguerite to Henri of Navarre. It would be a shame he would see them, but they would do their best to praise the virtues of the cloth. He could look for them in the crowds around the platform outside Notre-Dame, where the ceremony would be performed. Yet what did it matter? They had toyed with him. He meant nothing to either of them. Then why had Madame Challon sent a letter? Well, ladies-in-waiting were obliged to acknowledge a gift and thank the giver, no matter what his station.

A thicker letter was from Uncle Babcock. The syndicate members were still at odds with their colleagues in the Merchant Adventurers. They had decided to seek the advice of the Privy Council on the issue, but the Queen was on her summer progress and they must wait until the Court returned to Whitehall. Hunter was to deliver the enclosed letter to Viscount Harduin, citing the Queen's progress to excuse the delay in responding. Whatever the outcome, he should return to England by the end of August. The syndicate could not afford to maintain him in Paris beyond that. His uncle hoped he could fulfill his responsibilities to Ambassador Walsingham by then.

Hunter's shoulders slumped. He walked to the window. He must soon leave the familiar angle of sunlight on the shop opposite. His days with Sidney, his nights with Marguerite, the sights and even the smells of Paris had become his reality. But there was no excuse to stay. He had done all he could do for the Rouen Syndicate. He had fulfilled his service to Walsingham as well. His pamphlets had been printed and shipped, and should serve as the bait to ensnare English Catholics. Might agents follow some of those pamphlets to Richard Spranklin, or Mary? She was no longer a Spranklin now, of course.

Although Walsingham and Beale might be satisfied, part of his self-imposed mission had not been completed. Pickering's killers had not been identified. Half-ear and his hooded master remained a mystery. If someone at the French Court had arranged Pickering's death, he could not penetrate that world. Were the rogues who had pushed him into the bonfire connected with Pickering's death? So many unanswered questions.

What would he say to Marguerite about *them*? She was the first woman with whom he had shared a bed. Not the first he had loved—Mary Spranklin had been that. Marguerite and he had never said, "I love you," yet they had spoken of love. Both knew that they could not fit into one another's lives in the long term, yet they had shared more than affection. What could he call it but love?

A rap on the door and Sidney's hearty, "Hello," pulled him from his reverie. Sidney set down a large bag with a thump. "What are you doing, ordering your papers or avoiding ordering them?"

"A bit of both," Hunter answered. "A letter from my uncle says I am to return to England by the end of August."

"I am sorry to hear you will leave," Sidney replied, "but I intend to leave a few weeks afterwards, so let us enjoy one another's company until then." He started to unbutton his doublet. "Are you ready for our afternoon bouts?"

Hunter was already in his linen shirt and venetians. "I am. Did you obtain the rebated swords?" He nodded towards the bag.

"Yes. Signore Coccitelli lent me a pair with points and edges dulled." Sidney straightened up and struck an exaggerated heroic pose. "I will have you know you are sparring today with a man who has been summoned to Court by the king himself."

Hunter raised his eyebrows. "Why?"

"I do not know." Sidney relaxed his pose. "Perhaps one of his pages has taken ill and he needs someone to hand him a handkerchief."

Hunter laughed. "When are you to wait upon His Majesty?"

"Next Saturday, the ninth."

"Perhaps he means to honor you."

"Perhaps, but not for anything I have achieved. Rather as a gesture to my uncle, or to Her Majesty. After Genlis's defeat, he needs English support more than ever if he is to act in the Netherlands." Sidney removed the rebated swords from the bag. "Did you ask Madame Moreau if we may use the courtyard?"

"She says we may, if we do not frighten the guests or the horses."

Their exercise had lasted only ten minutes when the Huguenot gentlemen sauntered out to watch. After cheering a few deft lunges, de Galion asked if they might join in the sport. Hunter introduced them to Sidney, and Mongaston climbed to their chamber to fetch their weapons. The men organized two matches, one using the rebated swords and the other with "sharps." The men not fencing served as judges. Every five minutes, they changed the roles of opponents and judges. Bernard Coran was surprisingly agile for a short, rotund man, but he relied on his strength. His dark expression made him appear angry, yet he was in control, tapping an opponent lightly when he saw an opening in his defense. Vincent de Galion was skilled in his parries, but not aggressive enough to take advantage of opportunities. Young Mongaston, in contrast, was all aggression. Despite the advice of his older companions, he seemed unable to resist the urge to attack, and lost most matches to his opponents' ripostes. Guillaume Poudampa proved to be the Frenchmen's best duelist, moving with quick reflexes and calm concentration. Both Hunter and the more skilled Sidney were able to hold their own against the Gascons.

Hunter touched Mongaston to win a match. Applause from a window. Marguerite Moreau was watching their exercise. How long had she been there? Was she proud of him? Poudampa saluted him. A feint and a lunge might score a hit while she was looking on. Poudampa was not fooled by the feint, and, executing a circular parry, lunged and tapped his sword against Hunter's chest. "A hit!" Sidney exclaimed. So much for impressing Marguerite.

At the end of an hour, all repaired to the taproom. After congratulations on particularly successful thrusts or parries, Sidney asked the Gascons how they had found Paris.

Mongaston smiled. "Coran has enjoyed its whores,"

"As did you," Coran replied.

"Yes, but I am not married," Mongaston countered.

"Would that I were not," Coran said. Hunter began to smile, but the serious faces of the Gascons told him Coran's marriage was not a laughing matter.

After an awkward silence, Poudampa said, "I hope you have been careful to avoid those with the pox." This produced another awkward silence.

Coran changed the subject. "I regret that the king has forbidden the carrying of weapons. I would use my sword to teach some taunting apprentices a lesson."

De Galion said, "We should follow the example of King Henri. When I spoke with the Admiral two days ago, he said His Majesty endured scores of scornful remarks and snubs from Anjou and his friends. He bears all with equanimity and smiles upon those who would rouse his ire."

Poudampa added, "The jibes of apprentices count for less that the actions of nobles. Next week the Prince of Condé will marry Marie de Clèves. A week later, Henri of Navarre will marry Marguerite Valois—two yokings of Catholic noblewomen with Huguenot princes."

De Galion picked up the jug on their table. "Gentlemen, let me refill your glasses. We should drink, Master Sidney, to your uncle the Earl of Leicester, a great supporter of Protestants throughout Europe."

Sidney said, "You are kind to honor him so." They raised their glasses and drank.

"I only hope that Queen Elizabeth will soon declare her support for the Dutch and send an army to Holland. Perhaps your uncle would lead it," Poudampa suggested.

"That too would be a great honor," Sidney said. "But keep in mind, gentlemen, that Her Majesty abhors war."

Hunter did not voice his thoughts. The last time the Queen had sent troops across the Channel to aid French Protestants, troops led by Sidney's elder Dudley uncle, the Earl of Worcester, she had been badly burned. The Huguenots they had come to help had joined with the forces of King Charles and besieged the English occupying Newhaven. During the silence that followed, perhaps the others were remembering that.

"We shall visit some of our friends lodged near the Admiral tonight," de Galion said to restore a positive atmosphere. "Will you two honor us with your company?"

They did. That evening, Hunter and Sidney met members of the Huguenot gentry who had accompanied Henri of Navarre to Paris.

Friday, 8 August 1572

A few days later, Hunter crossed the Seine with Poudampa and Coran to visit Saint-Germain-des-Prés. Near the Porte de Buci, they were passing Wilkes's lodgings when Robert opened the door, nodded in recognition, and crossed to them.

"Good day, Master Adams. I bear a message for you," he said. "Seeing you here saves me trudging across Paris in this heat." He held out a folded letter.

"Sir Gregory received the money I sent two days ago, did he not?" Hunter asked.

"Yes, sir." Robert cocked his head at Coran and Poudampa and switched to French. "Pardon me, gentlemen, I bid you both good day, as well."

Poudampa returned his greeting with a smile; Coran, with his customary crustiness. Robert's manner altered as he heard their responses. "Have you gentlemen come from the South with the King of Navarre?" he asked in a neutral tone.

"Aye." Coran's growl made a challenge of the affirmation.

"Well, welcome to Paris. I hope you enjoy your stay." Robert's voice held a trace of irony. He turned to Hunter. "As you have obliged me by passing by, I can return to my master's service straight. He has a long list of tasks for me." He bowed slightly and left.

"That was a servant of some English acquaintance of yours?" Poudampa asked.

"Yes. My service to English merchants has led me to meet Englishmen living in Paris." Hunter could not explain his true business with Wilkes to these Huguenots.

Wilkes's note had asked to meet soon. Had something gone wrong after the pamphlets reached Sandwich? Would Sir Gregory request more information about Sidney? After Robert's report, he would need to explain his association with the Huguenots to Wilkes, as well. Surely the loyal Catholic Paul Adams would be using his acquaintance with Huguenots to gather information that might be used against them.

At Saint-Germain-des-Prés, Hunter met Count Montgomery and other leading Huguenots. All the time he was conversing, he imagined himself a papist spy, gleaning bits of information he could feed to Wilkes. He declined an invitation to dine with the Huguenots, deciding to go directly to Sir Gregory's. It was better to find out what was on his mind immediately than to gnaw on the bone of uncertainty.

Robert opened the door. "Master Adams!"

"Is your master in?" Hunter asked. "If it is convenient, I can attend him now."

Robert's eyebrows knit. "If you will come in, I will check with my master."

He waited in the entryway, smiling to himself. Such an immediate response was unexpected, which might give him an advantage. Robert returned with a crisp, "Sir Gregory will see you now."

Wilkes was dressed formally, in a gray satin doublet with silver embroidery. "I was not expecting such a prompt response, Master Adams, but I am glad you have come."

Hunter waited for Wilkes to reveal his reasons.

"Have you heard from Francis Reddan that your pamphlets have been received?" Wilkes asked.

A question Hunter had not expected. "No."

"It has been almost a week since Captain Baudin returned. He said your Thomas Miller was most accommodating and effectual, so I presumed your pamphlets would have arrived in London by now, and Master Reddan would have confirmed that—either by Michael or some other messenger—hopefully writing in cypher this time."

"I do not expect he would notify me immediately," Hunter improvised, "unless the pamphlets did not arrive. When I received your message saying they had been delivered to Miller, I supposed all would be well." To deflect Wilkes, he asked, "Do you know if your catechisms have reached their destinations safely?"

Wilkes's eyes flashed suspicion, then he smiled. "Those bound for London and the southeast arrived safely. I have yet to hear from farther north and west."

"Then our mission was a success," Hunter said. "Thank you for advancing Captain Baudin what I owed him."

"Thank you for reimbursing me so promptly," Wilkes said. "When you were last here, we drank to the success of our mission. It seems appropriate now to have another glass to celebrate its outcome." He called to Robert to bring wine. "My servant informed me you were with two gentlemen from the South, Huguenots who are in Paris for Navarre's wedding."

The query Hunter had anticipated. "They are guests at the inn where I lodge."

"And they think you are a Protestant?"

"They do."

"Have you spent some time with them?"

"Only this past week."

"A few hours may be enough time with a man, if he takes you into his confidence," Wilkes said. "Robert said you were headed to Saint-Germain-des-Prés. Many Huguenot nobles lodge there."

This was Hunter's invitation to tell all. He listed those he had encountered that afternoon. As he finished, Robert entered with wine.

"Paris is full of rumors of a second assault on the Netherlands, led by Coligny. What did the Huguenots say about that?" Wilkes asked.

"They all expect him to lead an offensive, but most believe it will not take place until after the wedding." Hunter was repeating common wisdom.

"Did anyone assert that such an offensive will be sanctioned by King Charles?"

"Opinions differ. Some say the king will openly declare war on Spain. Most think he will nod to Coligny but tell King Philip that the Admiral acted against his orders."

"As he did with Genlis," Wilkes said. "Did they speak of where this assault might be launched?"

"There was much speculation, but no one spoke as though he had knowledge of a plan, not even those who bragged of their close friendship with the Admiral."

"What was the speculation?" Wilkes pressed.

"There were almost as many opinions as there were men," Hunter said. "Some thought it best to march through Flanders and join the rebels in Zeeland and Holland. Some said Strozzi could transport an army from Bordeaux to join them. Others said it was wiser to link with the Prince of Orange and march on Brussels from the east. Others promoted a conjoined attack—Coligny through Hainault, Orange from the east, and a third force from the coast—though they seemed uncertain whether that would be made of rebels, Strozzi's army, or an English army."

"Some still hope Her Majesty will involve herself, do they?" Wilkes said.

"Yes."

"Has your companion Sidney heard anything from his uncle?"

"I do not believe he has had any letters from him in the last week."

"Did the Huguenots speculate who might command which units in the expected offensive?" Wilkes asked.

Hunter balanced the necessity of giving some information with the danger of repeating details. "Those who had commanded troops in the past were all mentioned: Montgomery, Briquemault, Piles, la Rochefoucauld, and Téligny."

"That agrees with my other reports," Wilkes said.

His comment suggested that Wilkes was in touch with informers in the Huguenot camp. Hunter must warn the Huguenot leaders through Walsingham, but now was the time to lean on Wilkes for information in return. "I fear that what I have learned is of little value to date, but perhaps I can gather more in the future. I hope your other sources are closer to the Huguenot leaders."

"Some are, I am glad to say," Wilkes said.

Hunter waited, but a few moments' silence made it clear Wilkes would offer no more. "Are they privy to Coligny's discussions with his lieutenants?"

Wilkes's mouth tightened, and his eyes hardened. "You will realize it is of great importance that I say nothing that might reveal anyone trusted by the Huguenots who is sympathetic to the Church of Rome. None of the other expatriates knows the identities of these men, and neither may you."

"I appreciate your need for secrecy," Hunter lied. He chuckled. "It would be ironical if, in the past week, I have myself spoken to one of those supplying you with information."

Wilkes's demeanor did not change to show whether this guess was on target. "If you had, I would betray my trust if I said so."

"It was but an idle thought." Hunter smiled. "I must content myself to know that any intelligence you obtain, whether from my feeble efforts or from those closer to the Protestant leaders, will reach the Spanish Ambassador, who will know best how to frustrate the plans of the Huguenots."

The tightening of Wilkes's body revealed he had guessed right. Sir Gregory said only, "I can do little with information that might help the Catholic cause, but must convey it to others, of whatever nationality, who can put it to better use." He drained his glass. "Master Adams, you must forgive me, but I have other business to attend to."

Hunter took his cue. "Thank you for seeing me at such short notice, Sir Gregory."

"Robert will show you to the door," Wilkes said. "Be sure to let me know when you hear from Francis Reddan."

As he left, Hunter bit his lips. The interview had begun and ended with Wilkes mentioning Reddan.

Saturday, 9 August 1572

"Lord Burghley sent you here with the intention of befriending Catholic expatriates and discovering French sources of popish pamphlets," Walsingham said. "Not only have you done that successfully, but your dealings with Sir Gregory Wilkes led to the discovery of a distribution network in England. Our men followed the shipments. They confirmed our suspicions of several Catholic families spreading texts and discovered other secret papists we had not known about. Ten have been arrested and dozens more brought in for questioning. I congratulate you on your part in this."

"I thank you, sir," Hunter replied. "It was a privilege to serve you, Lord Burghley, and Her Majesty." He remembered his hopes that Mary Spranklin and her father might hear him praised. But she was now married and, as Catholics, Walsingham's praise for unearthing 'papists' would not sound sweet in their ears. A thought struck him. "Was Francis Reddan among those arrested?"

"Yes. A great store of pamphlets was found in his home, as we suspected. As he served our purpose in your story, we no longer needed to delay arresting him. Why do you ask?"

"Sir Gregory seemed particularly concerned about Reddan. He again reproved Reddan for not writing in a cypher, and expected that he would write me immediately confirming the delivery. How long after the catechisms arrived were the arrests made?"

"I see," Walsingham said. "Wilkes must ask those who receive his shipments to write to him immediately. Miller reported two large chests of catechisms. At a house in Rochester, the contents were divided into several bundles. Those went in several directions: London, Portsmouth, Bristol, and many farther north. I would guess some of those at the distribution points wrote to Sir Gregory, but I doubt if each individual recipient was expected to." He shuffled through papers on his desk and extracted one. "Arrests were made within a few days of the delivery of the catechisms.

We did not want the evidence to disappear. But the catechisms arrived at different places at different times." He pursed his lips. "It is hard to tell. If his distributors wrote immediately, he would have news of safe delivery, but not of any arrests. Within a week, he will most likely know. You are right to suppose this will make him suspicious of you."

"I fear he may already be so."

"As you are to leave by the end of the month, you may be able to avoid him for the next few weeks," Walsingham suggested. "If not, commiserate on his bad luck and rail against the spies and informers the Privy Council employs at all ports. You may use Reddan's arrest to prove that your plan was also frustrated." He pulled out a fresh sheet of paper. "But now, tell me all of your conversations with both the Huguenots and Wilkes."

Hunter did so, ending with his belief that Wilkes had an informant in the Huguenot camp.

Walsingham nodded. "We have suspected it. Not every man is motivated by faith. Favor with those in power, personal gain—these also are at work among the Reformed. Alva appeared to know details of Genlis's movements in advance. Halston, the wounded man staying here, said it seemed as though the troops under Toledo were waiting."

A knock at the door. Alain Brune announced Philip Sidney. He entered, beaming and holding a roll of parchment with dangling seals. "Good afternoon, Your Excellency. And how fortunate to find you here, Paul."

"I believe you have news to tell us," Walsingham said with a knowing smile.

A look of embarrassment passed over Sidney's face. "King Charles has honored me by creating me a Gentleman of the King's Chamber and a Baron."

"Congratulations," both said.

Sidney addressed Walsingham. "You knew His Majesty was going to do this, did you not?"

"I did. And I told him that Her Majesty does not take kindly to her subjects receiving titles from foreign princes."

"I know, but I could not offend him by refusing."

"No," Walsingham agreed. "But I would not style myself Baron Sidney in England."

"I do not plan to. I know the king honors me only because of my family. In fact, my patent says as much." He handed Walsingham the roll.

"I would that this honor might sway Her Majesty to support the cause of Reform in the Low Countries," Walsingham said, untying the ribbon, "and I know your uncle does as well." He sighed as he unrolled the document. "But I hear she plans to recall her subjects who have gone to the Netherlands. I must write her again."

"I realize King Charles hopes to gain influence with my uncle by this, but he mentions only the Sidneys, not the Dudleys. Yet," he smiled at Hunter, "I will gain some personal advantage this next week, and perhaps you may as well."

"What?"

"As a Gentleman of the King's Chamber, I will be invited to view the royal nuptials from a balcony overlooking the platform outside Notre-Dame. That evening, I am invited to a supper at the Louvre, and to each of the festivities to take place on the four days following the wedding."

"No one does spectacles like the Queen Mother," Walsingham said.

"I am pleased for you," Hunter said, "but more interested, selfishly, in how your new station may be of advantage to me."

"I may bring a servant or guest with me to each of the occasions," Sidney said. "And I thought you might wish to witness the wedding and attend some of the festivities."

Hunter gave a low bow. "I am at your command, master."

10-15 August 1572

During the week before the wedding, the nobility escaped from the Paris heat to their country estates. As Hunter walked the streets, he observed the increased tempo of activity. Carpenters constructed the platform outside Notre-Dame and triumphal arches at important intersections. Drapers measured yard upon yard of damask and cloth of gold. Seamstresses and tailors sat in their shops, sewing the gowns, robes, and doublets their clients had ordered for the wedding festivities. Carts laden with all manner of food and drink jostled one another in the hot, narrow streets. Carters came to blows, each refusing to back up so the other could deliver his load. Bags of flour and casks of wine toppled into the road and exploded. Everyone complained that his order arrived late and shouted at those who delivered it. Fistfights broke out between the young Huguenots who had come to town with the King of Navarre and the Parisian apprentices, among the servants of rival aristocrats, all quick to defend their master's honor, and, as usual, among the students of the Latin Quarter.

The inns of Paris filled the week before the wedding, and L'Échiquier was no exception. One Monsieur Grattard from Bordeaux arrived with his young wife, a boy of fourteen, and a two-year-old child, followed by a spice merchant from Brussels, a merchant and his wife from Lyon, and couples from Angers and Troyes. Finally, four German students, unable to beg a bed or even a pallet from their friends at the university, arrived and pleaded with Madame Moreau to rent them her top story room. She set strict rules before she agreed: no girls in their room, they must return by 10:30 each night or be locked out, they must not annoy other guests, and they could only drink in the taproom. As L'Échiquier filled, Madame Moreau forbade fencing in the courtyard. She temporarily hired a neighbor lad to help Auguste and Pierre in the kitchen, and asked Marie to bring her younger sister for two weeks to help.

Hunter noticed that, in her busiest week, she found time to speak with Monsieur Grattard. Their smiles and laughter suggested they had known each other before. Speaking to Grattard confirmed his suspicions. A wine merchant from Bordeaux, Grattard came to Paris twice a year. He always stayed at L'Échiquier. This was the first time his wife had come. She was his second wife. His son Gaston was the product of his first marriage, but his first wife had died about the same time Monsieur Moreau did. Yes, he had first stayed at L'Échiquier when Monsieur Moreau was alive. He liked the chamber Hunter now occupied, and had lodged there often.

Hunter smiled and bid him farewell, but his imagination wove a story of Marguerite, a lonely widow, and the widower Grattard meeting during his visits to Paris. He had stayed in Hunter's chamber. Had he also used the secret staircase to visit Marguerite at night?

Other thoughts plagued him that week. Sir Gregory Wilkes was sure to learn of the arrests in England. Despite Walsingham's advice, he sent a vague note, saying he had received worrying news, and received a similar note from Wilkes the same day. He quickly sent another arranging a meeting.

Saturday, 16 August 1572

"You wrote of worrying news from London," Wilkes began without a preamble. "What have you heard?"

Hunter dove in. "Francis Reddan has been arrested and the pamphlets I sent him have been seized. What is your news?"

"I have had three letters. Several of my contacts in England have been called by officers of the Privy Council to answer questions. Some men have been arrested and books seized." Sir Gregory's face was grim, his eyes hard. His vague terms, not mentioning any names or places, spoke suspicion.

"Our venture has gone seriously awry," Hunter said. "I had heard Lord Burghley had agents in every town and every port, but I thought the claim was exaggerated."

"Yes, Cecil has many informants," Wilkes spat out his enemy's name, refusing to use his recent title. "But they have not detected those I deal with until now." His eyes spoke accusation. "Perhaps your Miller in Sandwich was one of Cecil's spies."

"That is hard to believe." Hunter's mouth was dry. "Reddan trusted him. You saw his letter."

"Yes, I did. A letter written in plain English instead of in cypher, delivered by a messenger you did not personally know. I fear Reddan has been too careless."

For the present, Wilkes was blaming Reddan and not him. "If so," Hunter said, "his carelessness has landed him in jail."

"And many others as well, who have done much for the Catholic cause." Wilkes fixed him with a stare. "Do you not fear you are in some danger? The first question they will ask Reddan is where the pamphlets came from."

Hunter adopted a worried look. "I believe he will not reveal that."

Wilkes shook his head. "I have known soldiers hardened in battle, who, when they were merely shown the instruments of torture, told all they knew."

Hunter remained silent, furrowing his forehead. Had Wilkes discovered he was to return to England soon? "At least I am safe in Paris."

"How long have you known Francis Reddan?" Wilkes asked.

"A little over three years. I met him shortly after I came to London to study at Gray's Inn."

"Yes," Wilkes said. "You are not from London. Where is your home?"

"Hertfordshire."

"Where in Hertfordshire?"

Hunter did not like where this was going. "Between Ware and Bishops Stortford. But I told you this when we were first introduced."

"Yes," Wilkes said. "Pardon my poor memory. I fear I have also forgot some facts about Francis Reddan. You said he was a merchant who trades with Spain and Portugal. Where does he live in London?"

Hunter doubted that Wilkes, who remembered the name of the fictitious messenger Michael, had forgotten the details he supplied about Francis Reddan, but he could do nothing but respond. "Reddan lives on Fish Hill Street."

"Is he married?"

"Yes. He has two sons nearing twenty, both unmarried, who assist him in his business, and a young daughter." Better to appear willing to give more information than requested.

"Are any of his neighbors or business associates zealous Protestants?"

"I imagine some are," Hunter said, "but why do you ask?"

"I am trying to identify the source of information that led to his arrest."

"That could have come from anywhere—a servant of his, a fellow merchant, someone he trusted to deliver pamphlets..." Hunter tried to turn the discussion. "Could the source have come from someone who was distributing the catechisms you sent?"

Wilkes appeared to consider this. "All things are possible, but these men have been faithful before." His face hardened. "As both our tracts were followed, it seems likely that someone at Sandwich knew of their arrival. Reddan recommended Sandwich. When did you last speak with him?"

"Before I came to Paris."

"Did he seem to take adequate precautions? Could any servants have overheard you?"

"No."

"And he was part of the syndicate you represent?"

"Yes," Hunter lied. He was walking on thin ice.

"Did the other merchants in the syndicate know you carried a manuscript from him?"

"I cannot know everyone Reddan took into his confidence, but I do not believe anyone else knew."

"Very well." Wilkes appeared to relax. "We cannot undo what is done. But before I risk another shipment, I must make enquiries. There is much damage to repair. How long will you remain in Paris?"

He does not know. "I am to leave near the end of this month."

"Soon, eh?" Sir Gregory said. "If I were you, I would not land at Sandwich. And you might ask your companion Sidney to write his uncle praising your good character and loyal Protestant beliefs. A word from him might spare you, if Reddan mentions your name to the Privy Council."

"Thank you for your concern," Hunter said. "If I may do you any service when I return to England, pray inform me."

"You do not consider your position dangerous enough?" Wilkes asked.

"I would risk any danger to promote the Catholic cause," Hunter said. Best lay it on with a trowel.

When he returned to L'Échiquier, Hunter found Captain Izard standing in the door of the office, speaking with Marguerite Moreau. "... full of Huguenots," he was saying. "Such an inn needs to be carefully watched."

"I provide accommodation for travelers who pay me," she replied. "I do not ask them about their beliefs. If my inn has Huguenot guests, it is not the only one in Paris; hundreds have arrived for the wedding."

"And yours is not the only inn being carefully watched," he said. "But it may be the only inn where Protestants are allowed to wield weapons and practice swordplay."

Marguerite's mouth opened in surprise. Hunter stepped towards Izard's back and said, "We were merely taking our exercise."

Izard turned. "Ah, the Englishman, Master Adams. Are you arriving to rescue Madame Moreau?"

"Is she in need of rescuing?" Hunter asked.

Izard smiled. "She is certainly in no danger from me. The Hôtel de Ville has ordered the militias to keep the peace in the city during the wedding."

"Is Madame Moreau endangering the city's peace?" Hunter asked.

"As her inn is full of armed Protestants, I thought it only prudent to remind her that she should be vigilant for any signs of disorder among her guests." He looked sternly at Hunter. "Even foreigners."

"I have heard her explain to the German students that they must behave peacefully and respectfully," Hunter said.

"I hope her English guests will also respect the honor of their host." Before Hunter could reply, Izard walked towards the door. "I have other establishments to visit, so you must excuse me."

Marguerite stepped into her office. Her troubled expression bid Hunter enter. After closing the door, he embraced her. "Was he threatening you?"

"Not directly. Just his usual—reminders that he commands the militia, that he could make trouble for me. It has been thus since I refused his advances after my husband died." She stepped back. "I wonder how he heard of your fencing in the courtyard."

"Any of your servants or last week's guests could have mentioned it," Hunter said. "I am sorry our exercise landed you in trouble."

"You meant no evil, and Izard knows it. But he will twist anything. He implies that if I have Protestant guests, I am not a faithful Catholic. Not all my guests are Protestants, but I would not say that to him. It is not his business."

"He seems to think everything that happens in this quarter is his business." Their eyes locked. "His comment about 'the honor of my host.' Do you think he knows about us?"

She turned away. "I think we have been careful, but a servant may have overheard something." She faced him. "As much as I long to lie in your arms tonight, the inn is full and the chance of someone hearing something is greater. I am tired, too, and cannot give you the love I would wish." Hunter saw the exhaustion in her eyes. "And," she hesitated, "you will soon be gone, but I will remain here."

"That argues that we seize as much joy together as we can, before I must leave."

She nodded. "But the greater the joy, the greater will be the pain at parting."

He held her again and kissed her. How much had she been frightened by Izard, how much was she worried about her reputation after he left, how much might she be remembering an earlier affair with Grattard that had ended with his departure, and how much was she pulling away now to protect herself from the pain of separation? "We will do as you wish for now," he said.

King Philip sat at his desk, candles burning all around him. He scribbled a note in the margin of the report. Affairs were going better in the Low Countries. Genlis's Protestant forces had been defeated. The army Orange had cobbled together threatened to fall apart because he could not pay them. Mons could not hold out much longer. Although the coastal towns in Holland and Zeeland still defied Alva, it could only be a matter of time.

Just now, France was a greater worry. The captured letters of Charles IX showed clearly that he was a party to Genlis's invasion. To tolerate Protestants in his own country, as Charles had done, was bad enough, but to encourage them to aid the heretic rebels in the Netherlands was unpardonable. He was tempted to declare war on the inconstant mother's boy, but he restrained himself. The defeat of Genlis should have dampened his dreams of conquest, but reports said Coligny still whispered in his ear that he should aid Orange. If Coligny led an army into the Netherlands, that would tip the balance. After Alva defeated Coligny, and Spanish armies occupied Picardy, Burgundy, and parts of Guyenne and Languedoc, what territories could he demand? Certainly the tiny kingdoms of Navarre and Béarn. Whether or not those were the French King's to give was immaterial. If Spanish troops held them, Charles had only to recognize that Philip ruled there. Then the plague of Protestant heresy near his borders could be exterminated. And Henri of Navarre, to whom, any day now, the House of Valois was about to yoke itself, would be a king without a kingdom. That wedding, if it took place, would surely be invalid. It was impossible the Pope would grant a dispensation, no matter the pressure.

He sighed and rubbed his eyes. God required so much of him. At least the Turks seemed quiescent this summer. Elizabeth of England was playing a double game, signing a treaty with France and at the same time making overtures to him to reopen trade with the Low Countries. Well, she had come to realize how much her second-rate kingdom depended upon his good will. Although he did not trust her, he would approve the opening of negotiations. One could not fight every heretic prince at once, even with God's blessing. Elizabeth could wait.

A memory tugged at him. A message from de Spes, one of the last from that poor ambassador before brigands had killed him on his way home, had told of a spy sent from England to Paris. He should have sent that along to Zuñiga months ago. With affairs so volatile in France, it would be good to forward it now. He called a secretary to retrieve the letter.

Monday, 18 August 1572

Hunter met Sidney near the east end of the Church of Saint-Christophe. With him was Leonard Halston, the wounded English volunteer who had escaped from Mons during the rout of Genlis's forces. The three approached the Gothic arcade facing the Parvis of Notre-Dame. Sidney showed a note to the guard at the door, then he and Hunter helped their companion climb to a large ballroom on the first floor. Servants bustled about, arranging sweetmeats on tables. They strolled to a balcony overlooking the Parvis and the platform where the wedding ceremony would be performed.

Gentlemen leaned over the balustrade, talking. These were not the actual members of the King's Household, Sidney explained. Those were all busy at the Louvre. Rather, these "gentlemen of the chamber" were a collection of minor nobles or gentry, who had purchased or, like Sidney, been given honors, without actual duties and often without any wages. As they waited, Halston told of his service with Louis of Nassau at Mons, how he had been sent as a messenger to Genlis and received his wound.

Below, the platform was draped with cloth of gold, and the buildings around the Parvis were hung with brightly colored tapestries. The sun rose behind the cathedral's towers into a cloudless blue sky, threatening to blind those on the balcony. Militiamen took their places around the platform, pushing back early arrivals who had positioned themselves too close. Hunter recognized the young militiaman who had pulled him from the fire on Saint John's Eve. So, Izard's company was to have a role in this wedding. There was Izard himself, strutting in his captain's uniform, finding fault with the tilt of a hat or the angle of a sash. Sidney fetched a stool for Halston, while Hunter surveyed the Parvis. People crowded onto balconies and at windows, and even risked infection by climbing to the roof of the Hôtel-Dieu. Below, hordes poured into the open spaces around the platform. It was scarcely nine, two hours at least before the royal procession would arrive.

"The pickpurses will have a good day of it," Halston commented.

"There are Bryskett and Madox." Sidney called to them and waved. He turned with an uncomfortable expression. "Paul, I know I asked you to accompany me to the revels following the wedding, but Lodowick has served my father faithfully for some time, and Madox has asked as well, so I have agreed he shall serve me at the Louvre supper tonight, and Bryskett attend me tomorrow. I hope you are not offended."

"Not in the least," Hunter said. "Both have a better claim than I."

"But you shall be with me the following days," he said. "Both agreed to that. Each is content to see one royal fête."

Hunter surveyed the crowd. He spotted Robert, with his strawberry birthmark, and his gang of boys entering the square. They spread out, each to his assigned territory. Halston was right. The pickpurses would have a profitable day. Jacques Crespin sat atop a balustrade and waved up at him. Timothy Heath and Barnaby Timmons joined scores of students streaming in from the Left Bank. Where were the other expatriates? Did they stay away because they did not condone the marriage of a royal princess with a Protestant, or had they secured a place at a window? He scanned the buildings on the north side when an unfamiliar voice, speaking English with a heavy French accent, caught his attention.

"Is one of you the Baron Sidney?"

They turned to see an older man, balding with a gray beard, wearing a dark blue doublet.

"I am Philip Sidney, and these are my companions, Paul Adams and Leonard Halston."

"Pierre Delorme, at your service." The man bowed. "I had heard Baron Sidney might be here, and I hoped to meet you. I visited your country several times with Michel de Castelnau, Sieur de la Mauvissière, when your queen first ascended her throne." Delorme then spoke enthusiastically of his experiences in London, including details of where he had lodged, the taverns he had frequented, and the officials he had known.

The Englishmen indulged him, affirming that a certain pie shop was still to be found just outside Newgate, and explaining who had replaced whom at Court in the decade since Delorme's visit. Delorme, enjoying speaking English again, though frequently asking for words he had forgotten, launched into an account of his time in Scotland, when Castelnau had accompanied the young Mary Stuart home after her husband Francis II died.

As the sun blazed down, the crowd on the balcony grew. Muttered comments of "Where are they?" and "Late." The mood turned from anticipation to frustration. Men craned their necks for any sign of the royal party. "Can you see anything?" a voice in the back asked. "No," answered a chorus from the parapet. "Then another cup of wine," the voice said. Laughter.

To amuse himself, Hunter scanned the packed Parvis again. Justin Lepage stood at a window on the south side of the square. Heath and Timmons spoke with Roger Barnes. Near them stood Landon and Vasse, the artisans he had met at the Horn after he had received Mary's letter. The four Gascons from L'Échiquier stood on the north side of the Parvis, near a group of somberly dressed men that included Pierre Merlet, the

Huguenot draper who specialized in linings. The window above them framed several women. He recognized the posture of one's back, then the sight of brown curls escaping a French hood confirmed his guess. Marie Challon turned, looked towards the balcony, and waved. He raised his hand in acknowledgement.

"Who is that?" Halston asked.

"One of the Queen Catherine's ladies-in waiting. I supplied her with some English cloth," Hunter said. "She said she would have it made into a gown to influence the Court, but I do not believe she is wearing it now."

Marie disappeared from the window.

"Whom are you talking about?" Sidney asked.

"Madame Challon. I believe you met her at a banquet after the treaty signing."

"Ah," Sidney said, "the curly-headed lady you were with at Nevers's banquet."

"Madame Challon," Pierre Delorme said in a knowing way. "Are you another who has fallen for her charms?"

"I enjoyed her company." Hunter remembered her hand running up his thigh.

Marie was back at the window, pointing at Hunter and speaking to a woman who stepped into view beside her.

"It is the Viscountess of Tours," Sidney exclaimed.

Both women waved, and Hunter and Sidney waved back.

"Charlotte de Sauve," Delorme said. "You gentlemen are indeed fortunate. Many courtiers' hearts would beat faster at a greeting from those two."

"They are indeed fine-looking ladies," Halston chimed in.

The women giggled together, then waved again and laughed.

"Are they laughing with joy at seeing us, or laughing at us, do you think?" Sidney asked.

"Either way, they are paying you attention," Delorme said.

"You know the Court," Halston said. "What can you tell us of them?"

"Both are ladies-in-waiting to Queen Catherine," Delorme said. "Madame de Sauve is the more important. Her husband is a secretary of state. They say he tells his wife of every conference King Charles has with Admiral Coligny, and she tells the Queen Mother."

Not quite the role Hunter had heard the women of the flying squad played, but serving the same end of informing Queen Catherine of everything that passed at Court.

"The Duke of Anjou admired her beauty," Delorme went on. "But her father, the duke's chamberlain, was not willing for his daughter to be his mistress. So she married the Baron de Sauve. Now, safely married to a man almost twice her age, she is free to become the mistress of whomever she wishes."

"Does her husband not object?" Sidney asked.

"He controls her fortune," Delorme said, "and is so involved intriguing to gain influence with the king, the Queen Mother, and Anjou all at the same time, that he has little time for his pretty young wife."

"What of Madame Challon's husband?" Hunter asked. When Sidney gave him a questioning glance, he added, "I have never seen him or heard of him at Court."

"He does not like the Court, nor the city. He prefers to stay at his estates in the Auvergne," Delorme explained. "His wife has given him an heir, a little boy he dotes on, so she has done her duty so far as he is concerned. He is over forty and, they say, he only married to ensure his line. In return for his wife's service to Queen Catherine, he received a grant that enlarged his estates, so he seems content to allow her to remain here. She enjoys the life at Court."

Indeed she does, Hunter thought.

"Queen Catherine seems to favor married ladies with older, compliant husbands for her maids of honor," Halston observed.

"She does." Delorme warmed to his new role of gossipmonger. "But the term 'maid of honor' is less appropriate than ladies-in-waiting. All those married are no longer maids, and few of those unmarried are either, and as for honor..." His lascivious expression left no doubt as to his meaning. "It is said they are truly ladies-in-waiting, waiting for the next attractive man to approach."

"So you believe the Queen Mother has a flying squad to seduce secrets from the men at Court," Hunter said.

"Believe? I know it," Delorme said. "I could name at least a dozen gentlemen of the Court who have told me of an alliance with one 'maid of honor' or another."

Was Marie Challon one of those?

"Men brag of their conquests, whether real or imagined," Sidney said skeptically.

"True," Delorme agreed. "Men often do, but they do not brag of confidences they had sworn to keep, foolishly told to a paramour in bed, and later thrown back in their faces. Such actions bring shame and dishonor."

Halston glanced at the sun. "I have become both hot and hungry waiting for the wedding party to arrive. I suspect they have decided to dine at the Louvre before setting off. A man can only survive so long on wine and sweetmeats."

"A servant said that they would bring bread and cold meats if the ceremony were delayed," Sidney said. "I will go to see."

"May I accompany you?" Delorme asked. He and Sidney squeezed past those behind them.

"I heard of the immorality of the Valois Court," Halston said. "Delorme says the queen's ladies seduce men to learn their secrets, then betray them. Could one be more dishonest?"

Wilkes and Walsingham had suggested possibilities to Hunter the previous week. "A *man* could swear to fight for his lord and his faith, then betray both and send hundreds to their death."

Halston was silent a moment. "Yes. I have seen such a betrayal first hand."

Two more hours passed before trumpets announced the approach of the royal party. The crowd surged forward, to be forced back by militiamen and a company of royal archers. People pushed and craned, squeezing into windows, scrambling onto stairs and bannisters, and stepping onto stools and benches to see over those in front of them. Boys clambered onto rooftops. Ambassadors, members of the Parlement of Paris, and royal officials filed onto stands erected between the cathedral and the bishop's palace. Even the rows of kings and saints on the west front of the cathedral, now lit by the afternoon sun, appeared to watch the proceedings.

Charles IX and his brothers Anjou and Alençon processed to the cheers of the crowd. Those near Hunter on the balcony spoke the names of the dukes and lords that followed softly, like a litany: Guise, Retz, Tavannes, Nevers, de Sauve, Cossé, Montpensier.

Hunter grasped Sidney and pointed. "Look, just ahead of the king's party. The two we spoke with at Saint John's Eve, the ones who pushed me into the fire."

Sidney looked. "I believe you are right."

The two they were watching took off their hats and cheered the king. So did the man next to them, a man with half a left ear. Hunter gripped Sidney's arm even harder. "What is it?" Sidney asked.

Hunter's half-forgotten suspicions—that a member of the Court had ordered Pickering killed, and that his enquiries about a half-eared servant had led to his singeing on Saint John's Eve—seemed confirmed as he watched Guillaume and Richard smiling and laughing with Half-ear. But Sidney knew nothing of Pickering's death or Half-ear and the mysterious Hooded Frenchman. "I was just remembering the pain of those flames." He turned to Delorme. "Do you know those men down there?"

"Where?"

"There," Hunter pointed. "Three men moving away from us. Two with black caps, one with a russet cap and doublet."

"Why should I know such men as those?" Delorme's tone indicated that he did not associate with common rabble.

"I thought one might serve some nobleman at Court," Hunter said.

"Not likely." Delorme squinted, then shook his head. "No. I have never seen them before. No gentleman at Court would hire such riffraff." He tilted up his nose and asked, "How do you know them?"

"We encountered two of them on Saint John's Eve in the Place de Grève," Sidney interjected. "My friend suffered an accident that night, and we believe they were responsible."

"Oh." Delorme seemed satisfied that gentlemen might encounter ruffians under the conditions described, but, if they had come to grief, it was their fault for associating with them.

The royal procession crossed the platform to retrieve Princess Marguerite from the Bishop's Palace. King Henri of Navarre arrived from the opposite side of the square, accompanied by Huguenot noblemen. The king's retinue returned with Princess Marguerite, wearing a gold gown sparkling with jewels and a blue velvet cloak with a long train, trimmed in ermine. King Charles and Henri, Duke of Anjou, walked on either side of her. Catherine de Medici, just behind, had forsaken her usual widow's weeds and wore a gown of dark purple brocade and chains of jewels. The Cardinal of Bourbon, who was to preside, followed with his clerical retinue. The crowd cheered as they took their places on the platform. The king and his brothers, as well as Henri of Navarre and Prince Condé, wore suits of pale satin material, cut alike and covered with silver embroidery and pearls. "I suppose this is to suggest they are all brothers now," Delorme commented cynically.

The crowd fell silent when a bell sounded to begin the ceremony. The couple knelt before the cardinal, who spoke in a voice that echoed about the square. Everything proceeded as expected until the cardinal asked the bride if she took Henri de Navarre to be her husband. In contrast to Henri's loud assent a few moments before, she remained silent. The cardinal looked nervously from side to side, then asked again. After a tense pause, King Charles stepped behind his sister and pushed her head forward. The cardinal took this as a nod of assent and proceeded with the ceremony. Around Hunter, men exchanged looks and muttered.

At the end of the nuptial rites, Henri and Margot, the royal family, and the Catholic noblemen processed into the cathedral to attend Mass. The babbling of the crowd grew to a rumble.

Halston asked Sidney, "Is Navarre attending Mass as well?"

"No. He accompanies his bride to the altar, then will return."

"Did you note Princess Margot?" Delorme asked.

"She did not seem eager to wed," Hunter said.

"They say her heart belongs to Henri, duc de Guise," Delorme said. "I wonder if it can be a valid marriage without her verbal assent."

A man standing nearby said, "If her mother the queen says she is married, she is married."

Below, men were shouting at Coligny and the Protestant lords, "Go into the cathedral. Go into the Mass." A soldier gestured with his halberd, and the chanting stopped, but the glowering continued. Henri of Navarre returned to walk about and talk casually to the taunted Protestants. The soldiers pushed the crowd away from the platform.

Above, men retired from the parapet. "There is little more to see," Delorme said. "The Huguenots wait for the Mass to end so they can feast at the Bishop's Palace."

Before leaving the balcony, Hunter turned to where Madame Challon and the Viscountess of Tours stood. He and Sidney waved a farewell, and they waved back. Delorme was right; they were dishonest, dangerous—and fascinating.

When the crowds had thinned, Hunter made his way back to L'Échiquier. He had considered searching the Île de la Cité for Half-ear, but his chances of success were small, and he was hot and tired. Marguerite stood near her office, engaged in lively conversation with Monsieur Grattard. Hunter retired to the taproom and sat where he could watch the exchange. As Grattard described the wedding, Marguerite smiled and nodded. Her eyes danced and sparkled. She laughed at his comments. Yes, Marguerite knew Grattard very well. Finally, they said goodbye, and he climbed the stairs, presumably to his waiting wife and children.

Hunter swallowed the last of his ale and approached Marguerite.

She smiled. "Good afternoon. What did you see at the wedding?"

"I suspect you have already heard all about it from Monsieur Grattard."

"Yes, he gave me a very thorough description of the ceremony." Then she added, "But you may have seen things he did not."

"I suppose you know who accompanied the king and princess," he said. "Yes."

"And what they wore?"

"Yes. Navarre wore a pale satin suit with pearls and Margot a gold gown, blue cloak, and over five pounds of jewels."

"You see, you do know everything."

"Monsieur Grattard said that the princess did not give her consent to the marriage, but her brother forced her."

"He pushed her head, making her nod."

"Poor lamb," she said. "A princess has less choice whom she weds than a shepherdess."

"Then she can plead compulsion later, when she takes a lover," he said.

"And she might be justified in doing so," she said, then continued in a lighter voice. "Did Navarre and Coligny stay on the platform during the Mass?"

"As I said, you have heard everything during your long talk with Monsieur Grattard. You seemed to be enchanted with his voice."

"He has a very pleasant voice," she said with a hint of defiance. "And I am accustomed to talk with whom I wish for as long as I wish."

"I gather you know him well."

"Yes. He is an old customer."

"He told me he was accustomed to stay in my room," he said, "so I assume you know him *very* well."

Marguerite's face grew red. She turned and stormed into her office. Hunter followed, catching the door she attempted to slam and closing it slowly. "I did not invite you in here," she hissed.

Hunter did not reply, but stared reproachfully. Marguerite clenched her fists and spoke with controlled intensity. "What business of yours is it what I did or did not do with Monsieur Grattard? You do not own me. You have no hold on me. And now you act as though I must answer to you, that you may judge me." Hunter opened his mouth, but she continued. "You will soon leave and move on to another woman, to other women. What happens to me will not matter to you. You will leave me and forget me."

"I will not," Hunter protested. "I care for you."

"You did." Her voice softened. "We shared love." She turned her head and her voice hardened again. "That will end now. Do not pretend you will always love me; we both know better. I have heard enough promises in my time. I am sure you already look at other women." She swiveled suddenly, and her eyes bored into his. "Yes, you cannot deny it."

"Now who is acting as if they own another?" Hunter's voice rose. She held up her hands and he continued in a hissing whisper. "You will tell me where I may look and what I must think? You tell me how I will feel in the future and charge me with deeds I have not yet done? Yes. I *will* leave, and when I am gone I will not have to listen to accusations such as these." He turned and stomped up the stairs.

Hunter sought out a rundown tavern to avoid seeing Marguerite. If Sidney and Madox had not been at the wedding festivities, he would have slept at their lodgings. After choking down bland pottage, he slunk back to the Chessboard Inn, relieved to see the doors to the office and Marguerite's chamber closed.

His dreams were plagued with visions of Marguerite in bed with Grattard, with Half-ear taunting, "You will never know who killed him," with Marie and Charlotte standing near a man in a hooded cloak. He awoke in a sweat with teeth clenched. Throwing off the sheet offered no relief from the heat.

His dreams returned. Wilkes decried the arrest of English Catholics. Mary Spranklin stood bound beside him, asking, "Edward, how could you do this?" Suddenly it was the day to leave Paris. Izard and his militiamen were in his chamber, threatening to seize his possessions. Marguerite snarled, "I knew you would leave me." How unjust she was! Now Crespin entered, asking why he was not ready. He awoke, sunshine pouring in his window. He had slept late, but had had no rest.

Tuesday, 19 August 1572

At breakfast, Hunter joined the drowsy Gascons, who told of the Count Montgomery's celebrations lasting well past midnight. Marguerite passed their table without a glance and placed bread and butter by the Grattard family. For a considerable time, she talked and laughed with them. Hunter frowned as Marguerite passed their table, but she kept her eyes straight ahead.

The day held further disappointments. When Hunter stopped by Crespin's lodgings to arrange for his chests to be shipped to Rouen, he suggested a journey to Montmartre. "I remember when you first showed me Paris. I have a desire to go back there before I leave. I have only ten more days."

"I can understand your desire," Crespin said, "but why climb the mount on one of the hottest days of a hot summer?"

"We shall hire horses."

"I am sorry, but I have an appointment with Master Cope, Lady Lane's son."

At Sidney's lodgings on the rue Saint-Martin, Bryskett answered Hunter's knock. Sidney was still asleep, having returned after one in the morning. He did not expect him to wake until after noon, at which time they must quickly prepare to attend today's festivities.

Very well, Hunter would ascend Montmartre alone if he must. Instead of trudging back to the horse market near the Bastille, he would visit a stable near the Montmartre Gate. He found several, but each reported their horses were hired, lame, or reserved for use later in the day. He sighed and strode on, towards the abbey on the summit. Conversation would have diverted him; now he was alone with his thoughts.

Images of Marguerite smiling and laughing with Grattard plagued him. They dissolved all too easily into scenes of the two rolling naked in bed. Though her coupling with Grattard had been in the past, before she knew him, it felt like a betrayal. She had always stressed they would part. Was he just another conquest in a list of temporary lovers? How many had she had since her husband died? Perhaps she had not always limited herself to one man. She had used men, maintaining her distance, making sure she was in control. And she dared accuse him of being false. He had known only her! She said he lusted after other women. The fact that she was right only made her words sting more. But why should he not look at other women? He trudged on, sweating profusely.

Marie Challon. There was a woman who had known lovers, and—was he mistaken to believe it?—had found him attractive. He should beware of her suspicions that he was more than an agent, but the danger made her more alluring. He recalled her hand brushing his codpiece and stroking his leg. Yes, she had used her station to taunt him, but was there not desire behind her teasing? Did Marie not enjoy his company? Might he dally with her at the celebrations tomorrow? Whether or not it pleased Marguerite Moreau, he could imagine her a lover, or at least take pleasure in her beautiful face and slim body.

He reached the abbey wall, where he had stood almost five months before with Crespin. Sweat ran down his back. There lay Paris. He picked out her palaces, churches, monasteries, and grand houses. L'Échiquier was somewhere out of sight, east of Saint Avoie.

He sought out the wine stall where Crespin had directed the servants. The pottage was surprisingly good. He lingered over several cups of wine. His mood ebbed and flowed like waves over rocks. He had impressed the French officials, but the syndicate merchants complained. He had discovered the printers of Catholic tracts, but not the truth about Pickering's death. He had revealed Wilkes's network, but might have caused Burghley's men to arrest Richard and Mary Spranklin. Marguerite had offered herself to him, but accused him unjustly and only had eyes for Grattard—the wanton bitch! No, anger was a sin. What sins had he committed in Paris? He had confessed and attended Mass, at times thinking like a papist; he had reveled in fornication and felt little shame for it; he had lived a lie for five months, betraying to some degree the expatriates, Philip Sidney, and all who trusted him; he had neglected reading his Bible and saying his prayers. And now, he had to admit, he had drunk too much.

He paid his bill and staggered back to the Chessboard Inn. Marguerite saw him and turned away. He cornered Laurent and asked him to bring up a pail of water and a towel. In his chamber, he stripped off his clothes, washed himself, and collapsed into bed.

CHAPTER 16

Betrayal

Wednesday, 20 August 1572

"THE WEDDING FESTIVITIES WERE SPECTACULAR," SIDNEY SAID. "THIS WAS after food and dancing, of course. There were wagons with the king and his brothers, and others with Neptune, Triton, and sea monsters. It lasted a long time."

"So I gather," Hunter said. "When I stopped yesterday, near ten, you were still abed."

"Madox and I were lucky to wake by noon. But before I tell of yesterday, I have more news of Monday. Admiral Coligny left early. Either he was ill, he dislikes dramatic interludes, or he was busy planning military exploits. And the Duke of Guise left soon afterward. No one said he was ill, but many whispered he was heartbroken that Margot married."

"I had heard that as well."

"Yesterday," Sidney continued, "when Bryskett and I arrived at the palace, they had loosed a bear and a lion on an ox in the courtyard. The ox gored the bear, but the lion pounced on the ox and tore out its throat. Guards could not make the bear and lion fight. The king was sore disappointed, as were those who had wagered that one would kill the other. Then there was tilting at the ring, but after a few passes everyone repaired to the Hôtel d'Anjou."

"What happened there?"

"Oh, the food was excellent, as you would expect. After supper, we returned to the Louvre for a ball. I danced with many ladies, the

Viscountess of Tours and your friend Madame Challon among them. Both asked about you. I told them you would accompany me tonight."

Hunter's heart sped. Could it be that one or both of these enticing beauties, desired by many noble courtiers, desired his company? But perhaps they merely wanted to show him their garments sewn from English cloth. No, he would be foolish to expect more than a polite greeting.

"Madame de Sauve is an unusual woman," Sidney said. "She mentioned *Amadis de Gaule*—have you read any of it?"

"No. I haven't the endurance to plod through a long romance," Hunter said. "But what about Madame de Sauve?"

"She spoke of various knights and ladies in the tale," Sidney said, "how some suffered from unrequited love, how others were so besotted they helped their beloved gain the hand of another, how a knight surrendered his will to his love, how ladies had to choose between love and honor, and so on."

"While you were dancing?"

"And between dances. But all the while she spoke, her eyes...her face... the tone of her voice..." Sidney's face flushed. "It was as though she was speaking of us...as though we might be lovers...as though she was asking what kind of a lover I might be."

"Yes." Hunter had witnessed Madame de Sauve at the Louvre. "She can ask that question with her face even when she is not speaking of love."

"I felt quite uncomfortable."

"You said you danced with Madame Challon as well."

"Yes," Sidney said. "She was charming, as usual. She asked how long I was staying in Paris, where I was traveling afterwards—just polite conversation."

"No talk of love that was abstract and concrete at the same time?"

"No. But she spoke of travel. Within the week she will leave Paris for her husband's château in the Auvergne."

A tremor of disappointment shook Hunter. Why should he react this way to the news of Marie Challon leaving? He was leaving soon himself. He must seek her out at the festivities. "When are we to arrive this evening?"

"Within the hour," Sidney answered. "I must call Harry to help me dress."

Sidney showed the guards at the Hôtel de Bourbon his invitation and introduced Hunter as his servant. As they entered, Téligny approached and said the Admiral wished to speak with Baron Sidney urgently. Hunter drifted slowly towards the great hall, hoping that no one would question his presence there alone.

"Master Adams!" a voice came from his left, full of surprise and delight. Marie Challon whirled towards him, her brown eyes sparkling.

A warm glow spread over Hunter as he bowed. "Madame Challon, what a great pleasure to see you again."

"And for me as well. Baron Sidney told me you would accompany him tonight." She glanced around. "Where is he?"

"Speaking with Admiral Coligny."

"Ah, a discussion of great import, no doubt. Perhaps he wants Sidney to ride with him. Everyone says he will set off to aid Nassau."

"You keep current with Court rumors."

"I suppose you, as a man of wide interests, continue to be interested in Court gossip and military matters."

Again, her intimation that he was more than a mercantile agent. Hunter ignored the remark and asked, "Are you wearing English cloth?"

She stepped back and spread her arms. "I am."

He regarded her from head to toe. She wore a tawny gown that opened to reveal a forepart that matched a low-cut murrey bodice decorated in gold braid. White silk showed through its slashed sleeves. A gold chain with pearls looped from one shoulder to the center of the bodice neck-line to the opposite shoulder. Pearls dangled from her ears and from the coronet she wore. Her eyes challenged and tempted him.

"It has been well dyed, cut, and sewn," he said. "However, the garments are minor players in a pageant of loveliness. They can only enhance the beauty of the one who wears them."

"Your honeyed tongue again," she said. "Has the Viscountess of Tours seen you?"

"No."

Marie's eyes flashed, and she smiled widely. "Then I might have you all to myself."

A wave of excitement washed over Hunter.

"You must forgive me for being forward," she said, "but I hope you can escort me to watch the pageant later. It is called the 'Mystery of Three Worlds' and the '*Paradis d'Amour*.' I think the latter sounds more interesting."

"It would be an honor I do not deserve, but it would please me greatly."

"We must first forgo one another's company for an hour," she said. "Her Majesty has asked that I dine with the Vidame de Chartres, but his wife will sit with him at the spectacle."

"I am honored that you ask me to accompany you for even a moment," Hunter said. "I cannot hope to spend all evening with you."

She smiled slyly. "You promise you will let no other lady entice you?"

"None other can compare with you."

"Suppose a noblewoman of high degree were to ask you to accompany her?"

"I would think I was dreaming," Hunter said, "but even in my dream I would tell her that I promised to be with the fairest lady in France."

"You flatter well enough to win a duchess," she said. "But if one does not sweep you away, I will meet you here after supper." Her huge brown eyes stayed glued to him as she turned. She flashed a smile, then swirled away.

Hunter stood watching the alluring sway of her gown. She really was attracted to him. His dream of yesterday was becoming real. His doubts had been foolish. He lingered in the vestibule, hoping Sidney would return, greeting city and court officials he knew and Huguenots he had recently met. Viscount Harduin, frowning, summoned him with a gesture. He prepared himself for an unpleasant conversation.

"Master Adams, I had hoped to hear by now that your syndicate merchants were sending someone to negotiate the final details of the staple agreement. It is four months since the treaty was signed and two months since its ratification. Their delay is verging on an affront."

"I must beg your forgiveness, sir. I have urged haste in my letters, but I fear my pleas have fallen on deaf ears. They are meeting resistance from other merchants."

"I am meeting with resistance myself. There are many, as you know, who object to closer ties with a Protestant nation, even though the ties are in the realm of trade. I shall write London again, demanding action. I hope you will do so as well."

Lepage's comment, that trade, politics, and religion were bound together, was proving true. "I return to London at the end of the month. I promise to put your case to every member of the syndicate I see, and tell them of your displeasure."

"Let us hope that will have some effect." Harduin's curt nod made it clear their conversation was at an end.

A moment later, Sidney summoned him to the first course.

During dinner, Sidney fretted about Coligny. King Charles had not given him permission to march to Nassau's aid, a promise the Admiral felt obliged to honor. The Admiral put great faith in Sidney's ability to convince his uncle, and in Leicester's ability to convince Queen Elizabeth, to declare her support for the Dutch rebels openly and send troops to their aid. Such action, Coligny declared, would convince King Charles to invade the Low Countries, and would assure the victory of reformed religion in Europe. Sidney did not feel up to the task imposed on him.

On Hunter's other side sat a *maître des requètes* whose main interest was the evening's entertainment. "I have heard it will be the greatest spectacle since Bayonne. Of course, nothing tonight will match the water spectacle there, which I witnessed. Sailors attacked an artificial whale; sirens sang; Neptune greeted the royal party in verse. Monday night was but a pale imitation. Chariots in a hall cannot compare with boats on a river," he rattled on.

Hunter half-listened. Delorme had said that many courtiers admired Marie Challon's beauty and desired her. Yet she had chosen him to escort her. At the Louvre, her thigh had pressed against his. After the shock of cool water, she had stroked his damp thighs.

When the guests progressed from the dining hall, Hunter lingered in the entrance hall, as arranged, and Marie Challon joined him. Together they climbed the stands in the great hall and seated themselves on the fringe of the queen's ladies-in-waiting and their escorts, near the entrance. The Queen Mother sat thirty yards away, in the midst of ladies without escorts. Marie ignored the questioning looks from those around them.

"Look," she gushed, "the three worlds. On the left is Hell with its devils, then over the River Styx—see Charon in his boat?—is Earth. There is Paradise." She pointed right.

A cacophony of cowbells sounded as a wheel in hell turned, powered by two demons walking inside it. At the same time, on the paradise platform, a huge wheel, painted with signs of the zodiac, the seven planets, and lanterns signifying the stars, began to rotate. Hunter gasped. The circular platform, full of grass and flowers, turned to reveal twelve women in gossamer gowns.

"Ahh," Marie said, "they take your breath away, do they?"

"I was surprised that the garden turned with the heavens," Hunter said.

"You did not notice the nymphs in the garden, in such thin garments?" she asked.

"What man could help but notice them? But what are nymphs doing in Heaven?

"If Charon is boating on the Styx, then that must be Tartarus, not Hell, and Paradise must be the Elysian Fields, not Heaven." She let out a small laugh. "That makes sense. It is not Heaven, full of sexless angels, but the *paradis d'amour*." She fixed him with her eyes. "Isn't that a better paradise?"

Was that a flash of desire in her brown eyes? "I cannot disagree with such a fine lady."

"Will you approve whatever I say? Have you no opinions of your own? Do you agree with your queen and our priests that all should strive for virginity, not a paradise of love?"

"You place me in a difficult position. I must either differ with my sovereign and the Catholic Church or the lady I am with."

"Still you avoid my question." She wrinkled her brows. "I expected a lawyer to be ready to take a stand and argue his case."

"Lawyers are also skilled at dodging questions," he said. "However, as Her Majesty is far away, and I see no clergy nearby, I will agree that a paradise of love is more appealing to me."

"Stated with all the care and craft of a lawyer." Her eyes sparkled with mischief.

A series of explosions caused the crowd to gasp, and Marie grabbed Hunter's arm. In a moment, both laughed. The Christian devils dancing about the pagan Tartarus had set off small fireworks. They lit more firecrackers from a slow match and capered and dodged in mock terror as they exploded. Sulfurous smoke floated over the crowd. Marie kept hold of his arm and nestled close to him.

The demons cowered as three knights in armor strutted out near the Elysian Fields. The audience recognized King Charles and his brothers. The nymphs executed graceful gestures of admiration for the knights.

"How lucky they are," Hunter said, "to have four maidens each."

Marie jabbed him in the side. "Surely they will not 'have' them. What an indecent idea."

"I simply meant there are four nymphs for each knight," Hunter countered. "You cloak my innocent verb in bawdy garments."

Marie pouted, then pointed back to the center of the hall. "Look, here come more knights. Perhaps each nymph will have a man." They exchanged looks. "Do not look at me so," she said. "My verb is as chaste as yours."

Henri of Navarre, Prince Condé, and a dozen Huguenot nobles stood before the king and his brothers. Henri pointed to the nymphs, and the Protestant knights strode forward.

"Perhaps their intentions are less innocent than our verbs," Marie said.

The king held up his hand to stop the Huguenots.

"The king will protect their virtue," Hunter said.

"He must keep the damned Huguenots out of Heaven," Marie said. "That is only right."

The knights on both sides struck threatening poses. Henri of Navarre challenged the Valois brothers. The audience applauded, while servants pushed out barriers and grooms led two caparisoned horses. Marie squealed with delight. "I love jousting! Do you?"

Hunter swallowed. "I must admit I have never attended a tournament."

"No experience?" she said. "Then I shall have to instruct you."

"Pray do."

"It will be my pleasure," she said with an impish grin. "These passes will be short; there is no room in the hall for the horses to gain the speed they do in the courtyard. They pass left side to left side. A good rider may unhorse his opponent, but as they meet with angled lances, it is more likely one will break."

Pages carried out helms and lances. Alençon would be the first to tilt. "That is Count Rochefoucauld," Marie identified the Huguenot knight. "He is more experienced, but perhaps he will be kind to the young duke."

The audience cheered the first pass. The riders' lances glanced off one another's shields.

"Have you much experience in the saddle?" Marie asked, devilment in her brown eyes.

"I learned to ride when I was nine." Hunter willed innocence into his face.

"Men do learn to mount horses at a young age," Marie said. "That is true."

A cry from the crowd. This time, both lances made solid contact and broke. "I thought that the memory of Henri II's fatal wound led Queen Catherine to forbid her sons from jousting."

"She did forbid tournaments for some years, but now the king is of an age, and cannot be ruled by his mother," she said.

Evidently the breaking of lances had been determined a sufficient outcome. Grooms led new horses in, and Anjou and Condé mounted. "A lady appreciates a knight who knows how to mount softly," Marie said. There was that impish grin again.

"But these knights tilt for the favor of nymphs, not ladies" he said.

"I know these nymphs," she said. "They bestow their favors to those who can mount gently and ride long and hard."

Hunter held her gaze. Could she mean what she seemed to mean? She returned a bold stare and a smirk. A cry from the crowd pulled their eyes back to the list. The prince and the duke cantered towards each other, and both lances shattered. Spectators cheered and applauded.

"These knights are only able to complete a short ride," he said. What would she respond?

"In this hall," she purred, eyes full of meaning. How well did she know Anjou?

The spectators applauded as the two kings mounted. They thundered towards one another, but hit only glancing blows. "That may not impress the nymphs," Hunter said.

"No. They prefer men who can aim well and strike home." This time she kept her eyes on the spectacle, but grinned.

The kings charged again. Henri's lance slid off Charles's shield, but the King of France broke his lance on Navarre's chest, knocking him off balance. The spectators cheered and applauded. Servants led the horses away, while others removed the barrier and the horse droppings.

"Will Henri's knights retire now?" Hunter asked.

"No," she said. "None of Her Majesty's spectacles is as short as that. There has been no singing or dancing."

The Huguenots again strode towards the nymphs. Again, the king forbade them. Again, Henri of Navarre challenged him.

"Perhaps they will win on foot," Hunter said. "They outnumber the king and his brothers."

"Have you ever seen a masque where the king is defeated?" she asked.

Common sense told him the answer. "No, but there are two kings in this masque."

"But it is King Charles's Court."

The noble actors drew their swords. The audience rose and shouted.

"You will see three defeat twelve," Marie predicted.

Sure enough, as swords swung in mock combat, King Charles, Anjou, and Alençon forced the Huguenots back towards Hades. The crowd roared their approval. The frowns of Coligny's party showed their displeasure at the plot of this masque.

"Look! They are sending the Protestants to Hell," Marie squealed, grasping Hunter's arm.

The Huguenot knights retreated to the blue cloth that represented the River Styx, dropped their swords, and pantomimed swimming to the far side, where demons seized them.

Hunter was surprised Henri of Navarre had agreed to his role, but kept that to himself. Marie held his arm tightly and bounced up and down.

The demons herded the Protestant knights into a large cage using tridents. The audience cheered. The Huguenots gathered about Coligny snarled and gestured. Beyond them, Queen Catherine's ladies hooted with laughter. One only, it seemed, did not share in the jollity. Charlotte de Sauve was glaring at them.

"There is your friend, the viscountess," Hunter remarked.

"Yes," Marie said. "She had to wait upon Her Majesty tonight."

The Valois brothers escorted the nymphs from their rotating garden and began a ballet.

Marie leaned closer and whispered, "This will take a long time. I am feeling unwell. Will you accompany me?"

He searched her face for signs of illness, found none, but answered, "Yes."

As they were seated near an entrance, they left without disturbing others. Marie led Hunter to the entrance hall of an adjoining building where servants stood. She whispered a request for the "necessary," and a servant directed her where two female servants stood on either side of a door. Hunter spotted two male servants standing by a door opposite. It would be wise to avail himself of this opportunity. He had drunk several goblets of wine and water.

After relieving himself, he waited in the entrance hall. A tall gentleman with an aristocratic bearing, one of the gentlemen who had watched the wedding from the balcony, recognized Hunter and frowned. "You are the English lawyer who has busied himself about Paris talking up the cloth trade, are you not?"

"I am. Paul Adams, at your service."

The man sniffed. "I do not need the service of a foreign lawyer, but I am surprised to see one so often in unexpected places, mingling with those above his station."

Hunter struggled for self-control. "I hope a man of any profession and any country is free to go where he is invited."

The tall courtier snorted. "That young Englishman Sidney is your voucher." He turned, but threw back, "Perhaps English gentlemen are less discerning about the company they keep."

Hunter stood, stewing. Marie appeared at his side again. "What is the matter?"

"Nothing, really," he sighed. "A courtier just informed me that a foreign lawyer should not be seen in such high places."

"Take no notice of such popinjays."

"At least he did not call me a rag peddler."

Marie's face grew serious. "Forget those words. No one thinks of you that way any more." She stepped closer and stroked his cheek. "Can this sooth your pain?"

"Such a soft touch could cure anything." Her touch aroused him. "And you, do you now feel less ill?"

"I still have an ache that needs remedy." She gazed straight into his eyes. Then she placed her hand on her head, sagged forward as though weak, and groaned. "I beseech you, come with me."

She led him down a dark corridor, leaning against him. His heart beat faster. "Where are we going?"

"You will see." She turned, all sign of weakness gone. "Will you help me feel better?"

"I am at your service." His desire overwhelmed any foreboding.

She shushed him, glanced back at the entrance hall, and turned to climb a set of spiral stairs. He followed without speaking. He wanted her. Was Marie toying with him again? Would she tempt him, then, when he attempted to kiss her, laugh at him or act offended? At the top of the stairs, he slipped his arm around her waist. She returned the gesture and guided him down an unlit, deserted corridor. She stopped in front of a door, pulled away from him, slowly turned the knob, and peeked in. "In here."

They stood into a small, dark antechamber with a tall chest on one side. Hunter shut the door softly. Marie stepped forward, embraced him, and held up her face with open lips. Heart racing, he put his arms around her, hesitated a moment, then kissed her. Her tongue darted about his mouth and her pelvis pressed hard against him. His penis stiffened.

After a long moment, their lips parted. This was no fraud.

"I am feeling better already," Marie said. "But this bodice is much too tight for such a warm night." She twisted sideways and touched the bow that tied the laces of her bodice. "Can you help me with this knot?"

Hunter stood panting and momentarily paralyzed.

"Don't be afraid." She puckered her lips playfully. "Have you never helped a woman out of her bodice?"

He laughed nervously and fumbled with the bow, "Of course I have." He must not seem inexperienced with this worldly lady of the Court.

"Good." Her laces loosened. "I have already given you a lesson in jousting tonight. I hope no lessons in love making will be necessary." She took his hands and slid them inside her bodice.

Was this really happening? Marguerite had been right; not only did he think of other women, he was about to be unfaithful to her.

"Are you afraid? What is the matter?" Marie asked.

"No. Nothing." He cupped her warm breasts and bent to kiss her. Marguerite had always said they were temporary lovers. She had had Grattard. Well, she was not the only one who could take another lover. His hands massaged. Their tongues tasted one another. His penis swelled.

They broke apart again. "I am feeling better all the time," she purred, "but that ache is still there." Her eyes bored into his. She slid her hands to his waist and pulled the laces that bound his codpiece.

He inhaled sharply as she grasped his penis. She laughed. "I will not hurt it."

"It does not hurt," he said. "It feels delighted."

"Quickly, help me up on this chest." As she hopped, he hoisted her. "We must not be gone too long." She drew her gown and petticoats up around her waist.

Hunter grasped her firm thighs, now spread apart. Seated on the edge of the chest, she was at nearly the right height. He rose on his toes and guided his throbbing penis. She moaned as he penetrated her. She clung to him and rocked back and forth. After only a minute, he exploded. She laughed.

"I am sorry that was such a short ride," he said.

"It is all we have time for, but it was enough to relieve my ache."

He backed away. She shook out her petticoats and slid off the chest. "You asked if Queen Catherine's ladies used their charms to draw out secrets. I told you no and now you have proof. This was not for secrets, but for pleasure." She kissed him again, lightly, and stepped back. "Help me with this bodice." She guided his hands to the laces. He pulled and tied them.

A sudden qualm. "What if you should be with child?"

"When the celebrations end, I leave for the Auvergne. Any child I bear in nine months will be my husband's," she answered. "You must lace yourself. You are so lusty you will stiffen again if I do it."

Hunter fumbled with his laces and his thoughts. He had just coupled with one of the queen's flying squad, a woman desired by many noblemen. She had chosen him as a partner. He must doubt himself no more. If a woman like this could desire him, then so might others he had thought beyond his reach.

"Come." She gripped his hand. "We must return. You came with me while I rested a moment in the dark to relieve my headache and dizziness."

"Will they not suspect that story?"

"We cannot help what others think," she said. "Just hold to this—I was taken ill, and after purging myself in the privy, I feared I might faint or be accosted by someone in my weakness. I asked you to accompany me to a quiet room. After some time, I felt stronger. That is what we will say of our absence. Now, I am sure no one saw us come up these stairs, and no one must see us descend. Will you go down first?"

Hunter crept down, making as little noise as possible. Light from the entrance hall filtered into the empty corridor at the bottom. "All clear," he said.

They made their way back to their place in the stands, Marie leaning against him and feigning weakness. The nymphs were still dancing. As they sat, a lady-in-waiting asked if she were ill. Marie told the story they had agreed upon and received a sympathetic look.

The warmth of Marie's body nestled against him sustained his glow. He had enjoyed one of the beauties of the Valois court. He felt superior to those men near them.

The nymphs froze in position as their dance ended, and the audience applauded. They knelt before the Valois brothers, making gestures towards the imprisoned Huguenot knights and raising their hands to the sky. To cries of amazement, a chariot pulled by cocks descended on ropes from the ceiling. A tall, athletic man in a winged helmet held a caduceus; a short, chubby boy carried a bow and arrow.

"Mercury and Cupid," Marie exclaimed, forgetting she was supposed to be ill. Hunter shot her a warning glance. Her shoulders sagged, and she leaned against him again.

As the chariot touched the floor, the gods sang, praising the royal brothers for their martial prowess. In a solo, Mercury sang that the haughty
knights who had dared to enter the Elysian Fields had paid enough for
their affront and should be freed. The king relented and demanded the
release of the Huguenots, but the devils shook their heads.

"Another battle looms," Hunter said to Marie. The royal knights fought
their way towards the prison, while demons threw firecrackers at them.
The devils defeated, Catholic and Protestant knights marched together
across the now-shallow River Styx. Perhaps the theme was one of reconciliation after all. A herald announced that the knights and nymphs would
process to the ballroom, where all the guests were welcome to join them.
An explosion of fireworks ended the performance.

"Shall we dance now?" Hunter asked, anticipating continued proximity.
"Did you not have sufficient exercise?" she asked with a smile.
"Only enough to whet my appetite for more."
"You are a glutton, and gluttony is a deadly sin."
"So is lust."
She gave him a sudden frown. "Remember I am ill. If we dance a gal-
liard, it will give the lie to that."
"I will be content to sit by your side." He offered his arm.
"Perhaps a pavane, then my poor disposition will force me to retire."
He raised his eyebrows.
"Alone," she said.

Thursday, 21 August 1572

Hunter slept late the next day. Lulling in bed, he relived his time with
Marie—their kisses, their embraces, their union in the dark antechamber.
Ah, the contours of her body, her soft but firm flesh. He could impress
Sidney by recounting her favors. Yet she was worried about her reputation, despite what she might actually do. And Sidney still stove for virtue,
though Bryskett chided him for his virginity. Perhaps he would hint of
his conquest to Bryskett.

At last he roused himself and dressed. In the corridor, he breezed past
Jeanne's longing eyes. He was late for breakfast, but perhaps he could
beg some bread and butter and small beer from Auguste. At the bottom

of the stairs, Marguerite sat in her office, a ledger spread before her. Her mouth curved into a smile. "Pray you, come in a moment." She signaled for him to close the door. "Paul, I must ask your forgiveness for speaking so sharply to you," she began.

Hunter's stomach sank.

"I realize your jealousy over Georges Grattard was not because you thought you owned me, but because of your affection." She stepped close, pressed against him, and spoke in a whisper. "Dare I say—your love?" Tears rose along her lower eyelids.

Hunter embraced her, but gazed over her shoulder into the pit of his own guilt. "How can you ask my forgiveness, when I spoke so cruelly to you?" And acted even worse.

"No," she said, "you were right when you said I knew Grattard well— very well. I admit it. But that was years ago."

"And I had no right to condemn you for that, or to be jealous of things that happened before we met." But she had every right to condemn him now.

"I was wrong about something else, as well," she said.

Let her not say she was wrong to accuse him of lusting after other women.

"We should not stay apart for these final days you are in Paris. Come to me tonight, as usual."

"I have promised Sidney to attend this evening's celebrations at the Louvre," he said, and felt her body tighten, "but I will leave early, I promise."

"Good." She tilted her head so he could kiss her. "Now go see Auguste. He has saved some breakfast for you. Later you can tell me about last night."

Hunter asked Laurent to tell Madame Moreau that he had gone to check with Crespin about arrangements for transporting his chests to Rouen. She only wanted a description of the previous night's festivities, but could he describe those calmly while remembering what had taken place between himself and Marie Challon? The late breakfast sat as a lump in his stomach. He had been wrong to become jealous. Marguerite's past affair was nothing compared to his dalliance the night before. She could confess what was past; he felt unable to admit what had happened in the present.

Instead of returning to L'Échiquier after seeing Crespin, Hunter wandered to the Port au Vin, where he sat near a mill and watched the river flow. He considered professing illness and telling Sidney he could not come tonight. But Marie had said she expected to see him. He had not satisfied her. Could he refuse her if she wanted him again? Could he copulate with Marie, then return to lie with Marguerite? Others might, but he could not. He would have to refuse Marie, to confess he felt obligated to another. His spirits sank lower. Why was his guilt limited to the thought that he had betrayed Marguerite? Should he not feel deeper remorse for his sins of the flesh? He had ceased to consider his relationship with Marguerite as sinful, but Marie was married. He had committed adultery with her. When was the last time he had prayed? Was he becoming more depraved, or merely growing into knowledge of the ways of the world? The Seine flowed quietly past.

He delayed returning as long as he could and was grateful to see Marguerite's office door closed. He refreshed himself, changed into his new black suit, and descended. His steps were not quiet enough. Marguerite opened the office door. His stomach tightened.

"You were away a long time." Not an accusation, but she was clearly disappointed.

"Matters arose I needed to see to," he lied.

"Are you leaving now for the Louvre?" she asked, eying his clothing.

"I must meet Philip Sidney at five." That at least was true.

She stepped close. "Be sure no 'matters arise' tonight. You promised to leave early. You will need a long time to tell me of all the spectacles—last night and tonight. And we must leave time for other activities." She smiled.

"I look forward to it." His insides churned. He leaned forward to kiss her quickly and walked into the street.

Hunter and Sidney were directed to the stands erected on the north side of the Louvre courtyard. Before them, mounted courtiers tilted at a ring the size of an apple, dangling between two posts. Sidney scanned the seats and frowned. "I do not see Admiral Coligny. He said he would press an audience with the king today. It may not have gone well."

Hunter looked for Marie Challon, unsure if he hoped to find her or feared it. "There is Delorme. Let us sit by him."

"The main celebrations are delayed," Delorme said. "They are filling the time tilting at the ring. Ah! Cossé aimed too high!" A sigh of disappointment from the crowd. Sidney asked for news of Coligny. "Yes, the Admiral saw the king today. He begged His Majesty to allow him to ride to the relief of Mons. Said his oath to Nassau bound him to leave immediately."

"And what did the king say?" Sidney asked.

"Evidently put him off, saying he was involved in a few days of merriment to celebrate his sister's nuptials, and would satisfy him when those were done. He did call him 'father,' they said."

"The delay seems reasonable."

"But the Admiral answered rudely, I hear. Muttered if he left Paris, it might begin a civil war rather than a foreign war. Oh, well done! Well done! Did you see d'Amboise spear that?" Delorme joined the crowd's applause.

In response to some signal, the courtiers rode from the courtyard, and servants cleared the posts and horse manure. A murmur from the crowd accompanied the arrival of Queen Catherine and her ladies. Marie Challon and the Viscountess of Tours walked near one another some way behind the Queen Mother.

Marie caught Hunter's eye. She nodded to him and smiled, then turned to Charlotte de Sauve. The viscountess glared at him as the Queen's party climbed to a reserved area. The Admiral still had not appeared.

The main spectacle began. Drums and cymbals sounded, and a troop of Turkish knights appeared on the left, dressed in reds and yellows, wearing turbans, and waving flags with crescents. Beneath the turbans, the audience could identify Henri of Navarre and other Huguenots who had been imprisoned in Hell the previous night.

From the right end, a fanfare blew, and another group of horsemen rode in. No, they were not horse*men*, or rather, they were and were not. The riders were costumed as Amazons, with one breast each and sporting bows, but their faces were those of King Charles, Anjou, and Alençon. A Turk issued a challenge to the Amazons. The groups of horsemen charged and swirled in a *mêlée* with scimitars, swords, and maces. The crowd shouted. The Amazons, predictably, prevailed over the Turks. As on the night before, the Huguenots were cast in the role of enemies of Christendom. Delorme expressed satisfaction, but assured Hunter and Sidney that they should not take offense at this.

The spectators stood as Queen Catherine and her ladies exited towards the feast in the Louvre. At a signal from a household official, other spectators descended and funneled into the palace.

Hunter, Sidney, and Delorme had scarcely entered when Charlotte de Sauve approached them. "Gentlemen, I hope you will excuse Master Adams. I would like a private word with him before supper."

Delorme regarded Hunter with raised eyebrows. "I will see you inside," Sidney said.

Hunter suppressed his surprise. "How may I serve you, madame?"

"You may accompany me down this passage"—she tilted her head— "where we may speak privily." When out of earshot of other guests, the viscountess turned to face him with a bland smile. "Did you enjoy the festivities last night?"

"Yes, indeed," Hunter said. "The spectacle was most impressive."

"You accompanied Madame Challon."

"It was an honor to escort her."

"But the two of you did not see the entire spectacle."

"Madame Challon felt ill," Hunter replied carefully. "I accompanied her until she recovered."

"I did not see you at the dancing." Her eyebrows knit in a question.

"As I said, Madame Challon was not feeling well, so after only a few selections, I accompanied her back here."

"To her apartment?"

Hunter touched his hand to his chest. "That would have been improper."

"And very probably witnessed," she said. "So it must have happened earlier."

He swallowed. "What are you suggesting?"

"Did you have her?" She stared directly into his eyes.

"I beg your pardon, madame. I do not understand what you are asking?"

"Do not play coy with me, Master Adams." Her voice was hard. "Did you fuck her last night?"

"I am shocked that a lady would ask me such a question."

"Be shocked if you wish. I am only trying to establish facts."

"Do you wish to spread gossip and sully her reputation?"

"No." She drew back. "She is my best friend." Her mouth curled into a smirk. "She said you fucked her. I am only trying to confirm that."

Hunter stood agape, then stammered, "I don't believe you."

"Your face says otherwise, Master Adams." She turned and muttered, "Damn her!"

"I insist you have misread my face," Hunter protested. "And it is outrageous that you accuse her and curse her."

She stepped closer, "I do not curse her in earnest, it is just that she has won the bet."

"Bet?"

"Fifty écus."

Hunter stared at her.

She stroked his cheek, as Marie had done the night before. "My dear Master Adams, the bet was about you."

Hunter could not believe what he was hearing.

"You remember that day you brought your cloth to the palace? Well, Marie suggested inviting you up. We hit upon the idea of a bet. The first one to kiss you would win five écus from the other. You remember, I kissed you on the temple,"—she touched him—"here, where you have this scar."

Hunter remembered the day well.

"But Marie does not like losing. She spilled water on your lap. She said, as she had touched your prick and bollocks, that more than canceled my kiss, and I should pay her. I refused. That was not part of our bet, just her invention. We argued long and hard about that."

Hunter suspected the next segment of the story, but stood frozen like a mouse before an advancing adder.

"Our argument faded until we saw you the day of the wedding," she continued, "and that night Baron Sidney said you would accompany him to an event. Marie and I agreed to raise the bet in body and gold." She licked her lips. "The first one of us to fuck you would collect fifty écus."

"Ah." Both a sigh and an expression of understanding. When he had first seen Marie that night, she asked if he had seen the Viscountess of Tours and said she had him to herself.

"I had to attend on Her Majesty last night." She paused as though realizing something. "Perhaps she arranged that too. Yes, she was cleverer than I. I thought we would both have a chance to seduce you at the dancing after the spectacle, but she arranged to have you before that, and her feigned illness assured that I would not meet you at all." She laughed. "She has won this time, but I shall get even."

"How?" he asked.

She looked him up and down, then laughed. "Not with you, dear boy." She placed her hand on his chest. "I will not take second place to Marie. We have counts and dukes aplenty to contest; we do not need lawyers for diversion."

Stung by her words, Hunter turned.

"Wait," she said. "I will not be left. You must escort me to the dining hall."

Hunter longed to shout that he was no toy, no mouse for cats to play with then devour, but he took a deep breath and swallowed. Whatever they had been, he had been the fool. There was no need to make it worse by storming out of the palace. He must use wit and self-control to salvage whatever self-respect he could. "It is a privilege for a mere lawyer to escort one of the Queen's maids of honor."

Charlotte smiled, and they began to walk back. "Marie said she enjoyed your conversation and your company, despite certain shortcomings." She lingered on the last words. Again their eyes met.

Stung again, he controlled his response. "She told me we did not have a long time, so I did my best to serve her rapidly."

Charlotte de Sauve laughed her throaty laugh. "So she said, Master Adams. Not the highest of ratings, but satisfactory under the circumstances." They reached the door of the dining hall. "Where are you sitting?"

"I am afraid I have lost my appetite," Hunter said. "I will bid you good night here. Tell Madame Challon to enjoy her winnings."

"I shall. Good night, then."

He bowed and turned. He exhaled and relaxed. He had escaped. He did not have to face Marie now that he knew the truth. He could keep his word to Marguerite and return early.

Walking back to L'Échiquier, he considered confessing all. But that would cause Marguerite pain. Better to deal alone with humiliation and guilt. At the inn, recounting the details of the spectacles was easier than expected. Afterwards, their lovemaking was long and gentle, filled with deeper passion, not the frantic excitement of the night before. Afterwards, he lay beside her, basking in the warmth of their bodies, content to hold her close. He was truly wanted and loved.

Friday, 22 August 1572

Hunter made his apologies to Sidney for the night before, saying he felt ill and decided to forgo another gargantuan banquet.

Sidney pressed a hand to his stomach. "It is difficult to keep up with the demands the Valois Court puts on one's digestion."

"And one's stamina," Hunter said. "How late did the dancing last?"

"I do not know. I left at half past midnight." Sidney looked around. "What time is it?"

"Near eleven," Bryskett said. "I heard a clock chime the quarter."

"I must go to the Admiral this morning," Sidney said. "He did not attend the spectacle, but Rochefoucauld said he wanted to see me today. He was to attend a council meeting in the morning, so there is no great hurry. After almost a week of revels, the king must make some time to govern the country, it seems. Will you accompany me?"

"I would be delighted," Hunter said.

"Fine. Harry, fetch me my hat, if you please." Sidney turned to Hunter. "I danced a gavotte each with Madame Challon and the Viscountess of Tours. Madame Challon told me to send you her regards and tell you she missed you."

She missed another opportunity to test her ability to manipulate a man. Or perhaps she and the viscountess had made another wager. "Did the viscountess not tell you I was ill?"

"No," Sidney said, "only that she had seen you briefly and wondered why you had not come to sup."

Both ladies were equally skilled at lying.

On the rue de la Verrerie, a rider in a gray cloak burst through a fleeing crowd and galloped towards them. Hunter and Sidney pressed themselves against the wall as he pounded by, crying, "*L'Amiral est mort!*"

They turned to one another wide-eyed. "The Admiral is dead!" They ran towards the rue de Béthizy. As they turned into the rue de l'Arbre Sec, two riders approached. The first recognized Sidney and reined in. "Baron Sidney, have you seen a rider?"

"Yes. Up the rue de la Verrerie. Is the Admiral dead?"

"Shot, but not dead."

"What happened?" Hunter asked.

"Others will tell you. We must pursue the villain!" He and his companion spurred their mounts.

"Saint-Auban, a gentleman of Dauphiné," Sidney explained. "Let us hurry."

They followed others to where a line of Protestants stood, blocking their way. In answer to shouted questions, one of the Pardaillon brothers said the Admiral was alive, but wounded in the hand and arm. The royal physician Amboise Paré was attending him. He begged the crowd to move away and spread the news, so others would not rush to find out. Recognizing Sidney, he shouted for others to make way. Sidney and Hunter shouldered their way to Pardaillon.

"We saw the assassin fleeing," Sidney said. "What happened?"

"The Admiral was passing the house on..." He broke off, glancing back at the crowd. "Pray pass. Ask Guerchy, who was beside him. I must keep this mob away."

They hurried through the gateway of Coligny's lodgings, and across the courtyard, where a crowd near a doorway blocked their progress. "Is Monsieur Guerchy here?" Sidney asked.

Two gentlemen turned to face them. "He is upstairs with the Admiral," said the taller, slender-faced man. His companion, with bushy eyebrows, nodded in confirmation.

"I would like to speak with him. I am Baron Philip Sidney." He used his new title in hope that it might gain him access. "This is my companion Paul Adams."

"I am Jules Coutreau, and this is Henri Tallon," the man with the bushy eyebrows said. "His room is crowded with his companions, and the staircase is full of those who wish to see him. I do not think you can reach Guerchy until later." Seeing Sidney's disappointment, he added, "We both serve Lord Cornaton, and were there when the Admiral was shot."

"What can you tell us?" Sidney asked.

"The Admiral was walking back from the Louvre with several gentlemen, including our master," Coutreau began.

"He had been watching the king and Téligny play at tennis," Tallon added.

Coutreau gave an annoyed glance and continued. "As he passed the house on the rue des Poulines, he stooped to spit..."

"No," Tallon interrupted, "he was adjusting his shoe."

"No matter," Coutreau continued, "his bending down may have saved his life."

"If the bullets are not poisoned," Tallon said.

"Who is telling this story?" Coutreau's face creased with irritation.

"You are," his companion said, "but you should be accurate."

"Pray continue, Master Coutreau," Sidney said.

"As I was saying, as the Admiral bent over, for whatever reason,"—he shot a glance at Tallon—"a shot rang out from a window. The Admiral wavered as the bullets struck, one in his hand and another in his arm."

"His right hand and left arm." Tallon was unable to stop himself.

Coutreau gestured in exasperation. "Go ahead. You tell it."

Tallon hesitated, then proceeded. "His right index finger was almost blown off, and the second ball—the assassin must have double loaded—was lodged near his left elbow." He looked at Coutreau, who remained silent. "He said, 'I am hit,' then 'Thus are honest people treated in France,' and his legs gave out. Guerchy and Pruneaux supported him, but he rallied and said he could walk to his lodgings. Then many things happened. I followed the Admiral and saw Pruneaux wrap his arm." He paused and looked at Coutreau.

"Are you suggesting I am competent enough to relate some?" Coutreau asked.

"Of course," Tallon nodded. "You stayed near the place of the shooting."

"When we realized what had happened, there was a cry to apprehend the assassin." Coutreau glanced at Tallon. "I mean the man who attempted to kill the Admiral."

Tallon nodded his approval of the correction.

"Pray continue," Sidney urged.

"Saint-Auban and de Séré rushed to the house where the shot had been fired. They broke down the door. Someone said the house belonged to a tutor of the Duke of Guise. Another said the Duke's mother owned the house." Coutreau looked at Tallon as if expecting an interruption. "They found an arquebus on a table, and a servant said the man staying there was Bondot, a friend of her master. In the back, a boy had held a horse ready for Bondot to escape."

"We saw this Bondot riding up the rue de la Verrerie," Hunter said.

"In truth?" Coutreau asked, open-mouthed.

"Yes," Sidney said. "He shouted the Admiral was dead."

"He did not wait to see if his shots struck home," Hunter said.

"Thank God they did not," Coutreau said.

Tallon said, "Word came down a few minutes ago that Paré removed the ball and cut off the damaged finger, and the Admiral is resting."

Sidney took a deep breath and turned to Hunter. "Ambassador Walsingham should learn of this as soon as possible. Can you take one of my horses and ride to the embassy, post-haste? I will stay here in hopes of seeing the Admiral."

As Hunter turned to leave, Téligny dashed towards him, his doublet unlaced. "Make way, I must see my father!"

Those gathered near the door stepped back, but Sidney asked, "May I go with you? The Admiral asked to see me today."

Téligny stared blankly for a moment, then recognized him, snapped "Yes," and started pushing his way up the staircase. Sidney followed.

Hunter ran to Sidney's lodging, ignoring the hubbub around him. He told Bryskett and Madox what had happened while Harry and John saddled a horse. As he rode across Paris, he could tell by the expressions around him how far the news had traveled. Half way up the rue Bordelle, the calm demeanor of those bustling in and out of the shops assured him that he had outrun the news of the assassination attempt. The second attempt this summer. Pray God this one would be equally unsuccessful. But this shooting was not the work of an apocalypse-crazed stableman, but of the House of Guise. Would the Huguenots attack them? Would the king have them arrested? How severely would he punish them? Would Coligny live? Would his death end the Netherlands enterprise? If he lived and the Guise were banished from Court, would the king openly espouse an invasion of the Low Countries?

In the ambassador's office, Hunter found Walsingham, Beale, and Lepage. Lepage's presence made him hesitate. But all of Paris would know within an hour. "The Admiral has been shot," he announced, and proceeded to tell what he knew.

Beale spoke first. "Everyone will suspect the Guises are behind this, seeking revenge for the assassination of Duke Francis."

"There may be other motives," Walsingham glanced at Lepage.

"Gentlemen," Lepage rose, "I am sure you have more pressing business just now than discussing staff with me. As you are satisfied with Alain and Christophe, I will take my leave."

Hunter asked, "Shall I leave as well?"

"Stay a moment." Walsingham's dark eyes flashed meaningfully. When Lepage had left, he began, "Though the circumstances seem to connect this shooter with the Guise family, they have sought revenge for years. Why act now?"

"Opportunity?" Beale said.

Walsingham shook his head. "Coligny has been in Paris before, with fewer followers. The likelihood of retaliation by hundreds of Huguenots is greater now." He looked speculatively into space. "Perhaps the Guises are thanking God even now that the Admiral was not killed. I believe this attack was primarily to prevent the assault on the Netherlands."

"The House of Guise would celebrate that as well," Beale said.

Walsingham nodded. "But so would the King of Spain. Their ambassador could easily hire an assassin."

Hunter, feeling like a fly on the wall, fidgeted in his chair.

"Master Adams, did you hear any word of the king's reaction?" Walsingham asked.

"No, sir," Hunter said. "Téligny had most likely been with the king when he got the news, but he said nothing in his haste to see his father."

"I would be interested to know the reaction of the Catholic expatriates," Walsingham said. "Might you deliver this news to them, and report their response?"

"I will be glad to do so," Hunter said, though he longed to return to Sidney, "but I think they will have heard the news by now."

"Perhaps," Walsingham said, "but you saw the assassin escape, and heard a first-hand account of the assault."

As Hunter prepared to leave, Alain brought in a rolled document with seals dangling and announced, "Delivered by a royal messenger."

Walsingham scanned the scroll. "The king commands all in Paris not to take up arms; he has ordered an enquiry into the attack; he asks Catholics near the Admiral's lodgings to leave their houses so that his Reformed followers might move close to him." He pursed his lips. "I doubt any enquiry will progress quickly enough to satisfy the more hot-headed Huguenots. Let us hope they do not take it upon themselves to mete out justice to the Guises as they see fit."

At the Antelope, Hunter found Kempson, Barnes, Timmons, Heath, Chandler, and Fisher embroiled in conversation. Disappointed that Wilkes was absent, Hunter nevertheless related what he had witnessed.

"Then you do not know that a great number of Huguenots appeared before the king and demanded justice," Heath said. "Some threatened they would take matters into their own hands."

"Everyone thinks," Sir James said, "that the assassin was hired by the House of Guise."

"All the evidence points that way," Chandler said. "I wonder if those Huguenots who pursued Bondot have captured him by now."

Several simultaneous discussions began anew. If the shooter were not captured, could a case against the Guises be proved? Would the Protestants be satisfied if King Charles did not arrest the Duke of Guise? What if he had not been involved, but his mother had? The assassin used one of her houses. Would the king dare act against the House of Guise, heroes to the Parisians, in defense of the Admiral, whom they hated? Could Anjou, Queen Catherine, or King Charles himself have known of this attempt and approved it? But the king admired Coligny. The Queen Mother and Anjou would be pleased at his death. Yes, but he was only wounded. Might there be another attempt on his life? Would the Admiral and his followers leave the capital tonight? The king had offered protection, even inviting him into the Louvre. Surely it would be an affront to refuse. Could he be moved safely with his wounds? How many Huguenots were lodging near him? If the Admiral were to die, would they attack the Guises or the royal family? Would the citizens of Paris rise and attack them?

"It appears at this juncture," Sir James said after the babble died, "that the Admiral must trust the king to protect him, and the king must trust the Admiral to control his followers, though that might be difficult for both of them."

Chandler eyed Fisher. "Today proves once again that a common man may influence a kingdom's affairs."

"You need not renew that argument," Fisher said. "I concede your point."

It was clear none of the expatriates had inside knowledge of the attack. A thousand similar conversations must be taking place throughout Paris, all speculation. No expatriate had expressed happiness that the Admiral had been attacked. Unlike Walsingham, none remarked on how Coligny's wounding would impact the offensive into the Low Countries.

At his lodgings, Sidney told Hunter the news of Coligny's condition and recounted all who had visited the Admiral during the afternoon—not only every important Huguenot, but also almost every noble at Court, including the king, the Queen Mother, Anjou, and Alençon. "The king looked genuinely concerned and swore to avenge the attack. It was more difficult to believe that Anjou or the Queen Mother wished the Admiral a quick recovery rather than a fatal infection. Someone said the assassin's arquebus came from Anjou's guards. The only person conspicuously absent was the Duke of Guise. Some said this showed his guilt, but others saw it as prudence. As even the king's brothers received venomous stares and jostling as they made their way to the Admiral's bedside, Henri of Guise would be taking his life in his hands to come into the midst of angry Huguenots.

"After all the well-wishers left, an argument began. The Vidame urged all to abandon Paris before assassins could strike again. Téligny said they should trust the King, and that the Admiral was too seriously injured to move. The physician Paré agreed with Téligny, and his opinion carried the day. Some moved into houses close to the Admiral, others thought it wiser to remain across the Seine, in the faubourg Saint-Germain-des-Prés, and a few thought it best to leave the city. Navarre, Condé, and many of their followers are staying in the Louvre.

"The Admiral, for all his pain, remained in good humor. He said he was fortunate to have been wounded for following God's word. He had faced death many times in battle, and had been condemned to death two years ago, so he was prepared for death whenever it was God's will."

"Do you believe the Vidame correct to distrust the king?" Hunter asked.

"Perhaps it is the Queen, Anjou, and the other counselors that they distrust," Sidney said. "Retz, Tavannes, Nevers—they have all opposed Coligny in the King's Council. Would they stand by and let the king arrest the Duke of Guise?"

"Will it come to that?" Bryskett asked. "Even if the assassin is apprehended, he may swear he acted alone, from some personal grudge against the Admiral."

"But how will he explain using the Guises' house and an arquebus of Anjou's bodyguards?" Sidney objected.

"He will claim personal connections with the housekeeper and a bodyguard. The Guises will deny any knowledge. The servants will be thrown to the wolves, but their masters will not be punished." Bryskett's tone was cynical. "You have not seen enough of the world to know how these affairs work."

Sidney turned to Hunter. "You would be wise to reach your inn before nightfall. We cannot be sure what may take place in the streets of Paris tonight."

Even in daylight, the atmosphere of Paris had changed. Hunter noted anxious movements, nervous sideways glances, and sudden stops to look over the shoulder. Near L'Échiquier, Izard's militiamen stood in doorways, heads together, eyes scanning the streets.

When Hunter entered, Marguerite Moreau started towards him, her face a mix of concern and relief, then she checked herself and glanced towards the dining room. She backed towards her office door, eyes asking him to follow. He glanced at the patrons intent on their food and did so.

In the office, they embraced. "I am glad you are safe," she whispered. "You were gone all day." They exchanged a kiss of longing and relief.

"I am thankful to be back as well, though I was in no danger."

"Laurent said you went to Master Sidney's. As he is close to the Admiral, I imagined you might be involved in the tumult. Two of the Gascon gentlemen returned and said their friends were staying the night near the Admiral. I thought perhaps you had as well."

"I admit to some involvement in 'the tumult' as you call it, but it is a long story. I can tell you tonight. Suffice it that I am here now. You must look to your guests, and I am ravenous."

"You may slake your hunger with food now," she smiled back, "and take care of other hungers later."

Hunter recounted his experiences of the day over supper with Coran and Mongaston, omitting his visit to the Antelope. In turn, they told how they had heard the news, rushed to the rue de Béthizy, and were finally able to see the Admiral for a few moments. They voiced anger at the Guises and recounted anxious discussions with other Huguenots. They had decided to return to the Chessboard Inn, while de Galion and Poudampa elected to stay near the Admiral. Perhaps tomorrow the king would punish those responsible, but they had little faith he would.

After the guests of the inn retired, Hunter descended to Marguerite's chamber to tell her of his day and find solace and comfort in her arms.

The Hooded Man and Zuñiga sat on either side of the ambassador's desk, glasses of red wine before them.

"Many in Paris speculate that Your Excellency had a hand in this," the Hooded Man said.

"I am glad to hear that the power of Spain is held in such high regard," Zuñiga said, "but I was as surprised as anyone at the news. More surprised than Queen Catherine."

"You were there when she received the news?"

"I was. Her face was a stone."

"I suppose she could not afford to show her joy." The Hooded Man sipped his wine.

"More likely her disappointment," Zuñiga said. "The shot did not kill him." He drank. "That made me suspect you might have had a hand in this second botched assassination."

The Hooded Man tightened his grip on his glass, then relaxed. "I only wish I could claim credit for such a design, but I know Your Excellency expects me to focus my energy elsewhere."

"So I do," Zuñiga said. "Though it is late and I am tired, I agreed to hear your ideas."

"And I assure you I am grateful for your time, Your Excellency." The Hooded Man shifted his glass to one side. "All of Paris is tense with fear. Hundreds of angry, well-armed Huguenots are in our midst. People hear and repeat the Protestants' cries for vengeance and their insults outside the Hôtel de Guise. Some have even threatened the king."

"Yes," Zuñiga said.

"I hope we might fan those fears, so that they might spill over to the English," the Hooded Man said. "Your agents might suggest that the English Ambassador is encouraging the Huguenots. *La Hache* could send similar messages to militia leaders."

Zuñiga nodded thoughtfully.

"Perhaps tomorrow some citizens might gather in front of the English Embassy to express their anger at such provocation."

"Hardly enough to break an alliance," Zuñiga said, "but such incidents do set the right tone."

"That was what I thought." The Hooded Man took up his glass. "Then if the Huguenots do act—even one of the Admiral's followers losing his temper and attacking a good Catholic might do—the good citizens of Paris may react. If a battle breaks out between Catholics and Protestants in the streets, the English may not be safe in their embassy. One of those opportunities we have been waiting for might develop."

"I shall ask those working for me to spread the word that English heretics embolden their French brethren to insult the king and his family, and to suggest they show their disapproval." Zuñiga smiled. "As to further opportunities, we must leave that in God's hands."

"Of course."

"I almost forgot." The ambassador sifted through papers on his desk. "There is a paragraph in a letter I received which may interest you. It seems Lord Burghley sent a spy to Paris some time ago. Here it is." He drew out a letter and read. "A young man named Edward Hunter."

The Hooded Man shook his head. "I do not know anyone of that name, but no doubt he assumed another."

"So the letter says," Zuñiga said. "But a description is included. 'Of medium height and build. Dark brown hair and eyes. Thick eyebrows. High cheekbones. Could be considered handsome. Aged 22 or 23.'"

"The description fits a man calling himself Paul Adams, who has been here since April." The Hooded Man sat back. "Well, perhaps it is time to make his life more difficult."

Saturday, 23 August 1572

A crowd stood at the corner of rue de l'Arbre Sec and rue de Béthizy, their way blocked by Huguenot servants who, in defiance of the king's edict, wore swords. They assured the crowd that the Admiral was alive and doing better, but needed rest, not visitors. Hunter and Sidney shouldered their way to the front of the throng, where Sidney produced a note from Téligny. The guard allowed Sidney through, but, as no Paul Adams was mentioned in the note, Hunter must wait. Sidney promised to speak with Téligny and return soon.

Hunter waited, certain that Sidney would obtain permission for him to enter as well. He edged sideways, away from the guard who had blocked his entrance, and asked another guard for news. Saint-Auban and de Séré had returned from their pursuit without the assassin. All now believed the shot had been fired, not by any Bondot, but by Charles de Louviers, Lord of Maurevert, a client of the Guises who had shot and killed the Huguenot captain Mouy three years before. The riders had followed his trail to a Guise château, where the sight of arquebuses at its loopholes forced them to turn back. The servants from the house where the shot had been fired were being questioned. Surely they would gather enough evidence against the Guises for the king to act. "Unless, as some believe," the guard whispered, "the king approved the attack."

Sidney emerged from between two guards.

"Did you get a note?" Hunter asked.

Sidney's face was grim. "I pray you, follow me. We must talk."

What had gone wrong? Frowning, Hunter followed him into a doorway that afforded some privacy. Sidney fixed him with a look of disappointment mixed with anger.

"What happened?" Hunter asked.

"Téligny received a letter early this morning." Sidney paused for a deep breath. "It stated you have a close relationship with a number of English Catholics who have settled in Paris, that you frequently meet with them, and..." Another pause. "...that you have attended Mass on several occasions. I said these accusations could not be true, but he said he cannot take the chance of letting you approach the Admiral."

The calamity Hunter had feared was upon him. "Who sent the letter?"

"It was anonymous." Sidney looked steadily into Hunter's eyes. "Tell me those things are all lies."

If he denied his association with the expatriates, Sidney could easily discover the truth. He longed to explain his service to Lord Burghley and his success uncovering the Catholic distribution network, but his role must remain secret. "They are not lies. I have good reasons for what I have done, but I cannot tell them to you now."

Sidney recoiled as though struck in the face. "Until you can explain your reasons, we must consider our friendship to be at an end. I am not accustomed to spend time with those I cannot trust." He spun and strode back towards the rue de Béthizy.

Hunter opened his mouth to cry after him, but could think of no way to explain himself and mend the rift that had opened between them. Had an expatriate written the note? Sidney did not accuse him of writing pamphlets, but perhaps Wilkes would not mention that, lest it reveal his own activities. Roger Barnes, his companion in the search for Pickering's killer, would not write a letter denouncing him. Thomas Fisher could, in one of his sober moments. Might Timmons, with his constant concern for the state of others' souls, want to make sure Paul Adams did not suffer for avoiding the True Faith? Sir James Kempson, Richard Chandler,

Timothy Heath—any of them might have written. They had all been at the Antelope yesterday, but none had said anything hostile to him. After holding his secret for months, why would they reveal him now?

He walked east, towards the pont au Change. He would march to the Antelope and demand if any expatriate had sent the letter. As he crossed to the Île de la Cité, he reconsidered. What would it profit him to find the source of the letter? It would not repair his friendship with Sidney. And he would be leaving Paris in six days. He would have no more to do with the Parisian expatriates after that, so best just avoid them for the next week. The anonymous letter could do him limited damage during the few days he remained in France. He would face the disapproval of the Gascons at L'Échiquier and exclusion from Huguenot circles. With the Admiral in danger and the fate of their faith in the balance, would they do more than disdain a Catholic Englishman who had deceived them? Coran might challenge him to a duel. But he would have to deal with that if it happened. He could regain Sidney's trust by revealing his mission. That must be his immediate goal, but he must obtain Walsingham's approval first. He turned his steps towards the embassy in Saint-Marcel.

In the Place Maubert, a friar harangued a crowd. "Why do we tolerate vipers in our midst? They pollute our city with their heresies. They strut among us, carrying weapons in contempt of the king's edict. They insult and mock the Church's holy rites." The crowd punctuated his sentences with angry snarls. "Because their leader has suffered a wounded arm, they threaten that our streets will flow with blood. If any blood is spilled, it should be the blood of heretics, blood that will cleanse Paris of their foul teachings..."

A large number of soldiers stood at the Port Bordelle. They checked Hunter's papers twice and reluctantly allowed him to proceed. A group of ragged workmen stood around barrels at a wine shop near the embassy, following him with angry eyes. One muttered, "*Chien anglais,*" as he passed, but he kept his gaze straight ahead.

After Hunter knocked twice, the porter Alain opened the door a crack, bid him enter quickly, and bolted the door. "I hope I might speak with the ambassador."

After looking into Hunter's determined eyes, Alain led him up the grand staircase. Following a muttered exchange at the door to Walsingham's study, he announced, "The ambassador will see you now."

Walsingham waved him to a seat. "Master Adams, what news of affairs in the city?"

"Less than I might wish." Hunter reported the return of Saint-Auban and the belief that Maurevert was the would-be assassin.

"I received a message to the same effect," Walsingham said. "Maurevert had been placed in the house prior to the attack by another Guise retainer. Their fingermarks are all over this crime. Did you see the Admiral?"

Hunter sighed. "I was not allowed near him. Téligny received an anonymous letter stating that I met with English Catholics in Paris and attended Mass. Not only was I denied entrance to the Admiral's lodgings, but I lost the trust of Philip Sidney by confirming the accusations."

Walsingham frowned. "Do you think one of the English papists wrote the letter?"

"Most likely," Hunter said, "yet I cannot understand the motive. Sir Gregory urged me to use acceptance by the Huguenots to discover their plans, and my friendship with Sidney to milk his uncle's thoughts from him. The others have kept the secret of my Catholicism for months."

"How did they react yesterday to your news of the attack?"

"It was clear that they had no knowledge of who had planned or carried out the attack. As everyone, they suspected the Duke of Guise."

"He and his cousin spoke to the king early this morning at the Louvre, then returned to the Hôtel de Guise. Clearly they were not arrested." Walsingham formed a steeple with his fingers. "It is hard to see why expatriate would want to sever your connection with the Huguenots now, when all of Paris is eager to know what they are saying and planning." He rested his lips on the finger steeple a moment. "This denunciation may come from elsewhere. A piece of sensitive but false information about English volunteers in Flushing was shared with the Huguenot leader Lord Damville a week before the royal wedding. At the ceremony, it was clear that the Spanish Ambassador had received it. Within a few days, Alva was acting on that false information."

"Do you suspect Damville, a Montmorency, of being in league with Spain?"

"No, but someone he trusted passed the information to Zuñiga. There are Frenchmen in league with Spain—including at least one Huguenot—focused on frustrating English interests. Since the treaty was signed, they have worked to drive a wedge between England and France. I suspect they were behind the man who jammed a pistol in my chest." He paused, as though remembering that morning. "Just now, the Huguenot leaders, and to some extent King Charles, long for a reassurance I wish I could give, that England will support an offensive into the Netherlands. Revealing Paul Adams as a Catholic might, in some small way, raise distrust of the English among the Huguenots."

"Can you guess who is responsible?"

"The interests of the Guises and Spain overlap. The list of noblemen in their camp is large. A weak Huguenot might see advantage in joining them. But which sharks within that vast sea hunt English fish, that is difficult to say."

Hunter hesitated. "I wondered, sir, if I might explain to Sidney the reasons I sought out the company of English papists."

Walsingham's eyes became flint. "Master Adams, there is more at stake here than your friendship with Philip Sidney. Having a friend of his status might be of great value to you, both now and in the future, but, Edward Hunter"—their eyes met as Walsingham pronounced his real name—"every informer who is revealed raises the wariness of our enemies. If Sidney suddenly resumes his friendship with a man discovered to be a papist fraud, how would that look? You would become suspect in the eyes of the expatriates. It is more important that they believe you than that Sidney does."

Hunter could not disagree.

"And you have done well as Paul Adams. There are other places in Europe where Adams might represent English merchants, places where exiled Catholics might welcome him, especially if their friends in Paris vouched for him."

Hunter should have been glad that Walsingham considered he might serve again as an intelligence agent, but would employment as a spy cut him off forever from any true friendship?

"I am sorry," Walsingham said, "but you must remain estranged, at least for the present. Perhaps when Sidney returns to London, after his tour of the Continent, Lord Burghley will explain your role here."

"Could you not tell him, after I leave?" Hunter asked.

Walsingham shook his head. "Too soon. Perhaps when he departs, some weeks hence."

"I would appreciate it if Sidney might know the truth before he leaves Paris."

"Will you visit with the English papists today?"

"I thought to confront them, then doubted the wisdom of that and came here instead."

Walsingham nodded. "That was wise. As a loyal Catholic, you could not be angry at being identified, only disappointed that you can no longer reveal Protestant plans to them."

Sensing the meeting was over, Hunter let himself out and immediately encountered Robert Beale.

"Master Adams," he said with raised brows.

"Good day, Secretary Beale."

"Are look about to leave. I would advise you to stay in the embassy just now. A hostile crowd is gathering outside," Beale said. "Ned, the son of my man Thomas, was set upon by ruffians as he returned from the bakery. They beat him when he tried to gather the scattered bread. They called him an English dog and said he wanted Huguenot heretics to kill all good Parisians. He was fortunate that Manucci came along at that moment."

"Manucci?" Hunter asked.

"Jacomo Manucci," Beale explained. "A Florentine gentleman who travels frequently between Paris and Lyon." He looked over his shoulder as steps sounded on the staircase. "Here he comes now."

A man in a brown doublet advanced towards them. His stocky, muscular body was a few inches shorter than Hunter, his bearded face was handsome, with high cheekbones, and his sharp eyes looked out from under heavy brows.

"Signore Manucci, may I introduce Paul Adams," Beale said. "I was just advising him to tarry awhile before leaving."

"Good day, Signore Manucci," Hunter said. "I understand you rescued one of the embassy's servants."

"The lad is downstairs with his father,' Manucci said. "Several idlers at the nearby tavern accosted him, but fortunately my servant and I were on our way here. The louts were less eager to deal with two men their own size. While they retreated to rally friends, we were able to pull young Ned inside. He has a broken lip and some bruises."

"The ruffians did gather reinforcements." Beale pointed out the window.

A crowd of about twenty men advanced towards the embassy. Alain bounded out the front door to close and lock the gate. His actions evoked menacing shouts. Stones whizzed past Alain as he nipped inside.

"It will be wise to close our shutters." Beale leaned out to grasp the handle. "As it appears you gentlemen will be here for some time,

I will ask Gilbert to prepare food for you. We will dine in an hour. Signore Manucci, the ambassador is expecting you. Master Adams, pray excuse me."

Manucci entered Walsingham's office. Hunter stood irresolute. Yesterday he had been in the midst of events; today one letter had excluded him. He faced the prospect of idly waiting—not explaining himself to Sidney, not speaking to the expatriates, and now, not even gathering information. So far as Walsingham was concerned, he had completed his task. So far as the syndicate was concerned, he had softened up some resistance to a Rouen Staple and fanned some enthusiasm for it. He wished that he were leaving for England tomorrow—except that would take away six nights with Marguerite, nights that had become more important now. If not for the rabble outside, he could have gone to her side, in case Izard threatened again.

He remembered Leonard Halston, wounded veteran of the Battle of Saint-Ghislain he had seen at the wedding, and sought him out. Halston answered his knock with a hearty greeting. They discussed the attack on Coligny and the taut state of the city until they were called to dinner. They shared a table with Manucci, Beale, and Ambassador Walsingham. They spoke of who was behind the attack on Coligny, of what the Huguenots, the Guises, and the king might do. Manucci held that it was impossible to predict what would happen. Walsingham said, in a somewhat irritated tone, that if affairs were impossible to predict, it was better not to make predictions. The others took their cue and ate in silence.

When they were nearly finished, Alain announced Walter Williams. A large man in his thirties with a ruddy face, Williams entered and bowed to Walsingham "I pray your pardon, Your Excellency, but I heard you were at table and, frankly, I have a powerful hunger."

"By all means, sit," Walsingham said. "André, pour some wine for Master Williams. I had hoped to see you today, but I feared you might be delayed by the tumult outside."

"I quelled the tumult," Williams announced, seating himself next to Manucci. "Good day, Jacomo, Secretary Beale." He looked enquiringly towards Hunter and Halston, and Beale introduced them.

"Master Williams," Walsingham said, smiling, "I know you to be a formidable man, but I am amazed that alone you have dispersed some two dozen rascals."

Williams wiped wine from his mouth. "If truth be told, I first came here some three-quarters of an hour ago and saw your unwelcome visitors. Realizing even I have limitations, I rode back to the city gates, where I had observed soldiers loitering about. I reminded them of their duty to keep the peace and told them of the clamor in front of your embassy. Several agreed to accompany me and disperse the rabble. It is thus I claim to have quelled the tumult."

"I must thank you," Walsingham said. "If the mob is gone, perhaps we can open the shutters and gain some relief from this heat." He looked to Beale, who rose to speak to the servants. "I was considering sending a message to the king, to ask for some protection, but you have saved me the trouble."

"Sir, I believe your idea a good one. Those who came with me could only stay a while before they returned to the Porte Bordelle," Williams said. Jonas placed a plate in front of him.

"When did you land in France?" Beale asked.

Williams cut himself a slice of beef before answering. "We docked two days ago at Dieppe. I left the Queen's progress at Kenilworth a week ago and I bring you," he reached into his doublet and pulled out a packet of letters, "messages from Secretary Smith and Lord Burghley."

Beale took the packet, wet with perspiration, between two fingers. He glanced at Walsingham, who shook his head slightly, and Beale deposited them next to his chair.

"I shall read those after you have slaked your hunger," the ambassador said.

Williams nodded his thanks, his mouth full of beef.

"Did you pass near the Louvre?" Beale asked.

"I did indeed. The Admiral is well and receiving many visitors." Williams stopped to chew and swallow. "The king has ordered fifty soldiers to guard him, but the Huguenots grumble. The colonel in charge of the guard is a sworn enemy of Coligny. There was snarling against the Guises and even against the King of Navarre, though he was at the Admiral's bedside, because he had married a 'popish princess.'"

"Master Adams was at the rue de Béthizy just after the Admiral was shot yesterday," Halston said.

Hunter was compelled to tell his story again as Williams cleared his plate.

"Gentlemen, I have correspondence I must attend to." Walsingham rose. "Master Williams, Jean will help you settle into a chamber upstairs.

Signore Manucci, might I prevail upon you to carry a request to King Charles?"

Manucci agreed.

"Master Adams, it is now safe for you to return to your lodgings," Walsingham said. "Master Secretary, if you would pen the request to His Majesty..."

Hunter trudged down the hill dominated by the Abbey of Sainte-Geneviève. The afternoon sun baked Paris. Men and women dragged themselves uphill towards him, their faces anxious. Porters panted by, sweat staining their clothing. Dust hung in the air. This heat would do nothing to cool the Huguenots' anger. At the Place Maubert, another priest railed against Huguenot treachery. On the Petit-Pont, a man with furrowed brows told another, "If Montmorency rides in with his troops, the Guises are done." With both sides full of fear, anything could happen. Would the Gascons at L'Échiquier have heard that he was a secret Catholic? He could not share a table with men who despised him. Best to have Marguerite bring food up to his room. What would he do for the next six days?

At L'Échiquier, Marguerite Moreau spun around and her face lit up. Then she observed him more closely, and the light in her green eyes faded. She glanced around to make sure no one else was near, drew close to him, and asked, "What is the matter?"

"I am hot and tired," he said, reluctant to explain the entire situation.

"Have you been at the rue de Béthizy all day?"

"No," he said. "The embassy again."

"They say the Admiral is recovering. Why did you need to go to the embassy?"

"It is complicated."

She regarded him a moment. "I will have Laurent bring up a basin and some water. You can cool yourself." She drew closer. "Then perhaps I could come up to dry you off."

He smiled. "What? In the afternoon?"

"We have few nights left us," she said. "We may have to use the afternoons and mornings as well. The guests from Lyon and Angers will leave tomorrow morning. The Grattard family departs Monday."

"Afternoons and mornings will be fine with me." Hunter paused and bit his lip. "Might I dine in my room tonight?"

Marguerite wrinkled her forehead. "You do not wish to dine with the Huguenots?"

"It might prove awkward."

She nodded towards her office, and he followed. "What happened today?" she repeated.

He sighed. May as well make the effort and explain now. "You know I have spent time among the English Catholics who live in Paris."

"Yes," she said, "to glean information for Walsingham."

"They believe I am one of them, and have not revealed my faith."

"That, too, I have gathered."

"This morning the Huguenots received an anonymous letter stating that I am familiar with those expatriates, and that I have attended Mass."

"Ah," she said. "So they consider you a traitor."

"That may not be the correct word, but, yes, they do."

"And that is why you wish to avoid the Gascons."

"Yes, but that is not the worst of it. Sidney believes I am a false knave as well."

"I am sorry this has broken your friendship with such a noble man," she said. "Do you know who sent the note?"

"No, and the ambassador believes that if I try to discover the author, I may create problems for myself and others."

"Go to your chamber now," she said. "I will send Laurent with water. I will tell other guests you are feeling ill and send food up later." She kissed him.

"What about drying me off?"

"On second thought, too many guests remain now."

"I could bathe again tonight, for the pleasure of your touch."

"We will see," she said.

Hunter finished wiping the sauce from his plate with bread when a loud knock sounded on his door.

Coran, the Gascon he had imagined challenging him to a duel, stood before him, his eyes dark with loathing. "I heard you were feeling ill. You should be, infected as you are with treachery. My companions returned from rue de Béthizy with news of you."

He had seen this coming, but had only prepared a weak defense. "I did not deceive you. You never once asked about my conscience. You concluded that, because I was English, I was Protestant."

"You were in the company of the Earl of Leicester's nephew," Coran said. "Did he never ask you about religion?"

Hunter felt stung. "My relationship with Master Sidney is my own affair."

"So you deceived him, as well," Coran snarled. "You can use your lawyers' equivocation, but I know you for what you are. Tell me, did you enjoy sharing everything we said with your popish friends?"

"I shared nothing that would harm you or your cause."

"Do you expect me to believe that?"

"You may or may not believe me." Hunter paused, weighing whether he should state what he knew. "I did not reveal anything, but there are those in your midst, trusted leaders, who are telling secrets to your enemies."

"You seek to excuse yourself by hinting at other traitors." Coran's tone accused, but his eyes registered doubt.

"I will say again that you may think of me as you like, but you do not know me," Hunter said. "I pray for Admiral Coligny's recovery and the just punishment of those who plotted against him."

"Many papists, even the king himself, say the same." The fury had faded from Coran's voice.

"I know you are angry with me," Hunter said, "but I ask you to respect my conscience as I respect yours."

Coran's eyes flared again. He spat on Hunter's chest. "There's for your conscience." He turned and stomped away.

CHAPTER 17

Massacre

Sunday, 24 August 1572, Saint Bartholomew's Day

HUNTER AWOKE TO VOICES SHOUTING AND BELLS RINGING. "WHAT'S happening?"

Marguerite sprang up beside him. "I don't know." She swung her legs off the bed and pulled on her shift. "Nothing good." She stumbled to the open window. "Perhaps the Huguenots have risen."

Hunter fumbled with his shirt. Shouting and the pounding of running feet drifted through the window. Marguerite leaned out. Torchlight from below flickered across her face. She held her breath and listened, then jerked erect and spun towards Hunter, her eyes wide with horror. "They are killing the Protestants! The militia is coming! I must warn the guests!" She grasped him by the arms. "Hide in the staircase. I'll say you spent the night with Sidney." She turned and struggled to straighten the covers. "No. I'll say you are at your embassy. They will not attack that."

"The papers in my chamber," he gasped. "They cannot fall into militia hands."

"Very well." She threw on her robe and kissed him. "But hurry!"

He opened the hidden staircase and felt his way up the ladder, his heart racing. Each sermon urging Parisians to cut out the cancer, all the fear and hatred, was bearing fruit. What can Marguerite do to help her guests? Where can they flee? He unlatched the panel and stepped into his room. Marguerite will say he is gone; he dare not light a candle. Below, she pounded on doors and shouted warnings. No time to dress and secure his papers. He dived into his chest. The black suits, brown venetians, hose, a pair of shoes. He threw them in the hidden staircase. He could dress later. As he stepped back into his chamber, loud knocking on the inn's door.

Marguerite began her descent to answer. Below, Laurent's sleepy voice. "Madame, should I open the door?"

"No! Wait!" A few minutes delay might give the students at the top a chance to climb out to the roof. Grattard and his son could arm themselves. What chance will they have against a dozen men?

The pounding grew louder. "Open up, in the name of the king!" Izard's voice.

Marguerite kept herself from rushing down the last flight of steps. Laurent and Martin stood, confused and frightened. "Go. Both of you, out through the stables. Run home and stay there." She pushed them and turned to the door. A fierce volley of knocks set it vibrating.

"Open the door, or we'll break it down."

"Who is it?"

"Captain Izard," a voice other than Izard's announced. "Open by command of the king."

"Captain Izard!" Marguerite tried to assume her most surprised tone. "I feared rioting thieves were assaulting my inn."

"Open this door immediately, Madame Moreau," Izard spoke. "Do not play coy with me."

"Captain," came a voice from the street, "they are escaping over the rooftop."

"Shoot them," was Izard's reply.

Marguerite opened the door. Izard stood before her, his face turned towards a militiaman fumbling with an arquebus. "Hurry, Georges!" he barked, and turned back. "Madame, I am here to carry out the king's orders."

"What are they?" She stood in the doorway, arms crossed, but knees shaking.

"To kill all the Protestants. I know some are lodging here. Did you warn that man climbing on your roof?"

"With your pounding and yelling, no one needs warnings from me," she said. "Do you have a warrant?"

"There was no time for warrants," Izard snarled. "Can you not hear the bells? That's the signal to act. Huguenots planned to kill the king, but the Duke of Guise struck first. The Admiral and his followers are dead. The heads are cut off the hydra, and now we must search out and chop to pieces the coils and tails."

A shot sounded, and a disappointed groan issued from the men. The shooter had missed "They're getting away!" someone shouted.

Izard jerked his head around. "Georges! Pierre! Head them off."

Marguerite pointed to a cross painted on the inn door. "What is that?"

"My men marked places where Protestants lodged late last night. Orders from the *Prévôt*, so we would not overlook any heretics. Of course, I would scarcely overlook L'Échiquier."

"Some of my guests are foreigners," Marguerite objected. "Does the king's order include them?"

A smile spread across Izard's face. "To be sure we are doing the king's will, we will kill them too." He stepped forward. "Move aside, madame."

Madame Moreau swallowed and took a half step back.

Izard stepped closer and whispered, "I will personally waken your English lover."

"He is not my lover," she snapped, "and he is not here. He has gone to his embassy."

"So early? I shall see for myself?" Izard pushed past her.

Marguerite grabbed his arm. "Is it the king's will to start a war by killing Englishmen and Germans?"

"A few dead students and a rag peddler will not start a war," he said smugly. "Release my arm. You are interfering with a captain of the militia who is carrying out the king's orders. I would be justified in killing anyone who does so." He stared hard into her eyes, and she let go.

"Quickly, Martin, lead the men up. Leave Jean and Gaston on this door, so no one escapes." The militia's ensign, gripping a sword, his sleeve wet with blood, slipped behind Izard. A dozen militiamen, bearing halberds, swords, and arquebuses, tramped up the stairs, laughing, eager to begin their bloody work.

Marguerite watched, helpless.

Hunter could not haul his chest of papers to the secret staircase—too noisy and liable to leave scratches leading directly to his place of refuge. He grabbed a bag near the bed and threw in handfuls of notes from the chest. Pounding and shouting downstairs. He lugged the filled bag to the staircase. More papers remained. He pulled leather saddlebags from under his bed. Below, Izard and Marguerite were arguing. Was she in danger? Could he help her? He stuffed the saddlebags. They would surely kill him if he appeared. As he carried saddlebags to the secret staircase, militiamen clomped up the stairs. He could not risk retrieving more papers. But there! His sword and hanger lay beside the bed, his dagger and bread knife on the stool. What a fool to forget them and worry about papers! He darted back into the room, closed the chest, and grabbed his weapons. Knocking on the door. He slipped into the hidden staircase.

Izard's voice called out, "Adams, open your door!"

He closed the panel door gently and turned the latches inside. More pounding.

"Open at once in the name of the king, or we will break the door down!"

Hunter stood immobile, sword in his right hand and dagger in his left, trying to breathe without making a sound. Above the beating of his heart, wood splintered as the militiamen kicked in his door. The flickering of torches played about the edges of the false panel.

"He's not here," said one.

Izard issued orders. "Look under the bed. Henri, look out the window."

Fists pounded on other doors down the hall.

The militiamen in his chamber reported. "Not here." "Nothing here."

Shouts from the hall. A scream. Hunter's grip tightened on his weapons.

"Captain!" a shout came from an upper floor.

"Damn the man!" Izard yelled. "Perhaps he *is* at his embassy. Look again, then follow."

Izard stomped up the staircase. Within the room, men banged about.

"No jewelry," said one.

"Some fine doublets here, and these boots will fit me," a higher-pitched voice said.

"Later," his companion said. "Let's go up."

A crash as a door down the hallway was forced open. More shouting and screams. The two men left.

Hunter stood frozen. They cared nothing for the papers he had taken such care to hide. Their only business was killing and grabbing anything of value. A woman's scream echoed in the hall. Had they harmed Marguerite? No, she was shouting not to kill her guests.

A door splintered. Shouts, a pistol shot, more screaming. Izard's angry voice. "Make way! He's hurt!" Descending footsteps and worried voices.

Thuds and crashes from the top floor. Reports of pistols. A shriek of unbearable anguish. More screams. The rhythmic thump of bodies being dragged down the stairs.

Hunter clenched his sword and dagger so tightly his hands began to ache. His heart pounded. He must act! But he could not. Any attempt to help could only result in his own death.

Renewed clomping on the staircase. A man almost shouted the *Ave Maria,* either proving he was a good Catholic, or effecting a conversion to save himself. More screams and crying. A plea for mercy. Another pistol shot. A woman's wailing that ended suddenly. The thud of a body landing at the foot of the stairs.

Anguish tore through Hunter with each sound. His jaw ached from clenching it.

The din continued several minutes, then died down. No more screams of victims, only the voices of the militiamen. Hurrahs and laughter from upstairs. Muffled thuds from outside. They were throwing corpses from the windows. Men tramped down the stairs, guffawing and shouting. Then, an eerie silence, with only distant bells and cries. A woman sobbed in a room above. Had the militiamen overlooked a victim, or was this someone who had proved herself a good Catholic, terrified at what had taken place all around her? Hunter's breathing slowed, and he strained to listen. Was it safe to come out?

The talk of the militiamen drifted up. Laughter mingled with shouts about gold and jewels. An argument with the word 'shares' repeated. Evidently the men had agreed to pool any valuables they found while about their gristly business. Now more cheers and the clink of cups. They had helped themselves to a cask of wine.

Near at hand, the squeak of his chamber door opening. Again his heart raced. He held his breath and tightened his muscles. At first, no sound. Then the swish of moving cloth, the creak of wood flexing as weight was carefully transferred from one floorboard to another. One man alone. A greedy militiaman, looking for loot on his own? But they had looked over his room before. Perhaps a junior member of the militia, trying to impress his captain by ferreting out a hiding Protestant.

Shoes scuffed and floorboards squeaked. His visitor approached the hearth. He must exhale as silently as possible. Was this one of the men who had searched before? Had he noticed some clue in the paneling?

Below, the murmur of conversation continued, but in Hunter's chamber all sound stopped. Both men held their breath and strained to hear. The militiaman knocked on the panels above the mantelpiece. He tapped his way from the fireplace towards Hunter. The next rap produced a hollow sound on the concealed door. Hunter clenched his weapons. A pause. The intruder sensed his hiding place. Would he call out? Leave to fetch his comrades? Should Hunter burst through the door and attack him? Could he descend to the floor below quietly? Would such a retreat gain him anything?

The door panel creaked as it bowed inward, but the latch held. Would the militiaman investigate the molding above the panel for a mechanism? Was it time to raise the latch and pounce? He would have to silence the man immediately to keep him from calling the entire company to his aid. He could muzzle the man with his left hand and slash his throat. But his right hand held his sword, his left his dagger. How could he manage it?

A sliver of light appeared. The panel's top edge flexed, and a knife point thrust through the opening. The intruder was trying to pry open the panel. He must act. He flicked the latch mechanism with his dagger. The panel door flew open and slammed against the chimney. A young man with sandy hair tripped over the bottom panel and fell forward. His left hand shot out to catch the far wall, and he hung, suspended and off balance. His eyes met Hunter's. It was the young militiaman who had pulled him from the Saint John's Eve bonfire. He raised the knife in his right hand and opened his mouth to shout.

Hunter lunged with all the energy he had held in check. His sword point thrust into the boy's throat. The blade hit bone. His wide eyes staring at Hunter, he emitted a sound between a cough and a swallow. His knife clattered to the floor. He twisted to his left as Hunter pulled back his sword, slicing his throat open further. Blood poured from his mouth and bubbled from the gash in his neck. A gurgling sound as he tried to inhale. A cough sprayed blood from his neck and mouth. He was drowning in his own blood. Hunter read a plea for help in his eyes before they glazed over.

Hunter's chest was tight and his throat dry. He had killed a man. Scarcely a man—a boy of perhaps sixteen. The boy who had pulled him from the fire. Thou shalt not kill. And to kill someone who had helped him in distress... But this boy had been set on killing him. He had acted to defend himself. Logic could not overcome his anguish.

Shouts from the floor below. Had the men in the dining room heard? The outer door of his chamber was open. So was the panel door to his hiding place, with one leg of the boy protruding.

He pulled the boy's leg in. A glance around his chamber revealed no trace of the intruder except for scratches on the panel. Feet and voices sounded on the stairs.

He wrestled the body free of the panel door and closed it. Had the militiamen heard the crash and come to investigate? Had they missed this boy? He leaned the body against the panel and waited in darkness, the sickly-sweet smell of blood in his nostrils, his hands sticky. He felt his gore rise. He could not allow himself to vomit. He concentrated on slowing his breathing as voices passed his door and climbed higher.

Downstairs, Izard shouted angrily at the men to leave their drinks and booty. A colleague had been wounded. There were more Huguenots to be hunted down. Loud cheering. "Good carving!" a man shouted. What was he talking about?

The men from above thudded down the stairs. Hunter tensed again. They paused on the landing and entered his chamber. He could not give way to nausea. Two men spoke of boots. Floorboards creaked. The rustle of clothes hitting the floor. These must be the men who coveted his boots and doublet. He prayed they would focus on plunder and not look at the scarred panel.

Izard continued his harangue. It was early. The coins and jewels should not be divided yet. Easy to carry them along. There was a Protestant jeweler in Old Temple Road and two rich Huguenots nearby. Did they want others to get there before them, while they drank? Shouts of *Non!* told he had prevailed, and the sounds of scraping benches and clanking metal followed.

In his chamber, a voice said, "Look, it fits well." Another, "So do these." Feet shuffled towards the door and down the stairs.

The militiamen clamored their way into the street. Hunter remained tense, still fighting down his nausea. Scraping on the floor above. Probably the Catholic lodgers who had survived the massacre. The weeping immediately below must be Marguerite. He must go to her. He turned from the boy's body and fumbled with his clothes in the dark until he found a pair of venetians to pull on. He stepped over his bags of papers to the narrow ladder that led to Marguerite's bedchamber. He descended, making as little noise as possible, and felt his way to the panel in her chamber. He listened. Only her sobbing. He rapped softly on the wall. The crying stopped.

She scuffed towards the panel and whispered, "Paul?" He turned levers and opened the latch. "Thank God you are safe," she sobbed.

He stepped through and held her. "Did they harm you?"

"No. No. But my inn is full of blood. At least twenty killed. Grattard's whole family." She began to weep again, but stopped. "You are not safe here."

"I know. Marguerite, I killed a man."

"Who? Where?"

"One of the militia. In my room."

Her eyes filled with dread. "When they find him, they will kill me."

"I hid him in the staircase. He discovered it and I had to kill him. He is not in my chamber."

"We must move him. When Izard finds he is missing, they will come back."

"Can we add him to the corpses they threw into the street?" Hunter asked.

"They will recognize him," Marguerite said. "Come, take me to him."

She lit a lamp and they climbed the hidden staircase to the second floor. There, with barely room to stand side by side, she raised the lamp and gazed at the body.

"My God," she muttered, "*Petit Nicolas*." She crossed herself. "God rest his soul."

The blank eyes and gaping throat sickened Hunter. "You know him?"

"He outgrew his nickname, but everyone still called him *petit*. From the rue des Rosiers. A new recruit. The baby of his family."

"The baby of his family," Hunter lamented. "He pulled me from the fire on Saint John's Eve."

Marguerite's jaw tightened. "It will not do for you to think on it. He is Nicolas no more, only a body whose soul is gone." She paused. "And my death warrant if they find him here. Strip his clothes off. Move him so I can examine your room. We must be quick."

Hunter opened his mouth to protest, but her analysis of their situation could not be disputed. He clenched his teeth, grasped Nicolas by the shoulders, and shifted him away from the panel door. Marguerite hung the lantern on a nail and stepped through. Hunter closed Nicolas's accusing eyes. Not Nicolas. A body that must be undressed. A task performed daily by those who deal with the dead. He must divorce his mind from what he had done and concentrate on practical necessities. Remove the shoes. Untie the rope belt. Slide the canvas breeches and russet hose down the legs. Roll the body over. Remove the bloody jerkin. Next, if he pulled the blood-soaked shirt over the loosely attached head... He shut his eyes and fought for control.

Marguerite was back at the panel door. "We are fortunate. No sign of a fight in the room. If I stain these scratches, no one will notice." She looked down. "We must look for birthmarks, scars, any identifying mark. Cut his shirt and turn him over."

Hunter struggled to move his leaden limbs. He picked up his knife and slashed the back of the shirt. He and Marguerite peeled the garment off both sides. Together they rolled the corpse onto its back.

Marguerite nodded. "Again, we are fortunate. No birthmarks. No scars." She stood. "Now you must cut off his head."

Hunter's head snapped up, eyes and mouth open wide. Desecrate a corpse?

She stared back with cold eyes. "If you killed him to save your life, you can cut off his head to save mine."

He still hesitated.

"You almost did so when you stabbed him in the throat," she added.

Hunter nodded and tried to swallow. "It will not be easy." Years of ingrained precepts fell before the logic of her argument and the exigencies of the moment, but his stomach turned at the thought of what he must do.

"Carry him down the secret stairs to the ground floor. I will fetch you a carving knife from the kitchen. If everyone is gone, I can clear a way to the secret door in the storeroom. After that..." Her face clouded. "Adding another body to the heap in the street may work—but all have heads. His head you must throw in the river." She glanced at the window. "But it is almost dawn. Disposing of the corpse must wait until dark."

"I can hide here until tonight," Hunter said.

"You will not be safe," she said. "One man has already discovered the hidden staircase. You should go to your embassy."

"But I would have to cross Paris to reach it."

"Take a boat from near Ave Maria. You can row across and throw the head in the river."

"If I can make it to the river."

"We have no time. Move the body now." She closed the panel and was gone.

Hunter heaved the bags of papers he had taken such care to hide out of the way. He grasped the body by the ankles and pulled it to the stairs. He did not want to hoist it over his shoulder. Embracing the body revolted him. He might lose his balance. He tore strips from the bloody linen shirt and tied the wrists and ankles together, then fashioned a strap under the armpits and around the chest. This was taking too long. He listened for any sound that the militia had returned, but heard nothing. He dragged the corpse so that its feet dangled over the stairs. Rapping at the panel door made him jump.

"Paul." Marguerite opened the panel. "What is taking you so long?"

"It is difficult to move a body down steep stairs. I had to tie him up first."

"The militiamen haven't returned. The guests are locked in their rooms and I told them to remain. Bernard and Bertha also. Laurent and Martin are gone. The street is quiet outside, but you can hear running, shouting, screaming farther off. Can you move the body now?"

"I think so."

"Good. Here is a knife to use." She handed him a large carving knife. "I will repair these scratches." She bent to pick up a bottle and a rag.

Hunter slowly lowered the body to the ground floor, using the linen straps, then climbed back to retrieve the lantern and knife. He opened the panel and asked Marguerite, "Is the hidden door in the storeroom open?"

"No. It will take time to clear everything away. Izard and his men will come back before long." She gestured to the top edge of the panel. "This is done." She scrutinized him. "You must change out of those clothes."

He looked down at his shirt and venetians. Blood in all states—dried, tacky, and fresh. "After I have...done what I must do," he replied.

"Ah. I must bring you some sacks," she said. "Wait here a moment."

Hunter was relieved not to descend to the dark closed space behind the storeroom, where Nicolas's body lay. Revulsion and guilt overwhelmed him. He had taken a life. Although every Christian Church said it was no sin to kill defending oneself, he was about to mutilate a body. Defile the dead. But Marguerite was right. This was no longer *Petit Nicolas*, but a corpse that must be disposed of to keep her safe. He must continue to consider the body a problem to solve.

Marguerite returned with five sacks. "One or two should soak up any fresh bleeding, then you can wrap others around the head. The last one should be dry."

Marguerite's stark recital chilled him. He took the sacks, carving knife, and lantern, and climbed down to the ground floor. On the grime-covered floor behind the storeroom, he knelt beside the body and murmured a prayer for forgiveness. He grasped the carving knife, forced himself to position it in the gashed throat, closed his eyes, and pressed down. His blade sliced between vertebrae and sank into the dirt floor. Unable to control himself, he turned and retched. After several convulsions, he brushed dirt over the vomit. He willed his breathing to normal. He must do this.

He lifted the head by its hair, the face turned away, and let the blood flow onto a sack. He wrapped it in one sack after another, ending up with a bag a foot and a half in diameter. He climbed back to his room with the grisly parcel.

Marguerite knelt like a washerwoman, scrubbing at the blood in the alcove where he had stabbed Nicolas. "The stain will not come out." She wrung her rag into a pail of water. "But after I finish it will not look fresh. If they discover the staircase, I can claim it was old." She stood. "If you change into fresh garments, you can take your soiled clothes with those." She pointed to the wad of Nicolas's clothes. "Then make your way to the river—a man carrying two bundles of bloody clothes to be washed."

"Are people going about their business on such a morning as this?" he asked.

"Let us hope so. But hurry. It is quiet nearby, but there are shouts towards the Temple and the Bastille."

He stripped off his bloody garments. She returned to her scrubbing. He picked a clean shirt, brown hose, and a beige suit from the floor, where the militiamen had scattered them. They had taken his gray suit, court shoes, and boots. Best to let the other clothing lie in a jumble, in case the militia returned. He considered donning his sword, but it would be little defense against a mob, and might slow him. He tucked his bread knife into his belt, but would have to rely on his ability to run or climb for safety. He noticed his empty chest. "Those papers in the staircase should be burned."

"I shall see to that if an opportunity presents itself." She placed the rag in the pail, stood, and wiped her hands. "Other rooms have been defiled, but I must empty this water first."

They closed the panel and descended the hall stairs together, he carrying the two bundles, she the pail of bloody water.

"I will dump this in the courtyard drain," she said, "and make sure Bernard and his wife are not watching. Then you may slip out the stable gate. Dispose of your burdens as quickly as you can, then, if it is safe, go to your embassy."

"But we must move the body. I will return and hide in the staircase until night."

"You will not be safe here."

"And you will not be safe until Nico—the body is out of your inn."

She pressed close to kiss him lightly. "Wait." She put down the pail and ducked into her office. "Take this key to the stable gate. If you must return, you can let yourself in. I pray you make it safely to the embassy. Tomorrow all may be sane again." She turned towards the courtyard door and held up her hand for him to remain. She carried the bucket to the gutter near the manure pile and poured out its contents. "Bernard," she called up. "It seems safe now. Both you and Bertha fetch pails and brushes and come help me clean the rooms."

"*Oui, madame*," Bernard called back. Marguerite signaled Hunter into the sunlit courtyard. He slipped from the doorway and followed her to the stable gate. He brushed her face with his lips, poked his head out, then slid into the street.

As he closed the gate, wings flapped behind him. He turned. Crows fluttered up from piles of bodies. His heart sank as he saw what in hiding he had only imagined—the guests who had been hauled out or pitched from the inn's windows earlier that morning. On top lay one of the German students who had not escaped over the rooftops, his distorted face smeared with blood. Coran lay next to him, lifeless eyes staring at the sky, a gaping bullet wound in his chest. Beneath him, the other Gascons lay as they had landed, bodies twisted and bent, tangled together, nightshirts stained a reddish-brown. The bottom layer contained the naked bodies of their servants. In the second mound, the couples from Troyes and Lyon with their servants, all stripped naked, their bodies rent with sword wounds, and the ring fingers sliced off. Examples of the "good carving" the militia-man had praised. On the far side lay Grattard, his head split open with a blow from a halberd. Only a few days ago, he had burned with jealousy. Now he could feel only pity for the man, and sorrow for his young bride, his adolescent boy, and the baby who lay beside her mother. Tears ran down his cheek.

He must not stand paralyzed, or he would join the slaughtered. He glanced towards Saint-Gervais, where a crowd of people roiled about in the Old Cemetery of Saint-Jean. Better to walk away from the throng. Glancing east along rue Sainte Croix de la Bretonniere, he saw only one figure scurry past at the next crossing. Would it be safer to proceed down larger, straight streets, which would allow him to see some distance either way, but might contain more people, or choose smaller, crooked streets where there might be fewer people, but a greater chance of ambush?

Hunter lifted his foot. The mud stuck to his sole. The Paris streets were not running with blood any more, at least not the rue Vieille du Temple. Here the blood had congealed. To his left another pile of naked male and female bodies lay twisted together in macabre embraces. The face of the young woman nearest him had been beautiful. Now her vacant eyes gazed up at the window from which she had been hurled. Sensing movement beyond the bodies, his head jerked back to street level. Figures in the distance slipped furtively away. A scream echoed from farther north, beyond the Hôtel de Guise. So the killing continued.

The city had become a slaughterhouse full of Protestant carcasses. If he encountered a neighbor who recognized him as the Englishman lodging at the Chessboard Inn, he would become another corpse, killed to advance that neighbor's reputation for religious zeal. Even if he did not meet anyone who recognized him, he doubted he could he reach the Seine without confronting someone who would demand to see what the two bundles he carried contained—one of bloodstained clothes and the other the head of the first man he had killed.

To the south, many houses had closed shutters. Some good Catholics had chosen to remain secure indoors and not take part in the slaughter. On the far side of the street, gateways and cul-de-sacs would allow him somewhere to dodge if a mob appeared.

He could at least make it as far as the next corner. A bold walk might attract less attention than slinking along. He marched with his two bundles, passing smashed doors marked with crosses. A crow hopped away from corpses he approached, shaking his head vigorously to loosen a bit of tissue. A wave of nausea. Better not to think what that beak might hold. He skirted the bodies of two men, both stripped naked, with gaping wounds in their chests and groins. Had he known these victims? No, best not look closely. On his left two men and two women, wearing only nightshirts, had been laid out carefully side by side.

At the corner of the rue du Roi de Sicile, he turned east and nearly tripped over a man bent over a body. With the flash of a knife, the man turned and snarled. Hunter stepped back and muttered, "*Pardon,*" his heart racing.

"You've got your booty," the man growled. "Leave."

The man's knife and his right hand were smeared with blood. With his left, he tossed a severed finger onto the corpse's chest and dropped a ring into a pouch on his belt. Next to him lay a bundle similar to Hunter's— bloodstained clothes. Harvesting jewelry and clothing from corpses, the man assumed Hunter was doing the same.

Hunter backed away. Up and down the street, other men and boys squatted, stripping bodies. Perhaps they were a gang, working together. He crossed the street and turned south on the rue Renault-le-Fevre. Another heap of naked bodies, several with missing fingers, lay in front of the Hospital Petit Saint-Antoine. The ghouls had finished their work here and moved north. How quickly he had become accustomed to the sight of corpses.

Approaching the rue Saint-Antoine, he tensed. Crossing this major thoroughfare, he would be most exposed. Shots and yelling to his left. He pressed his back against the house on that side of the street. A movement and flash of color to his right. Marching from the Place Baudoyer came six of the king's Swiss Guards, carrying halberds. He bounded from the left side of the road to the right. Had the soldiers seen him? Although the shouting of the horde in the east reached him, they were beyond his sight. He hugged the wall, praying the soldiers would march past. Their steps grew closer and closer. They stopped. He held his breath a moment, then risked a peek around the corner. The soldiers stood outside a house across the rue Saint-Antoine, only a few doors away. He remembered what Crespin had said about it months earlier. The soldiers were guarding the house of Marie Touchet, the king's Protestant mistress. Here at least would be one Huguenot left unharmed on Saint Bartholomew's Day.

If he faced no danger from the soldiers, he still had to cross the rue Saint-Antoine. Shouts echoed from crowds out of sight both to his right and his left. If the corpse robbers had mistaken him for one of them, others might as well. He took a deep breath and strode into the rue Saint-Antoine. West, beyond Marie Touchet's house, a crowd was moving away from him, towards the Place de Grève. A tall man carried an infant above his head, taunting the parents to beg for its life. The rabble around them hooted and mocked.

He shuddered with the helpless anguish he had felt all morning, and turned his head east. That crowd was further away, bunched in three smaller packs. At this distance, he could not determine whether those they carried were dead or alive. He veered south to the rue de Jouy. The street was deserted, save for an old woman and a boy, bending over a corpse in front of the Hôtel des Abbés de Chaalis. As he approached, the boy fixed him with a look. He murmured something to the old woman, who also stared at Hunter as he passed.

When he turned towards the Seine on the rue Nonnains d'Hyères, he heard the boy scurry away behind him. Had he been recognized? Could the boy be summoning pursuers? Before him, the street held no one, living or dead. He hurried towards the river. If the boy summoned others to hunt down a Protestant Englishman, he would reach the river first. He only had to untie one of the boats there and row across between the Île aux Vaches and the Île Notre-Dame. If the current was not too strong, perhaps he could row up the Bièvre to near the embassy, staying safely outside the Left Bank's walls. He crossed the rue de la Mortellerie at a trot. Just a small alley before the steps that led down to the boats.

Behind him, a man called out. He took no notice, but hurried past small warehouses to the top of the steps. Below, more than a half dozen boats were tied. The two on the left were chained to poles. So were the next two. Five steps down, he froze. All the boats were chained. Above him footsteps crunched on gravel.

"Master Fine Gentleman," a caustic voice called. At the top of the steps stood two men with shaggy beards and ragged clothing. "Too fine to answer when an honest workman calls to him, but not too fine to help himself to dead men's clothes," the speaker continued.

"Let's take a look in those bundles, Pierre," suggested his comrade, a taller and leaner man wearing a hat with a white cross.

"I bet there's a good doublet in that one." Pierre pointed, advancing.

"But maybe he's hiding something more valuable in that dirty sack." His companion indicated the bag that held Nicolas's head.

Hunter retreated a step towards the Seine. He could throw the bags into the river and take his chances fighting these two men. He should have worn his sword, but the dagger in his belt would give him a chance.

"Let's see what you have, gentleman." Pierre sneered the last word and stepped down.

"I would rather not." Hunter took a step backwards. Should he drop his bundles now and attack the men? Crunching gravel. Three more men appeared at the top of the stairs, one holding a club. Hunter's mouth was dry.

"What have you found, Pierre?"

"A gentleman corpse robber."

Hunter bristled, though that was the identity he had relied on to reach the river.

"Why, he is that Englishman," a bald man on the top step said, "the one who lodges at the Chessboard."

"An Englishman?" Pierre said. "Then he is another Protestant. Instead of beating him and taking his bags, we can just kill him." He strode forward and the three men at the top clomped down to join him. Two drew knives.

Hunter retreated two more steps. Now he faced five men. He must throw away the bundles. Even if he were to die, at least there would be no evidence to link Marguerite with Petit Nicolas's killing. He tossed the bundles into the nearest boat, and stepped in after them.

"What in Mary's name are you doing?" Pierre asked. The others joined in cries of bewilderment.

Hunter pulled his own dagger and faced them, the boat rocking beneath him. He held a better defensive position, but he needed to make his way to the stern of the boat to toss the bundles far out into the current. They must not float to shore. He shuffled backwards, crouching low and kicking the bags behind him. Without turning, he lifted them over the first thwart and stepped over it himself.

His pursuers reached the bottom stair, but hung back, their advantage in numbers now nullified. One threw a stone at Hunter. He ducked and nudged a bag back with his foot. A rattle of metal. A chain lay in the bottom of the boat. Another rock whizzed past his head. A third hit his shoulder as he knelt and wound the chain around the sack containing Nicolas's head.

"Go on," Pierre urged.

The bow of the boat dipped when his tall companion stepped aboard. Ignoring the pain in his shoulder, Hunter grasped both gunwales and rocked the boat from side to side. The tall man teetered, lost his balance, and fell. The chain of the neighboring boat scoured the side of his head.

His companions first laughed, then advanced to aid him. While they were distracted, Hunter scrambled over the second thwart to the stern and threw the chain-weighted sack as far as he could into the river. He almost lost his own balance, but recovered. The boat held no other objects to weigh down the bundle of bloody clothes, so he launched it into the river, hoping it would sink as it absorbed water.

Behind him, his pursuers howled. The fool had thrown away whatever loot he had been carrying. Their only joy now would be to kill him. They huddled together, talking and gesticulating. When they spread apart, their plan became clear. Two men pulled the boat on Hunter's right close to the shore and stepped in; two executed the same maneuver with the boat on Hunter's left. Pierre stood at the bow of Hunter's boat, smiling. The men on both sides pushed their boats towards his. He was surrounded. He might wound one or two men, but the blade of at least one would strike home in the off balance fight he faced. He muttered a prayer to himself.

A voice from above shouted, "Pierre!"

His pursuers looked up. At the top of the stairs, Hunter recognized the strawberry face of Robert, surrounded by a dozen members of his gang. Among them stood the boy who had gazed at him so intently at the Hôtel de Chaalis.

"Don't bother me now, Robert. I am busy killing a Protestant," Pierre answered.

"He is not a Protestant," Robert said.

Pierre and his men looked at one another in consternation. "What do you mean?" Pierre asked.

"Wait, I'll tell you." Robert and his comrades jumped down the steps. In the boats, the armed men shifted their eyes between Hunter and the shore, but made no move towards him. Robert related his first encounter with Hunter. "He's a cloth seller. Said the prettiest *Ave Maria* and gave us a douzaine." The other boys nodded their concurrence. "Confessed his faith right there in the street, and paid a tribute to Our Lady every time we saw him."

"Is this true?" Pierre asked Hunter.

"Yes."

"Why did you not say so?"

"Would you have believed me?"

"I say we should kill him anyway," the tall man with a bloody face yelled. He gripped the gunwale of Hunter's boat and pulled himself closer.

"Giles Courtin," a shrill voice cried from above, "you should be ashamed of yourself. There are Huguenot maggots breeding in Paris. You should be slaying them, not threatening this good Catholic. He left England to come here." It was the old woman from the Hôtel de Chaalis.

Giles released the gunwale and hung his head. Was the old woman his mother?

She waddled down a few steps. "You are wasting your time here. A nest of Lutheran vipers is barricaded in their house on rue des Lions."

"The grand one?" Pierre asked.

"Yes."

"Come on then," Pierre gestured to his men. "We'll get more in the rue des Lions." As they started to climb the stairs, he looked back. Did he regret not killing Hunter, or was he just curious about the contents of the bags?

Loud cheers erupted downstream, near the pont Notre-Dame. A trail of smoke floated from the bridge into the morning sunshine. Two unmoving forms fell into the water, amid cheers. Splashes echoed. Corpses of slain Protestants were being pitched into the Seine. Nearer, his second bundle floated on the shimmering water. There was no trace of the first bag. Hunter made his way towards the bow. Being saved by a boy and an old woman was not very heroic.

Robert addressed him as he stepped ashore. "It is dangerous for you to go about the streets without the signs."

"Signs?"

"Don't you know? You must wear a cross on your cap and a band around your arm." Robert turned to the short boy next to him, the one who had carried the gang's money at their first meeting. "Do you have more armbands, Armond?"

Armond dug into his large satchel. "A band, a cross, and a pin to fix it to his cap."

Robert handed Hunter the armband. "Here. Tie this around your left arm." Yes, the men who had menaced him had such bands and crosses. In his preoccupation with disposing of the bundles, he had overlooked the emblems the Catholics had adopted.

"If you bend down," Armond said, "I can pin this cross on your cap." Hunter did so. "Now you can come with us to see them cut the Huguenots' throats and throw them in the river." Armond nodded towards the pont Notre-Dame. The other boys voiced encouragement.

Grateful Robert had spoken in his defense, Hunter was nevertheless unwilling to observe more bloodshed. "Even with the signs, for which I thank you, it is wiser for me to stay within. There are many who believe me a Protestant. You are some of the few who know my secret."

Robert's face fell. "You will miss some good sport. You will never see a day like this again."

Hunter hoped Robert was right. He pulled out a teston. "I am grateful to you for saving my life."

Robert smiled. "Thank you. But you should give it to Madame Latour. She is the one who scolded them away."

Hunter drew out another coin. "Then give this to her, Robert."

Robert's eye glinted. Then, overcoming temptation, he said, "I swear by Saint Bartholomew that I will."

His gang murmured their admiration for his noble act, but Armond said, "Let's go. They will have killed them all before we get to the bridge."

Robert judged the other boys' restlessness. "All right. We will go now." He turned to Hunter. "Be safe." They bounded up the stairs.

Hunter gazed across the Seine towards Mount Sainte-Geneviève and the embassy beyond. Would there be safety there? Only yesterday a mob had gathered to shout insults at 'English dogs.' Would a crazed mob respect the embassy of a Protestant country?

A hundred yards of chained boats convinced him that all must have been ordered chained to the Right Bank, so no Protestant could escape that way. To reach the embassy, he would have to cross the pont Notre-Dame, where a mob was slaughtering Huguenots. Were they doing the same on all the bridges? How many gauntlets could he successfully run, even with his white cross and arm band? He had told the truth when he said many Parisians knew him as a Protestant Englishman. Why leave Marguerite with the problem of the body, when there was so little promise of safety? His chances were better hiding at L'Échiquier. The thought of Nicolas's headless body made him shiver. But he had put Marguerite in danger. He must stay near her and make certain she came to no harm.

He climbed towards the rue Nonnains d'Hyères. Rather than passing by the gang stripping corpses again, he would continue north, towards the rue Pavée. The widow of Francis, Duke of Guise, lived there in the Hôtel de Lorraine. Surely no mobs would search out Huguenots in that neighborhood.

Crossing the rue Saint-Antoine, someone called his name. His hand went to his dagger, but the voice held a tone of greeting rather than of threat. Georges Landon and Gilbert Vasse, the stonecarver and leather worker he had shared drinks with at the Horn, approached with a group of six men. "Master Adams," Landon called, "you wear the cross of the faithful. Will you join us?" The men all held weapons: mallets, cleavers, a sword, and a bloodstained club.

"Join in what, Master Landon?" Hunter believed he knew the answer.

"We aim to save some Huguenots," Landon replied.

Save? Hunter was confused. "Has the king not ordered that they be slain?"

"Oh, yes," Vasse replied with equanimity, "but Georges insists that we first give them a chance to recant. If they agree to go to Mass, we escort them to a church. If they remain obstinate heretics, then we are obliged to kill them." His friends nodded their agreement.

"We have saved four souls this morning," Landon said.

"And killed six," Vasse added.

"I thank you for your invitation," Hunter said, "but I feel that, as an Englishman, I must not harm any of King Charles's subjects."

"Oh, you need not take part in the killing," Landon said, "but you could help convince them to go to Mass and save themselves. You could speak as one who was surrounded by the reformed religion, but saw its errors."

Should he accept the invitation? Could he save some Huguenots? Could he urge them to abandon the Gospel for popery? Would they buy their lives at the cost of eternal torment? What price would he pay for his false witness? Practically, any delay might endanger himself and Marguerite. "I pray you will excuse me," Hunter said. "Each man must follow his own conscience and make his own decision."

"Very well," Landon said, regret in his voice. The men looked hard at Hunter and whispered something. "No," Landon replied, "Henri Lascot said the same thing and stayed at home, and we all know he is a devout man."

"I wish you success in saving Huguenots." Hunter backed towards the rue Pavée.

After a few moments, he turned left onto the rue des Rosiers, the shortest route back to L'Échiquier. No one moved on the street, but two bodies lay just past the statue of the virgin, where Robert's gang extracted tribute from Huguenots. Petit Nicolas had lived on the rue des Rosiers. Had one of these houses been his home?

The bodies still lay in front of the Chessboard Inn. He had seen many corpses, but he had known these men and women. A sob caught in his throat. He inserted the key in the stable gate and pushed gently, listening for sounds in the courtyard. Nothing. He slid in and locked the gate. He listened again at the back door. Movement on an upper floor, but nothing nearby. He entered, transferring his weight carefully from board to board. Where was Marguerite?

Footsteps crossed the hall above him. He sprang into the kitchen and darted to the storeroom door. He opened it gingerly, hoping it would not grate. Steps on the staircase; the clanking and sloshing of pails. Bernard hummed as he carried what must be buckets of blood-tinged water. He passed by and entered the courtyard. As it would take him some moments to pump fresh water, Hunter scurried on tiptoes up the staircase to Marguerite's bedchamber. Its door stood ajar, her room empty. Above, Marguerite spoke to Bertha, evidently still cleaning. He would conceal himself in the secret staircase off her chamber until he heard her enter.

As he waited, he thought of Sidney, and reproached himself for not considering his friend's welfare until now. Sidney's lodgings were nearer to the rue Béthizy, where the killing had begun. Surely King Charles, who had so recently honored Sidney, would not now target him. Yet the king had promised to protect Coligny, and fear of Huguenot violence had overcome that promise. He could not have thought Sidney a party to any Huguenot plot. But the king's will might have no bearing on Sidney's fate. Izard's militia was no respecter of foreign Protestants. Would Sidney and his companions try to reach the embassy? What chance would they have to cross Paris? Hunter fretted until he heard Marguerite's bedchamber door close.

When he turned the latch, she jumped in surprise, then ran to him and embraced him. "I kept hoping you were safe at your embassy, yet I wanted you here. What happened?"

Hunter told of his encounters in the streets, his disposal of the bundles, his rescue by Robert and an old woman, and his decision to return to L'Échiquier. "And now I am safe," he concluded.

349

"Neither of us is safe while that body lies behind the storeroom door," Marguerite said, "yet we cannot move it until dark." She sighed. "Even then, it will be difficult. Three guests and their servants remain. Neither Bernard nor Bertha can learn of the corpse or the secret staircase. We must be sure no one sees us carry the body out."

"I can clear a way through the storeroom, if you keep the ostler and his wife out of the inn." That task would be preferable to cowering in the secret staircase with the corpse.

A roar outside caused them to spring to the window and peer through the partially closed shutters. At first they could see nothing, but the whooping of the crowd increased. "You should hide," Marguerite said.

"No. I want to see what is happening." Hunter pushed the shutters wider, but stood to one side.

Three young boys, perhaps six years old, skipped into sight, pulling a doll by a rope. No, it was not a doll, but a baby's corpse. A crowd came dancing behind them. As the mob in the rue Saint-Antoine that morning, they were in a carnival mood. Hunter gasped. Below, a man pushed a wheelbarrow with the body of Pierre Merlet, the Huguenot draper who specialized in linings. Merlet's head dangled awkwardly, mouth open; his doublet was stained with blood. Beside the barrow, a burly man carried the corpse of the family's nurse slung over his shoulder. Two men dragged the body of Sarah Merlet between them. Hunter feared what would see next. Rachel and little Rebecca, the daughters who had greeted him in English, hung lifeless as dolls on the backs of women, their heads lulling back and forth. He began to sob.

Marguerite pushed him from the window. "What is it?"

He was unable to answer for several minutes, then explained.

She held him for a long time as he wept. Finally, she said, "Most of the Protestants we know will have met that fate. We can only save ourselves." She led him to the secret staircase. "Wait here. I must speak to Bernard and Bertha. Try to rest until I can return."

How could he rest when the world had dissolved into chaos? Sobs wracked his body. He must stop himself. If his crying revealed his presence, even to such trusted servants as Bernard and Bertha, Marguerite would not be safe. Who could keep a secret when armed men threatened them with death? He must remain silent. He lay down. One floor below lay the headless body of Petit Nicolas. He must not think of that, either.

Marguerite opened the panel. "Come, Paul. Bertha and Bernard have gone to tend to the horses." They embraced for long minutes without a word, then she said, "Come to the kitchen. I have promised to prepare food for the guests if they stay in their rooms. This is your chance to clear a passage in the storeroom."

Hunter was surprised to find a table covered with loaves of bread. "Did they bake bread on such a day as this?"

"Bakers lit their ovens before the tocsin at Saint-Germain l'Auxerrois began at ring," she said, "and people still need to eat. The boy delivered these as usual while you were out." She broke off a piece. "Here. You will need your strength." She extracted half a round of cheese from a cupboard. "Cut yourself some. I will heat some pottage to carry to the guests with bread and cheese. If this madness ends today, then Auguste may return tomorrow."

He forced himself to eat as she examined the storeroom. "You must move some barrels into the kitchen for the moment," she said. "Then you can shift the boxes and sacks away from the door."

He squinted. "Where is it?"

"The last five boards on the left wall," she said. "You cannot see the hinges from here. After you clear things away, you will see a small hole at the bottom. Insert the cross-shaped key on the wall to release the latch."

Rearranging the storeroom contents was a relief from helpless inactivity, but the knowledge that Nicolas's body lay behind the wall haunted Hunter as he worked. By the time Marguerite had retrieved plates from her guests, he had cleared a way to the secret doorway.

Marguerite nodded approval. "There will be enough space to bring out the body. If you roll these two barrels from the kitchen back, anyone looking in will not notice the gap behind them."

Hunter grasped the rusty cross-shaped key. "When was the last time this door was opened?"

"Not since my husband died. He hid wine casks there to avoid the tax."

Hunter stared at the dirty, cobwebbed boards of the concealed door, in no hurry to join the headless corpse on the other side.

"Mistress!" a voice sounded from the courtyard. "Are you there?"

"I will help you draw the water," Marguerite called back. She drew close to Hunter. "Bertha will help me clean the dishes. You must move those barrels and hide in the staircase while I keep her talking." She kissed him with passion and left.

He waited until he heard the women pumping before he repositioned the barrels and closed the storeroom door. He inserted the cross-shaped key, and, with some difficulty, turned it. With a grating sound, the door opened a crack. He grasped its edge, lifted so that it would make no noise, and slowly opened it. A wave of sweet putridness drifted out. Although it had only been a few hours, and this day was less hot than the previous week, decomposition had begun. He gulped air from the storeroom, held his breath, and stepped through.

He stumbled over the body, now stiff with rigor mortis. Without pausing, he climbed two floors to his chamber. He changed into his black suit of Lancaster fustian, to prepare for his nighttime excursion. He retreated to the hidden staircase and sat in the dark. Guests moved and spoke elsewhere in the inn. One woman continued to cry. Conversation and clatter of dishes rose from the kitchen. Shouting filtered in from the street. Exhaustion washed over him, and he drifted into unconsciousness.

Marguerite watched Bertha cross the courtyard to her lodging. Now was the time to fetch Paul and move the body.

A loud knocking sounded at the front door. "Madame Moreau! Open at once!" Izard's voice.

Her heart pounded, but she forced herself to open the door and welcome the captain calmly. "Captain Izard, what brings you back? Are you done with your bloody business?"

"My business is now to proclaim the king's edict: all are to return home and keep the peace." He stepped inside.

"Then the killing is over?"

"Some Huguenots on my list were missing. They may be hidden away."

"But if the king has ordered all to keep the peace, then they are safe."

"Do you wish heretics and traitors to be safe?"

"I did not say that. But if the king has called for an end to the killing, then they will be safe, whether I will it or not."

"If every man in Paris hears the king's edict, that may be," he said philosophically. "But some may not hear the edict, and keep acting on this morning's instructions." His voice became hard. "But I have other business with you. One of my men was wounded here and another is missing."

"I know of the wounding. He bled all over a table in my dining room."

"One of your guests fired a pistol at Henri Marlin when he opened the door this morning. Thankfully, he survived, but his shoulder is wounded. I had to take him to his mother."

"Those who remained were quite able to continue their carnage without you," Marguerite said coldly.

"Yes, they did their duty admirably," Izard said, "though they were distracted by wine and booty. Yet I suspect that the man who shot Henri had been warned by you, and you are responsible for his wound."

"Warned by me? With the clamor in the street and your men pounding and shouting, I did not need to warn anyone that the city had gone mad." She rounded on him. "And as an innkeeper, is it not my duty to protect my guests from murderers?"

"Be careful what you say, madame. My men were carrying out the king's orders."

"The king ordered all Parisians to respect and welcome those who came for the wedding," she countered.

"That was before Huguenots plotted to kill the royal family and make Henri of Navarre king."

"My guests did not plot that. But your men made my inn into a slaughterhouse. I have been cleaning all day."

"You may have more to worry about than bloodstains," Izard said. "One of my men is missing."

"What has that to do with me?"

"We last saw him here."

"Well, none of your men remained here. Maybe he had sense enough to be sickened by the bloodshed. Or perhaps he decided to go looting on his own."

"He would not do so," Izard replied.

"Who is this paragon in your militia?"

"I do not like your tone, madame"

"I do not like what you did to my inn, captain."

"I and my men were following orders, as you know." He sniggered as though a thought struck him. "We did save wear and tear on your staircase by throwing some of the bodies out the windows."

"Am I to thank you for that?"

"You are to inform me if you have seen any sign of Petit Nicolas."

"Petit Nicolas? Have you asked his mother if he returned home?"

"No," Izard said. "I did not wish to alarm her."

"It is more likely he is at his home than here."

"Captain..." his ensign Martin appeared in the doorway.

"Yes."

"We found him and brought him here." Martin moved aside. A militiaman pushed Jacques Crespin through the door.

"Master Crespin," Izard said, "you guide Englishmen about Paris. You are used to touching heretic flesh. I was going to ask my men to cart some bodies to the river, but they are tired and need a rest. Have you a barrow, Madame Moreau?"

"In the courtyard."

"Then Crespin can do his part in cleansing Paris of heresy." Izard chuckled. "Cart those Protestant bodies in the street to the pont Notre-Dame."

"Of course, I am always willing to help the militia." Crespin spoke with overemphasized politeness. "But if all are to observe a curfew and be in their homes after sundown, I will not be able to move all the bodies by then by myself."

"And you expect my men to help you?" Izard asked. "I shall write you a pass saying you are working for the militia, all night if need be. You can show that to any who question you after dark."

Crespin sighed and nodded.

"I regret your Mister Adams was absent this morning." Izard turned back to Marguerite. "Do you miss him?"

"Miss him?" Marguerite said.

"My lady," he pronounced the title with irony, "you may act pure, but do you think your maids do not have eyes, your lads do not have ears. They say you serve him often at meals, that you make eyes at him and his English friends. When he was burned, you stayed by his bedside into the night." He leaned close to her face. "I think you must have climbed into bed with him and played the whore."

She clenched her teeth and raised one hand, then stopped herself. Crespin stepped towards Izard, but Martin gripped his arm.

"Is slander part of your duties, captain?" she asked, relaxing her body. "I have seen my maids giggling and looking at Master Adams. I have rebuked them for making advances, advances he has spurned, as a virtuous bachelor should. Their disappointment, I see, has turned to bile. They saw me nursing an injured man and spread false stories. I need not answer their scandalous tales, but I am not surprised that you believe them." She looked meaningfully at him. "You know well how spurned desire can turn to hatred."

Izard's face flushed. His eyes grew cold. "Martin, tell the men to come in. We did not totally clear the possessions of those Protestant snakes from this inn. We will do so now, and divide those items the dead can no longer use." He turned back to Marguerite. "As they are dead, they will not need their horses. I am sure Bernard will identify those of your deceased guests. We will take them tomorrow."

Marguerite opened her mouth to protest, looked into Izard's eyes, and closed it.

"And Martin, tell the men to look in every room. Perhaps Madame Moreau has failed to notice Petit Nicolas, or is hiding her Englishman under a bed. And clear his room as well. I will assume he has been captured and killed somewhere between this inn and his embassy." He looked to gauge Marguerite's reaction, but she gazed stoically ahead. "And ask those guests who remain if they have seen anything of Petit Nicolas or the Englishman."

"Yes, sir," Martin said.

"Crespin, go fetch the barrow from the courtyard," Izard ordered. When Crespin had left, he said, "Tonight the men are eager to divide those items which the dead Huguenots no longer need. But I will return tomorrow. If Petit Nicolas has not appeared by then, I will search every cupboard, every armoire, every mattress, every barrel in your cellar, every mound of hay in your stable. If Petit Nicolas or any sign of him is here, I will execute justice on the spot."

The militiamen tramped up the stairs.

"I will retire to my chamber," Marguerite said, "if you give me your word that your men will not take the bedclothes and furnishings."

Izard assumed a shocked expression. "How could you think such a thing, madame? Of course, you may retire. But to make sure that no one is hidden there—someone who might do you harm, of course—I will accompany you and check all corners of your rooms." He smiled. "I would ask

Crespin to chaperone us, in case you try to seduce me, but he has other duties."

Awakened by Izard's knocking, Hunter had listened at his chamber door during Marguerite's conversation. He seethed at Izard's remarks, but returned to his hiding place when militiamen entered the inn and stood motionless in the dark. He heard Marguerite enter her chamber on the floor beneath him.

"Here you are," she said. "Look about as you wish."

"I will," Izard said. Would he dare to ransack Marguerite's chamber?

"You may look under my bed if you wish. You are welcome to anything you find in the chamber pot."

Hunter stifled a laugh.

"You continue to try my patience, madame," Izard said, "but I may not have to endure it much longer." He banged about. "You have many fine gowns in this chest. This inn must be more profitable than I thought. It would be a good investment for someone, should anything happen to you." After a pause, he added, "As you have no children to inherit."

"I have nephews," she said quietly.

"Perhaps they will be willing to sell at a good price, especially if the inn has suffered some damage during these disturbances," Izard said.

Hunter edged towards the staircase, jaw and fists clenched. If he heard sounds of a struggle, he would bolt downstairs. He would kill Izard, even if it meant his own death.

"Are you checking this room for my safety, or appraising it?" Marguerite said.

"As I said, I want to be sure no one is hidden here." Izard paused. "Anyone, living or dead."

Did Izard suspect Petit Nicolas had been killed? that Hunter had remained? If the militiamen inspected every inch of inn, they would discover the secret staircase.

The door to his chamber opened and militiamen entered. "Look in the chests," one man said. Their thumping and banging drowned out what was taking place in Marguerite's chamber. "Dump those papers. We can load the chest with clothing. Take care with those ruffs."

They scraped the chests along the floor, then lifted them and clomped down the stairs. Hunter heard nothing from Marguerite's chamber. Voices and banging came from rooms further away. Izard barked orders to his men and questioned guests. The commotion continued for some time, then the militiamen descended. Izard promised, "I will be back tomorrow."

As Hunter lowered himself to the first floor, he heard Marguerite weeping. When he stepped in, she ran to his arms.

"I am undone. I am undone," she sobbed.

"No, Marguerite." He stroked her hair. "No. I will remove Nicolas's body tonight, if I have to carry it to the Seine myself."

"I was so frightened," she wailed.

"I heard what you said. You were brave."

"They will investigate every inch of my inn tomorrow."

"Quiet, dear. I heard his threats."

"They will discover the secret stairs."

"They may not. And if they do, the body will be gone."

"I fear Izard will find something—bloodstains, a piece of Nicolas's clothing, what you hid in the staircase—and he will accuse me of hiding you, of killing Nicolas. You heard what he said, that he would be sure I was hiding no one—living or dead."

"I heard him."

"We must thank God his men were eager to divide the plunder. He would have had them tear my inn apart today."

"After I dispose of the body, come with me to the embassy."

She pulled away. "And leave my inn?"

"Yes," he said. "Ambassador Walsingham will protect you."

She shook her head. "And what would become of me? I cannot stay at your embassy forever." She dried her tears and stood pensive. "No. I must stay. If Laurent and Martin come back, and Auguste and his son, even Marie and Jeanne, those ungrateful bitches... If we are all here, we can open every door and cupboard to Captain Izard. We can be so cooperative he will think we want him to move in. Yes. If we help his investigation, his men will have no excuse to tear and destroy."

"But the secret staircase," Hunter said.

"That was my fear speaking. I cannot let him win. The staircase has been a secret for years. I must take the chance."

Hunter longed to carry her away and protect her from danger, but what real protection could he offer? Accompanying him across Paris would put her in danger she would not face at her inn. And he could not offer her a future. They had been through that before. He sighed. "What can I do?"

"We must search the secret staircase again, looking for any stains or bits of clothing that could betray us."

"But if they discover the passage..." he began.

"It will support his accusations that we were lovers." She suddenly smiled, "Which we are." She embraced him again, not leaning on him for support this time, but pressing her body into his. She kissed him deeply. "That is a scandal I can bear, if it comes to that." Her hands slid to his buttocks, her breath hot in his ear.

His breathing became short and his penis stiffened. "Marguerite," he said, "if we could only..."

"We can," she breathed back, holding him tight. "I may never see you again. We must seize the time. The militia is gone. Bertha will not return for an hour. Love me now."

Still pressing against one another, they stumbled towards her bed. They stood for a moment in a passionate kiss, then broke apart and shed their clothes. All the fear and tension of the day found release in furious, rapid lovemaking.

Both lay panting in one another's arms. Hunter said, "I am grateful I could love you again. If anything should happen..."

She put her hand on his mouth. "I know. We both have one more time to remember. Let us lie another moment together." They did, saying nothing, basking in one another's warmth.

After long minutes, she slapped his buttocks. "Now, to work."

CHAPTER 18

Night

Hunter waited in the dark storeroom. Sitting hidden behind barrels for what seemed like hours, he listened to Bertha and Marguerite prepare an evening meal, serve it to the guests, and clean the kitchen. As time passed, the fetid odor from the other side of the secret door increased. Finally, three raps on the storeroom door, then three more. Marguerite's signal. He stood, muscles objecting their long-cramped position.

"Is it dark?" he asked.

"Not dark enough," she replied, "but Crespin may come soon. We must move the body into the storeroom before he does. He can't learn of the secret stairs." She leaned over a barrel to kiss him. "Move these, I can help you carry it."

"No," he said. "I can pull it through. You need not touch it."

Hunter barely finished repositioning the barrels and dragging the corpse into the storeroom when he heard Crespin call Madame Moreau. He closed the door.

She bid Crespin enter the kitchen and offered him bread and broth.

"Madame, it were better I take the food outside. I smell like a charnel house."

"All of Paris begins to smell like a charnel house," she said. "What is happening now?"

"It is quiet nearby, but people still crowd the river banks to see bodies thrown off the pont Notre-Dame."

"But the houses on either side..." Marguerite queried.

"The houses of the Protestants have been ransacked," Crespin said. "I wheeled your barrow through the front door of the Golden Hammer—or where the front door once was—straight to the gallery over the river, to dump the corpses."

Marguerite shuddered. "Has the king not ordered everyone to return home and keep the peace?"

"People have not returned home," Crespin sighed. "I suppose they might argue that watching Protestants being tossed in the river is not breaking the peace."

"Do others bear the dead to the pont Notre-Dame?"

"Yes, from as far as the faubourg Saint-Martin. Householders do not want their air tainted by the bodies of their neighbors." He drank from the bowl. "And they do not want to be reminded of what they did to their neighbors—or let others do."

Marguerite walked to the storeroom door. "I must beg your help and your silence."

"You have shown me many kindnesses, and endured great misfortune today," he said. "What I can do for you?" He took a bite of bread.

She opened the storeroom.

Catching sight of Hunter, Crespin recoiled and almost choked. "Adams!" he sputtered. "I thought you had gone."

Hunter almost laughed at the sight of Crespin's face. He stepped forward and clasped his hand. "And I am glad to see you as well."

"Where have you been hiding? In that storeroom?"

"No. That would have put Madame Moreau in too much danger. I have been nearby, but cannot tell you where."

Crespin screwed up his face. "You cannot tell me?"

Hunter spoke earnestly. "In a city where men are threatened with death if they do not tell where a Protestant is hiding, it is best to be ignorant."

Crespin nodded.

"If you are to help Madame Moreau, and me," Hunter said, "you must reconcile yourself to ignorance in other matters."

Crespin looked from one to the other. "Very well. Keep your mystery to yourselves. What would you have me do?"

Hunter stepped aside and gestured to the body. "We would ask you to add one more corpse to your barrow."

Crespin stepped closer to the storeroom. "Headless. I guess his identity is one of those matters I am not to know."

"It is," Hunter said. "Who it is, and how it comes to be here. But its disposal is a matter of life and death for Madame Moreau."

Crespin turned to Marguerite. "If one more trip to the river will save you from danger, I shall be glad to make it. But Izard left a boy to watch me. I told him I must come in and eat, but he is waiting by my barrow. We cannot carry the body there."

Hunter sighed.

Marguerite asked, "Has he eaten?"

"No. His companions seem to have forgotten about him."

"Then I shall invite him to sup with me," Marguerite said.

"Are you mad?" Hunter blurted.

"Not at all," she said. "While he and I break bread in my dining room—and share glasses of wine—you two will move the body."

"That puts you at great risk," Hunter objected.

"We are all at great risk now, if the lad comes to look for Jacques." She nodded towards the corpse. "Can you move that to my office, then go invite the lad—what is his name?"

"Claude," Crespin said.

"Tell Claude I have prepared some refreshment for him," Marguerite said. "Lead him into the dining room. I will seat him so he cannot see the front door. You can take the body from my office out to your barrow."

"Let's waste no time." Hunter grasped the body by the shoulders. Crespin lifted the legs. Both turned their heads as they carried the corpse to Marguerite's office. Hunter remained there while Crespin invited Claude into L'Échiquier.

When he was seated, with Marguerite chatting coquettishly, Crespin quietly opened the office door. "There is no one on the street," he whispered.

They hauled the body out the door and six paces to the barrow. Hunter lowered the shoulders over the wheel, the legs pointing towards the handles. He cut linen strips from the wrists and ankles.

"No other lacks a head," Crespin said. He indicated the body of the Lyon merchant's wife. "Help me lift this one to cover it. She will be light enough. I can manage both."

They positioned her body on top of Nicolas's corpse.

Hunter glanced both ways. "You must leave before Claude returns."

"And you must disappear again, as well."

"I must order some things at the inn, then I will go to the embassy."

Crespin raised his eyebrows. "You cannot take any bridge. They are crowded with mobs. Militias are gathered at Cemetery Saint-Jean and Place de Grève. Guards are posted on all the gates."

"I feared as much." Hunter pressed his lips together. "I must try to swim across."

"You can swim?"

"I learned in Lake Geneva."

"Good luck, my friend," Crespin said.

"Quickly, have you heard anything of Sidney?"

"I haven't heard that any English gentleman has been killed."

"Any word about the embassy?"

"No."

Footsteps on a cross street. A figure flitted past, heading north.

"We must both leave." Hunter clasped Crespin by the shoulders, then slipped back to the inn's office.

"I am glad you reached here safely," Zuñiga said.

"As am I." His visitor shed his hooded cloak.

"We must thank God that the people are cutting out the tumor of heresy, but a mob can be unpredictable."

"The streets are quieter tonight. Heralds shout that the king orders all to keep the peace." The man shrugged. "At least a few have heeded his commands."

Zuñiga ushered his guest into his study and poured glasses of wine. "Your message said you wished to speak of an opportunity we have long sought."

"This bloodlust is the opportunity," the man said. "In the midst of such chaos, an embassy might be stormed, and an ambassador killed."

"Are you trying to frighten me?" Zuñiga smiled.

"You know I am not speaking of Your Excellency. The Ambassador of His Most Catholic Majesty, the staunchest defender of the faith, would scarcely be a target of Parisians. I was thinking of the English. The angry men who shouted and threw stones yesterday might gather there again tomorrow."

Zuñiga nodded. "I heard you roused some elements in Saint-Marcel, but a few city guards chased them away. Did they return today?"

"I imagine they were busy killing and looting today," the man said. "Tomorrow they will be looking for new targets. I think they can be inspired to focus on the English Embassy again. *La Hache* has promised them each a double sol for their trouble."

"There may be a further problem," Zuñiga said. "The king is to send guards here tomorrow. Some may be dispatched to the English Embassy as well. How will your undisciplined rabble react to royal guards? If they succeed in entering, what will they do—grab the first valuable they see, and not bother to find the ambassador?"

"I will not depend on the mob of Saint-Marcel," his visitor explained. "*La Hache* has connections with Captain Izard, one of the most active militia commanders in Paris."

"I know of him," Zuñiga said. "Most zealous in arresting Huguenots during the last war."

"He was very active today, as well. I propose to meet with him after I leave you, if you approve of my plan."

"Pray continue." Zuñiga sipped his wine.

"The rabble of Saint-Marcel will gather before the embassy, as yesterday. They will shout and threaten and distract the attention of any guards the king may send, as well as those in the embassy. That will allow Captain Izard and his men to enter the courtyard gate at the side. As I have said, I have a man inside who can open that gate. The captain has a disciplined force who will dispatch the ambassador and all Englishmen at the embassy."

"I understand many have sought asylum with Walsingham," Zuñiga said. "Your militia may encounter more men than they expect."

"Armed militiamen can match anyone he shelters. And once they have entered, they can let the mob in. All those inside will be overpowered and slaughtered." The speaker's eyes glittered. "This is the opportunity we have looked for. Let King Charles try to explain to Elizabeth why his guards were unable to protect her ambassador."

Zuñiga pursed his lips. "This Izard, is his militia not on the Right Bank? Can he be counted upon to march across Paris? What will you promise him?"

"Captain Izard is a man eager for gold." He fixed his eyes on the ambassador.

"I thought so," Zuñiga said. "That is why you have come to me."

"I would not think of proceeding without your approval," His tone became obsequious. "If I offer him sixty écus, he will have his share and enough to reward his men. Is it not a cheap price for destroying the treaty between England and France?"

"Before agreeing," Zuñiga said, "I would know more of the refugees at the embassy. How many? How well armed? Are there any Huguenots? If so, Walsingham can be discredited for interfering in His Majesty's affairs. If you have men inside, you should be able to find out."

"We must act quickly," his visitor argued. "Although the people are giddy butchering heretics today, if the king's heralds keep proclaiming the killing should stop, their excitement may wane."

"That is another problem in your plan," Zuñiga said. "We do not know what tomorrow may bring. Now that the Huguenot leaders are dead, the king may command Montmorency to march troops into Paris and restore order."

His visitor set his mouth. "Very well. I shall go to the embassy tomorrow. I shall see for myself who is there, and inform the militiamen. And I shall make sure a man will be with them to guide them to their victims."

Zuñiga smiled. "Then I agree to supply the funds, if you yourself see that the conditions are right. But you had best be gone when the mob breaks in."

"I will visit near midday, then take my leave," his visitor said. "But I must contact Izard tonight, so he will be prepared. After I investigate the embassy, I can send him a message. He will be ready to enter at two tomorrow, unless I send word he should stay."

"We are agreed." Zuñiga raised his glass.

Hunter stood on the bank of the Seine, his back against a warehouse wall, the towers of the Hôtel de Sens to his right. He breathed deeply, gathering his strength and will power.

He regretted leaving Marguerite to face Izard. They had reviewed the matter again, as they strewed herbs where the body had lain and shifted barrels and boxes back to the storeroom. He could not help by staying; confronting militiamen would result in his own death and make her position worse. She would not abandon her inn for a dangerous and uncertain journey across Paris. Walsingham could not legally shelter her, a subject of the French king. Neither had voiced what both knew: they had no lasting future together.

So they had turned to the practicalities of his escape. He stuffed the white cross, armband, cuffs, and collar in his black garments. He smeared his face and hands with grease and ashes, the better to blend into the shadows. He shoved a few coins in his pocket and left the rest with Marguerite. He could not swim with his sword. Marguerite swore she could hide it and his remaining clothes where they would not be found, even if the secret staircase were opened. He secured his dagger and a long carving knife in scabbards looped on his belt and tied around his thighs.

Together they had reviewed his route. If he swam to the Île aux Vaches, walked to its eastern end, then swam on, he might reach the Left Bank beyond the Porte Saint-Victor, near the mouth of the Bièvre. From there, he could proceed to the embassy outside the walls of Paris. He had never swum fully clothed before, but he could not arrive at the embassy naked, or in only his breeches.

Hunter slipped off his shoes, covered with the *boue de Paris*, and now augmented with the blood of those slain. He cleaned them as best he could, scraping them against the wall, then stuffed them into his doublet and buttoned it to the neck. He waded a few steps into the river, moving from the wall's shadow into the light of the rising moon, striding slowly so as not to splash. He shivered as the water lapped his thighs. Voices resounded on the bank above.

"Well, I killed four today," a nasal voice bragged, "so I am one ahead of you."

"But one was a woman and another a child," his companion objected gruffly. "All three of mine were men."

"But all unarmed," the first said. "One of my men had a sword."

Hunter crouched down in the water.

"He had a sword, but you had your arquebus," his companion said. "That was no contest."

"As much a contest as you with a sword and a Lutheran with empty hands," the first voice whined.

"Well," the gruff voice struck a conciliatory tone, "let us drink to both our successes."

Their footsteps receded in the direction of the Hôtel de Sens. Hunter pushed into the river and began to stroke towards the willows on the island. The current pushed against his left side and his clothes pulled him down as they absorbed water. He stroked and kicked harder.

"Look!" the gruff voice sounded, "A man swimming."

The men had not gone away. But they could do him no harm. By the time they raised an alarm, he would have reached the Île aux Vaches.

"A Huguenot escaping!" Gruff shouted. "Quick, prime your weapons!"

Weapons? More than one arquebus? Hunter gulped in air and kicked harder.

Cries echoed from the Right Bank. Had the speakers met others?

The report of an arquebus rang out. The water to his right hissed as the shot skimmed across it. He was within range. Now a second explosion, and a closer splash. At least two had guns. Hunter's arms and legs were heavy clay. A third shot sounded, and the bullet whizzed within inches of his head. His heart beat faster. How many armed men were there? How long would it take them to reload? How many strokes would get him beyond their range? Another report echoed. The ball whistled overhead. An idea! He might deceive them. Hunter cried out and rolled onto his back.

"You struck him!" a man cried. Others cheered.

Hunter floated on his back, fighting to keep his nose and mouth above water as his soaked clothes pulled him down. Do not panic. Breath slowly. The ruse had worked. God, do not let them fire again to make sure of their victim. How long would it take to drift out of range, or out of sight? He dared a few kicks underwater, and stoked his arms slowly, in what he hoped would pass for drifting in and out with the current. How far downstream could he drift? Would he hear the millwheels in time to avoid them? Beyond the mills was the pont Notre-Dame, with its bloodthirsty crowd. He willed himself to delay another minute, then rolled over, raised his head above the water, and gulped in air. Ahead to his right, a millwheel slowly turned in the Seine. Beyond it, torches flickered at the Place de Grève and the pont Notre-Dame. He could not see where he had entered the water. He was out of sight of the shooters, but also well beyond the Île aux Vaches. He swam again, now for the Île Notre-Dame. Although the current strengthened as he neared the island, he soon touched bottom. He waded out, whispering a prayer of thanks, water streaming off him.

A scuttling in the grass. Hunter stepped back, stumbled over something, reached down, touched soft, swollen flesh, and recoiled from the stench. Another corpse, no doubt thrown in upstream, had come to rest on the island. Moonlight revealed that rats had begun gnawing it. He skirted it, climbed the bank, and collapsed under the willows, exhausted.

Waterwheels beat, voices murmured from the Place de Grève, and the crowd on the pont Notre-Dame shouted.

After some time, he rose and looked downstream, past the fields where washerwomen spread their laundry to dry, to the cathedral Notre-Dame rising above the Île de la Cité. He turned and crept to the island's north-eastern end.

Upstream, the Île aux Vaches lay low and dark in the water. To reach it, he would have to swim against the current. But swimming fully clothed had proved more difficult than he anticipated. If he stripped off, perhaps he could reach the Île aux Vaches and the Left Bank. But what then? Could an almost naked man, skin gleaming in the moonlight, hope to avoid detection? Could he take clothes from a corpse? The idea repelled him, and most bodies had by now been stripped. Might he find a boat on the south side?

Fifteen minutes later, he reached the end of the tree cover. No boats, but the jumble of branches and logs that had snagged themselves on the south side of the island gave him an idea. Instead of swimming to the Left Bank, he would find a suitable tree branch, cling to it, and keep afloat. Drifting with a branch and kicking, he could attract less attention.

He tried to estimate where he might land via a floating log. Certainly past the Tournelle and inside the wall, probably on the mud flats of the port near the Bernardins, where wood and hay were stacked. He dared not drift further downstream, to end up among the houses and ware-houses near the Petit-Pont, where torches flashed. Shouts, laughter, and the occasional firing of an arquebus floated across from the Left Bank. The king's orders to keep the peace appeared even more ineffectual among the students than among the bourgeois of the Right Bank, continuing a long Paris tradition.

Hunter found what he was looking for, a section of a young tree, about seven feet long, lying half in the water. The thicker end, some eight inches in diameter, rested on the shore. About one foot from that end, it forked, and smaller branches rose from both forks. He could position himself in the fork, the branches arching over him, and guide it to the opposite side. He waded in, tugged the log into the water, and settled himself in the fork.

He pushed off and glided away from the island, the log parallel to the shore and the current. Five yards out, the current caught the longer left end and began to turn the tree broadside to the river's flow. He kicked hard towards the farther shore, but the Bièvre's flow pushed him back to the middle of the Seine and spun the log further to the right. His struggles only steered the log perpendicular to the shore with the full current behind it. His panic grew as the wood port and the Bernardins slipped past on his left; to his right, the bishop's palace and the cathedral. He was racing downstream, out of control. The river narrowed and the current increased. Ahead loomed the three stone arches of the Petit-Pont, with its bloodthirsty horde.

He kicked furiously, trying to steer the log. Would he be spotted from the bridge? Torchlight reflected on the water and shouts echoed around him. Clinging with both hands, he shot towards the middle arch. When he was almost through, the end of the log hit the side of the arch. It spun, and he gulped a deep breath as he turned over. He held tight as the log pulled him underwater on his back. He was in the heart of city. If he surfaced to breathe, he would be seen. A splash to his left. The body of a naked old woman spun underwater beside him. They were throwing corpses from the quai. He strained to hold his breath. His lungs would burst.

With a jolt, his log struck a wooden trestle supporting the pont Saint-Michel. He lost hold and flailed about. His hand struck a piling, and he wrapped his arms around it and hung on, gasping for air. His log and the old woman's body drifted downstream. His plans had ended in disaster. He was under a bridge in the middle of Paris. Wild shouting and laughter echoed around him. The body of a bearded man with a missing arm floated past.

Downstream stood the Tour de Nesle. If he could pass that, he could reach the faubourg Saint-Germain. But close at hand, along the quai des Grands-Augustins, a crowd danced around a bonfire. The throng opened a corridor as a cheer arose. Three men pushing wheelbarrows piled with corpses dashed through. At the edge of the quai, people regrouped around the barrows, shoving one another aside to grasp the bodies and fling them into the Seine with loud hurrahs. Hunter could not hope to pass these ghoulish revelers unnoticed.

Houses backed onto the river nearer the bridge. In the open cellars beneath them, skins and cloth hung from rafters above huge vats. Hunter was cold and exhausted. If he could reach those workshops of dyers and leatherworkers, he might hide and rest. Perhaps the rejoicing killers would tire, or run out of corpses to hurl, and meander home. Staying in the darkness under the bridge, he kicked away from one piling and reached the next with a few strokes. After each effort, he embraced the newly-gained timber, caught his breath, and listened for any sign that he had attracted attention.

He launched himself from the final trestle and fell onto the muddy bank near a dyer's workshop. He scurried into its depths and cowered behind an enormous tub, listening for sounds of pursuit over the beating of his heart and his own deep breathing. The rabble downstream continued to whoop and shout, but the workshop was silent. He gave thanks to God. His body shook. With great effort, he unbuckled the belt with his knives, removed his soaked clothes, squeezed them out, and draped them over the tub to dry. Wrapping himself in dry undyed cloth, he collapsed on the floor. As warmth gradually returned to his limbs, he took refuge from a city of corpses in unconsciousness.

Monday, 25 August 1572

A loud thump awoke Hunter. After a moment's confusion, he remembered where he was, and became instantly alert. Had he slept long? Was the dyer coming to begin his morning's work? He reached for his clothes. Still damp. The moon rode high. Shortly after midnight. He had slept only a few hours. Whatever sound had awakened him, it was not repeated.

What was his best course of action? He must abandon his refuge before the morning work began. He could return to the river to float or swim past the Tour de Nesle. That idea filled him with dismay. He was ashore on the Left Bank. Perhaps yesterday's madness had run its course. Perhaps the king's orders would be obeyed, and the gates would open again. With an armband and cross-adorned cap, he could brave the streets of the Latin Quarter. Better to start towards the Porte Saint-Jacques. What he would do to get through the gate would depend on what he found when he arrived. He donned his damp clothes.

The door of the dyer's workshop was unlocked. Hunter peeked into the street. Deserted in both directions, at least for the moment. He slid along the façades, away from the pont Saint-Michel. Three men meandered towards him. Despite his pounding heart, he assumed an indifferent air and greeted them. They returned his greeting and passed by. Perhaps walking the streets would not be so dangerous. After two more encounters, he passed Saint-André-des-Artes and headed down the rue Hautefeuille.

"Adams!" someone called. Roger Barnes and Thomas Fisher emerged from the rue de la Serpent. Both sported white crosses. "My good man," Barnes exclaimed, "I am glad I have found you. You must come with us to safety."

"If anywhere in this town is safe for anyone," Fisher added, tottering beside Barnes.

"What has happened?" Hunter asked. "Are you in danger?"

"All Englishmen are suspect," Barnes said. "Come. I will tell you as we go."

Hunter did not want to accompany them, but what plausible reason could he have to refuse their offer of safety? Whatever had befallen the other expatriates might inform him of conditions on the Left Bank that could help him reach the embassy. "Where are you headed?"

"We are gathered at Sir Gregory's." Barnes set a brisk pace. "It seemed the safest place. His servant Robert knows the local militia leaders."

"Why are you abroad now?"

"I went out to find Thomas," Barnes said.

"I thought the Antelope safe enough," Fisher said, "but they were worried I might fall foul of the mob."

"You avoided them all day?" Hunter asked.

"I slept until mid-morning," Fisher said, "which was a good start. When I came out to see what all the uproar was about, I found stacks of bodies by my door, and went back inside. When things quieted down, I wound my way through the corpses to the Antelope. There I met a college servant. Seems he was thirsty after killing a dozen Huguenots. He gave me the cross. We retired to a back room and drank to the destruction of all Protestants."

"He and his friend had slept away most of the evening, according to the barman," Barnes said.

"Unless you enjoy killing, it seemed a good way to spend yesterday," Fisher said. "And even Hugh—my friend—tired of it soon enough. He never went back."

"Were you in danger, Roger?" Hunter asked.

"Knocking awoke me this morning," Barnes said. "There were armed men, asking my neighbor where the Protestant was. He said there were no Protestants in our building, but the man said he had heard an Englishman lodged there. My heart stopped. I shut the door and held my breath. Thank God Laurens spoke up in my behalf—said I was a good Catholic and attended Saint-André. Said the priest would tell them, if they didn't believe him. They still marched up to my door. I said a prayer before I opened it, believe me. They wanted to hear me say an *Ave*, then insisted on searching my rooms. Barnaby and Timothy had close escapes as well, but they can tell you. Here we are."

Robert leaned against Wilkes's door. "Good. You've returned. Now maybe I can get some sleep." His eye rested on Hunter. "You fetched back more than you went for."

"We encountered Master Adams in the rue Hautefeuille," Barnes said. "Let us pass, Robert. Then you can sleep."

Robert grunted. He let them in, then locked the door and lowered himself onto a pillow on the floor of the entry.

At the top of the steps, Richard Chandler opened the door. "Did you find him?"

"Yes." Barnes stepped past him. "And Adams."

Chandler embraced Fisher. "Thomas, I began to fear I would have no one to argue with."

Fisher laughed. "You are not so lucky."

"Paul, you have made your way here as well." Chandler touched his arm. "You are wet."

There was no use lying. "Crossing from the Right Bank was a dangerous affair," Hunter said. "The bridges are crowded with those cutting throats. I had to swim across."

Heath stepped close. "Thank God you are safe."

"Thank God we have all survived this madness," Timmons said.

"Is it madness to kill heretics?" Chandler asked.

"No," Timmons said, "but the Parisians are mad. You heard what happened to Timothy and me."

"Nothing, once they knew you were not heretics," Chandler said.

"You would not say 'nothing' if a man had held a knife to your throat," Heath said with heat.

"And not all those slain have been Huguenots," Timmons added. "The Catholic jeweler near the Collège Bourgogne was killed."

Chandler shrugged. "Some mistakes may have been made."

"What happened to you?" Hunter asked Heath.

"A mob invaded the college this morning," he said, "shouting they knew Lutherans were there. There were hundreds of them. Barnaby and I were making for our chamber when two men grabbed us. 'You are not

Frenchmen,' one cried. 'Those lads said so.' I don't know who he meant. 'The king has ordered that all heretics be slain,' one said, pressing a knife covered with blood to my throat."

"My God," Hunter said.

"Barnaby pleaded with him, saying we were faithful Catholics, and telling him not to kill us or his soul would suffer torment in hell for his mistake. I think that was what stayed them."

Timmons nodded vigorously. "Thank God he heeded me, for his sake as well as ours. But the man who held me would not let go. He said any heretic might say the same. I said, 'Take us to the principal of Collège Mignon. He will swear we are Catholics.' And that was what he did."

"You are right to speak of madness," Hunter said.

"If you have made your way here from the Right Bank, you must have seen your share of madness as well," Heath said.

Images flashed through Hunter's mind: the corpses outside L'Échiquier; the crowd carrying the Merlet family in a macabre carnival procession; the corpse robber holding a severed finger; the woman pleading with the man who held her baby out of reach; the rat-chewed corpse on the Île aux Vaches. Overpowering all other memories, the shudder up his arm as his sword pierced Nicolas's windpipe. "Yes," he said quietly. Expectant faces surrounded him. "But I do not wish to speak of it now." He looked around. "Where are Sir James and Sir Gregory?"

"Sir James is safe at his house," Chambers said. "Sir Gregory retired to his room to rest."

As if on cue, Sir Gregory entered. "I thought I heard more voices. Thomas, welcome. I was sure that you would be unharmed. Roger, did I not say you were foolish to endanger yourself?"

"You did," Barnes said, "but I was in little danger. The city is quieter now."

"I am glad to hear it." Wilkes eyed Hunter. "Master Adams, I am surprised yet delighted to see you here."

"I thank you, as I am sure everyone does, for providing us refuge on such a day as this," Hunter said.

"You came here for protection?" Wilkes asked. "There must have been places closer to your lodgings."

"Militiamen came. I escaped while the innkeeper was telling them I was not there, and I hid in a cellar all day. As you know, you are the only ones in Paris who know my true faith. Those near my lodgings know me as an English Protestant. This is the one place in Paris I was sure I would be safe."

"Yes. You have attracted some attention in Paris with your barrow of English cloth," Wilkes said. "I can well believe that the killing squads that roam the city would dispatch you with pleasure."

"I fear they would," Hunter said.

"Master Adams, pray seat yourself over here." Wilkes indicated a large, extravagantly carved wooden chair. His manner made Hunter uneasy, but could think of no reason to object. The others seated themselves in semi-circles on either side of Hunter and Wilkes.

"Gentlemen," Wilkes addressed the room, "it is fortunate indeed that Paul Adams has come to us for protection now." He smiled. "We can provide what he needs and deserves. He is at this moment our guest of honor." The benevolent looks of the expatriates did nothing to counteract the insincere tone in Wilkes's voice. "I shall tell you what Adams has recently done for the Catholic cause. Last month he printed a pamphlet titled—what was it, Paul—'The True Duty of English Catholics'?"

"Yes," Hunter said. Why was Wilkes telling them this now? Was this why he called him a guest of honor?

"Listen, by your leave, while I read you the contents of two letters." Wilkes opened a wooden box on the table next to his chair and withdrew the letters.

Hunter's muscles tightened. Could he hold a letter revealing him as a Catholic, or as a Protestant spy?

"Not only did he cause the pamphlet to be printed," Wilkes continued, "he paid for it to be shipped to London where a Catholic merchant, Francis Reddan, would distribute it to those of our religion who long for words of guidance and comfort."

Timmons looked at Hunter with admiration.

"Unfortunately, his efforts did not meet with success. The pamphlets Paul sent were seized and Reddan jailed."

The expatriates looked with sad, sympathetic eyes. Hunter gripped the arms of his chair.

Wilkes stood. "I feared Paul might be in danger—that Reddan might reveal he was working on his behalf, that he might lose his position here, or that he might be arrested when he returned to England. But this letter put my mind at rest." He unfolded it as the expatriates exchanged glances.

"Although Reddan is in jail, he was able to smuggle out this letter in answer to mine." He reached into the box again, pulled out a wheellock pistol, and pointed it at Hunter. The expatriates gasped. Wilkes's stern voice rose. "Reddan writes he never knew anyone named Paul Adams."

Hunter felt a fool. He should have seen this denunciation coming. Wilkes's questions at their last meeting should have put him on guard. He should have followed his instincts and not come with Barnes. Perhaps he could still talk his way out of this. "Sir Gregory, you wrong me! I told you Reddan would not betray me. Of course he would deny knowing me, to protect me."

"Before we discuss this further," Wilkes said, "I will ask Barnaby and Richard to relieve you of those knives on your legs. Stand slowly. Remember this pistol is aimed at your heart."

Hunter had no choice; he stood. Timmons hesitated a moment, looking back and forth from Hunter to Wilkes, then he reached down and pulled the dagger from its sheath. On his left side, Chandler extracted the carving knife tied to his thigh.

"You may sit again," Wilkes said. "I can understand why Reddan might deny knowing you to Her Majesty's torturers, but why should he deny knowing you to me?"

"He could not be sure who might read his letter," Hunter replied.

"True," Wilkes said, "but I did not mention this letter was encrypted. Gentlemen, Master Adams had previously shown me a letter he said was from Reddan, but it was not in a cypher and was written, oddly enough, in a completely different hand." He waved the letter. "My conclusion is that the supposed letter and the pamphlet were both part of a plot against the Catholic cause."

Hunter's heart beat faster, but he had to continue arguing his case. "It makes sense that Reddan took extra care in writing from prison. And how can you call the pamphlet part of a plot?"

Wilkes stepped back, but held his pistol steady. "Gentlemen, I must confess that I fell into the trap baited with this pamphlet. Thinking it genuine, I sent a shipment of Vaux's *Catechism* together with the pamphlets, and as a result many good Catholics in England have been arrested. I must apologize for my mistake and ask your forgiveness." He dropped the letter on the table.

"We both knew Burghley's spies watch every port and that sending a tract to England ran the risk of discovery," Hunter said.

"Your argument grows weaker and weaker," Wilkes said. "But I have not yet shared the contents of the second letter." He retrieved it from the box. "Roger, I beseech you, open this." Barnes took the small letter and unfolded it. "That is from the Spanish ambassador. He writes that the same Lord Burghley just mentioned sent a spy to France in April, a man—pray read the underlined words, Roger. I must keep my attention on Adams."

"A man of medium height and build, dark brown hair and eyes, thick eyebrows, high cheekbones, aged twenty-two or twenty-three, who might be considered handsome. It is believed that the man calls himself Paul Adams, but his true name is Edward Hunter." Barnes stared in disbelief.

Wilkes pointed at Hunter and proclaimed, "This man is a spy and a traitor!"

The expatriates rose, eyes burning.

"Do you deny this?" Chandler asked

Hunter stared at the pistol barrel. He had struggled through a city gone mad, eluded bullets, almost drowned, and it had come to this. At least he had succeeded in his mission. He had done what he could to protect Marguerite. Perhaps his family would learn that he had died serving his queen and protecting his religion. He might have to answer to God for fornication, adultery, and murder, but he would not perjure himself now. "No," he said.

"You lied to us all," Heath hissed. "We should kill you here and now."

"No," Timmons said. "We cannot stoop to the acts of the mob. Our souls must not bear the sin of his murder."

"And we must not soil this fine floor"—Wilkes regained his composure—"nor our hands. We shall simply turn him over to Robert's friends in the militia and tell them we discovered a Protestant spy. I understand they are in the rue Saint-Jacques, near Saint-Séverin."

"Have you any rope?" Chandler asked. "We should bind his hands."

"The cords on the bed curtains will serve," Wilkes said.

Chandler left the room.

"Timothy," Wilkes said, "pray remove the handkerchief from his arm and the cross from his cap. He has sailed under false colors long enough."

"Gladly." Heath tore the cross from Hunter's cap and untied the handkerchief.

"Sir Gregory," Barnes said, "I feel responsible for bringing this conspirator into our midst. I trusted his lies. I must apologize to you all for my error." The others muttered their forgiveness. "To help make amends, I will deliver Adams, or Hunter, to the militia."

Hunter's anguish grew. Barnes, with whom he had sought Pickering's killer, who had visited him after he had been pushed into the bonfire, was volunteering to take him to his death. Sidney loathed him. He would die despised by both Catholic and Protestant friends as a false traitor.

"Thank you," Wilkes smiled, "but you cannot undertake it alone."

"Timothy, will you help me?" Barnes asked.

Timmons looked surprised.

"Perhaps someone stronger," Fisher muttered under his breath.

Timmons bristled, "I am strong enough to walk a man with his hands tied a furlong up the street." When Wilkes hesitated, he added, "And we can carry your pistol."

"Very well," Wilkes agreed.

Chandler entered with cords and a knife. Fisher and Barnes stepped to Hunter's right side; Heath and Timmons to his left. They pulled him from his chair.

"Best tie his legs so he can walk but not run," Fisher said. Chandler knelt and tied Hunter's feet, allowing him a two-foot stride. Barnes forced his hands together, as though clasped in prayer, and wrapped a cord around his wrists.

"Better to bind his hands behind him," Wilkes said.

"It is but a short way." Barnes pulled the knot tight. "He cannot get loose."

"Very well," Wilkes said. "No need for delay. We are all weary, and I will sleep easier knowing that Paul Adams, or Edward Hunter, is reaping a proper reward for his acts." He handed Barnes his pistol.

Barnes seized Hunter's right arm and pushed him forward. Timmons, on his left, did the same. Chandler opened the door and said, "I will go down first, to be sure there are no accidents on the staircase."

Barnes backed slowly down, pointing the pistol at Hunter's chest. Timmons followed, holding Hunter's dagger. Below, Chandler explained what was happening to Robert.

Hunter pondered. Would his treatment by the militia be less painful than being shot here, or breaking his neck in a tumble down stairs? Something within him clung to life, though it might be measured in minutes. He prayed silently.

Timmons and Barnes took his arms and stepped into the street.

"Shall I come with you?" Chandler asked.

Timmons turned. "Do you, too, think me too weak?"

"No, Barnaby," Chandler said, "I just...I am sure you and Roger can do the job."

"You will find Captain Girard and his men in front of Saint-Séverin," Robert said. "Do not fare well, Master Adams." He laughed. "Fare-unwell, Master Adams." He laughed louder, and nudged Chandler to notice his cleverness. As Barnes and Timmons started up the rue Saint-André-des-Arts, he called again, "Fare-unwell."

Judging they were beyond earshot, Hunter murmured, "Roger, I was surprised you were the most eager to take me to my death."

Barnes's hand lashed across his face. "Silence!" Blood flowed from Hunter's lips. Behind them, Robert and Chandler laughed.

The trio trudged in silence along the rue Saint-André.

"Turn here," Barnes ordered at the rue de l'Éperon. After several yards, he signaled a halt. He kept the pistol trained on Hunter as he backed towards a body lying near the cemetery of Saint-André-des-Arts. He kicked it, then returned. "That way." He indicated the dark, narrow street beside the cemetery. After a few steps, he turned to Timmons. "We must not do this."

Hunter stared at Barnes. "Roger," he breathed. Had he heard right?

"What?" Timmons gaped.

"I will not have this man's death on my conscience," Barnes said, "nor upon my soul. Did you not say his killing would blacken all our souls? Will our guilt be less if we lead him to his killers?"

"No," Timmons said softly, "but what will we tell the others?"

"That he escaped," Barnes said.

"How?" Timmons asked.

"The corpse," Barnes explained. "I kicked it to make sure it was not someone sleeping in the road. We will go back and play out a scene, in case anyone is watching. I will trip over that corpse in the dark. As I fall, I will drop the pistol. Let us pray it doesn't go off. Seeing an opportunity, Paul—or Edward—will push you, Barnaby, and dive for the pistol. He will point it at my head and demand you cut his cords. When he is free, he will strike us both and make his escape."

"May God bless you," Hunter said. "But I cannot strike those who save my life."

"I had to strike you, to make Chandler believe I would take you to your doom. You must strike us, for us to be believed. Our wounds will keep us from suspicion," Barnes said. "As far as saving your life, I can only give you a chance to save your own. You will have a pistol with one shot, and a dagger, but you still might be slain." He turned to Timmons. "But we shall have no part in it."

"Again I thank you from my heart," Hunter said.

"Can you play your part and take a blow?" Barnes asked Timmons.

"Yes. A wound will heal."

"Then let us go," Barnes said. "It will be best if you strike me on the face with the butt of the pistol, but use only your fist on Barnaby."

"I can take a hard blow," Timmons said.

"I will try to do as little harm as I can," Hunter promised.

They turned into the rue de l'Éperon. After a few steps, Barnes let his foot catch on the body, and fell against the cemetery wall. The pistol sailed from his hand.

Hunter plowed his right shoulder into Timmons as Barnes fell. He tensed as the pistol spun towards the dirt, but it did not fire. He sprang forward and scooped it up as best he could. Barnes lay as though stunned. Perhaps he was. The left side of his face bled, where it had scraped the wall.

Hunter pointed the pistol at Barnes, his finger outside the trigger guard to prevent an accident. "Timmons," he hissed, "Cut me loose or I will blow his head off."

Timmons rose, his face a mask of fear.

"Free my hands first." Hunter demanded. Above, a window creaked. A head ducked back. "Quickly!"

Timmons struggled to cut the cord.

"Someone at the window," Hunter whispered.

"Then your blows must be genuine," Barnes whispered back.

"My feet," Hunter snarled aloud, "or he dies."

Timmons sliced the cord.

"Forgive me," Hunter murmured. "And drop my dagger when I strike you." He shifted the pistol to his left hand and swung his right to catch Timmons in the face. He fell with a stifled cry.

"Roger, forgive me. I owe you my life," he whispered, then raised the pistol and struck a glancing blow. Barnes crumpled. Hunter could not tell if the blow had rendered him unconscious or whether he was acting. He could not stay to find out. He retrieved his dagger, glanced at the window, and ran towards Porte Saint-Germain, breathing a prayer of thanks.

Hunter had passed only a few streets when he heard shouts and laughter to his left. He ducked into the doorway of a grand house. Four drunken voices grew louder.

"...would not have thought such a little fellow would have had so much blood in him," a thin, high-pitched voice said.

"When it sprayed all over you, I thought I would wet my breeches laughing," his baritone companion said. The group guffawed as they passed, heading towards the Porte Saint-Germain.

Could the gate be open? Hunter untied the cords from his ankles and peered around the corner. Four soldiers guarded the Porte Saint-Germain. Two stood, leaning on halberds, while the others sat on the ground, backs against the gatehouse wall, arquebuses propped between them.

"Halloo, halloo," the thin-voiced man called.

"Halloo, yourself, Étienne," the taller halberdier said. "Is it not time you were abed?"

"Much, much too early," Étienne replied. "We wish to pass through."

"On what business?"

"Well," Étienne slurred his words, "we have killed all the Huguenots we could find in the Latin Quarter, but Jean says he knows where to find some in the faubourg Saint-Germain."

"You are hours too late," the guard said. "They all galloped off at dawn, with the Duke of Guise in pursuit."

"So I heard," said the baritone, Jean, "but that was just the nobles. The Huguenots I know cannot afford horses. Let us go through so we can see for ourselves."

"You know that the king has ordered that the killing stop," the guard said in a mock serious tone. The other guards and the revelers broke into laughter.

"We are not to open the gate until dawn." An arquebusier struggled to his feet. "Why don't you nap and come back later?"

"If we wait till dawn," a third voice said, "the Huguenots may have fled. We want to surprise them in their beds."

The halberdier looked at the arquebusier. "What do you say?"

"We are to keep the Protestants from escaping the city," the arquebusier said with a shrug, "but these are good men doing God's work, as I see it."

"Very well," the halberdier said. "Étienne, from the looks of you, you have been at God's work all day." The revelers laughed again.

"Oh, we took time out to eat and sleep away the afternoon," Étienne said. "That is why we are awake now."

"You need to find a clean shirt," the halberdier said.

Étienne gestured to his bloodstained clothes. "This only happened tonight, after curfew."

The door in the gate creaked as the guard opened it.

"We will find him another in some Huguenot's house," Jean said, passing through.

Hunter leaned against the wall. There was no hope of getting through here. By now, Barnes and Timmons would have returned to Wilkes's house, and the other expatriates might start a search for him, or ask the militia to do so. He must move. Might another gate be open? Or its guards sleeping or drunk? A thin chance, but he must find a way out of Paris. He slipped away from the gate. Here, the street was free of corpses. The barrow men from the quai des Grands-Augustins had done their job well.

At the corner of the rue Hautefeuille, the flicker of torchlight and voices approached. He spotted an iron ring and a torch holder above it. Using them, he clambered onto a cornice over a door and stretched out on top. He prayed the men would not be look up.

Richard Chandler appeared below, with two militiamen. "...not surprised you have not seen him," he said. "He would be a fool to run towards your post at Saint-Séverin. He'll head for a gate, I'll wager."

"A fat lot of good that will do him," one militiaman said. "All are guarded well."

They passed beneath Hunter and headed south on the rue Hautefeuille. So, the militia was looking for him. He lowered himself slowly, then leapt from the bottom ring. As he jumped, the pistol tumbled from his belt and flew spinning through the air. He held his breath.

The pistol hit the ground. The spring unwound with a hiss, but it did not fire.

He dived for the pistol, flattened himself against the wall, and examined it. The priming powder had leaked out. He whispered a prayer of thanks.

Another twenty minutes of slinking from door to door, detouring away from any voices or torches, led him to a passage off the rue des Cordeliers, which ended at the cemetery behind Saint-Cosme. Here was the church where he had first convinced the expatriates he was a Catholic, and the cemetery where Pickering was buried. Ahead on the rue de la Harpe, the clop of hooves and the creak of a cart. An ass came into view, pulling a wagon with two men.

"Here's three more, Gaston," the driver said. "I thought we cleared all the bodies from here."

"We did," Gaston said. "Some bastard must have brought these out in the last hour."

"Some neighbor searched 'em out when the smell come through his walls, most likely." His companion halted the cart in front of Saint-Cosme.

"Well, let's get 'em. 'Two sols for each body,' Captain Girard says." The cart creaked as Gaston climbed down.

"Only one sol for babes." The driver climbed down in his turn.

"May as well get these on the way out," Gaston said. "Then we'll fill up along the rue d'Enfer. Captain said they were scattered all the way to the Carthusians."

The shuffling of feet. Grunts as they lifted a body. A thump as it hit the back of the cart.

"If they're lyin' out there on the road, why don't they bury 'em in the monastery cemetery?" the driver asked.

"Bury heretics in holy ground! Are you daft? They need to be baptized in the Seine. Are you trying to argue us out of our money?" Gaston said.

"No. I'm glad you struck the deal with Captain Girard. I'm just tired, that's all."

These men were taking their cart outside the walls to load bodies. This was Hunter's way out of Paris. If he could bring himself to share a cart with corpses... If he could board the cart without its driver noticing... If the guards at the gate did not look too carefully among the bodies... There were too many 'ifs,' but he could think of no better way. The third body hit the bed of the cart. He slipped to the edge of the church and glanced around the corner. The back of the cart was only a few feet away. The men were about to climb aboard. He must act when they were least likely to feel the cart shift with his weight. If they raised a cry, he would have to overpower them—probably kill them. This was what his mission had become—kill or be killed.

Before him gaped the open cart, a canvas cover arching above the three bodies in its bed. Now was the moment. The men swung themselves up.

Hunter bounded out, placed his hands on the cart bed, and listened. The driver clicked to the ass. As the cart jolted forward, he leapt. His chest and hips landed on the floor of the death cart.

The smell turned his stomach. The dead eyes of the woman on his right stared into his. If he retched and revealed himself, he would never see his family again, never return to England. He closed his eyes and thought of his mother's flower garden in Hertfordshire. He must stand the odor, the touch of cold skin. He squirmed further in, pulling away from the bodies on the right side. He rose on hands and knees and crawled forward on the sticky bed. When his right hand landed on a soft slimy object, he jerked it back, stifling a cry. He was afraid to imagine what he had touched. Again his gorge rose, and again he fought it down. He gained the front corner, where his hand closed on a coarse cloth, crushed and pressed down—a winding sheet, stiff with dried blood and God knew what else. He could hide under it. With luck, a guard peering in would see only darkness. He buried his nose in his sleeve and pulled the stiff cloth over himself. In a few moments, the cart jolted to a halt.

"More?" Gaston said.

"Let's go on," his companion said. "They are only worth a sol."

"But they'll take less room," Gaston countered. "Come on."

The bed of the cart rose as the men jumped down. They walked to the rear of the cart. Suddenly a body landed on top of Hunter with a thud. A light body. They had thrown in a child's corpse. Another, even lighter, followed. When the cart jerked forward, Hunter shrugged his shoulders so the small bodies slid to the side. How could God forgive the men who had slain these children? How could He allow what was happening in His name? He would not lift the shroud and look at the children's bodies. He pictured his mother's garden again and bent all his will to lying quietly. After minutes that seemed endless, the cart stopped.

"What's in the cart?" a voice asked. They had reached the Porte Saint-Michel.

"Protestants," Gaston replied. Hunter tensed and reached for his dagger.

"What?"

"But they're dead," Gaston laughed.

"Don't jest," the guard said.

"But you know me, Antoine," Gaston remonstrated. "And after a day like today, we all need a jest or two."

"I've got my orders." Antoine said. "And the sergeant is a strict son-of-a-bitch," he added in a lower tone. "I'll look in the back." He paced to the rear of the cart.

Hunter held his breath. Rays from a lantern flowed beneath the shroud and wavered from side to side.

The guard grunted. The light disappeared. "Where are you going, Gaston?"

"Collecting more bodies outside the walls. Be back in an hour. Here's a letter from Captain Girard. We are to clear Huguenot bodies from the city and faubourgs."

"I'll show the sergeant." Long minutes passed, then the gates creaked open and the cart jolted forward.

Hunter had never prayed so much in such a short time. He gave thanks and began to breathe again, despite the fetid air. The cart bumped along. As he raised the shroud, a light body fell against his arm. He beheld a boy's face. Thank God the eyes were closed. On top lay an even smaller body, a child of perhaps three. In the presence of these small bodies, the other corpses in the cart, and the piles of the massacred he had seen this day, what could he feel? Disgust? Outrage? Despair? He was so drained and numb that he no longer feared for his own life. Survival had become a grueling job that would never end.

He crawled towards the back of the cart. He must wait long enough to be beyond the sight of the guards, yet not delay until the driver stopped the cart. The torches at the gate faded. He swung his feet over the back and waited for a jolt. When a wheel thudded into a rut, he slid from the cart and staggered into the doorway of a house. By the light of the setting moon, he examined himself. His doublet and venetians were covered in slime that reeked of blood, urine, feces, and unnamed fluids that had seeped from corpses. He brushed his hands down the front of his clothes and smeared the wall behind him with the residue. He wiped again, harder, but his hands remained sticky. This unsatisfactory cleaning was all he could accomplish now. He had to make his way east through unfamiliar streets, avoiding any packs of killers who roamed beyond the walls of Paris.

CHAPTER 19

Besieged

THE EASTERN SKY GLOWED BEHIND THE EMBASSY. COCKS CREW. COMPARED to crossing the Seine, his capture by the expatriates, and his ride in the death cart with corpses, Hunter's irregular trip across the faubourgs south of Paris had occasioned frustration, but not danger. He had followed roads that took him too close to a city gate, and others that veered off into the countryside. He had backtracked, stumbled upon the inns he had visited months before with Barnes, and backtracked again. At approaching footsteps, he had ducked into doorways, dodged around corners, and flattened himself into ditches between road and field, but those he encountered were not killing squads, but drowsy apprentices opening bakeries, laborers making their way towards the city, and farmers driving wagons filled with vegetables to market. Those who had spent Saint Bartholomew's Day slaying their neighbors were sleeping late.

The embassy's shutters were closed. At the front, the gate in the iron fence was chained and locked. Given his filthy condition, Hunter thought it best to approach the gate that led to the courtyard. He rapped on its doorway, waited, then knocked again, louder.

When a hatch opened, Hunter recognized the porter, Christophe. "Open the gate. I have traveled all night to get here." Christophe looked him up and down. "I am Paul Adams. I was here only two days ago."

A look of recognition. Christophe closed the hatch and drew back the bolts on the doorway. When Hunter stepped through, Christophe regarded him with obvious distaste. "You'd best wait here, sir. I'll fetch Master Secretary."

The dried grime on Hunter's clothes was beyond cleaning. He would have to borrow garments from someone at the embassy.

Beale appeared. "Thank God you are safe, Paul. You look as if you have undergone an ordeal to reach us." Hunter noticed he kept his distance.

"I have. There is much to tell. The expatriates know my true identity, as does the Spanish Ambassador."

Beale frowned. "That may not matter now. After what happened yesterday, our main concern must be to survive."

"Is everyone at the embassy well and safe?"

"We are," Beale said, "though the count of 'everyone' has vastly increased."

"Did Sidney and his party reach you?" Hunter asked.

"Yesterday afternoon," Beale said. "But there will be time for you to tell your story and to meet the others. First, pray avail yourself of the well in the courtyard." He called to a stableman carrying hay across the courtyard. "Philip, can lend you a brush and some towels to this gentleman?" Philip nodded his assent. "My man Thomas is about your size," Beale continued. "I will ask him for some clothes you might borrow. I fear those are beyond redemption."

"I would be grateful," Hunter said. Beale disappeared, and he crossed to the well and hoisted a bucket of water.

Philip appeared with a stiff brush and two towels. "You can use that empty stall over there for some privacy."

Half an hour later, Beale led Hunter, now scrubbed and attired in Thomas Howell's brown trunk hose and tan doublet, to Walsingham's private office. The ambassador greeted him with tired, worried eyes, but a sincere smile. "I am relieved you have made your way here safely. Robert says you have a long tale to tell."

Hunter related his experiences of Saint Bartholomew's Day. He omitted killing Nicolas and disposing of his body, saying Marguerite Moreau hid him all day in the storeroom.

"There was always the chance Wilkes would contact Reddan," Walsingham said. "I feared it might happen before the pamphlets were shipped."

"We must write to his jailors to be more vigilant." Beale made a note. "Visitors must be searched before and after they speak to him."

"Some visitors may be of such rank that they would be insulted by such a demand," Walsingham said. "We must ask as well for a list of those who have visited him." He exhaled a mirthless laugh. "Though God knows when we shall be able to venture out of this house, let alone send a messenger to London."

"Praise God that Roger Barnes was among the expatriates," Beale said.

"I am forever in his debt," Hunter said. "His Catholic faith is strong enough that he left England, yet his humanity is strong enough to forgive an enemy of Catholicism who deceived him."

"You said in your first reports that he had a brother in Worcestershire who remains loyal to the English Church," Walsingham said. "That brother may have been in his thoughts when he freed you."

"I hope both he and Timothy do not suffer for their kindness," Hunter said. "I hope my blows, much as I regretted giving them, provided them a credible explanation."

"You did what you could," Beale said.

"Your tale echoes that of others," Walsingham said, "hiding, donning cross and handkerchief to pass through the streets, avoiding murderers, witnessing unspeakable acts..." He sighed.

"Secretary Beale said Sidney and his party are safe here," Hunter said.

"Yes," Walsingham said. "The Duke of Nevers delivered them yesterday afternoon."

"Nevers?"

"Yes. I will let him tell you himself."

Hunter bit his lip, remembering Sidney's disdain when they parted.

"Do not worry," Walsingham said. "I will explain your role to him. He can meet Edward Hunter, the queen's servant, not Paul Adams." He turned to Beale. "Will you bid Master Sidney come here?"

"I am grateful that you will reconcile matters between us," Hunter said.

"We discussed that only two days ago." Walsingham said. "Since then the world has gone mad."

Beale returned. "Sidney should be down in a moment."

"How many others have come to you for shelter?" Hunter asked.

Walsingham looked Beale. "Some two dozen, is it not?"

"At least," Beale replied. "More if we count those here before yesterday—Halston, Manucci, the historian Bizari. And we must now include Master Hunter."

Walsingham nodded. "And the new groom in the stables," he said with a meaningful look. Could the young boy in the courtyard be whom they meant?

"Dean Watson, Lord Wharton, Bright, Cope, Faunt." Beale ticked off each on his fingers. "And their servants; add four. Sidney's group; add five. Five Dutchmen. Three Germans. I make that twenty-seven."

"In addition to our staff and my family," Walsingham addressed Hunter. "You see we are more crowded than usual."

"You need only point out a palliasse on the floor for me," Hunter said.

"That may be all we can offer," Beale said. "Our guest rooms are occupied by those of higher rank who came yesterday; others slept on the floor of the great chamber and the conference room."

"That will be far more comfortable than any of the places I slept yesterday."

A tap sounded on the door, and Philip Sidney entered. When he saw Hunter, every muscle in his body tensed. "You have come here?" he asked, frowning.

"Master Sidney," Walsingham said, "I must reacquaint you two."

"Your Excellency," Sidney said, "I have recently come to know Master Adams all too well."

"You think you do," Walsingham said. "The man before you is not Paul Adams, but Edward Hunter, recommended to me by Lord Burghley for his service to your uncle, the Earl of Sussex, during the Northern Rebellion. And I commend him as well for insinuating himself with an English Catholic here in Paris, one who was sending treasonous tracts against the Gospel."

Sidney's stern expression changed to surprise, then understanding. "That is why you consorted with Catholics and attended Mass." He stepped forward and embraced Hunter. "Why did you not tell me yesterday?"

"I could not," Hunter said. "I swore to maintain my role as a secret Catholic throughout this mission. But last night the man His Excellency mentioned, Sir Gregory Wilkes, discovered my true identity."

Sidney stepped away and nodded. "Saint Bartholomew's Day has changed everything."

"At least we are friends again. Though that small good has less than a feather's weight balanced against the ton of Protestant corpses in the streets."

"Tell me," Sidney said, "when did you arrive? How did you get from the Chessboard Inn to the embassy?"

"You gentlemen have much to say to one another," Walsingham said, "but I suggest you tell it over breakfast."

They followed Beale to the formal dining room. Walsingham introduced Hunter by his true name to three Dutch merchants, Scholten, Rensink, and ten Haken, who sat with their bread and small beer at one end of the table. At the other end, a gray-bearded man was seated next to a distressed-looking youth with sandy hair and a pale complexion. "John Watson, Dean of Winchester," Walsingham indicated the older man, "and Philip, Baron Wharton, meet Edward Hunter, one of my agents who has been in Paris these past five months."

The men exchanged greetings, and Hunter and Sidney sat, but Walsingham and Beale excused themselves, saying they must attend to duties before breaking their fast. As they left, three young Englishmen entered. Timothy Bright, Nicolas Faunt, and Edward Cope introduced themselves as students at the University of Paris.

As the latest arrival, Hunter was obliged to tell his experiences on the day of the massacre first. Then, as they shared bread, butter, and small beer, the men around the table retold their own stories of danger and escape.

Faunt and Cope had been protected by their French classmates, who at first hid them, then accompanied them to the embassy. Dean Watson, a guest at the Collège de Navarre, had been escorted to safety by its principal.

At the pleading of his friends, Bright, a medical student, had donned a cross and armband and participated in the sack of a bookstore, in order to blend in with the rioters until he could slip away. "At least the bookseller escaped before the mob reached his shop," Bright said. "I did not have to witness a killing with my own eyes." He nodded at Wharton, who stared at the table ahead of him. "Lord Wharton was not so fortunate."

The others looked at Wharton, as if it were his cue to relate his experience, but he merely shook his head.

Sidney whispered in Hunter's ear, "I will tell you later."

"When did you arrive?" Hunter asked. "Beale said the Duke of Nevers delivered you."

"He did, yesterday afternoon." Sidney recounted how Madox had wakened him with the news that a massacre was underway. "We closed the windows and locked the doors. We were in agony, hearing screaming and shouting and imagining what was happening outside. After an hour or so, we could hear that a crowd had gathered. There was pounding on our door and shouts for the 'English heretics' to open up. We armed ourselves, waiting for the mob to force the door. Then we heard horses and someone giving orders. The mob quieted. Then there was a knocking at the door and a voice said that the Duke of Nevers would escort us to safety. At first we were reluctant to open the door, but when we did, we saw the duke and his men. He bid us mount behind them. He even allowed us our weapons." Sidney paused. "I know you gentlemen have already heard my story," he apologized to the others at the table, "but Master Hunter has not."

"It is a tale worth hearing again," Cope said.

"The duke and his men rode to the rue de Béthizy, where he showed us...what was left of Admiral Coligny. He pointed out the corpses of other Huguenot noblemen—Téligny, Rochefoucauld, Piles..."

"Why?" Hunter asked.

"He kept saying we must report what we saw to Ambassador Walsingham. I believe he wanted him to have definite information, not rumor. He said those who had been killed were plotting against the king. Despite our position, I said I did not believe that. He swore he had heard Piles threaten the Queen Mother, and that a Huguenot who was loyal to the king had revealed the plot."

"Do you believe him?" Hunter asked.

"I know that the Huguenots were becoming impatient on the eve of Saint Bartholomew's. Many spoke of revenge and taking matters into their own hands, but their rage was more against the House of Guise than the king," Sidney said. "As to His Grace's account of a Huguenot leader who betrayed them, Walsingham says he believes it."

"But the Duke of Nevers could not claim all those killed throughout Paris were part of any plot," Dean Watson put in, feeling the duke should be given no benefit of any doubt.

"He only said the king had ordered all Huguenots to be killed," Sidney said.

"A statement difficult to believe," Watson said. "Either the duke and his ilk made it up, or His Majesty quickly changed his mind, as his proclamation of yesterday afternoon ordered the killing to stop."

Hunter remembered Nevers's criticism, that the Huguenots' protestations of loyalty to the king were false and they should be exiled. Had those opinions, so moderately expressed under the sycamores of his park, led him to approve of the wholesale slaughter of the Huguenots of Paris? The duke put a high regard on loyalty. If he believed the king had ordered the killing of all Protestants, he would not have hesitated to do so.

"I am grateful you arrived safely, no matter at whose hands," Hunter said.

Bright turned to Baron Wharton. "As we have broken our fast, will you oblige me in the chess game I proposed yesterday evening?" Wharton nodded, and both rose. All took this as a cue to leave the table.

"Has the ambassador determined where you will stay?" Sidney asked.

"No," Hunter said. "I might need to sleep on the floor of the great chamber."

"Nonsense," Sidney said. "Some slept there last night, but you can squeeze in my chamber. Bryskett and I fill the bed, but there is room on the floor next to Madox."

"I appreciate the offer, but should you not consult Bryskett and Madox?"

"They will not object."

As they climbed to the top floor, Sidney told the story of Philip, Baron Wharton.

"He saw his tutor killed before his eyes yesterday. The poor man had just arrived in Paris two days before. The killers would have slain Wharton too, but the principal of his college arrived and swore Wharton was a loyal Catholic, named for his godfather and mine, Philip II of Spain. That stopped them in their tracks."

"Yet, despite his religion, Wharton came here for safety," Hunter said. The expatriates, though they had also been in danger, did not consider coming to Walsingham for help.

"The ambassador must look out for the welfare of all Englishmen in Paris," Sidney said. "After seeing his tutor slain, Wharton was paralyzed with fear. His servant led him here." They arrived at his vacant room. Evidently Bryskett and Madox were still eating breakfast. "You look exhausted. Why not use the bed for a few hours?"

The bed, simple as it was, held great appeal. "Will you and your companions have no need of the chamber?"

"I will gather the few things I need," Sidney said. "And I dare say, if we all return in a quarter hour, we might dance a jig and not disturb you."

"I am, as I have so often been, in your debt." Hunter lay down and was asleep within moments.

"We are at your command, Captain Izard," Madame Moreau smiled. "Although I believe your men searched through every room yesterday, I have prepared my staff to assist you today. There will be no need to break anything. They will open any cabinet or chest, move any bed or table, unlock any door." She turned to her employees, standing in a line with their most accommodating faces on.

Izard frowned. "Very well. My ensign and Robert will search the ground floor."

"As most of this floor consists of the kitchen and dining room, Auguste can assist them."

"What about your cellar?" Izard asked.

"It is dirty and musty, but Pierre can show you anything you wish," Marguerite said.

Izard scrutinized the men behind him. They avoided his eye, not wishing to spend time below ground. He pointed at the young militia-man, who had drawn the duty of watching Crespin move corpses the night before. "Claude, you will search the cellar." He returned to those who had avoided his gaze. "Jean, Gaston, and Arnaud—the third and top floor."

"Marie and Laurent will accompany them," Marguerite interrupted.

Izard cast an annoyed glance and continued, "René, Gaspard, and Jacob, examine the second floor, especially the Englishman's room."

"Jeanne and Martin, show them every inch of the second floor," Marguerite instructed. She turned to Izard. "I told you he had gone to his embassy, and your men took all his possessions yesterday."

A malevolent smile spread on Izard's face. "I will check the truth of your statement today. Meanwhile, I will investigate the first floor, starting with your room, Madame Moreau."

"As you wish. Bertha will be with us."

Izard ignored the insinuation. "Guillaume, Richard, and Jerome will search your stables; the rest of you, take the horses of the dead to René Touchart at the horse market. I will see him tomorrow." The men detailed to the stables smiled. They had drawn the best duty.

"Bernard will show you which horses are which," Marguerite said. "The bay is mine, the grays belong to the merchant from Brussels, and the roan mares belong to the guests from Angers."

The search had barely begun when shouting arose in the street. "Hallelujah!" "Praise God!"

Izard strode to the door. A voice above asked, "What's happening?"

"Keep at your work!" he shouted at the men leaning out of the windows.

A crowd dashed by, brandishing axes and knives. Izard and Marguerite strode to the rue Bourg Tibourg and stopped an excited woman in a ragged dress, pursuing the armed group.

"It is a sign. A sign from God. A miracle!" she babbled.

"What are you talking about?" Izard asked.

"The hawthorn at Holy Innocents," she said through broken teeth.

"A hawthorn?" Izard tried to make sense of her words.

"A dead hawthorn tree in Holy Innocents burst into bloom last night," she said, finally stringing together a sentence. "I spoke to one who saw it."

"Is that the miracle you speak of?"

"Yes. Yes. It shows God's blessing on our work. The priest said so. Those who stopped killing have taken up their knives again."

Izard smiled. "Then I will not keep you from your holy work."

"Thank you, sir." The ragged woman made a slight curtsey. "The porter knows where Huguenots are hiding, and I don't want to miss it." She rushed off.

"Though the king changed his mind, it seems God has not," Izard said.

"If you believe He shows His will by hawthorn blossoms," Marguerite said.

"Who are you to question a priest?" Izard asked.

"I am a woman who sees priests are not always holy, and often contradict one another."

Izard snorted and turned back to the inn. "Well, we have learned what the clamor was about. We must complete this job quickly." He told a militiaman to inform the others of the miraculous hawthorn, then stamped up the stairs and ordered Marguerite to empty her chests.

"Did you not get enough of a look yesterday?" Marguerite asked.

"Yesterday I did not look closely enough. One of your gowns may be stained with Nicolas's blood."

"I am sure you may find bloodstains," she said. "Bertha, Bernard, and I spent hours scrubbing up after your men. It would be a wonder if our clothes did not become stained."

"Just empty that chest," Izard said.

An hour later, the militiamen gathered in the dining room. Those assigned to the stable reported the horses delivered to the horse market. Others reported, floor by floor, that they had found no trace of Nicolas, nor any sign that the Englishman was hidden. Claude emerged from the cellar, cobwebs hanging from his cap.

"What were you doing down there, sampling the wine?" Izard asked. His men laughed.

"I was following your orders to search every hiding place," Claude said proudly. "I knocked on every barrel and marked those that sounded hollow or half full. It took a long time."

Izard's eyes sparkled with an idea. "Claude, you have done well." He addressed his men. "We may not all have been as thorough as this lad. Each one of us needs to return to his area and investigate the walls and floors. What better place to hide than in some cavity or alcove? I have heard some inns have them. Paul and Charles, you take some axes, go down, and open the casks that are not full."

Marguerite's heart sank. It would be only minutes until someone discovered the secret staircase. She followed Izard upstairs and stood in her chamber, straining to hide her anxiety, as Izard pulled his dagger from his belt and began knocking on the wall with the hilt. He started on the interior wall, but would reach the hollow outer wall in moments. Could she claim she did not know of the hidden staircase? That was not credible. He would discover the stairs leading to Paul's chamber and accuse her again of playing the harlot.

Izard stamped on the floor. Another momentary reprieve before the wall echoed hollow under his dagger. When he climbed the secret stairs, he would see the stains behind the false panel and declare Nicolas's blood had made them. What difference would her denials make? He had said yesterday he would execute justice on the spot—his justice, where he was both judge and executioner. No one would question the death of an innkeeper, if a militia captain swore she hid a foreign Protestant and collaborated in a militiaman's murder. Her hands trembled.

Izard smiled at her. He was enjoying her discomfort. He stepped to the wall that concealed the secret staircase and raised his dagger.

A voice called his name from below.

Marguerite's head swam. One of his men had discovered the secret before him. This was the end. She leaned against the wall and fought to stay conscious.

Izard stepped to her chamber door. "What is it?"

"A messenger," the militiaman answered. "He is coming up."

A boy bobbed up the stairs and handed Izard a letter. For a moment, his face registered indecision, then he shouted, "Men, break off your search. We are summoned to a more important and more lucrative task. Down to the entrance—now!" He handed the messenger a coin and turned to Marguerite.

"Madame, it grieves me to leave you so hastily, but duty calls me to the Left Bank. If I should happen to see your Master Adams at the English Embassy, I will give him your regards. But do not fear, we shall return."

Marguerite continued to lean against the wall. Her breath came in short gulps. As the militiamen tramped down the stairs, relief flooded over her, and she began to weep. The threat had evaporated. Voices below shifted outdoors. Izard had mentioned the English Embassy and Paul Adams. Had the message summoned him to attack the English? Would they run slaughtering through the embassy as they had through her inn? Izard had promised to return. Her momentary relief turned to despair.

Screams and shouts echoed. Steel clashed on steel and a body struck the door with a thud. They were coming to kill him, Hunter knew. He jerked upright. His hand flew to his belt. He had no weapon! He looked right and left in panic, then his breathing calmed and his heartbeat slowed. He was safe in the embassy, in Sidney's bed. There was his dagger, where he had placed it. Judging by the light at the window, it was after noon. He must have slept several hours.

After a visit to the jakes, he headed for the stairs. He passed the open door of the Walsingham family parlor. Sidney knelt inside, spinning a top for the delight of the four-year old daughter, Frances. Her nursemaid sat watching.

Hunter entered. "I see you have another talent I had not discovered."

"Ah, you are finally awake," Sidney said.

"Again, I pray you," Frances gazed up at Sidney.

"You can see I am obliged to entertain this lovely lady," Sidney said.

A loud cry filtered in from the street. Frances's little head snapped up with a worried look. "Are those angry men coming back?"

"I do not think so." Her nurse crossed and knelt next to her. "You know the streets of Paris are always loud."

Frances draped her arms around Barbara's neck and buried her head in her shoulder. "But yesterday you said some people were hurting others."

"I don't think they are doing that again," Barbara said, yet her eyes showed Hunter and Sidney that she feared the killing had begun anew. "Would you feel better if Master Sidney went to Gilbert to fetch some marchpane?"

"No, no. I want him to stay here," Frances said.

"I can go to the kitchen," Hunter offered. "Master Sidney can spin your top again."

Frances smiled.

The two lads, Étienne and Ned Howell, were washing pots and pans. Gilbert, the cook, spotted Hunter. "Ah, Master Adams, I heard you came early this morning." He paused. "But I understand you are no longer Master Adams."

"My name is Edward Hunter. I used the name Adams to do some work for the ambassador."

"Ahh," Gilbert said with a knowing nod, "secret work for the ambassador. But you come to me because you are hungry, no?"

"No. I am on a mission for Mistress Frances. Have you some nuggets of marchpane?"

"I must offer her my apologies," Gilbert said. "I have only three left. It was too dangerous for the usual suppliers to come yesterday. You know what happened to Ned two days ago?"

"Yes. I heard he was beaten."

"Look at him," Gilbert turned the boy's face towards Hunter. His left eye was blackened and his lips puffy and split.

"I look terrible, I know," Ned said, "but I feel much better. At least I am alive."

"You cannot see the bruises on his arms and ribs," Gilbert said, retrieving the pieces of marzipan from a cupboard.

Shouting sounded outside. "Are things no calmer today in the city?" Hunter asked.

Gilbert shook his head. "Master Lepage came before noon. He said the killing has begun again. A dead hawthorn bloomed at the Holy Innocents, and they say it is a sign that the Lord approves of yesterday's slaughter."

"You sound as if you do not agree."

"Would God send a sign for Christians to slaughter their neighbors?" Gilbert asked.

"I cannot believe He would," Hunter said. "Yet He allowed the Hebrews to slaughter their neighbors—the Canaanite, the Midianites, the Philistines..."

"So argue some priests," Gilbert said. "We Huguenots are modern worshippers of Baal, according to them."

"I didn't realize you were reformed."

"I have not always been brave enough to confess my faith," Gilbert said, "but God is testing those of us who have been too timid." He glanced at the boys' alarmed faces. "Not that I would be fool enough to proclaim it in the street, but I have witnessed to the other Frenchmen serving the ambassador. After this madness passes—I am sure God will not allow it to continue—I will leave and go to La Rochelle. I have had enough of this city's hatred."

"Are all the other staff Roman Catholic?"

"André the butler and Jacob the coachman are also *reformé*," Gilbert said. "The rest are Catholic, but loyal to Master Walsingham." He handed Hunter the marzipan.

"I hope so," Hunter said. Was the embassy truly secure? Surely Walsingham and Beale would have made certain that the staff was loyal when they first engaged them. And Lepage was here checking that the embassy was secure. Looking after his clients, as he had said repeatedly.

Sidney sat with Frances, building a wooden block wall. Her eye sparkled when Hunter returned. "Did you get the marchpane?"

"Gilbert only had three pieces. I will entrust them to Barbara to give to you."

Frances's lips contracted into a pout, and she looked at Barbara with large, pleading eyes.

"Very well," Barbara said. "You may have only a small piece now, or it will spoil your dinner."

While the nurse broke off a piece of the sweet, Hunter knelt by Sidney. "Did you hear the news of the hawthorn blooming?"

"Yes," Sidney said. "The ambassador asked me to distract Frances from the clamor outside. Ned is her usual playmate, but he has not come since his beating. They fear his wounds will frighten her."

"You appear to be doing well," Hunter said.

"If my knees hold out," Sidney said. "Pray try to find out what is happening."

As Hunter reached the first floor, Walsingham emerged from his study with Beale and Lepage. All wore long faces.

"There are still only four guards," Beale said. "And a crowd is forming."

"Then I shall go to the Louvre myself," Lepage said. "Good day, Master Hunter—for I hear you have been new baptized—I understand you had quite an ordeal to reach the embassy."

"Indeed I did," Hunter said. "Thank you for your concern."

"A trip across Paris will be dangerous," Walsingham addressed Lepage. "And you sent a message near noon, under an hour ago. His Majesty might not have had time to respond."

"But you need more protection," Lepage argued, walking towards the top of the grand staircase. "The Palace may have become distracted by the tumult at Holy Innocents this morning, but His Majesty must recognize the need to protect diplomats."

"I wish we could offer you protection for your journey," Walsingham said, "but if those here were to accompany you, they would attract violence to your person." His head swiveled as a stone cracked against a shutter.

"You are correct," Lepage said. "I will be safer alone as a Frenchman wearing a cross and armband, than one accompanied by a squad of armed foreigners."

"But no one is safe on the streets," Beale said.

"My concern just now is for the safety of your ambassador," Lepage said. "And therefore, I must hasten to His Majesty."

As Lepage turned to descend the stairs, he caught his heel on the top step. With a shriek, he plunged headlong, stretching out both arms to break his fall. His left hand hit with a muffled crack, and he screamed in pain. He slid a few more steps and lay face down, moaning.

Walsingham, Beale, and Hunter rushed after him. Hunter knelt on his left side; Beale and Walsingham, on his right. Alain, the porter, started up the staircase, his face full of concern.

"My arm!" Lepage cried. When Hunter tried to unbutton the cuff above his oddly-twisted hand, he cried out in pain. "Do not touch it!"

"You may have broken your arm," Hunter said.

"Lift him carefully," Walsingham said. He and Beale grasped Lepage's right side, while Hunter and Alain slid their arms under his left shoulder and chest, trying not to touch the broken forearm. Others gathered to help lift him.

"Ready?" Walsingham asked. Those supporting Lepage assented. "Now."

As they lifted Lepage upright, his left arm swung down, struck Alain's back, and twisted. He screamed in agony and went limp.

Beale said. "Let us carry him to the great chamber while he is unconscious." He turned to those watching from the landing. "Jack, fetch the couch from the ambassador's study."

Hunter changed his grip to support Lepage's forearm, unbuttoned the cuff, and peeled back the sleeve to reveal a bulge, where bone threatened to pierce flesh. "It is clearly broken." The others nodded.

As missiles thumped against the embassy's façade, they carried Lepage up the broad steps and across the landing to the great chamber. At a signal from Beale, they lowered him onto the requested couch. Hunter laid his broken arm across his chest.

Walsingham addressed the crowd that had gathered. "Give him room. André, go fetch a surgeon. Let us move him against the wall beside the fireplace. Jack, can you devise a sling?"

"He cannot go to Court today," Beale said. "Master Williams, can you and Halston accommodate a third in your chamber?"

"I can move to the floor of the great chamber, if needed," Williams replied.

"Let us see what the surgeon says," Walsingham said.

Ned appeared at Beale's elbow. "Sir, Gilbert says that dinner will be ready soon."

The announcement caused the knot of curiosity around Lepage to loosen. Servants left the great chamber to help prepare. The gentlemen refugees became aware of their hunger and headed towards the dining room. Hunter left to report to Sidney.

When Jack returned with a cloth, Beale and Howell positioned it under Lepage's arm. The notary moaned. "Forgive me if I cause you pain," Beale said. "If you raise your head I can tie this behind your neck."

As Lepage did so, his eyes opened and snapped into focus. "What time is it?"

"Almost one in the afternoon," Walsingham replied.

"I must go." Lepage swung his legs off the couch and immediately howled in pain.

"Your arm is broken," Walsingham said. "Stay still. We have sent for a surgeon."

After a moment, Lepage unclenched his jaw. "Not only my arm. My foot. I can put no weight upon it."

"May it please you, lie back until André returns with a surgeon," Beale said.

"But I must go to the king." Lepage breathed heavily. His eyes bulged. "I must request help, so that you will be safe."

"You must think of yourself," Walsingham said. "You cannot leave with your injuries."

"Can you not spare me your carriage and driver?" Lepage asked, alarmed.

"Let us wait for the surgeon's opinion," Walsingham said. "A carriage ride is not a gentle experience, as you know. And today the streets offer more peril than usual."

Lepage sighed. "Very well. I will wait for now."

A crash of breaking glass. Howell left to investigate while Beale and Walsingham lowered Lepage onto the couch and adjusted a pillow under his arm.

"A rock thrown by one of the rabble," Howell reported. "The mob has grown larger."

Beale shook his head in exasperation. "Only one broken corner on the shutters, and a stone finds the gap."

"I am even more concerned that His Majesty must send more guards," Lepage said. "If I cannot go, I can write a message one of your men may carry. My right hand is still sound."

"We have already sent one request," Walsingham said, "and I doubt if anyone can cross Paris with surety."

Beale turned to his servant. "Thomas, as discreetly as you can, ascertain who here have weapons. Take stock of the arms store under the staircase and report back to me."

"But we must send a message to His Majesty," Lepage entreated. "Pray bring me pen and paper. Your man need only reach the nearest wine shop with a silver coin. Any of the men there will willingly run across all Paris."

"Most of those loiterers are throwing stones against our shutters," Walsingham said.

Lepage groaned and clenched his teeth. "Would that this surgeon would come!"

As if to answer his request, André led in a broadly-built, ruddy-faced man.

"This is not the surgeon we are wont to call," Walsingham said.

"I am sorry, sir," André said, "the surgeon was not at home. This is Raoul Guerin, a bonesetter."

"Good day, Your Excellency." The bonesetter doffed his cap and set down a large bag. After a glance at the doubting faces, he added, "It is true I cannot bleed the patient, but I know bones. You can ask anyone in the neighborhood."

"That's true," André said. "Many who gathered while I knocked at the surgeon's door said Master Guerin was better than the surgeon."

"Very well," Walsingham said. "Let him have a look at Master Lepage." The men moved aside, and Guerin approached the couch.

The bonesetter addressed Lepage. "Good day, sir. May I examine your arm?"

"Take care not to twist it," Lepage said.

"To be sure." Guerin leaned to untie the sling. "How did this injury occur?"

Lepage described his fall. The bonesetter nodded. "I must touch your arm to see if the break is clean. Can you stand the pain?"

"I will do my best," Lepage said.

Guerin felt along his forearm with a surprising gentleness for such a coarsely constructed man. Lepage first grimaced, then yelped in pain.

"You are fortunate," Guerin said. "The bones do not feel shattered, nor have they punctured the skin. And your foot was also injured?"

"Yes."

Guerin stooped and manipulated the foot, and Lepage cried out.

"It is difficult to tell, with all the small bones in the ankle," Guerin said, "but I do not think any are broken. Just strained sinews. I can bind it with a cloth for support. The swelling will go down in a few days if you do not walk on it. It may take a few weeks to heal."

Lepage groaned. "Master Bonesetter, how soon may I leave the embassy?"

Guerin's eyebrows shot up. "Leave? Sir, after I set your arm, you might be carried anywhere slowly and carefully. But on such a day as this, I would advise you to stay here."

"I shall make my own decisions about that," Lepage replied. "Just proceed with your business."

"Very well, sir," Guerin said. "As it will be impossible to remove your doublet without causing you great pain, may I cut along the seams where the sleeve meets the shoulder."

Lepage nodded.

The bonesetter guided a thin sharp blade around Lepage's shoulder. "I will first set the bones in your forearm. This may take several attempts. Then I will wrap the arm tightly, position splints, wrap it again, and finally pour melted wax between the bandage and the splits, to render the arm immobile. Most patients find this procedure painful. As you are a gentleman, you might wish that I administer some opium. It is expensive, but you will be unaware of the pain."

Lepage fixed him with an angry stare. "I do not wish to be unconscious for God knows how long. I will endure the pain. Just carry on."

"Very well, sir." Guerin carefully slid the sleeve down Lepage's arm, then turned to Walsingham. "Pray ask one of your men if he could melt some wax for me." He rummaged in his bag and extracted bandages, splints, a bowl, and large pieces of wax. "Are you ready, sir? Are you sure you do not want some opium?"

"Just get on with it," Lepage snapped.

"Very well, sir," Guerin grasped Lepage's elbow firmly in his left hand, his wrist in his right, and pulled. Lepage let out an ear-splitting scream that echoed through the embassy and fainted. Guerin looked apologetically at Walsingham. "I tried to give him opium."

In the distance, the bells of Saint-Médard's chimed one thirty.

"How can your arm break, Master Sidney?" Frances Walsingham asked.

"You know you have bones in your arm, do you not?"

"Yes," she said. "I can feel them under my skin."

"Well, if you fall very hard, they will break."

"That is why you must take care not to rush about, especially on the staircase," her nurse Barbara put in. Frances pursed her lips in thought.

Hunter smiled at Ursula Walsingham. "You have a clever daughter."

"Sometimes," Ursula said. "Frances, do you remember when we ate larks? You were able to break the lark's bones."

"Yes, mama, but they were very small."

"But any bone may break, big or small. Master Lepage must have fallen with great force, you see?"

Frances pursed her lips again and looked towards the ceiling.

"You are a pleasing sight when you ponder," Sidney said.

The sound of breaking glass caused Frances and her nurse to jump.

Hunter excused himself to see the cause. He descended to the balcony of the entrance hall, where Jean, the usher, knelt, picking up shards of glass.

"A lucky throw," Jean said. "All the windows are protected save that one hole in the shutters." The glass pieces tinkled as he dropped them in a basket.

Stones thudded against the walls. "It sounds as if the mob is growing," Hunter said.

"It is. We are lucky the king sent guards to keep them back." Jean picked up another shard. "And that there are not more stones in the street."

As Hunter headed back to the Walsingham's parlor, he met Thomas Howell coming out of the great chamber. "Master Howell, I must thank you for clothing me."

"It pleases me to be of service."

"How does Lepage?"

"He attends the surgeon impatiently," Howell replied. "Master Hunter, did you bring weapons with you?"

"Only my dagger and a wheellock pistol," Hunter said. "I left it with your master, to see if his spanner and shot were the same size."

"You have no sword?"

"No."

"My master has two."

"Does the ambassador wish all to be armed?"

Thomas Howell hesitated a moment. "I am to discover what weapons we have and to report to him. I am on my way to the arms storeroom."

"May I accompany you?" Hunter asked.

They hurried down the wide staircase. Howell obtained the key from Alain and opened the storeroom. A helmet rolled out with a clang and a cloud of dust. Several cuirasses lay on the floor of the dark, shallow closet. Four spears, several quarterstaffs, and two matchlocks leaned against the wall. Together, they cleared away the cuirasses and found two bucklers, three crossbows, a dozen bolts in a quiver, a partisan with a broken staff, and a sword with a broken tip.

"When was the last time anyone opened this?" Hunter asked.

"I think Pierre and Henry Roberts made inventory when the Ambassador first arrived."

"Over a year, then. How many men do you hope to arm with this?" Hunter's hand swept the room dismissively.

"That is what I must ascertain," Howell said.

"Those spears look made for ceremony, not for battle," Hunter said.

"Even a blunt spear is better than no weapon."

Further searching produced a pouch of bullets and match cord for the arquebuses, but no gunpowder. "Sydney has some powder." Hunter said.

"What arms do Sydney and his men have?" Howell asked.

"Three swords and one pistol altogether, as well as daggers and knives."

"I must report what I have found," Howell said.

A scream of pain came from the great chamber. Hunter hoped it had not frightened little Frances.

"Are you Captain Izard?" the thin man in the ragged doublet asked.

"Yes." Izard looked back to see if all his men had passed through the Porte Bordelle.

"Good. I am Philippe. They wait for you and your militia at *La Vieille Vigne*, close by the embassy. I was sent to bid you hurry."

Annoyance passed over Izard's face. "Very well. We will follow as rapidly as we may."

Fifteen minutes later, Philippe led Izard past the barrels that served as tables outside the wine shop, and approached a tall man with a protuberant nose who bowed slightly. "Captain Izard, call me Richard. We are pleased you have come all the way across Paris to join us. *La Hache* assured us your militia was a force he could depend upon."

"We are honored that *La Hache* asked us to take part in such a noteworthy endeavor." Izard did not to mention how much gold he had been promised. This man, whose hair reminded him of hay, might have been purchased for far less. He scanned the crowded wine shop. "I understand we are to cooperate with your men."

"That is so," Richard said. "I am glad you have arrived. Those who have been making a demonstration in front of the embassy for several hours are becoming tired. Now that you are here, we can proceed."

"And how exactly are we to proceed?" Izard asked. "*La Hache* gave me no details."

"Pentel is a close associate of *La Hache*," Richard said. "He promised to explain his plan to both of us when you arrived."

A large, rough-looking man stepped forward. His oval face, dark brown beard, and thin lips were unmemorable, but the scar on his left cheek led one's eye to his ear, the top half of which was missing. "I am called Louis Pentel. *La Hache* sent this message just after noon."

Pentel unfolded the letter and read. "There are near forty-five people now in the embassy. Four are women: Walsingham's wife and daughter, a servant, and the nurse. The Ambassador, his secretary, and their servants will all be armed. The staff of seven men and two boys should offer little resistance. Two other staff are with us, and will open the doors as planned. Many others have taken refuge there: three English students, lightly armed; two German students, one with a pistol; three Dutchmen, also armed, with two servants; Dr. Watson, old and no danger, with two servants; an Italian scholar of no account; Philip Sidney, with an armed companion and three servants; an unnamed gentleman with a pair of pistols, his servant. Then there are four of Walsingham's agents: an Italian who has some experience with arms, and three Englishmen: Halston, ill; Williams, considered dangerous; and an English spy who has been in Paris, calling himself Paul Adams."

A smile spread over Izard's face.

"You know those men?" Pentel asked

"Adams and Sidney are familiar to me."

Richard nodded. "I met both on Saint John's Eve in the Place de Grève, doing a job for *La Hache*."

"Well, in summary," Pentel said, "you and your men will face fifteen to twenty men who may be armed and can offer resistance. How many do you command?"

"Thirty-two," Izard answered.

"I shall be with you," Pentel said, "and twenty or more of Richard's best fighters can join us, by your leave, so we will outnumber them. And we will have surprise on our side."

"So long as your men will obey my orders," Izard said.

"Of course," Pentel said. "It is near half past one. Richard's companion Guillaume is directing the men shouting before the embassy. As the hour approaches, these men here, as well as others of the faubourg, will join them and create a great uproar, assaulting the king's guards and tearing at the fence. Before that, Captain Izard, you and your men will be in position by the side of the embassy, near the courtyard gate. I will lead you by side streets so that neither those in the embassy, nor those shouting in front of it, will see you.

"When the clock strikes two, a man inside the embassy will unlock the courtyard gate. All in the embassy will attend the clamor at their front door. That will allow you and your men to enter and surprise those inside. We will have Pierre with us. He used to work at the embassy." He indicated a large man, who smiled nervously at Izard. Under his breath, Pentel said, "He believes that we are somehow an army of God, who will bring on Armageddon, so do not be surprised at what he says. What is important is his knowledge of every room and closet in the embassy."

Pierre drew near and extracted sketches of the embassy from his doublet. He named each room with growing enthusiasm. Then Pentel spoke again. "On the ground floor, we should encounter only a few servants in the courtyard and the kitchen. From the kitchen, a staircase leads to a first floor serving area that will put us in the heart of the embassy. Doors off the serving room lead to both the dining room and the great chamber. Back this hallway are the offices of the ambassador and his secretary, and rooms for guests. Towards the front are the ambassador's study and the entrance hall. It is most likely we will find the ambassador and his spies on this floor. However,"—he shifted to the third sheet—"they might seek shelter on the top floor. Here, as Pierre said, are the private rooms for the ambassador and his family, his secretary and clerk, and a few guests. I suspect by the time we reach this level, we will find only the weakest cowering in closets.

"La Hache has confidence that you and your men can locate and kill the ambassador and his secretary, and those who have taken refuge. He wants to be sure they do not escape in the confusion. That is why the militia will enter first. After you have killed our principal targets,

Pierre will tell the porter to open the front door, and Guillaume and his men will rush in. They are to slay any the militia may have left alive. When all are dead, they, as well as your militiamen, may plunder whatever they wish. Do you have any doubt that your men can complete their job?"

Confronted with this challenge, Izard could only reply, "No. My men are well trained."

"Saint-Médard's just rang the half hour," Richard interjected. "Captain Izard and his men should move to their position."

"Let us be quick." Izard clutched Pierre's sketch. "I must show this to some of my men and organize them before the clock strikes two."

Shortly after the dinner dishes had been cleared, everyone in the embassy heard the sound. Some afterward described it as the crashing of a huge wave on a sea cliff; others compared it to the roar of a savage beast, accompanied by a fusillade of missiles striking the façade.

In the great chamber, Beale, Walsingham, and the medical student Bright were watching the bonesetter Guerin pour wax between the splints and Lepage's bandaged arm. He jumped at the noise, spilling wax on the floor. Beale and Walsingham leapt to the double doors and ran across the landing to peer through the shutters.

In the dining room, Dr. Watson, discussing Seneca with Edward Cope and Baron Wharton as though they were in a college dining hall, spilled his glass of port. Cope and the Dutchmen sprang up. They reached the gallery at the same time as Manucci, Halston, and Williams, coming from the great chamber.

Beale turned from the window. "There are hundreds of them. They are tearing down the fence. The king's guards are surrounded. Everyone, arm yourself!" His located Howell below. "Thomas, Jean—pass out arms to those who lack them!"

On the second floor, Philip Sidney's story of Reynard the Fox was distracting Frances's attention from the cries of pain and banging of stones. When the mob's cry echoed through the parlor, Frances clutched her mother. Hunter jumped up, blurted a word of excuse, and sprang into the corridor by the stairwell. A stream of men ran up the stairs.

What has happened?" he asked Cope's servant.

"We are under attack," the man said. "I must fetch my master's pistols. Each man must arm himself." As he spoke, others pushed past them.

Hunter opened the parlor door carefully and caught Sidney's eye.

"And that is how Reynard outwitted Ysengrin the Wolf," Sidney concluded. "I am sure either your mother or your nurse knows another Reynard story, but I must go with Master Hunter just now."

"What was that noise?" Frances asked.

"The crowd in the street is very excited about something," Hunter said. "I am not sure what, but it is best you stay with your mother. We will make sure you are safe." His tone explained the threat to Madam Walsingham and her servants.

"Fetch your weapons," Hunter said. "All are preparing to defend the embassy. I must find Beale." He dashed to the first floor and almost collided with the secretary, who pressed his pistol and a flask of priming powder into his hand.

"Here. My spanner fits your pistol. It is loaded and wound, but not primed."

Hunter took the pistol. "Thank you. Thomas said you had two swords. Might I beg one?"

Beale struck his forehead. "How foolish of me to forget. The other is behind my desk." Another roar sounded "I must go to the entrance hall."

Hunter pocketed the flask and raced to Beale's office. He drew the baldric over his right shoulder, pulled the sword from its scabbard, and weighed it in his hand. Its balance was very like his own. He resheathed the blade and headed back to the entrance hall.

Dr. Watson was puffing his way to the second floor, followed by Baron Wharton and his servant, carrying two sheathed swords. "Ambassador ordered us to protect the women," he wheezed.

"Good," Hunter responded. Walsingham's request was for the dean's own safety, and Wharton was in no mental condition to take part in fighting. The gallery was lined with men. Next to him, Walter Williams rammed a ball down the muzzle of an arquebus. Further along, others with wheellock pistols were winding, loading, or priming. Faunt passed Hunter, blowing on two match cords. He handed one to Williams, who nodded towards a matchlock leaning against the ambassador's study door.

On the ground floor, Howell and Jean distributed the last of the storeroom weapons. Bizari received a quarterstaff, much to his displeasure. Henry Roberts waved a crossbow with a broken string. Howell shook his head and offered him a truncheon.

Another roar arose outside.

At the far side of the gallery, Walsingham and Beale stood, heads together. As the howl outside faded, Beale shouted, "Are all loaded and primed?" Choruses of "yes" and a few "noes." "Load your weapons and take your positions!" Beale bellowed.

Hunter poured the priming powder into the pan of his pistol. He closed the cover and blew away the excess powder. Where was the gunpowder and shot he would need to reload? What was his 'position?'

Williams and Faunt shuffled along the gallery, headed for the front windows. On the landing opposite, Cope and Halston were doing the same. Evidently a plan had been devised to fire at the mob and drive them off, orders he had missed as he searched for the sword.

"What positions are we to take?" he asked Sidney.

"Follow Reinhardt." Sidney gestured to the German student who followed Manucci.

As he moved into position, Hunter saw a dozen men below, bearing a variety of weapons, arrange themselves into a line facing the entrance. Madox and Bright shouldered crossbows; Gilbert stood with a butcher knife and a cleaver; the line bristled with swords, spears, and quarterstaves. Alain, Henry Roberts, and two Dutch servants pushed a heavy chest against the front door.

Before him, Ned Howell stood near the first-floor window, holding a rod that would swing open the exterior wooden shutter. Walter Williams waited closest to the window, his matchlock arquebus across his chest. Behind him stood Manucci and Reinhardt.

"Are all ready?" Beale shouted from the far window.

"Yes," the men cried.

Williams blew on his match cord.

"Open the shutters!" Beale shouted.

Ned and those at the other three windows swung open one of the pair of shutters. Williams raised his arquebus and fired. At other windows, Faunt's matchlock thundered, and Beale and Walsingham fired their pistols. Smoke rolled back into the entrance hall. Screams and shouts of anger rose from the mob. Those who had discharged their weapons stepped to the rear, and the next in each file moved forward. Ned handed Williams a powder flask and a pouch of balls to reload. After he fired, Hunter would need to find Beale for powder, shot and spanner. Manucci and the others in the second rank fired, and Reinhardt's rank stepped to the window. Hunter thumbed the dog on his pistol from safe to operating position. The German fired and spun away from the window. Hunter stepped forward through the smoke.

Below, the crowd cried and howled, some running, a few resentfully backing away from the embassy. Faces of fear and anger stared up at him. Near the embassy, one of the king's guards lay on the ground. Two men knelt over a boy whose face was full of blood. Where should he aim? He did not want to kill a child. Should he intentionally aim to miss? As he hesitated, knots of men halted, ready to make another assault. He must make his shot count. A stone whizzed past his face and cracked against the closed shutter to his left. He brought his pistol to bear on a cluster of men near the fence, beyond the collapsed guard. There were so many he would surely hit one.

Shouting behind him. A high-pitched voice. Then an answering chorus of alarm. Williams placed a hand on his shoulder. "Hold. Do not waste your shot."

Hunter turned, confused. "The courtyard," Williams pointed, and turned to run away from the entrance hall.

Nicolas Faunt, matchlock in hand, barged between Hunter and Reinhardt, who was fumbling to reload his pistol. Sidney followed. "They have broken into the courtyard!" he shouted.

Hunter followed him to the back stairwell. After descending three steps towards the kitchen, they halted. The invaders had forced the door from the courtyard. Izard's militiamen! Why were they here? They clashed in the kitchen with defenders who had rushed in from the entrance hall. Gilbert wielded his cleaver and butcher knife. The coachman Jacob, wielding only a truncheon, clubbed away swords. Bizari whirled his quarterstaff. Jean and Jonas jabbed spears at the attackers. As Hunter raised his pistol to find a target, Madox and Bright ran up the stairs towards them, spun, and fired their crossbows. One militiaman fell and another screamed, a bolt protruding from his shoulder. Gilbert and Jacob fell, as more attackers pressed forward.

"Reload behind us," Williams roared at the crossbowmen, unable to get a clear shot at the invaders. As Madox and Bright shouldered past, Hunter spotted Captain Izard himself, sword in one hand and pistol in another, inclining his head to listen to—yes, that was Pierre, the old embassy porter. What was he doing there? Pierre pointed up the stairwell. Izard followed his gesture and his eyes met Hunter's. He smiled, then shouted orders to the attackers, who surged towards the stairs. Beside him, Faunt, Williams, and Sydney fired. Three attackers fell back upon the others. Through the smoke, Hunter aimed at Izard and pulled the trigger.

Sydney shouted, "Up!" He retreated to behind where Cope, Reinhardt, and Manucci stood, pistols now reloaded.

"I need powder and ball," Hunter shouted.

Sidney poured powder down his pistol. "I have powder. My shot may fit."

Cries from the kitchen. Howell and others advanced to engage the attackers.

Through swirling smoke, Hunter saw Izard, unscathed, aim towards the staircase. He had missed! To Izard's left, a man with half an ear raised a pistol. Half-ear!

"Look out!" Hunter shouted.

The defenders jerked away from the top of the stairwell as shots flew past. Cope, Manucci, and Reinhardt swiveled back, descended a few steps, and fired their pistols.

Hunter took Sidney's flask and poured a charge down his pistol's muzzle. To his right, Walsingham, Halston, Beale, and the Dutchman ten Haken emerged from the great chamber, each carrying a pistol.

"What is happening?" the ambassador asked.

"They are taking the kitchen." Williams primed his arquebus. "We defend the stairwell."

The ball Sidney offered was too large. "May I use your shot and spanner?" he asked Beale. Beale handed across his pouch.

As Hunter reloaded, a bellow announced another assault on the stairwell. The defenders delivered a fusillade from the top of the steps.

Hunter rammed home a ball and cranked the wheel. From below came moans and cries of pain. He passed the pouch back to Beale, pulled the priming powder from his pocket, and poured. His pistol loaded, he looked for a target. Izard and Half-ear had vanished. At least seven attackers lay at the foot of the stairs; only two were moving. Others rushed past their fallen companions. Firing sounded from the corridor to the entrance hall, where defenders were retreating.

The men around the stairwell began to stumble towards the gallery of the entrance hall, pausing every few steps to load and tamp powder and ball, to wind wheels, and to prime their weapons.

"We should not all go," Walsingham said. "Williams, Faunt, Cope—stay and guard these stairs. They cannot be allowed to reach the top floor. Ned, you stay too."

Hunter gained the gallery of the entrance hall before those reloading. Below, defenders were fleeing towards the grand staircase. Their pursuers flooded the entrance hall, Izard, Pierre, and Half-ear in their midst. Near Izard was another familiar figure, a tall man with a bulbous nose, whom Hunter recognized from Saint John's Eve. Richard? Guillaume?

The defenders gathered at the bottom of the grand staircase. Jean, Jonas, André, and Harry White extended their spears to keep the invaders at a distance, but ensign Martin waded through his colleagues, bearing a halberd. Here, he had space enough to wield the weapon. He swung it against the spears. White's spear shattered. The rest flew from the defenders' hands and rattled across the floor. The militiamen with swords pressed forward.

Behind them, Alain and others were pushing the chest away from the door. Why was Alain aiding the invaders? Outside, the crowd roared again. If that mob broke into the embassy, their fate was sealed. Why hadn't the rabble followed the militiamen through the courtyard entrance? Had stablemen closed the gate, or had all in the courtyard been slain?

Those who had finished loading their firearms, as well as the two crossbowmen, joined Hunter in the gallery. Walsingham and Beale stood to his left; Sidney to his right.

"Do not aim at the foremost," Walsingham shouted. They all understood; too great a chance of hitting their own.

At the sound of the ambassador's voice, Pierre grabbed Izard's sleeve and pointed at Walsingham. Hunter aimed at Izard again and fired. A thin militiaman behind him cried out and dropped. Izard coolly raised his pistol, cried, "Shoot the man in black," and fired at Walsingham. The shot hissed past and struck the wall. Half-ear and two others aimed at the gallery.

Hunter and Beale seized Walsingham by either shoulder. "Please you, sir, get back," Hunter said. Should he be handling an ambassador like this? Walsingham submitted to their pressure.

Defenders in the gallery and invaders on the floor fired simultaneously. Reinhardt shouted in pain, dropped his pistol, and staggered back. Bullets from his pouch rolled across the gallery and rained onto the ground floor. Smoke filled the entrance hall.

"Help him to the great chamber," Beale shouted. "And reload." He handed Hunter his pouch and powder flask. "Meet me on the landing." He sped towards the top of the grand staircase.

Hunter and Walsingham, supporting Reinhardt on either side, headed back down the corridor. Sidney followed.

Williams, still guarding the back stairwell, asked, "What is happening?"

"They are storming the grand staircase," Walsingham said. "But stay here for now."

In the great chamber, they sat Reinhardt in an oaken chair. Blood dripped from his right arm. "I will be all right," he said.

Walsingham looked to where Bryskett and Jack stood, near Lepage and Guerin. "Bonesetter," he shouted, "come here and staunch this bleeding."

Jack, carrying the broken partisan, escorted the terrified bonesetter to his patient while Hunter and Sidney crossed to Bryskett and Lepage. Bryskett, face filled with frustration, addressed Sidney. "Sir, the ambassador told me to stay with Master Lepage, but I can help defend him better outside."

"Mine is not to overrule the ambassador," Sidney said.

"You may go for all I care," Lepage said. "I will not have to hear your complaints then. Give me a pistol and I can defend myself."

Hunter grasped the warm barrel of his pistol and reloaded.

"Bryskett longs to join the fight," Sidney said to Walsingham when he joined them.

"Anything which may offer us the shadow of a chance of surviving," Walsingham said.

"I appeal to you again, Ambassador," Lepage pleaded. "Let me speak to these invaders. I know I can convince them to stop."

Walsingham's expression showed he thought Lepage was out of his mind.

"I assure you I am not mad," Lepage said, anguish in his voice.

"I can equally assure you that no one in that rabid mob would be able to hear you," Walsingham said. "As you sought to protect us, I must now protect you."

The door to the landing opened and Jonas staggered in, supporting Scholten. The Dutch merchant's face was full of blood.

"Bonesetter," Walsingham called out, "another patient." He turned to Sidney and Hunter. "It is time we joined Beale on the landing."

Sidney remonstrated, "Sir, you should not endanger yourself."

"I must do what I can," Walsingham said, "not cower in a corner." He opened one of the double doors and they stepped onto the landing.

Beale had lined up the crossbowmen, arquebusiers, and those with pistols a few steps from the top of the stairs. He signaled Walsingham, Sidney, Hunter, and Bryskett to join the line. The defenders on the staircase had retreated more than three-quarters of the way to the top. Only six of them bore swords, including Howell's broken blade. White held the stump of his spear. A militiaman slashed the leg of a Dutch servant, and André caught him as he fell.

Ten Haken broke from the line, shouting "Jan!"

"Hold your position. We will tend him," Beale said.

Although invaders lay in the entrance hall, at least thirty advanced up the stairs, against nine defenders. With a loud crash, the entrance door swayed in. Alain stood to one side of it, key in hand. Martin looked to Izard for an order, held up his hand to restrain Alain, and stepped towards he staircase. Once Alain turned that key, they could not hold out for long.

"On my command, you on the stairs," Beale shouted. "Down!" The defenders dove backwards towards the line on the landing. The gunmen and crossbowmen stepped forward and fired into the attackers. Several fell as smoke obscured the scene.

"To the great chamber!" Beale shouted.

The defenders walked or limped towards the chamber. How many had fallen to their volley? Even if every shot struck true, some twenty or more might remain. That would mean almost even odds. But once Alain released the mob...

"Quickly," Beale hissed in Hunter's ear, "inside. We must reload." As Hunter reached the door, four figures materialized from the smoke. He turned and squeezed past Jean, who slammed the door and called for trestles to block it.

"No," Walsingham said. "If they are stopped, they will turn to the back stairwell." The path to his wife and child. "Hold the door until we can reload. André, Jack, those with swords, flatten yourselves against the wall and stab them as they enter."

Hunter pulled his pistol's dog to safe and poured powder into the muzzle. It was even hotter than before. How long before one of the wheel-locks exploded in its owner's hands?

Walsingham continued. "Those with firearms, form a line between the door and the wounded."

On his couch, Lepage called for a pistol. At his feet sat Reinhardt and the Dutch merchant Scholten, his head bandaged. Guerin was dressing Jan's leg wound.

"Roberts," Walsingham said, "ask Williams if the back stairwell is secure."

As Hunter placed a ball and patch on his pistol barrel, the doors to the great chamber bowed in and parted. Jean, Jonas, Howell, and Bizari leaned their backs against the doors, and pushed them closed again. Hunter rammed his charge home. Another surge hit the doors. They inched inexorably wider as the attackers increased the pressure.

"Hold on!" Sidney yelled, pouring priming powder.

"I still load," Halston said.

"And I," Bryskett added.

"My last bolt." Madox raised his crossbow.

"Get back, sir!" Beale shouted to Walsingham.

Manucci took aim. "You on the door. Leap aside!" he shouted.

The men holding back the doors dove to either side.

The pressure released, several invaders tumbled through onto the floor. Jack plunged the partisan's blade into the militiaman's back nearest him. André skewered another with his sword.

Izard, wheellock in hand, tripped over fallen men as he rushed in, and his pistol discharged into the ceiling. His stumble saved him; Manucci's shot whizzed into the space his head had occupied a second before. Martin strode behind Izard with his halberd. Several swordsmen followed. A crossbow bolt sailed over their heads. Beale's shot struck one.

Sidney rushed his shot, pulling the trigger before moving the dog to the firing position. The wheel spun, harmlessly. Hunter dropped his unprimed pistol, kicked it behind him, and drew his sword. Others who had not finished reloading did the same. The defenders formed a line across the great chamber. Martin's halberd buzzed near their faces. They retreated from the swinging blade. Swordsmen advanced on either side of Martin, his halberd guaranteeing the defenders could not reach them. Behind the attacking line, Izard reloaded his pistol. Beside him, Half-ear spoke and pointed to where Lepage watched them with terrified eyes. Izard shouted, "Traitor!"

Manucci called something to Bryskett in Italian. Both retreated from the line, dropped their swords, and grasped the tall candelabras on either side of the fireplace. "Make way," Manucci cried. He and Bryskett ran forward, holding them as spears, candles dropping as they charged. Martin's swinging halberd blade rang as it clashed into the many arms of Bryskett's candelabra. Manucci stabbed from the opposite side, trapping the halberd. Together, they jerked the candelabras towards them, pulling the halberd from Martin's grasp. The tail of the trapped halberd swirled left and right as the Italians wrestled to untangle their locked candelabras. "'Sblood," Manucci shouted in frustration. He and Bryskett looked at one another, dropped the tangled metalwork, and reached for their swords. Ensign Martin drew his sword and rushed towards the two who had disarmed him. The line of intruders surged forward with him.

A dark-bearded man in a stained doublet advanced towards Hunter, but from the corner of his eye, he saw Izard step behind Martin and level his pistol at Walsingham. Hunter leapt to his right and swept his sword up under Izard's pistol. The shot soared to the ceiling and the wheellock sailed from his hand. Hunter's plunge exposed his left side to the dark-bearded man, who drew back his arm to thrust. A hand struck Hunter's back hard. He stumbled forward and fell, dropping his sword. As he landed on both hands, swords clanged above him. Manucci had parried his attacker's blade, and held it while he stepped over Hunter's legs.

Over the noise of fighting, a voice dripping with loathing said, "You!" Hunter looked up into the snarling face of Captain Izard. Izard drew his sword. Hunter recovered his own and scrambled to his feet.

"I had hoped to do this yesterday morning." Izard slashed at him.

Hunter parried the blow. "It may prove harder than stabbing sleeping men."

"You are awake, but you are still outnumbered." Izard wove back and forth. "By the way, Madame Moreau sends her regards."

Hunter clenched his teeth. "You still threaten her?"

Izard laughed. "When I have finished with you, I will give her what she deserves."

Hunter lunged at the captain, felt his blade twist aside, and winced as the Izard's blade sliced the edge of his left ear. He recovered in time to block Izard's next blow. He could not afford to strike out in anger. Blood trickled down the side of his head. Perhaps he would end up like Half-ear.

To Hunter's right, Bryskett, Howell, Halston, Sidney, and Madox formed a line protecting Walsingham and the wounded. Behind them stood White with his broken spear and Jack with his partisan. Beale and Bright primed the discarded pistols.

Izard lunged again. Hunter parried and counterattacked. Izard blocked his blade, and both paused, eying one another. Militiamen were slipping left behind Izard. Manucci, Jean, and two Dutch merchants were engaged there. The shifting militiamen would soon outflank them. "They are coming on the left!" Hunter shouted.

The door from the back stairwell burst open. Cope, Roberts, Faunt, and Williams fired their weapons. Two militiamen fell, and their comrades stumbled over them in retreat. Cope and Roberts handed their pistols to a servant, drew swords, and joined the defensive line. The attackers dropped back. Perhaps the tables were turning.

The fusillade had distracted Hunter and Izard for a moment. Izard recovered first and lunged. Hunter barely reacted in time to push his blade aside. They slammed together, guard pressed against guard, body pushing against body.

"As close as you lie to Marguerite each night, Adams," Izard snarled. He jerked his knee up. Hunter twisted aside and shoved Izard away.

To his right, Bryskett slipped on one of the candles. Martin lunged as he fell, but missed. He strode forward to stab the fallen Bryskett, but Thomas Howell stepped in to block him. Howell now faced two opponents with his broken sword. A short militiaman stabbed at his right side. When Howell defended, Martin thrust his sword into Howell's left chest. Howell cried out and fell. Bryskett leapt up, slashing at both attackers.

Shouting crescendoed in the entrance hall. Glints of triumph sparkled in the eyes of the attackers; fear clouded those of the defenders. No matter what happened now in the great chamber, when the hordes poured in, all would be lost.

Rage overpowered Hunter. He gritted his teeth. Blood pumped loud in his ears. After all he had endured, now he would become another corpse dragged into the streets, stripped, and thrown into the Seine. Heavy footsteps sounded on the grand staircase. Izard smiled and glanced towards the front hall. The bastard had lowered his guard! Hunter thrust forward, driving his sword into Izard's chest. The captain's eyes swiveled back, amazed. His knees buckled.

Hunter's anger turned to icy satisfaction. Izard would not live to see the embassy fall. He would neither ravish Marguerite nor take her inn. Whatever fate might befall him in the next minutes, he could take comfort in that. He might be a sinner about to face the Divine Judge, but he would not repent killing Izard.

The report of a pistol deafened him. Beale had fired over Bryskett's shoulder, and Ensign Martin fell, his face a mass of blood. Those on either side of him held swords at the ready. Hunter was not the only man who would die fighting. He turned to face an attack, but the invaders had stepped back. Why should they risk death when at any moment the rabble would arrive to aid them?

Hunter glanced back at Walsingham. He stood stoically behind the line of swordsmen, in front of the wounded. Behind him, Lepage raised his pistol and aimed at Walsingham's back. For a moment, Hunter doubted what he saw, then shouted, "Ambassador! Get down!"

Both Walsingham and Lepage stared directly at Hunter. Lepage clenched his teeth in anger; Walsingham opened his mouth in surprise. "Behind you!" Hunter cried, leaping towards the ambassador. Walsingham had half turned around when Hunter collided with him. He scrambled to cover Walsingham's body with his own, expecting a bullet to pierce his back at any moment. The shot did not come. What had happened? Above him, Lepage stared across the room, frozen.

Hunter followed his gaze. Inside the great chamber's double doors stood, not the rabble of the streets, but armed men, wearing breastplates and carrying polearms and swords. A loud voice called out in French, "Put down your weapons. The king commands you stop. This embassy is under his protection."

What was happening? Who had spoken? The report of a pistol rang out above Hunter. He tightened his body in expectation, but felt nothing. Across the room, Half-ear staggered back with a shocked face. Pierre, gazing at Lepage in astonishment, caught Half-ear as he fell.

"Drop your weapons," the voice repeated. Through the double door, limping slightly, came the Duke of Nevers. The attackers and defenders regarded one another, reluctant to be the first to obey.

Walsingham stirred beneath Hunter. Had he offended? Hunter said, "I'm sorry."

"You saved my life," Walsingham said. "Lepage was aiming at me."

Another shot rang from Lepage's couch. He had a second pistol. Walsingham and Hunter instinctively flattened themselves. The bullet whistled past Pierre's head. His expression changed from disbelief to determination.

The Duke of Nevers repeated his injunction. "Put down your weapons now, in the king's name, or my men will compel you." Slowly, those in the facing lines lowered their weapons. Nevers's men advanced between them.

Hunter and Walsingham helped one another to their feet and turned to face Lepage. He still gripped a pistol, his face a picture of frustration. "Trying to defend you," he said between gritted teeth.

"You were not," Walsingham began.

Hunter heard a commotion behind him. Pierre dashed past Nevers and dodged between defenders. He pushed Walsingham and Hunter out of his way, pulled a knife, and pounced on Lepage. Lepage struck Pierre's head with his pistol butt at the same time Pierre plunged the knife into his belly. Together, they rolled off the couch. Lepage's scream swelled through the great chamber. Hunter reached down and pulled Pierre off. He rolled onto the floor beside Lepage and lay there limp.

CHAPTER 20

Revelations

"For the last time," Nevers's voice rang, "put down your weapons."

Swords and knives clanked on the floor.

"Where is the ambassador?" Nevers asked.

"I am here." Walsingham turned from Lepage and Pierre. "I am safe, Your Grace."

"Thank God." Nevers walked towards him.

"I thank you for our lives." Walsingham tensed and turned to Roberts. "Pray see that my wife and her women are unharmed. Find if any of the staff has been killed or wounded." Roberts headed for the stairwell.

Hunter knelt beside Lepage. Blood was spreading over his doublet, but he still breathed. Lepage must live and explain himself.

Kneeling next to Pierre, Madox said, "He is alive, sirs."

Walsingham called, "Bonesetter, there are wounded over here."

"Are all these members of your staff?" Nevers's arm swept the great chamber.

"No," Walsingham said. "Many Englishmen sought refuge here on Saint Bartholomew's Day, as well as German students and Dutch merchants."

As Walsingham identified individuals to the Duke of Nevers, Hunter surveyed the room. Nevers's men were pushing the militiamen towards the door. Several attackers lay on the floor, some dead, some unconscious, some moaning in pain. Nearby, Beale held Thomas Howell's face between his hands and wept. This generous soul, who had clothed him, lay dead.

"This man was porter here until June," Walsingham concluded, nodding to Pierre. "Lepage insisted we dismiss him. He may have sought revenge."

"Ambassador, he must have come seeking revenge on you," Sidney said. "He could not have known Lepage was here."

"We shall disentangle this web later," Walsingham said.

"We dispersed the mob outside just as your porter opened the door," Nevers said. "I believe he meant to admit them."

"Your Grace, might your men bring up our porter. He should have a chance to speak for himself."

Bryskett tapped Hunter on the shoulder. "Your head is bleeding"

Hunter put his hand to his ear. "I know. It is not serious."

A cry rose from across the great chamber. "A priest! I need a priest." Half-Ear, slumped against the wall where he had fallen, coughed after the exertion of shouting.

One of Nevers's men asked, "May I fetch a priest from Saint-Médard's?" Nevers nodded.

Hunter took a step towards Half-ear, then turned to Nevers and Walsingham. "I have sought this man for months. He may know who murdered Pickering. May I question him?"

Walsingham exchanged glances with Nevers; both nodded.

Hunter knelt beside Half-ear. His breath was labored, and blood oozed from a wound in his chest. "What is your name?"

"Louis Pentel."

"Did you go about the inns of Saint-Marcel this spring, asking after an Englishman?"

Louis nodded.

"Who employed you to do that?"

"*La Hache.*" His eyes swiveled towards where Guerin knelt by Lepage. "The bastard that shot me."

Hunter's mind spun. Half-ear had not been working for some courtier, but for Lepage. Pentel coughed and sprayed blood in his face.

Hunter wiped it with his sleeve. "Why did he hunt Pickering?"

Pentel looked puzzled.

"The Englishman," Hunter explained.

"Heard him plotting," Pentel said.

"Pickering heard Lepage plotting?"

Pentel nodded.

"Do you know who killed Pickering?"

Pentel looked at him with sad eyes. "Where is the priest?"

"Do you need to confess Pickering's murder to him?"

Again Pentel coughed up blood, then nodded.

"Has the priest come yet?" Hunter asked those crowded around him.

"No," was the chorused reply.

"Two men attacked Pickering," Hunter said. "Who was the second?"

"Guillaume."

"Does he have a last name?"

"Don't know. Outside."

"One of those attacking the embassy?"

Pentel nodded.

"On the night Pickering was killed, who led him to you?"

Pentel inclined his head towards Lepage.

"Justin Lepage hired you to kill him and led him to you?"

Another nod. A cough. Blood flowed down his chin.

"Why did you attack the embassy today?"

Another slight inclination of his head towards Lepage.

"He called you?"

Pentel's nods were becoming weaker.

"Why, if he summoned you, did he shoot you?"

Pentel coughed and choked. His eyes rolled back in his head.

"The father is here," a voice said.

Hunter stood, hoping Patel would hold on long enough to cough out a confession. He had been taught that it was superstition to believe that priests could absolve sins, but what Patel believed could provide him an easier death, even if he would soon face divine justice. The same justice Hunter had escaped by a miracle. He murmured a prayer begging forgiveness and strode across the room to where Nevers and Walsingham bent over Lepage.

Henry Roberts was reporting, "...are all safe. Dean Watson and Lord Wharton will be down soon. Gilbert is dead, cut down in his kitchen. Philip took a bad crack on his head, and Sidney's man Fisher has a deep cut on his arm. Jacob has a shoulder wound. The rest of the staff is here with you."

"Thank you," Walsingham said. "Take Master Guerin to see to the wounded." He turned to Hunter. "What have you learned?"

"Pentel is confessing to the murder of George Pickering," Hunter said. "He named Justin Lepage as the man who employed him to find and kill Pickering."

"Why?"

"He said that Pickering overheard Lepage plotting, and Lepage summoned him to attack the embassy today."

Walsingham glanced at Lepage. "I have been blind. Pickering knew Lepage wanted to silence him, but I dismissed his call for help as another plea for money." He paused again. "Lepage has been plotting for months. Alain was his recommendation for porter. He was about to aid the mob. Christophe, who he said would add security, must have opened the courtyard gate." He turned to Roberts. "Did you see Christophe?"

"No, sir," Roberts replied. "Philip said he fled when the duke arrived."

Hunter asked Guerin. "Is Lepage still alive?"

"Breathing, but unconscious."

"Your Excellency," Nevers interjected. "I do not understand. Master Hunter, whom I met by another name, says that Lepage is behind this attack. Why would a man invite an attack on the place where he was?"

"He did not intend to be here," Walsingham said. "He was to leave over an hour ago, but he fell on the stairs and broke his arm. His agitation when we kept him increased with every minute. He knew this attack was coming."

"That is why Pentel was shocked when he saw Lepage here," Hunter said.

"But Lepage shot him," Nevers said. "If he was a confederate, why shoot him?"

"I believe I can explain," Hunter said. "The moment before Your Grace entered, Lepage aimed his pistol at Ambassador Walsingham. He believed the mob was about to enter. Killing the ambassador would fulfill his plan and demonstrate he was with the invaders. When Your Grace arrived, he realized the changed situation and decided to silence his confederate."

"If Lepage had Pickering killed because he knew too much," Walsingham said. "He shot Pentel for the same reason."

Those around Pentel crossed themselves as the priest intoned the last rites.

Nevers's men marched in, holding Alain. The porter would not meet Walsingham's eyes.

"Alain, others have reported you opening the door to those who attacked the embassy," Walsingham said. "What have you to say for yourself?"

Alain fell to his knees. "I...I beg your mercy, sir."

"Do you admit to opening the door?"

"Yes," he whispered.

"Why?"

"I was promised a large reward."

"By whom?"

Alain glanced to where Lepage lay. "By him."

"But you were obliged to serve the ambassador," Nevers said heatedly. "To forsake your duty for money is base. Disloyalty deserves the severest punishment." He turned to Walsingham. "Your Excellency will be obliged to remain in the embassy until the disorders in Paris cease. With your permission, I will take charge of this porter."

Walsingham looked long and hard at Alain, then agreed.

Ursula Walsingham entered, with Dean Watson trailing behind. She beheld the great chamber and gasped, then rushed to embrace her husband. "They said you were safe, but I had to see for myself." Tears ran down her face.

"Are you and Frances safe?"

"Yes, though she is frightened."

"Anne? Barbara?"

"Yes, yes."

Walsingham noticed Dean Watson and broke his embrace. "Doctor, I thank you for staying with my wife and daughter."

"It was my honor," Watson replied.

Walsingham turned back. "Dear, I would not have you stay here among the dead and wounded..." he began.

But she stepped past him and touched the kneeling Beale on the shoulder. "Not Thomas."

Beale stood. "He is dead."

As he uttered the words, Jack led Ned Howell into the great chamber, his bruised face wet with tears. He walked to his father's body, and stood sobbing.

Even after twenty-four hours filled with death, Hunter could not stop his own tears.

Ursula held the boy in an embrace. After several minutes, Beale asked, "May he come upstairs with you?"

Walsingham placed a hand on Ned's shoulder. "Frances is frightened. You were always able to make her happy. Will you return with my wife and comfort her?" Ned sniffed and nodded. Dean Watson escorted them both upstairs.

Halston, kneeling next to Pierre, said, "This man is coming around." Walsingham, Hunter, and Sidney drew near. "He has no wounds, only a massive lump on his head."

Pierre opened his eyes, raised himself on his elbows, and looked about in confusion. "Where is God's army?"

"What do you mean, Pierre?" Walsingham asked.

Pierre's eyes fixed on Walsingham and his mouth gaped in astonishment. He groped the floor on either side of him. "My knife! Walsingham must die!"

Halston, Sidney, and Hunter threw themselves on Pierre. He thrashed about, calling, "Where have the servants of God gone?" but they hung on.

Nevers called men-at-arms to help. It took the combined efforts of eight men to subdue Pierre. As they wrestled him to the heavy oak chair near the stairwell door, he called out "Does Satan still hold sway?" After they bound him to the chair with stout ropes, he asked, "Must we wait eighteen months?" He fixed his eyes on the Duke of Nevers. "Sir, I see you are a nobleman of great rank and authority. Why do you help the servants of Satan?"

Nevers spoke to Walsingham *sotto voce*. "Is this the man you said was your porter?"

"Until this June," Walsingham replied. "We always thought him a loyal servant until we learned he was a member of a confraternity with the mad groom who tried to kill me. At Lepage's urging, I dismissed him."

Nevers nodded. "He appears to trust me. With your permission, I will try to extract his story."

Walsingham assented.

Nevers began. "I was not aware I was aiding the Prince of Darkness. Perhaps if you explain, I will understand. How came you to attack the embassy?"

"Master Lepage told me the time had come."

"The man you assaulted?" Nevers asked.

Pierre looked over to where Lepage lay. Without emotion, he asked, "Is he dead?"

"No, Pierre," Beale said. "Master Guerin staunched the bleeding."

"Oh." Pierre's syllable expressed neither disappointment nor remorse.

"Why did you try to kill him?" Nevers asked.

"He must be a false prophet," Pierre said. "The captain called him a traitor and he shot at the servants of God."

Those gathered around exchanged looks of confusion.

"Perhaps you could start at the beginning," Nevers said, "and I will better understand." He signaled his men to bring seats. Nevers settled on a stool in front of Pierre; the other auditors sat on benches on either side.

"When did you first become porter at the embassy?" Nevers asked.

"Over three years ago, when Ambassador Norris was here."

"Did Notary Lepage recommend you?"

"Yes."

"How did he know you?"

"Master Poillard, an advocate, knew me through the Confraternity of the Holy Name of Jesus."

"Ah, yes." By raising an eyebrow, Nevers asked Walsingham if this was the confraternity he had just mentioned. Walsingham nodded. "Did Lepage tell you to report embassy affairs to him?"

Pierre registered surprise. "Oh, no!"

"Well," Nevers asked, "what did he want you to do at the embassy?"

"Just serve well as a porter." He recited his duties. "Question anyone who wanted to enter. Treat those who were welcome with respect. Perform any duties I was assigned to the best of my ability."

"And that you did admirably for as long as you served us," Beale put in. "How does that connect to 'God's army' and the 'Servants of Satan?'"

"You do not see," Pierre said smugly. "Neither did I at first. But one day Master Lepage spoke to me about the words of John in his Apocalypse. He knew I had studied the prophecies and saw that The End was coming soon. He said I had an important role to play."

As he spoke, Pierre grew more animated. "I was a porter—one who opens doors—and that was like the opening of the seven seals. He said I was one of those Servants of God spoken of in Scripture, who was marked on the forehead. Draw back my hair and you will see." Beale leaned forward and raised the hair falling over his forehead to reveal a darker patch of skin, a birthmark. "I have always had that, but he told me what it meant."

"Was this after Ambassador Walsingham came?" Nevers asked.

"No," Pierre said, "before. But that did not matter. I knew God was working in the world to fight the Beast of Heresy. I told him the signs Father Antoine had talked about. He said I was right, and that I needed to keep myself ready to open the door of the embassy when the time came, so the Servants of God could destroy the Servants of Satan." He leaned forward as far as his bonds would allow and spoke as though explaining to a child, "Those are the ambassador and secretary and all who serve the Great Whore—that is what Saint John calls Elizabeth of England."

Those around him gasped at his words.

"Why did you continue to serve the ambassador?" Sidney asked.

"I asked him if I should leave such an evil place," Pierre explained, "but he said no. I must keep my knowledge secret until the right time. God needed servants in the enemy's camp, like Judith and Esther."

"What happened then?" Nevers asked.

"Nothing for a long time," Pierre said. "Even when I told him the signs that were there to see, he always said the time was not yet right, that we could not hurry God. Then, this past spring we met at the Pentacle, the day after Easter. He said the moment might be right for me to open the door. We talked of how someone might enter and set a fire, or kill the ambassador."

Again, the listeners exchanged glances. "Did you hate the ambassador?" Nevers asked.

"Oh, no!" Pierre answered, appalled. "He always treated me well, but," he continued as though he were stating that the sun rose in the east, "he was a heretic and the destruction of those who worship the Dragon and the Beast is part of God's plan. This was my chance to serve God and advance Christ's thousand-year reign."

"Lepage asked you to kill Ambassador Walsingham?" Nevers asked.

"No, no." Pierre was emphatic. "I was a porter. I was only to open the door."

"When was this to happen?" Nevers asked. "When Lord Lincoln came from England?"

"I do not know," Pierre said. "Pickering came upon us as we spoke."

"George Pickering overheard you talk of killing the ambassador?" Hunter asked.

"Yes," Pierre said. "I tried to follow him. Lepage said to tell him we were talking about possible threats to the ambassador, in order to protect him." He shook his head. "But I lost him in the crowds on the rue Saint-Jacques." His face took on a puzzled, thoughtful look. "I never saw him again, but the next time I met Master Lepage, he said he was mistaken at the Pentacle. He said the time was not right, and that we must wait."

"Did he say anything to you about the man who attacked the ambassador in the king's coach?" Nevers asked.

"Guillaume Nadeau, you mean," Pierre said. "He came to the confraternity meetings with Father Antoine. I knew him. And just because I knew him, Master Lepage said I must leave my job. I was surprised. I asked if Nadeau, too, was doing God's work and hastening the Millennium. He said he might have thought he was. When I asked why I must leave the embassy, he said the Servants of God had to suffer before the final triumph. He said that the Beast would hold sway for forty-two months, and those chosen by God would be ground under the Dragon's heel."

"He mixes all parts of Revelation," Beale said to Walsingham.

"That was when I first thought he might be a false prophet," Pierre continued, "that he had made me leave my duties as porter for no reason. Though he kept me at his house for ten days, which was kind."

It was hard to keep up with Pierre's switches and changes of tone, though it was clear Lepage had used Pierre's preoccupation with the Apocalypse to further a plot against Walsingham. Had Lepage been behind Nadeau's attempt as well?

"During the time I was at his house, I watched him. He went out at night in his great hooded cloak, and I began to suspect he was meeting with the devil. Then he found me a position at one of his friend's houses—Master Hillairet—so I thought again that he was a true prophet. But there I was not a porter. Master Hillairet said I must clear the horse manure from his stables and scrub his floors. So then I thought perhaps I was right that Lepage was a false prophet after all."

"You left the embassy in June. But Lepage called you here today?" Nevers asked.

Pierre appeared to wake from a dream, then continued in an excited tone. "Yesterday a message came from Master Lepage, with the axe symbol he said he would use. Master Hillairet would not let me leave his house, but the message came in. My friend, his steward, can read. It said the time had finally come for me to do my part. John's Apocalypse says the armies of heaven will wear white linen and," a smile lit his face, "that has come true in the streets of Paris. Those who kill the heretics wear white linen on their arms. He said I was essential—*essential*. It was I who knew the embassy and could direct the Army of God. It was more important than opening the door. Someone else would do that.

Pierre wore a beatific smile. "I was filled with joy. I knew the End Time was near. I paid a dixaine to the master's porter to let me out. Soon gold and silver will be of no use! I met Captain Izard at the wine shop, as the message said. I marched beside him. I knew we would plunge the Beast of Heresy into the fiery pit."

Pierre's face clouded. "But when we entered this room, I saw Master Lepage. Why was he here? Captain Izard called him a traitor, and then he shot that man who came with us. Then I knew for certain he was a false prophet. But what he said before, some of that was the truth. Yet there he was. He shot one of the army of God. He shot at me. I had to stop him."

Nevers nodded. "Thank you for explaining to us. I believe you are right that Lepage is a false man, so you should not have listened to what he said about killing the ambassador."

Pierre stared back, confused. "No...Yes... He was false. He fought with heretics against God... But it is true that the Army of God wears white linen and destroys the Beast of Heresy in the streets of Paris." Suddenly, he began sobbing.

Nevers exchanged looks with Walsingham. "Do you want to ask him more?"

"When you stayed with Master Lepage, you say he went out at night," Walsingham said. "Do you know where he went?"

"No."

"Did anyone go with him?"

"No."

Walsingham shook his head. "I have nothing further to ask him."

"Then my men will take him to the Châtelet. If Lepage dies, he must be tried."

Hunter held a bitter laugh quiet in his throat. How would the Paris authorities find time to try one murder, when thousands had been committed in the past day?

"Master Lepage seems to have devoted himself to your destruction," Sidney said to Walsingham. "Do you think he was behind Nadeau's attack?"

"If he could use the millennial hopes of Pierre, he might have done so with Nadeau as well," Walsingham said. "If he lives, we shall ask him."

"He deceived us all this time." Beale shook his head.

"How could a mere notary weave such a net of influence?" Sidney asked.

"Another reason I hope he lives," Walsingham said. "We might ask him who supplies him with the money to buy porters, militiamen, and assassins."

The curé of Saint-Médard approached and bowed.

"Thank you, father, for coming at our request," Nevers said.

"I thank you as well," Walsingham added.

"It is my duty," the priest said. "The man I was called to tend has died, and I have taken the liberty to administer Extreme Unction to several others in this chamber."

Walsingham thanked him again, though Hunter was sure he regarded the rite as popish superstition.

"Louis Pentel requested that I look after his daughter Martha, and that I ask Your Grace if you will do so as well. She has but twelve years and lives in the rue Montmorency near the cemetery of Saint-Nicholas."

"I will do what I can for her," the duke promised.

"With your permission, I will look after the souls of those who lie wounded below," the priest said.

"That would be fitting and proper," Walsingham said.

One of Nevers's men reported to him. He nodded and surveyed the room. "Your Excellency, my purpose in coming here was to ensure your safety and that of your staff. I am sorry I was too late to save some. My men say those who intended you harm have dispersed, and all the invaders who were slain have been removed. I will leave a dozen of my men here to remove the wounded and to defend you until either the king can provide adequate guards or Paris returns to normal. Captain Ducasse will be in charge." He indicated a tall man, who touched his helmet.

"We all owe our lives to your arrival," Walsingham said. "I do not know what I can do to repay you."

At that moment another man stepped beside Nevers and whispered a message. "Bring him in," he said, then turned to Walsingham. "Your Excellency, while searching your courtyard to be sure no invader lurked in hiding, my men discovered a subject of King Charles concealed in your coachman's quarters."

Walsingham's face held its dignity, but his eyes spoke regret with a hint of fear. Through the stairwell door strode an old man, dressed as a stable hand. His beard was white, and his face deeply lined, but his eyes burned fiercely. His bearing bespoke strength.

"Seigneur de Briquemault," Nevers said. "I thought you had ridden forth Sunday morning."

Hunter recognized Briquemault as one of the Huguenot leaders he had seen at Saint-Germain-des Prés, who had fought alongside Coligny throughout the religious wars.

"I was lodging near the Admiral rather than in Saint-Germain," Briquemault said. "I imagine you expected to see me in a pile of corpses there."

Nevers's brows showed he did not like Briquemault's tone. "I heard your role in the Huguenot plot was to kill me."

"No such plot ever existed," Briquemault said.

"That is not what the king says," Nevers replied.

"The king..." Briquemault paused, "has not always proved trustworthy."

"Nor have his Protestant subjects, who have taken up arms against him," Nevers said.

The men stared at one another with animosity, then Nevers turned to Walsingham. "Your Excellency, though you may offer refuge to your own countrymen, or those of other states, it is a breach of diplomacy to harbor a subject of His Majesty. I request that you surrender him to me."

Walsingham's face tightened. He had just stated that he could not repay Nevers adequately, yet to turn Briquemault over was to surrender him to certain death. As he opened his mouth to speak, Briquemault said, "His Excellency is not to blame. When I presented myself here, he bade me go further. He even offered me a horse. It was I who begged to enter, as I was too exhausted to proceed. I am content to go with you now, whatever you have in store for me."

"May I enquire," Walsingham put in, "what you intend? I am sure you will protect Seigneur de Briquemault from the fury of the mob."

"Indeed I shall," Nevers said. "My intention is to turn him over to His Majesty's justice. He must answer for his crimes."

"My alleged crimes," Briquemault interjected. "Though I doubt the fairness of any court I may face, I will have a chance to answer my accusers, which is more than those who awoke to soldiers plunging swords into them."

"I must accede to this." Walsingham's face was pinched with pain. "I ask you, Your Grace, to do all in your power to assure he receives a fair trial."

"I shall do so," Nevers promised.

"I thank you for your protection," Briquemault said to Walsingham. "You only took me in out of Christian pity. I know you are obliged to His Grace for saving all those in this embassy, and I would not choose to endanger them again."

"I entrust Seigneur de Briquemault to you. I am sure you will preserve his safety as you have preserved that of my embassy," Walsingham said.

The duke nodded. His men marched Briquemault away. Nevers turned back. "Your Excellency, it is my hope that you and your household will continue to be secure. If you need my assistance again, pray send one of the guards I will leave with you. I hope that, despite the plotting of this Lepage and the disrespect shown by the rabble who attacked your embassy, the relations between our two countries may continue to exhibit mutual love and respect."

"As do I," Walsingham said, yet doubt flickered in the corner of his eyes. "I again express my gratitude and that of all in the embassy for rescuing us when we were in dire jeopardy."

The ambassador and Duke Nevers bowed to one another. The duke and his men left the great chamber.

Walsingham spoke to Beale in a low tone. "I doubt that Briquemault will receive a fair trial. King Charles and the Queen Mother will need his confession to justify the massacre, and they will not flinch at using torture to obtain it." He sighed, looked about him, and spoke loud enough for all to hear. "Now we must do what must be done. I call upon all of you, despite your rank, to help in this work."

Someone tugged on Hunter's sleeve. It was Guerin, the bonesetter. "Sir," he said, "your ear and your scalp have wounds that need attention."

CHAPTER 21

Return

T<small>HE NUMBER OF THINGS NEEDING IMMEDIATE ATTENTION SEEMED OVER-</small>whelming. The dead needed burial, the wounded needed tending, the floors and walls damaged in the fighting needed washing and repair, and everyone needed nourishment.

Among the wounded, Hunter recognized the pale face of Claude, the boy of Izard's militia who had watched the mound of corpses outside L'Échiquier. Had that really been less than twenty-four hours ago? Izard had mentioned Marguerite. Had he ransacked her inn? Was she safe? Hunter knelt near the bandaged boy and asked, "You call yourself Claude, do you not? In Captain Izard's militia?"

"Yes. But the captain is dead. I saw them carry him out."

"Yes." Hunter's satisfaction mingled with guilt. "I was surprised to see his militia here."

"He stopped our searching the inn and told us we could earn more by coming here. He promised me a gold écu."

"What inn?" Hunter thought he knew the answer.

"L'Échiquier, on..." Claude looked at him again. "Aren't you the Englishman who stayed there?"

"I am. What happened there today?"

"We went there. Captain said we would tear it apart, show that bitch that runs it she could not get away with her sauciness."

Hunter controlled his tone with difficulty. "Did he harm her?"

Claude laughed. "She surprised him. When we showed up she was all 'Welcome. Come in.' Had her servants open everything. I went down to the cellar. Captain said I was smart for knocking the barrels to see if they was full."

"What did the militia find?"

"Nothing," Claude said. "At least, not the first time. We had just started to go 'round again, tapping on everything to find some secret hollow wall or something."

Hunter's heart quickened.

"Then Captain got a message to come here, and we broke off and come across town."

"And the landlady was unharmed?"

"Yes."

Hunter relaxed. "Do you know who sent the captain the message?"

"Maybe one of the men at the wine bar. We waited outside while he talked to 'em."

"What did they look like?"

"One tall fellow with a big nose. Another with a chopped-off ear. Maybe you seen 'im. They come with us to the embassy."

"I saw them."

"Think they both got shot," Claude said.

"The man with half an ear was killed," Hunter said.

One of Nevers's guards approached Claude. "Can you walk?"

"If you help me up."

"Where are you taking them?" Hunter asked, helping the guard lift Claude.

"Those with the worst wounds go to the Hôtel-Dieu. Others we'll drop by Saint-Gervais."

Hunter wandered towards the courtyard. He wanted to return to L'Échiquier, to see Marguerite, to tell her he had killed Izard, that Martin was dead, and that she was safe. He wanted to visit the wine shop nearby, to look for Guillaume or Richard. He wanted search Lepage's house, sure he could find Spanish reales in a chest, or letters hidden in a secret drawer. Yet these were fantasies. He could not set foot out of the embassy. Considering the events of the day, he could not even be sure he was safe inside. The Parisians' taste for blood was not slaked, and they knew that here was a building filled with Protestants.

After the evening meal, the crude coffins, quickly constructed to hold the bodies of Thomas Howell and Gilbert Morin, were laid on trestles in the great chamber. Dean Watson intoned the burial service from the Book of Common Prayer.

Jacob, the embassy coachman, had contacted a cousin who owned a small farm two miles out the road towards Bicêtre. A Protestant, he had agreed that the dead could be interred on his land. Walsingham chose Williams and Hunter to ride with Jacob and André and two of Captain Ducasse's men, all wearing Nevers's livery.

The sky was clear and the moon only a few days past full. Though well-armed, all were anxious as they rode. The entire party tensed when horses approached, but it turned out to be a farmer's cart much like theirs, whose driver regarded them with eyes more frightened than their own.

During the ride back, Hunter shuddered as he relived forcing a knife through Nicolas's vertebrae. Nicolas should have had a funeral. As his horse plodded on, he remembered Izard's surprised expression when his sword pierced his chest. Images of the dead from the past day clouded his mind. He shook his head and his horse balked. He could not allow his thoughts to run in those channels.

Instead, he considered Lepage. Had he played a part in Nadeau's attack on the ambassadors? Why not have Pierre simply leave a door unlocked one night, for an assassin to slip in? Why had he not acted sooner? Had his questions to Lepage about Half-ear caused the Saint John's Eve attack? Did he send the message to Téligny denouncing Paul Adams as a Catholic?

When they arrived back at the embassy, Philip opened the courtyard gate and told them the news. Justin Lepage had died. His questions would go unanswered.

Tuesday, 26 August 1572

The embassy received a copy of Charles IX's declaration to the Parlement of Paris that all that had been done in Paris had been done by his command, and that Coligny and the chief Huguenots had been plotting against him. A royal edict arrived simultaneously, proclaiming that no harm should henceforth be done to Protestants. "His Majesty wants to have it both ways," Walsingham said. "He desires peace in his capital, but wants to harvest the people's approval of these heinous acts for himself."

That afternoon, royal troops replaced Nevers's men. When Walsingham expressed his thanks to King Charles, the captain of the guard said the capital was calm enough that he might do so in person. Secretary Beale went instead, with an escort of the king's soldiers. He returned to report the mood of Parisians had changed little. He was jeered as he rode through the streets, and saw a crowd dumping corpses into the Seine. At Court, he learned that Henri of Navarre and the Prince of Condé were held in the Louvre, expected daily to convert, and that Briquemault was imprisoned at the Conciergerie.

That evening in Walsingham's study, Hunter recounted his conversations with Pentel and the militiaman Claude. When he finished, Beale said, "Combining all the statements, it is clear Lepage had been plotting for a long time to harm Your Excellency."

"We inherited him from Norris without question. When I return to London, I must ask him how Lepage first presented himself." Walsingham shook his head. "Norris must have found him useful, as we did: recommending staff, arranging services at good rates. His insistence that I replace Pierre was more evidence that I could trust him. I fear I did not scrutinize Alain and Christophe as I should have."

"The fault was mine as well," Beale said. After a pause, he said, "I am amazed that such a simple fellow as Pierre could keep his secret for so long."

"To him it was a holy mission," Walsingham said. "Lepage appealed to his longings for the Apocalypse. That is why I believe he was behind Nadeau's attack as well."

"It is hard to put everything together," Hunter said. "Lepage placed Pierre as the embassy porter before Your Excellency assumed the post of ambassador. He might have let in a cutthroat at any time. Why delay? Why enlist Nadeau? Why finally organize an assault on the embassy?"

"We cannot be sure," Walsingham said. "I believe the original plan was to admit an assassin one night. But I was often away that first summer, attending His Majesty's Court in one or another château, while he hunted in the Loire Valley. Then I succumbed to illness most of the autumn and winter."

"But that would have made you an easy victim," Beale said.

"Perhaps the presence of Killigrew and Sir Thomas Smith made the task more difficult," Walsingham said. "Too many targets. And when Pickering overheard him speaking to Pierre, that set back his plans. He could not be sure Pickering had not warned us."

"So that was a reason to change to a plan involving Nadeau," Beale said.

"That is my speculation," said Walsingham. "And the failure of that attempt caused another delay. Lepage was again in danger of being discovered."

"So the idea of storming the embassy was not part of his thinking at all," Hunter ventured. "He simply took advantage of the chaos."

"And I have another thought," Walsingham said. "A single attack in the night might be regarded as simply the work of some burglar. Nadeau's attempt and the assault of yesterday were more public. If successful, they would have produced the deaths of many ranked Englishmen, deaths more embarrassing to His Majesty than some random criminal act. If Nadeau, a servant of King Charles, had killed us all in the king's coach, it might have scuttled the treaty. If a Paris mob had slaughtered all in the embassy, overwhelming the king's meager protection, that would bring about a major rift between our nations. The massacres in Paris will bring shame enough on the king, of course, but I hope the treaty's clauses for mutual defense will hold."

"I doubt the Rouen Staple will go forward," Hunter said. "Who will be eager to move to a country where Protestants have been slaughtered in their thousands? All my work here has been for naught."

"I fear you are right," Walsingham said.

"You make sense, sir," Beale said. "Lepage's efforts were not only against you; they are designed to separate England and France. I suspect his funds came from the one monarch who would profit most if England and France mistrust one another."

"Lepage must have been angling for a Spanish pension, or may already have been receiving one," Walsingham said. "When it is safe to venture from this embassy, after his widow has had time to bury him, we could request that the king's men question her about his activities, especially the night visits Pierre mentioned. For now, we have other duties."

Late August, 1572

Over the next few days, the embassy returned to as near normal as could be expected, considering it was too dangerous to venture out. Occasionally men gathered in front of the embassy to hurl insults, but they kept well away from the guards.

News leaked in through the cracks in the door. Butcher's boys brought gossip along with the meat. Walsingham's informants tucked notes into baskets of bread. Gangs of killers still roamed Paris, searching for Huguenots in hiding. The Princess Margot had saved her husband's Protestant followers, who fled to her bedchamber and clung to her night-gown the morning of the massacre. King Charles would lead a procession to view the miraculous hawthorn blooming in the Holy Innocents and the remains of Coligny's body hanging at Montfaucon. Massacres had taken place in Meaux, Bourges, and Orléans. "The madness is spreading," Walsingham sighed.

One day a letter from Jacques Crespin arrived. Since news of the death of Captain Izard and twenty of his militiamen had reached his quarter, the mood had changed to dejection and confusion. Although Izard's partisans gave him an impressive funeral, some relatives of the militiamen who had died blamed the captain. They asked what was he doing in Saint-Marcel, attacking a foreign embassy. In a postscript, Crespin assured Hunter that all was well at L'Échiquier and Marguerite was unharmed.

Saturday, 30 August 1572

Hunter found Sidney sitting at a table in a conference room, a book, paper, pen, and inkwell before him.

"What are you about?" Hunter asked.

"Rendering Livy into French," Sidney replied. "Walsingham lent me this. I left all my books at the rue Saint-Martin. I hope some have survived."

"So, you study even here," Hunter said. "Latin to French, then French to Latin."

"I do. Though that fills only a few hours a day."

"Yes. I have the same problem. I listen to Manucci's tales of serving the Duke of Tuscany and the Dean's views on Cicero. I review in my mind each conversation I had with Lepage. I think of the Huguenots I met in the city and wonder if any survived. I worry that those who allowed my escape might have suffered for it. Though I do not call to mind the horrors of the massacre, they visit me at night."

"Time will ease your mind."

"Yes, but time drags. This embassy feels like a prison."

"The turmoil cannot last forever. Each day there is less."

"But each day, Protestants continue to be slain. Walsingham only dared travel to the Louvre today with an armed escort."

"Will you leave France as soon as you can?"

"I had intended to be in Rouen two days ago," Hunter said. "I left what few possessions the militiamen did not steal at the Chessboard Inn. I have only a few testons, salvaged from the putrid clothes I discarded. I must return to England as soon as possible."

"I am eager to leave as well," Sidney said. "I am sure when news of the massacre reaches London—and it may have already—my uncle will ask Walsingham to pack me safely home. Though I will not regret leaving Paris, I do not wish to give up seeing Germany, Austria, and Italy. If I leave before I receive an order I must obey, I can continue my tour."

"I envy you your travels."

"Come with us," Sidney said.

"I wish I could," Hunter said, "but I have described my pitiable state. You do not need a penniless beggar as a companion."

"True. And I cannot offer to pay for you. In fact, I must write and appeal for funds to make good whatever I have lost here. I do not even know if I will be able to search our lodgings in the rue Saint-Martin before I leave."

"Are you committed to your Livy," Hunter asked, "or shall we see if the chessboard is free?"

"Livy has waited fifteen hundred years for my attention." Sidney closed the book. "He should not mind another hour."

Monday, 1 September 1572

Walsingham addressed Hunter in his study. "A week and a day have passed since the massacre—what His Majesty chose to call a 'lamentable accident' when I waited upon him at Court. He provided passports so that messengers might journey from here to London. I intend to send three, each with a copy of my letters: Williams, Faunt, and yourself. I hope all may travel quickly, but as one or two may encounter delays, I am dispatching all of you to make sure the information arrives in a timely fashion. Each will go to a different port: tonight Williams leaves for Newhaven, tomorrow you will start towards Boulogne and Faunt towards Calais. In case the correspondence falls into the wrong hands, I have committed little to paper, but each of you witnessed what took place in Paris, you most of all. Whatever time you arrive in London, go immediately to Whitehall Palace and deliver my letters and your report to Lord Burghley."

Sending three messengers was wise, but Walsingham's words were not reassuring. The 'delays' each of them might encounter could be fatal.

"I am sure Ambassador La Motte will tell Her Majesty that the Admiral and his followers plotted to seize the royal family. He will defend as best he can the king's decision to give the Admiral's bitterest enemy the task of dealing with him. I cannot offer an opinion on that in writing. Diplomats must remain diplomatic, even when speaking of princes with blood on their hands. You, however, know my thoughts. There was no reason Coligny, or his followers, could not have been arrested and brought to trial for their alleged plot, rather than murdered in their beds. You can explain this to Her Majesty's Council.

"In my letters, I mention the kindness of the Duke of Nevers, but give no details of the attack on the embassy. There, too, I rely on each of you to tell your story. I commended your service in earlier letters, and I have done so again. You continued to investigate Pickering's death when I had abandoned the search for his killers. Your timely questioning of Pentel proved Lepage a villain. You showed bravery in the embassy attack. I owe my life to your quick action, and I hope to employ you again when I return to England."

"Thank you, sir. I did no more than others." Hunter's hopes for future favor overcame for a moment his worries about reaching the coast.

"As for practical matters, Beale has selected some of Thomas Howell's clothing, in addition to the suit you are wearing, and he will provide you sufficient funds to reach London. You shall have Beale's second sword and the pistol you brought with you. We have hired a mount, and the king has agreed to provide escorts for two leagues out of Paris. I pray God that will be enough. You may wish to join with others traveling to Boulogne for safety."

"I am grateful to you and Secretary Beale," Hunter said. "I will send a draft from London to reimburse Master Secretary for his sword and young Ned for his father's clothes."

Walsingham stared into space a moment. "Our sins deserve punishment—that we acknowledge. What have we done so to enrage Almighty God that He suffers the murder of so many followers of true religion and the triumph of idolaters? I hear that scores of those who had professed the reformed religion now pack the churches, abjuring their faith. Has their frail faith caused God's displeasure? Do they not go to Mass merely to prevent their children becoming orphans? Would I have the courage to profess the Gospel at the cost of my life?"

Hunter followed Walsingham's thoughts. Was this massacre God's will, or the misdeeds of sinful men and women? How could it have come to pass if it were not part of God's plan? He remembered Crespin's chain of logic from their day on Montmartre. Drought, floods, plague, or the high price of bread must all be God's judgment on France because the king allowed Huguenots to live among the faithful. The Parisians who killed their neighbors thought they were doing God's will, and saw hawthorn blooms as a sign. Pierre thought he would do God's will by opening the embassy's door to assassins. The Dutch sailors who impaled the Benedictine on their swords thought they were doing God's will. How could any man, born to sin, be so arrogant as to think he knew it was God's will to kill another?

"...would you?" Walsingham asked.

"I beg your pardon," Hunter said. "Would I what?"

"Would you go to Mass and renounce your faith to save your life?"

Hunter reflected. "I believe I would. I have already done so to convince others Paul Adams was a Catholic. That is a lighter reason than to save one's life."

"Your actions were part of an effort to stop sedition in Her Majesty's realm," Walsingham said. "If England remains at peace instead of the chaos we have seen here, I believe that God will forgive your deceit."

"During the attack on the embassy, I killed the militia captain, and I may have killed more when I fired into the mob," Hunter said. "But I cannot be sure I was doing God's will."

"Surely, He does not expect us to allow the slaughter of innocents," Walsingham said. "We are to defend them and ourselves."

"I pray I will not have to kill again," Hunter said. "But if I must, let it always be defending the innocent. If I ever believe that it is God's will to slay others..."

"It is hard to know what one might do in every situation," Walsingham said, "and so we pray daily that we are not led into temptation."

Tuesday, 2 September 1572

Early the next morning, Sidney entrusted Hunter with a letter to his uncle. Walsingham said a prayer for their safety, and Hunter and Nicolas Faunt rode from the courtyard as a morning mist rose.

Gilbert Kerr, one of King Charles's Scots Guard, had been assigned to accompany them through Paris. "Don't know who I crossed to get this commission," he complained, "guarding Protestants so they can sail back to England and keep Queen Mary from her rightful throne."

"We thank you for your service," Hunter said, judging it unwise to comment on Kerr's words.

Faunt was less cautious. "It was your fellow Scots that fought with Queen Mary, and she herself that fled to England."

Kerr bristled. "Her cousin Elizabeth, you'll notice, has not been quick to take her part. She's been prisoner now five years."

"It is not reasonable to expect Her Majesty to help one who plots..." Faunt began, but their horses drew up before the Porte Bordelle. Three soldiers with pole arms stepped forward.

"Who are these men?" one asked Kerr. He did not answer, but eyed Faunt sharply.

"The situation between our queens is a complex one," Faunt said. "I grant that you see things differently."

The Scot smiled and addressed the guards in French. "These are Englishmen with passports from His Majesty. I am commanded to see them safe through Paris. They are leaving France."

"Good riddance to them," the guard said. "Pass through."

They observed only normal activity as they rode. Carters unloaded, shopkeepers opened their doors, and servants lined up at bakeries. Perhaps the madness that had overwhelmed the city for days might finally have run its course.

As they crossed the pont Notre-Dame, Hunter spoke to Kerr. "I have a proposal."

"Aye, what is it?"

"Before the massacre, I lodged at an inn only a little way off the rue Saint-Martin. If we stop there for a few moments, I might gather some of my possessions. In return, I can offer you a fine cup of wine. Perhaps that might sweeten the distasteful duty of escorting Southrons."

"It might take several cups to do that," the Scot replied, "or perhaps a little aqua vitae."

When Laurent answered Hunter's knock, his mouth dropped. "Mistress! Master Adams has returned."

Marguerite Moreau emerged from her office, relief and joy on her face. She rushed towards Hunter, then checked herself when she saw men standing behind him.

"Madame Moreau," he said calmly, though his eyes spoke his own delight at seeing her, "I am only able to stop a few moments on my way home to England. I ask that Laurent draw my companions each a cup of wine, while I gather my possessions and bid you farewell."

Marguerite donned her best innkeeper-hostess smile. "I bid you enter, gentlemen. Our taproom is just here. Laurent, pour two cups of our best wine."

When Kerr and Faunt were served, Marguerite bid Laurent to run and fetch Crespin. Once inside her office, she threw herself into Hunter's arms. "I was so frightened."

"And I for you."

They kissed and held one another tightly.

"I was sore afraid when Izard left for the English Embassy, and relieved when word came he was dead."

"Young Claude said he came here first."

"He did." She held him tighter. "He was knocking on the walls just as the message came to leave. I thought it was over."

He tightened his embrace. "I killed him, and I am glad."

She kissed him again. "How can I thank you?"

"You already have. You gave me your love."

They kissed again, longer and deeper. "I must tell you who I really am before I leave. Paul Adams was a false name, and the time it was needed is past. I am Edward Hunter. When you remember me, remember me as Edward, not by a name designed to deceive."

"Edward," she said gently, and raised her lips to his. "But you have been true to me, despite your false name."

Hunter's conscience stung. "You were always honest with me. You always told me we must enjoy what time we had, but that we must part."

"I will not forget you," she said.

"Nor I you."

She loosened her embrace. "You are wounded." She touched his left ear.

"It has already healed. Do not worry."

"Your sword, clothes, and ink stand are under my desk. I brought them down when I heard Izard was dead." She pulled away with an apologetic look. "Many of those slain had not paid. I had to use some of your money to pay my creditors, but I will fetch the rest. I have had no guests since the massacre. I may yet ask the Hôtel de Ville to repay me for my losses."

"Thank you. I can repay Secretary Beale for the funds he supplied." He took off Beale's sword. "This must be returned to him. Can you send Crespin to the embassy when it is safe to do so?"

"You may ask him yourself," came a voice from the office door.

"Jacques!" Hunter whirled around and embraced him. "I am relieved to see you."

"So am I," Crespin said. "But excuse me. You have taken off your baldric and belt. Am I interrupting something?"

"Jacques!" Marguerite struck him playfully on the shoulder. "I sent for you because I knew you would want to bid him farewell. I did not expect to be repaid with ribaldry."

"Forgive me, madame."

"To atone, you may delve under my desk and retrieve the sword and clothing hidden there. *That* is the reason Master Adams removed his belt."

"I accept my penance." Crespin bent down.

"I will fetch the money from the strongbox in my chamber," Marguerite said.

As she left, Crespin emerged. "One sword and hanger, two fine black doublets, one pair of breeches, and hose."

"I thank you. I must reveal my true name to you, as I did to Madame Moreau. I am Edward Hunter."

"I knew you were not Paul Adams," Crespin said. "But why tell me now?"

"Everyone at the embassy knows, as do those I deceived with that name," Hunter said. "But tell me, how were you able to keep safe during these days of fury?"

"After the night of carting corpses, I lodged with a friend near Porte Saint-Denis for a few days, to avoid other macabre tasks. When I heard that Izard and his men had been killed, I returned to my lodgings. By then, one could walk about with caution. You only had to avoid the squads searching out hidden Huguenots."

"The ambassador and I thank you for your letter."

"Are the ambassador and secretary well?"

"They were unharmed in the attack, but Beale's man Thomas was slain, and Gilbert the cook. Many others were wounded."

"I am sad to hear that. I understand Sidney's party found refuge at the embassy."

"Many did." Hunter listed the refugees. "How soon will you be able to go there safely?"

"When two days pass without gangs of killers roaming the streets," Crespin said.

"After last week, you can embellish your tour commentary with limitless tales of death," Hunter said. "At almost any corner you can say 'So-and-so was killed here.'"

Crespin's face turned grim. "I know I used tales of gore when I took visitors about the city, but tales of slaughter a century old are more fascinating than the murders of those whose blood still stains the walls."

"I suppose you cannot expect many English visitors in the near future."

"No. But when they do come, I fear they will ask me to describe the 'Notorious Massacre of Saint Bartholomew's Day'." Crespin sighed. "I am not ready to do that yet."

Hunter finished fastening his sword. "I have little time. A royal escort and another messenger are taking a cup in the taproom."

Marguerite entered with a purse. "I have counted it out. Seven écus, five testons, some sols." She emptied the coins into her hand.

"Three écus and two testons should repay Ned Howell for his father's clothing, and cover part of what the ambassador loaned me to reach London," Hunter picked out the coins and handed them to Crespin.

"Do you not need the rest for your journey?" she asked.

"No. I have enough."

"Thank you for your kindness," she said, but her eyes spoke more.

"Are ye not finished in there?" came Kerr's rasping voice. "If I drink another cup, I'll not be able to sit steady on my nag."

Behind him, Faunt's eyes shifted from Marguerite to Crespin to Hunter, weighing possible relationships.

"I thank you both for your patience." Hunter turned to Marguerite. "I am indebted to you, Madame, for keeping my possessions safe, and for your kind attentions during my Paris stay." Her smile showed she understood his meaning. "Master Crespin, I could not have completed my task here without your assistance. I leave you both reluctantly and hope to see you again" Could circumstances change so greatly that he might return to Paris safely at some time?

They mounted and set off. Hunter turned to imprint and hold a final picture of Marguerite Moreau's dark hair, green eyes, and smiling face.

Kerr's mood had improved with two cups of wine. From the Porte Saint-Martin to Saint-Denis, the Scot regaled them with stories of Bannockburn, then of endless raids into England by various Border clans. In all his tales, the Scots were sly and courageous and the English stupid and cowardly. Hunter occasionally voiced a "Quite brave!" or a "Very clever." He saw Faunt seething, but with a look warned him to keep his silence.

On the far side of Saint-Denis, Kerr drew in his horse. "Gentlemen, this is as far as I am bound to take you. You must make your own way to the coast. If ye chance upon those who seek Protestant blood, ye can wave your passports at them. Perhaps they can read, and perhaps they will choose to read before they stick a sword through ye. I care little, now ye are no longer my charge."

"I thank you for your service," Hunter said.

"And I thank you for your lessons in Scottish history," Faunt said.

Thursday, 4 September 1572

After hiding in woods and sleeping beside his horse to escape bands of riders intent of intercepting escaping Protestants, Hunter gave thanks for reaching the coast. He had separated from Faunt outside Boulogne and surrendered his horse at the livery stable. Standing at the harbor and breathing in the odor of salt water, he recognized the familiar lines of a French barque against the setting sun. He made his way forward, unable to believe his eyes. When he was within the ship's shadow, he read her name, *Constance*, and again thanked God for his good fortune.

"Hello there," he shouted to a man at the rail. "Is Captain Tide on board?"

"Aye, sir. What would you be wanting?"

"Passage to England."

"I'll go and fetch the captain."

In a few minutes, Captain Tide's familiar face, framed by dark curls, appeared at the railing. "Are you the man wanting passage to England?"

"Yes, sir. I sailed with you before. You know me as Paul Adams."

"Adams. Yes. Dropped you at Rouen in April."

"That's right."

"Well met, Adams. I sail for Dover early tomorrow. Come aboard and we can discuss your fare."

Hunter ascended the gangplank, glad to leave the jeopardy of French soil for an English ship.

"Welcome aboard." Tide placed a hand on his shoulder. "Where have you come from?"

"Paris."

"Ah," Tide raised his eyebrows. "One of the lucky ones to escape the butchery."

"I am, thank God."

"Come to my cabin. You must tell me about it."

Over a glass of Bordeaux, Hunter related his experiences, holding back information Walsingham would not want known.

Tide listened with keen interest. "I am astonished. Yours is the only first-hand report I have heard. The truth is as bad as the rumors." He shook his head. "I tell you what—you shall sail with me free of charge. Your story has paid for your passage, Master Adams." He downed the last of the wine. "But I cannot offer you a bunk. You must bed down among the cargo."

"If you do not carry wet sheepskins," Hunter said.

"No, no," Tide laughed. "Only paper and playing cards."

"Then I accept your offer."

Tide raised a hand. "I recall that on your previous passage we chanced upon a Spanish caravel in the Narrow Seas and you were troubled by the treatment a Dominican received at Dutch hands."

"Yes. I remember that well."

"So I am wondering," Tide said, "After what passed in Paris, are you now so concerned about the treatment of Catholics?"

"I saw horrible deeds committed by Catholics on their neighbors," Hunter admitted, "but I do not believe that allows me to do the same to any Catholic. Although I killed some defending myself, the sins of murderers are not license for me to sin."

Tide nodded. "Well, may you be able to hold on to your scruple. Of course, those you saw killed were not your family."

"I pray I am not led to such a situation. May Her Majesty's realm never know such slaughter as France does."

Tide poured more wine. "We must both drink to that."

Saturday, 6 September 1572

Hunter reached London the afternoon of the day after he landed at Dover. At Whitehall Stairs, he presented Walsingham's letter to the guard, who escorted him to Burghley's office. Though his clothes were dusty from the ride north, Lord Burghley did not seem to notice. Instead, he gazed at him expectantly.

Hunter bowed. "Lord High Treasurer, I bring you letters from Ambassador Walsingham and my own report."

"We have all been most anxious for reliable news from Paris." Burghley took the packet. "I pray the ambassador is well."

"He is, thanks be to God. He sent three messengers. Am I the first to arrive?"

"You are." Burghley broke the seal, read each letter in silence, then turned to Hunter. "He says you can relate events he was loath to put in writing. Pray pull that stool close and tell me your story." He turned to his clerk. "Thomas, record Master Hunter's narrative."

Hunter related his experiences, starting with the day of Coligny's wounding and continuing through Saint Bartholomew's Day and the following week. Occasionally Burghley asked a question, but for the most part he listened. Hunter could see his mind churning, pondering the best way to inform the Queen and Privy Council. Occasionally he cast an eye to the clerk, indicating that Hunter's words should be carefully noted. At other times his eyes spoke disappointment. Any hopes he might have had for the unlikely marriage of the Queen and the Duke of Alençon had disappeared with the massacre. The possibility of creating a stronger alliance with France against Spain receded. England was more alone than she had been two weeks before.

Hunter finished his report an hour and a half later. Burghley was silent a moment, then said, "Ambassador Walsingham and Secretary Beale have served Her Majesty well, at great danger to themselves. I must also compliment you on your report." He sighed. "The ambassador had mentioned Lepage in his letters, as providing assistance. And all that time, he was plotting against us. I agree with the ambassador's opinion. He must have been in the service of Spain.

"I am surprised the Duke of Nevers proved such a valuable ally. You say he approved of the slaughter of Protestants in Paris, even encouraged it, yet he defended all the Protestants who were sheltering in the embassy. But then he demanded Briquemault."

"I cannot be sure how the duke reconciles his actions to himself," Hunter said, "but I know he respected Walsingham for his loyalty to the Queen. In fact, loyalty seemed a virtue he placed above conscience. He thought the Huguenots disloyal subjects and suggested those who could not agree with their sovereign's religion should leave the realm."

Burghley shook his head. "Whatever his reasons, we must be grateful to him for saving those at our embassy." He paused. "No doubt many others in the coming days will ask you to tell them of your experiences in Paris. I need not tell you that any private conversations you had with the ambassador should remain private. You will not reveal the work you undertook to discover those who printed seditious tracts and sent them into England. Though your uncle knows you undertook a secret mission, he does not know what it was. And the details of Lepage's betrayal of the embassy and the attack on it—it is better as few people as possible know of those things." He nodded to his clerk, who put down his pen. "It has become late. May I offer you some refreshment before you leave?"

"I thank you, sir, but I would like to see my aunt and uncle as soon as possible."

"Very well." Burghley rose. "Thomas, ask a guard to summon a boat to take Master Hunter downstream. I shall send Sidney's letter to Lord Leicester. He may want to speak with you tomorrow. I assume you will be at your uncle's on Cheapside."

"I will, Your Lordship," Hunter said.

Evening was falling when the Babcock's maid, Dolly, opened the door and shrieked, "Master Edward!"

As Hunter stepped in, his uncle and aunt came clattering down the steps, both calling his name. Aunt Kate embraced him, her body shaking. Uncle George placed his arm on his shoulder and said, "We feared you had been killed."

"Thank God," Aunt Kate sobbed. "Thank God for protecting you. If anything had happened to you, your mother would never forgive us."

Had Aunt Kate not believed he was in Germany?

"I had to tell her where you were," his uncle said. "Your mother and father as well know that you were in Paris, negotiating important agreements for the syndicate." Uncle George's eyes told him that he had not revealed Hunter's work for Lord Burghley. "And much blame I received for deceiving them for so long. Your mother does not appreciate the subtlety of commercial discussions."

"I must also apologize for deceiving them." Hunter pried himself from his aunt's grip.

"But come upstairs," his uncle said. "You must be hungry and exhausted. Have you just reached London?"

"I had to deliver letters from Ambassador Walsingham to Lord Burghley at Whitehall." Hunter's glance hinted there was more to tell.

"Oh, my word!" Aunt Kate opened her eyes wide at the mention of royal officials. Then she remembered her role as nurturer. "We were just preparing a supper of cold meats, salad, and cheese. Pray you, come up. Dolly, call Alfred to take Edward's bag to his old room."

Over his meal and several tankards of ale, Hunter told an abridged version of his time in Paris. His narrative of the Saint Bartholomew's Day massacre still included the morning slaughter at the Chessboard Inn, heard from inside "a closet" where he was hidden, and his sight of bodies piled on the streets of Paris, but he neither mentioned swimming the Seine nor his encounter with the expatriates. In his telling, he crossed Paris at night and reached the safety of the embassy, where he stayed secure until he could return. Even this expurgated telling brought tears to Aunt Kate's eyes, and vows that he should never again place himself in such danger. This was only a preview, he knew, of what he must face with his mother.

After supper, Uncle George escorted Edward to his chamber. Aunt Kate, he suggested, must calm herself with a draught of cordial. In Edward's room, Uncle George asked, "Did your mission for Lord Burghley go well?"

"Yes," Hunter said. "And I must thank you for the opportunity to serve him and Her Majesty."

Uncle George smiled broadly. "I knew you were cut out for more than sitting in a cramped room pouring over old deeds."

Hunter saw himself as he had been some months before, reading extracts of cases, listening to pleadings at Queen's Bench, longing to establish himself as a lawyer so that he would be worthy of Mary Spranklin's hand. Now he had lived the life of an intelligence gatherer in Paris, tasted intimacy with women, befriended Philip Sidney, discussed political maneuvering with Ambassador Walsingham, and delivered reports to Lord Burghley. Returning to Gray's Inn was far less appealing. "What am I to do now?" he asked his uncle and himself.

"I believe there are promising possibilities," Uncle George said.

The End

Author's Note

The second Edward Hunter novel contains a larger proportion of fiction in its history-fiction mix than the first. The coach attack on Walsingham did not occur. The invasion of the English Embassy was reported by Ambassador Zuñiga, but is unconfirmed by any other source. Otherwise, the events of the novel conform fairly well to the historical record.

For those who are interested in the events leading up to the Saint Bartholomew's Day Massacre, I recommend the sources I found most helpful. N. M. Sutherland's *The Massacre of St. Bartholomew and the European Conflict 1559-1572* explains the political background. Barbara Diefendorf's *Beneath the Cross: Catholics and Huguenots in Sixteenth-Century Paris* is outstanding in communicating the feelings of 'the man (and woman) on the street.' Biographies of Catherine de Medici, Francis Walsingham, and the Guise family necessarily contain chapters about the massacre. I consulted many books, but I will not turn this note into a bibliography. The *Bâle plan de Paris*, about 1550, by Truschet and Hoyau (available online), and Hillairet's two-volume *Dictionnaire historique des rues de Paris*, along with a few trips to Paris, allowed me to trace the steps of Edward Hunter.

One mystery I wrestled with was the location of the English Embassy. Though many historians place it in Saint-Germain-des-Prés, I agree with Professor John Cooper that Tomasso Sassetti's account, written within a decade of the massacre, correctly places the embassy in Saint Marcel.

DougAdcockAuthor.com
Facebook.com/DougAdcockAuthor

Acknowledgements

I am indebted to family and friends for their encouragement and patience. Special thanks to David Smith for reading this manuscript twice, and discovering some errors that had eluded me. Thanks to Professors Barbara Diefendorf and John Cooper for receiving my phone calls and answering my questions. Thanks to Hilary Davidson of the Museum of London for showing me some sixteenth century cloth and helping me understand the textiles of that era. I am indebted to the New York Public Library, the British Library, the *Bibliothèque Historique de la Ville de Paris*, and the Prospector System of the Colorado System of Research Libraries.

Printed in Great Britain
by Amazon

36121659R00270